To Beloved
Melinda

Thank you for sharing your
light with me.

@ Angelinaa

PRAISE
FOR
THE TEACHING OF LITTLE CROW

"Like a fine wine, *The Teaching of Little Crow* is a novel that should be savored. Just as the human soul, this story is multidimensional in its scope; addressing the evolution of man from ego consciousness to his Christ consciousness. Although the story alone is compelling and the characters endearing, the layers of esoteric teachings within the text beg for a second and third reading with a highlighter pen in hand. Little Crow is not only thought provoking, but soul provoking -- encouraging the reader to honestly appraise his own journey. There is a language spoken in this story that bypasses the conscious mind and communicates directly with the heart, where all things are remembered. Truly a treasure trove!"

Valere Althouse, "Adviser to the Stars," and until her retirement, for thirty years, a lecturer and consultant at The Greenhouse Spa in Arlington, Tx. Co-author with her husband, Larry, of *What You Need is What You've Got; Discover, Develop and Use Your Inner Resources,* and *You Can Save Your Breast: One Woman's Experience with Radiation Therapy.*

"A beautiful book! Exciting, brilliantly woven and most of all, profound. *The Teaching of Little Crow* is a magnificent love story that stirs deep memory in each of us -- memory of our Twin Flame and of the role that Twin Flames will have in returning the world to Love and unity. Angelina Heart is a compelling writer who holds your attention every moment, whether unfolding a good story or spiritual truths. The presence of this book affirms what I have received through the Messages from God -- that it is now time for uniting Twin Flames here on Earth as part of humanity's awakening."

Yaël Powell, author of *Say Yes to Love, God Explains SoulMates* and *Say Yes to Love, God Unveils SoulMate Love and Sacred Sexuality.*

The Teaching
of
Little Crow
the journey of the soul

by
Angelina Heart

heart flame
PUBLISHING

Cover Design and Typesetting: Randy Hansen,
The Idle Chicken Design, Dammeron Valley, Utah

Editing: Story Content, Cambridge Literary Agency
Text, DeAnne Moyle, Bethany Lopez Despain

Library of Congress Catalog Card Number:
2004110195

ISBN
0-9726618-0-8
Printed in the United States of America

Dedication

I gratefully acknowledge and dedicate this story to God,

☯

The I AM Presence anchored in all men's hearts,

☯

All those who seek at-one-ment with God and a reunion with their beloved twin flame, and

☯

All the glorious masters and teachers I have known in this lifetime and others

A note from the author...

Although *The Teaching of Little Crow* is a fictional work, it is also a gentle course providing instruction and insight into ancient esoteric teachings about universal laws. Crow's adventure not only represents the soul's journey into the depths of illusory material density, but also its awakening from the dream.

Since the story is heavily layered, some will simply enjoy the surface story, while others may recognize its deeper value. Calling it a "New Age" tale would be a misnomer, for it contains the most ancient of teachings upon our planet. For those who have had no exposure to esoteric terminology, a glossary of brief definitions has been provided.

It is no coincidence that you are reading this book. There are no coincidences. It has been said, "When man desires a manifestation and asks for the assistance of spirit, we call it Co-creation. When Spirit intends a manifestation and asks man to carry it out, it is Co-incidence." So be it. Immerse yourself in the Co-incidence and enjoy the ride.

The Teaching
of
Little Crow
the journey of the soul

by
Angelina Heart

BOOK I

Chapter 1

"Get up, you poor excuse for skin on bones! You knew we were leaving at sunrise. Get down to the stream and fill our containers!" Don Pedro barked his command with his thick Spanish accent, rolling the child over with his dirty boot. "Pack up the camp just as soon as you get back. I'll leave the jenny and the pack mules and you can catch up with the gear."

Angel had met Don Pedro's wrath too many times to hesitate, so he scrambled to gather the skins and head for the stream. If he could fill the skins quickly, the men could get away and he'd be left in peace to break camp without their cruelty and incessant orders. He decided not to take the wooden casks, but to come back later to fill them in order to hasten the men's departure.

☯

A gypsy named Grendor found three year old Angel abandoned and crying in the streets of Barcelona. The old nomad hoped to please his barren mistress with the gift of a child. Though nurturing and kind, she died prior to Angel's seventh birthday and Grendor had no further use for the lad. Ten days after his mistress died, Grendor told Angel they were going hunting and then to town to sell their game. Instead of the game, however, the child was presented for sale in the slave market.

By the time Angel turned eleven he had been bought and sold three times. In a tattered and filthy state, he was purchased by Don Pedro—a hard, former captain of the Royal Guard.

A group of Spanish explorers intent on mapping out the Americas employed Don Pedro to act as both guide and protector. He was known to be fearless, but cruel and ruthless as well. Though several members of the team objected to his tactics, the fact that he had made one previous trip to the new world weighed heavily in his favor.

Because Don Pedro received no advance for the journey, he purchased the cheapest slave he could to serve as his cabin boy aboard ship and his attendant on the long and arduous journey ahead. With a little soap and water on the outside, and some food in the child's belly, he felt sure he could make a useful servant of Angel.

Crow dog-eared the corner of the page, closed the book, placed it on the empty seat next to him, and stared out the window at the wispy clouds. Leaning on the armrest and propping his chin in his hand with forefinger gently placed over lips and thumb resting on the jaw line, his vision zigzagged around the ethereal formations like a slalom skier.

The stewardess passed through the narrow aisle of the puddle-jumper, hoping to offer a non-intrusive smile of recognition. Familiar, however, with the pose of a man deep in thought, she postponed the friendly, "Do you need anything?" interruption.

Crow reached into his vest pocket, withdrew a small silver flask and took a quick sip of his favorite Irish whiskey, followed by a whispered "Ahhh," as he slid it back into its cache. Ajusting the seatback and unlatching the tray in front, he propped the book far enough away to read clearly. Although bifocals had been recommended by his optometrist, his pride kept him from admitting that a natural aging process had begun. Crow began reading where he left off.

Sixteen months passed as the small group explored and mapped out the new lands. Even though the journey originally commenced in Central America, they now turned their attention to the north with more on their minds than map-making.

On several occasions they heard tales from various Indian tribes about a sacred place—the place of beginning—the heart of the earth where treasures untold were stored—a place of majestic red mountains and valleys so deep, the only way to descend into them was with wings—a place God hid from the sight of man, where only the pure in heart could enter.

The legends drew the explorers to the extraordinary place where they now camped, each of them hoping to prove the legends true. Their relentless avarice compelled them through many physical perils as the expedition turned from peaceful exploration into a mysterious treasure hunt.

The original expedition began with seven men, a cook, and three young men to tend to the camp needs, with Angel being the youngest among them. Nine months into the adventure the cook died when struck by a snake. The other two boys met their deaths at the hands of some curious, hungry Indians. Angel witnessed helplessly from a distance as the young men failed to defend the camp against the intruders.

After their untimely deaths, the sole responsibility for meeting the needs of all seven men was thrust upon the remaining child. This included cooking, tending campfires, laundry, food gathering, hunting, making and breaking camp, and hauling water. Singularly performing the difficult tasks of multiple people made the boy strong and independent.

Some of the explorers demonstrated genuine kindness, but those who had been hired to "defend and protect" the explorers were downright cruel to Angel. Paulo, a particularly foulsmelling creature, proved worse than the others. His unyielding lack of consideration for Angel was exhibited through daily humiliations, large and small. Angel never quite understood why Paulo felt such animosity toward him, for he served all the men with faithful attentiveness.

☯

Angel returned from the stream with the water skins as fast as he could run. Don Pedro, loading his horse with supplies and ammunition for the day, acknowledged the offering with a mere grunt. As the sun peeked over the mesa, the call sounded for departure and without further word to Angel, Don Pedro swung into the saddle and set off with the others.

While the sun filtered down through the trees, the entire camp transformed into a fairy kingdom similar to one Angel's gypsy mother had once described. A meadowlark paid homage to the rising sun with its lilting song. Squirrels and rabbits rustled through the brush unaware he would soon stalk them as prey for the evening meal.

Enormous cottonwood trees, with the majority of their leaves having already donned their bright yellow autumn color, graced the banks of the stream. He remembered seeing these trees further south in the springtime and marveled at the copious amounts of cotton that wafted down from their branches, collecting like layers of fluffy snow on the ground. He wondered if it could be harvested and spun into cloth.

Angel spent the next hour breaking camp and loading the mules before he set off into the high grasses to flush out their dinner. The hunt took but minutes and after he slit the throats of the rabbits, he hung them by their hindquarters on the side pack of one of the mules so their blood would drain before he began the journey. He didn't like killing anything and never killed more than necessary to sustain their little party.

Aquada, his best-loved mule, had been assigned the task of bearing the heavy weight of the water casks. Leading his friend to the stream to fill the empty containers, he stopped short at the sight of two small cougar cubs. Where there were cubs, there was bound to be a mother. Quietly, he waited for her to join them. The cubs appeared scrawny, as if they hadn't eaten well for quite some time and Angel wondered if their mother had abandoned them.

The sun rose higher and the boy knew he must depart soon to make camp for the explorers in a timely fashion. Waiting another quarter hour, he watched the cubs play. Their attempt at hunting lizards by the stream met with failure time and time again. They're starving, he said to himself.

Quite certain no mother stood guard, he ventured forward to fill the casks a goodly distance upstream from the frolicking duo, though they were still in sight. At first they appeared nonplussed by his presence, then unexpectedly sprang with enthusiasm up the bank of the stream heading straight for him. The wind had shifted and the scent of rabbit blood on his hands drew them like magnets. They approached like domestic kittens, licking his fingers and nudging them with their foreheads. Patting them tentatively, Angel scanned his surroundings again. One cleverly discovered the jerky in his shirt pocket and snatched it greedily.

Aquada suddenly whinnied and brayed loudly as he bolt-ed down the pathway toward the camp. Angel looked up just in time to see a snarling giant of a cat leaping through the air toward him. With nothing but his hands with which to fight off the beast, the cat tore and ripped at his arm and neck while he struggled to release himself from her enormous weight. An expert at dropping her prey, she went directly for his throat, which she tore so deeply that he fell unconscious.

The threat to her cubs now eliminated, she considered burying the intruder for a later meal. However, the smell of the creature offended her. The cat found the scent and flavor of her daily game more appealing, so she abandoned the tro-phy with a distasteful growl. The three cougars headed toward the camp where something smelled infinitely more promising. The female easily found the rabbits Angel had hung on the tethered mule and while the tied beasts brayed and kicked, she managed to tear part of of the rabbits free. Smarting from a well-placed blow, she called to her young ones to follow her away from the striking hooves.

By sunset the explorers realized the boy had not followed, so the chore of determining the problem fell to Paulo. The far-ther he traveled, the angrier he became. Long after darkness fell he understood a return to the beginning point of the day's journey would be required. With each plodding step of his horse he conjured up new ways to make "that lazy boy" pay for this inconvenience!

Because the moonless night made travel difficult, Paulo camped and waited for morning to complete his task. By the pre-dawn light he set off again. His empty stomach com-plained bitterly, but he knew when he located Angel an easy meal could be supplied from the stores of food.

He approached the campsite only to find all the mules packed and ready to go. The water mule, however, grazed nearby without any tethering at all. Dismounting, he hollered, "Hey, you stupid boy, why haven't you left yet?"

When no answer came Paulo began investigating more closely. One of the mules had parts of a rabbit tied to it, though most of the game had been torn away. The poor animal had large gouges on its side and had bled a great deal during the night as evidenced the by the pool of blood beneath its feet.

Heading toward the stream with his rifle in hand, cocked and ready for action, he yelled again. "Boy!" Still, no one answered. Keen awareness piqued every sense as he gingerly moved toward the water, rotating his head from side to side.

There, along the stream, lay the torn and mutilated body of Angel in a puddle of blood. The child still breathed, but Paulo believed he would surely die. Unwilling to let the others get ahead of him, the greedy man had no intention of nursing the boy. Probably just get eaten by whatever killed him, he thought. With his foot he rolled the boy partially into the stream and abandoned him without ceremony.

He marched back to camp, led the water bearer to the stream and filled the casks. After freeing the mule that had lost so much blood, he tied Aquada to the end of the line. Gathering the reins from the lead jenny, the foul smelling man made his way to his comrades, certain Angel's death would throw the camp care to him for the remainder of the expedition. He angrily cursed the stupid boy as a plan to abduct a young Indian to perform the chores slowly formulated in his thick brain.

❧

Crow laid the book down on the tray so he could stretch a bit. It always helped him to read the book from which the screenplay had been inspired. Although the screen version would utilize pictures to replace hundreds of words, he believed there were things he could not portray about his individual character without knowing the whole story. In the early 1900's Richard Eckerhardt wrote *The Teaching of Little Crow* as a gift for his son. It had not been published until after Eckerhardt's death, but once in the public domain the story received great praise for depicting a moral rarely portrayed in writing or on screen. Crow felt the writers had done a bang-up job of the rewrite.

Earlier that afternoon Crow caught a flight to Las Vegas from Los Angeles where he transferred to the small twin-engine, turbo prop Brasilia which now sped him to his final destination. He was probably the only Oscar-winning movie star who did not travel in his own jet with a full entourage—a luxury he could surely afford, but considered ostentatious. The plane would deliver him to the little town of Kanab in southern Utah where filming of his scenes in the movie version would ensue. He'd check in and let them know he'd arrived a couple of days early to get a feel for things.

The trick, of course, would be achieving his goal without being accompanied by the security task force assigned to him by the studio. Due to a death threat a few years earlier, Crow's employers insisted on watching over him. Although similar to being incarcerated for one's own protection, he had become adept at sneaking away unnoticed.

Chapter 2

She stroked his muzzle and, with a soft kiss, bade Pegasus good morning. "Come on boy—let's greet the sun."

A gentle whinny indicated the horse's willingness to share the ritual to which he'd become accustomed over the last year. He loved her, for she treated him with awe and respect and there was no doubting the sincerity of her affection. They seemed to meld together as they rode, always relaxing into a bond of true friendship in one another's presence. Never unkind or impatient, sometimes she even allowed him to lead the way and take her on an adventure. Instead of a pet or beast of burden, she treated him as an equal.

☯

Several years before he died, her husband, Scott, had given Pegasus to her as a gift. She loved animals, but the size and power of horses intimidated her. Having been thrown her fair share of times, Nikki had declined to ride ever since they bought the Red Rock Canyon Ranch.

The eight-gaited Peruvian Pasafino was beautiful to behold; bay with a deep black mane, long tail, and intense bright eyes. He had a glorious ancestral heritage from which both beauty and intelligence had been bred in the bone.

Nikki laughed the first time she saw Scott ride him. His massive feet flinging sideways made him look like a *lerp*; a term she used to indicate his appearance of instability. She had no idea his gait would make her feel as if she were in the comfort of her Lexus.

His previous owner, Cody Mullen, owned more than twenty horses and hadn't spent much time with him. One day the big horse was loaded in a trailer and hauled four hundred miles south to the Red Rock Canyon Ranch, a beautiful place nestled in a valley beneath the towering mesas of Zion National Park in Utah. A stream meandered through the narrow green valley. While barns, stalls, and paddocks were available, a lush pasture became his newly assigned home. He made casual friends with a jenny named Lucy and two rather rambunctious yearling fillies that ran free in the adjacent meadow. Four months passed without much contact with humans, save for their driving or walking by to admire him.

Scott had agreed to board the horse over the worst of the winter months, but in the springtime, phoned Mullen and offered to buy him. Mullen had called the Pasafino "Pecos Pete," but after riding him, Scott renamed him "Pegasus." "It's like riding a horse with wings," he declared to his wife. "How would you like him for yourself?"

Always grateful for her husband's generosity, she accepted the gift, but never had the courage to take the immense horse out of the arena. In fact, the only quality time spent with him was reaching over the fence for an occasional pat on his snout. Turned loose on the stream to roam the open pastures on the east side of the ranch, Pegasus passed another two years with little interaction among humans.

One day, however, something changed the course of his dreary life on the ranch. About a year ago, Pegasus stood idly in the shade of a cottonwood near the stream where a cool breeze blew gently over his back. He liked this particular spot on the ranch. Though free to roam over sixty acres of bottomland, he often stayed in this section for it was cooler than the open areas and the water easily accessible. Sometimes other horses came and stayed a few days, and sometimes the jenny, but he had not bonded with them much, preferring the quiet of the northeast pasture. Hearing an odd muffled cry upstream, he wandered over to investigate.

There she sat, arms wrapped around her legs, holding them tightly to her chest, head down, and sobbing. The heart-rending sound compelled the Pacifino to approach and nuzzle her head. Thus began a beautiful friendship between Nikki and Pegasus. She had lost her husband of twenty-three years. When the great horse found her she was crying for the first time since his passing. It had been a good life with Scott. Nikki believed his spirit now resided in a peaceful place, but also believed that overly grieving his passage would only bind him to her sphere. She truly felt it was the ultimate selfish act to be sitting there crying for herself, but the deluge of burning tears could not be checked.

As per his last wishes, Scott had been buried on the ranch less than a month before. That particular day, however, Nikki's whole world turned on its edge. It proved difficult enough to adjust to her husband's passing, but her beloved son, Sam, had boarded a plane that morning to attend Stanford. Although a strong person, she felt truly alone for the first time in her life and totally unprepared for the overwhelming void that surrounded her.

Something nudged her head, startling her out of her private misery. Towering above stood the estranged Pasafino. Where she gathered the courage to pull herself up bareback onto the horse was a mystery to both of them. As her hands gently and tenderly caressed his flesh, Pegasus stood still in shock. Leaning forward with arms wrapped around his neck, she fell asleep from emotional exhaustion. The horse began sauntering slowly around the northeast pasture. Arriving at the road that crossed the stream and led to the barns, he splashed into the water, waking Nikki with a start. As he climbed out of the stream she grasped his mane with both hands and held tight until he stopped in front of an old metal gate, cocked his head, and snorted.

After a somewhat clumsy dismount, Nikki looked deep into

his eyes. "You're not an angel, are you?" she whispered while stroking his neck. "Thank you. Thank you for your kindness." He lowered his head and allowed her to kiss his muzzle.

All her fear of him dissolved that day, that day when compassion was offered from another species.

"So, let's see where the wind takes us this morning, dear friend," she cooed as she threw her favorite blanket over his back. She had an internal sense of what provided comfort for Pegasus and always used soft, gentle ways with him. Using only a hackamore, she guided him without force of any kind. In fact, she but had to think the direction and he seemed to pick it up intuitively. She never jammed a metal bit into his mouth, nor burdened his back with a heavy saddle. They were just friends. He gladly carried her anywhere she desired, and when he led, she willingly went along for the ride.

The long paved road throughout the ranch ran relatively flat around the pastures and homes. However, the main entry road that dropped from the Byway into the ranch was a quarter-mile long and terrifically steep. Arriving at the base of the precipitous entrance road, she dismounted and led her friend up the hill to stretch his legs. They would explore the canyons on dirt roads just as soon as they crossed the Byway and headed east.

Nikki loved to ride in the early morning just before the sun rose over the Angel peaks and cast its rays over the ancient land she reverently adored. In the crisp air their breath hung like gossamer mist. Something about the days between summer and autumn made her glad to be alive. Mornings were cool, but the daytime temperatures still quite hot in the desert. Excitement hung in the air as they cantered down the road toward the *Stairway to Heaven*; stairs carved long ago with dynamite to facilitate the herding of cattle over the mountains. Here,where no cacti grew, Pegasus ran with no inhibitions, enjoying the challenge of climbing the steep rock stairs that delivered them to the overlook from the west side of Zion.

Once atop the mesa, Nikki slid off his back, stood to face the rising sun, and closed her eyes. The ritual, frequently performed when they rode together, caused Pegasus to wonder what she felt in the embrace of the first rays of the sun. She became enlivened and joyous after her dance with its glimmering light, and he wished he could hear the song the rays sang to her. Nikki turned to him, winked, and then walked to the edge of the mesa where her voice broke into song. Sometimes she would do this, as if the song used her to free its heart upon the winds, which, falling to the earth, blessed all life.

When the rite was complete she offered Pegasus a gift of gratitude, an apple from her backpack. After he finished his treat, she mounted and they wended their way back toward the ranch.

Approaching the Byway, she could see a car parked at the overlook above her spread. Upon its hood sat an overly large crow who took flight as they neared. She assumed the car belonged to either a curious tourist peeking into her private domain, or someone with car problems. The pair remained still and silent, waiting to see if someone would emerge from the overlook and head for the car.

The man stood about five-foot eleven, clad in new denim jeans, an expensive leather coat, polo shirt, sunglasses, and a black ball cap embroidered with a Warner Bros. logo. He sported a rather bushy, unkempt black beard, but the quality of his clothing and the way he held himself, however, made her think he was probably pretty well heeled. She prided herself on her ability to sum people up before they even opened their mouths and had very rarely been wrong. "Another locations manager, I'd wager," she muttered under her breath as she encouraged Pegasus toward him.

"Hey," (as opposed to 'hello') she said softly as she approached. "You just enjoying God's country or are you in trouble?"

"Aye, a bit o' both, ma'am," he replied with his thick Irish accent.

Because her ranch was four miles from the nearest anything, and radio waves impossible to pick up in the mountain range, she chuckled at the cell phone in his hand.

"Desperate for a phone, are you?" She smiled kindly, though in her heart she could never understand why anyone would seek communication with the outside world when they had the opportunity to dance among the spirits in Zion.

"Can't seem to get the bloody thing to work here!" He began shaking the phone as if it were simply disobeying his will.

"Drive back about a quarter mile to the Red Rock Canyon Ranch and I'll let you use my phone."As she turned Pegasus toward the Byway, his comment stopped her short.

"If I could get mi damn car to work, I'd be glad to. If I could get the bloody phone to work, I wouldn't need to bother anyone!"

Nikki had traveled to and worked a great deal in Ireland. She noted with interest his use of "mi," commonly used by the country folk in place of the word "my." It sounded much like the word "me," but in Ireland it was common to nearly drop the "eee" sound and practically say only the "m." Those who were raised in upper crust society of the larger cities rarely said "mi," but used the proper English "my" instead. *Clearly, this man either claims his origin in the Irish countryside, or was raised a rustic in the city,* she thought.

"Rental?" She pointed to the old blue Celica with severe rust holes dotting the bottom edges. The car simply did not match the man's attire or demeanor.

"Borrowed," he shot back tersely while kicking the tire. "It's making me contrary!"

"Mind horses?" She laughed inwardly at his odd statement as she offered her arm to lift him.

He tentatively scanned the breadth of the horse, noticing the lack of saddle, stirrups, and bit. "Is 'e calm enough to take us both?" he asked timidly.

"Pegasus is quite a gentle angel. I'm sure he'll be glad to fly us both home."

"I doubt a wee bit of a lass such as ye has the strength to pull me up to that height. We'll both end up on the ground!"

Spurred on by his unintended challenge, she bent and extended her foot in lieu of a stirrup.

He looked about to see if a boulder or tree stump could raise him to the height of the horse's back. Seeing none, he took her offered arm. Her strength felt like being lifted with sure swiftness in perfect balance, as if some unseen force had swung his full weight without the slightest effort.

The absence of a saddle and the slight sway of the horse's back pulled him so close to her that he blushed. She sensed his discomfort and asked if he would prefer to ride in front and have her behind.

"Nay, ma'am, 'tis all right," he answered hoarsely, betraying his embarrassment at having her read his thoughts so easily. "If ye don't mind, may I hang onto ye? Haven't been on a horse when I didn't have control before!"

Hmmm, she thought, *surprise, surprise—another man who wants to be in control.*

Pegasus turned sure-footedly and headed home as if there were no additional weight to bear. Something felt right about the two of them on his back, like a long awaited, pleasant reunion. During the mile ride to the main house he didn't object in the slightest.

The man appeared strong, and his hands were large, with fingers that looked too beefy for the rest of his frame. He wore a rather gaudy gold ring on his right baby finger, and Nikki smiled inwardly, remembering all the different "star types" who had been in movies filmed on her ranch. They dressed like that: incognito, but standing out like a tall red tulip in a field of yellow pansies. She decided not to pry.

As they entered the gate to her ranch the sight of the towering Zion mesas and monoliths in the distance striking a great contrast to the valley beneath overwhelmed him. Bordering the road cut out of a volcanic mesa were tumbled, black porous rocks lining the mountainside to his left. The opposing mesas of red sandstone, however, showed no signs of volcanic activity. Deep green pastures, old, tall cottonwood trees, and a meandering stream filled the narrow valley beneath. Many of the leaves had turned a bright yellow and as the sun shone through them, they looked like dancing gold rimming the fields. The lush green of the pastures seemed out of place in the high red desert, otherwise filled with junipers, sage, and cactus. The effect provided a feast for the eyes, softening the overpowering majesty of Zion. Even though it made him feel small, he felt completely welcome in the great park.

The long, steep, red driveway always looked forbidding, even in a car, for its eight-foot width dropped off sharply on one side about a hundred feet to the bottom of the canyon. Nikki heard the man whistle under his breath and guessed he was holding it just a tad. Just then, Pegasus stepped on a pebble and his weight thrust forward, adjusting his cargo. The man's arms swiftly made their way full round her midriff as if he trusted her to save him.

"Bloody 'ell!" he cried out.

She felt his heart beating furiously with his chest pressed tightly against her back.

"It's all right." She spoke gently as she leaned into him. "Just a pebble in his soft spot, I expect. He seems all right now." Pegasus recognized the tone of her voice; the same she used to calm him when he shied near a snake or anything he perceived from fear. "We're almost to the bottom of the hill and quite close to our destination. Just relax and trust me and I'll take you safely home."

What is it about this woman? Quietly, the Irishman became absorbed in his own thoughts. *She just appears from nowhere at the crack of dawn, astride this beautiful horse to rescue me. Damn lucky coincidence, lad!* He had become so accustomed to people catering to his every whim that he was shocked to find himself thinking any thoughts leaning toward gratitude.

He relaxed his grip slightly, so as not to appear a coward. Leaning back, he noticed her chestnut hair hung in a very long, thick braid down her back. It caught the morning sunrays while a thousand colors flashed from within each strand. Her braid was tied with a thin leather lace, at the end of which, dangled one malachite bead. The unusual adornment in her hair triggered an odd but powerful impression. He suddenly wanted to turn her around, right on the back of the horse, and embrace her with all his might. The feeling engulfed him, holding him slightly paralyzed as his chest seemed to expand with a blast of energy that radiated outward. Every nerve in his body began to tingle as he was held astounded by the sensation. The pleasant feeling, both physically and emotionally, led him to dismiss the possibility of heart failure. The moment passed and he attributed the odd experience to low blood sugar, for his breakfast consisted only of coffee and a cigarette. He laughed at himself and thought, *Hey, ol' man, just get to the damn phone and get a driver here as soon as ye can.*

She guided the horse before the most serene pastures, dotted with a border of cottonwood trees and lined with ancient, wide fences made of thick wood. The structures of the ranch were obviously old, but did not detract from the remarkable beauty. In fact, the white fences, in dire need of fresh paint, added to the rustic flavor of the place.

To him, Pegasus seemed unusually calm for a horse returning home. It had been his experience that most horses were barn sour, displaying infinitely more enthusiasm upon returning home than when they left their comfort zones.

They rode past a large, open wood structure with a metal roof, under which partitioned sections held ranch equipment. A black wooden profile of a cowboy, hat tilted forward, wearing a red bandana around the neck, leaned against a post.

A backhoe protruded from one section and the next held a tractor, apparently under repair, for parts and tools were strewn about it. Stacks of wood, both for burning, as well as building and repairs, filled the next section. Chainsaws, tools, mowers, and all the implements required to run a ranch were in full display. Only one area benefited from the protection of four solid walls, though secured only by a piece of wire through an old hasp on the door. *They're obviously not too concerned with security here,* he mused.

On his left appeared a number of gas tanks, each labeled properly for the different grades. Adjacent to the tanks sat a little gray building of clapboard construction with teal trim and shutters. A Rhode Island Red rooster had been painted on a round wooden plaque and bolted to the teal door. A fully caged area to house the chickens was attached to the building, but the high dry grasses inside indicated no animal life within.

They meandered around a wide bend in the road and past three more pastures. Two horses looked up nonchalantly as they passed, and when Pegasus whinnied, they answered. As the horse reached the top of a small hill, a pond with ripples of dancing light reflecting the morning sun came into view. Occasional weeping willows edged the pond along with little stone pillars between which were braced poles of cedar logs. In the center of the pond another willow on a tiny island shaded several sleeping ducks. Anchored to a purple dock, a blue-and-white canopied pedal boat swayed in the water.

Opposite the pond a sizeable vegetable garden surrounded by a purple picket fence mirrored the dock's bright color. *That's funky,* he thought as he twisted to get a better look. Most of the garden had been cleared, but signs of pumpkins, tomatoes, carrots, and squash still remained.

Uneven, winding rock wall gardens guarded the entrance to a small cabin situated north of the vegetable patch. The autumn flowers within them bloomed profusely. An unusual purple gate separated the rock walls, allowing entrance to the pathway toward the home. The cabin, built of old logs, had a front door constructed of heavy wooden planks, hinged with large ornamental iron. Charming paintings hung on the exterior of the house, and little flower boxes hung perkily beneath the windows. Petite sculptures of angels, fairies, and animals were placed throughout the yard as if they were somewhat shy and hiding. The sum of the picture did not appear tacky, but rather innocuous and tasteful, creating a most inviting little space. It beckoned with a strange peace and coziness missing from his busy life. *If I could but sit in that garden for a minute, I know I could take that feeling with me,* he wished silently.

When she steered the horse past the cabin, he assumed it

belonged to a caretaker. He feared his opportunity to visit the magical garden would be lost in the shuffle of phone calls in his attempt to contact someone to take him back to the set.

Apparently, his rescuer didn't understand his anxiousness to complete his task, for she headed the horse down yet another steep hill. To his relief, this one appeared shorter than the entrance road. Finally arriving at the barn, they dismounted and she led Pegasus to a breezeway for some feed and a rubdown. The stranger stood at her mercy, not wanting to seem ungrateful for her assistance. While he strolled around exploring, biding his time while waiting, he noticed none of the twelve stalls had occupants. Thick cobwebs indicated they had gone unused for some time. Beyond the barn he passed a horse walker, an indoor arena, and a large outdoor arena, complete with lights.

When he returned to the breezeway, he saw she had finished. The little woman untied the horse from the heavy metal braces on the wall and after removing the rope halter and blanket, turned and walked away from the horse. Pegasus followed her like a puppy until she reached an old metal gate that led to the stream. She unlatched the gate and it squeaked on its hinges as she cleared a space wide enough for both of them to enter. He heard her whisper, "Thank you, my friend," as she gave the horse's rump a friendly pat. Pegasus nodded to her, issued a little snort, then ambled slowly to the stream for a good, long drink.

Nikki turned to the Irishman while removing her jacket, exposing her slight, but strong looking body. She wore a gray sweatshirt with black riding pants and running shoes instead of boots. He had the impression he already knew her and removed his sunglasses to get a better look.

For the first time in forty-five minutes their eyes actually met and her heart exploded with joy. *It's him!* she screamed to herself.

It's him! I'd given up hope of finding him in this lifetime, but I'd know those eyes anywhere throughout eternity. She wanted to dance and squeal, grasp his arms and hold him close to celebrate their reunion, but she knew better. She called upon her higher self to send forth a rush of harmony and calmness, but could see beyond her restraint that he must have recognized something too. Not daring to break the spell, they both silently stared into each other's eyes. After a considerable pause and willing his eyes to look downward, he found his voice.

"I thank ye for ye'r kindness and help—and phone."

"Of course, it's not every day one gets to rescue Dylan Crow." She laughed out loud, for both of them knew he was no longer anonymous. "I heard rumor a movie crew was filming in Kanab, but I hadn't heard who the stars were. And, from your performances, I would never have guessed you were Irish! I've never heard your accent in any of your films. How do you change from one voice to another?"

"To be honest, I've spent a lot o' time with voice coaches. I can do anything from a New York cabbie to an Australian outback alligator wrestler!" What may have appeared as braggadocio was actually well earned, and he was proud of his achievement. He changed his accent like other men changed their clothes, depending on the need of the moment. Hollywood loved him because they could cast him into any mold. Unlike some of the great stars, he did not play himself—he played his character.

He seemed to shift into "I'm a movie god" mode, which she recognized instantly from her less-than-pleasant experiences with other movie stars. Her ranch had been used as a primary location for any number of films and she had observed that great talent was often accompanied by great pride. It made her uncomfortable, so she made a perceptible effort not to fuss over him.

"I thought I'd explore the area today to help me get into the head of the character I'm playing. That's why I borrowed that stupid car and why I'm out here in the middle of nowhere this morning."

"Come on up the hill to my humble digs. We even have electricity and running water out here in 'the middle of nowhere.'" Although she pretended offense, he could see it was just a ruse. She reached out her hand to make him move, for he seemed cemented to the earth. When their hands met, an undeniable jolt hit them both.

Is it he, or am I just recognizing some movie star who seems familiar because his face has appeared on everything from my television to every magazine that has crossed my desk? She wasn't sure if she could trust her impressions.

Only the frantic beating of Crow's heart outpaced his thoughts. *Crikey! What was that? What's going on in that head o' yers Dylan, ol' man? Ye'd best slow this pony down, lad, or ye'll be doing something else to show up on the 'bad boy' tabloid pages.* He had never married and possessed a notorious reputation for womanizing, though lately it had been more gossip than real.

She released his hand, aware his feet were finally moving, and they hiked the thirty-three steps to her log home. Her muscular yellow Lab and another hairy monster of a dog she called Bear, rose to the occasion with the warning growls they served up to every stranger. The hairy one struggled to his feet with obvious pain in his hips. "It's all right boys. It's just a movie demi-god passing through," she explained in mock humor.

"I take it ye're not overly fond of people in m' profession?" Before giving her a chance to pass judgment aloud, he changed the subject and pointed to Bear. "What kind o' beast is that?"

"He's a cross between a Great Pyrenees and a Bernese. I used to have four. Bought the whole litter from Robert Redford twelve years ago. He's the last, and I'm afraid he stays on just to comfort me. I love him to death. The Lab belongs to my son."

She smiled. "In answer to your first question, this beautiful spot has drawn more than its share of location managers and movie crews to my door. I always vow never to let them come again, and then I cave. Haven't had any since my husband died, though. Somehow it seemed to be too much of an invasion on my privacy—which I value greatly."

"Ye know Redford personally, then?"

"Not really. Met him a few times at openings and fundraisers with the obligatory friendliness. In fact, when he and Newman filmed Butch Cassidy around here in the sixties, he tried to buy this ranch from the previous owner. Unfortunately, the owner was a rather self-important, obscenely rich alcoholic, who insulted the hell out of Redford. Rumor is that Redford told him he'd own the ranch one day anyway." She reached down and scratched Bear's ear. The dog obviously loved her. "I bought the dogs from the kennel manager at Sundance. I don't think Redford even knew about the sale or cared who bought them."

He couldn't help noticing that her eyes matched his almost identically—not the shape or the brow, just the iris itself. Their deep green color, spotted with flecks of yellow, were rimmed with a striking bluish violet. Looking into her eyes reminded him of a time in his childhood when he spent many hours staring into a mirror, trying to see his soul through his eyes. He dismissed the odd thought and drew his brows together in apology. "I didn't mean to invade ye'r privacy, ma'am. I do appreciate ye'r help, though. If ye'll just show me to a phone, I'll make mi exit stage left so's not to burden ye with mi company."

"My name is Nikki…Nikki James." She bowed as if presented to royalty. "Somehow hearing you call me 'ma'am' makes me feel like you think I'm a really old woman!"

"Aye, just being the respectful lad mi mum raised, ma'am—I mean, Nikki," he stammered.

They both laughed with their eyes. She had a youthful ageless-ness about her and, from all appearances, looked near his age or slightly younger.

She led him to her home, the old cabin he deemed belonged to a caretaker. He was charmed by the little rock wall gardens over-flowing with the colors and aromas of flowers. The crooked stone pathway that greeted him as he entered her space felt like a bit of a fairy tale.

The outer door was constructed of thick, heavily lacquered wooden planks. At eye level a small, round, wooden plaque paint-ed in an almost medieval design lent a great deal of charisma to the entry. A padlock, which hung on a less than secure hasp, appeared to be the only security for the door. He wondered if it had ever been locked. A miniature hand-pull doorbell hung on the wall above the window box.

A large forged bell inserted into the top of a wooden post to the left of the door was nearly hidden for all the honeysuckle that had entwined around it. Its pull rope connected to the interior of the house through a small hole. *The dinner bell?* he wondered.

She opened the heavy outer door, and then a wooden screened one as they entered directly into the kitchen. His thoughts deep-ened as he assessed the architectural arrangement. *Aren't old ranch houses wonderfully functional? No pretense. Just get on in where the heart of the home lies!*

"You can have some privacy right through there." She pointed right of the kitchen to a small office. "There's a facility there as well, if nature is calling. You need a phone book?"

"Blast!" he cursed under his breath. "They all have cell phones over there and the only one I had memorized was m' assistant's.

She dropped it at the airport last night. I'm sure she hasn't had time to replace it yet."

"So, you want me to find a tow truck or something?"

"I think I can reach m' agent. He'll get all the right numbers for me. May take a few minutes, though. Do ye mind?" Uncertainty flooded his voice, knowing she didn't much seem to care for his type of people or the intrusion into her private space.

"Go right ahead. I'll just go change clothes and be back in a jiff."

He entered her little office, filled with pictures and sculptures of angels, flowers, cottages, and crystals. *Oh God, another New-Ager!* he thought, as he scrounged around the top of her desk hunting for pencil and paper. He spied a stone angel holding a writing pen. A sticky pad was next to the phone, so he accepted the proffered pen, picked up the receiver, and dialed.

As the phone rang on the other end of the line, he tapped the pen impatiently on the antique French style desk. Exquisite gold handles graced the drawers. While certainly not ranch-esque, it suited this little shrine perfectly. A rectangular wicker basket held a shallow pile of pamphlets advertising the Red Rock Canyon Ranch. A beautiful business card was stapled to the top with Nikki's information printed in an elegant font bordered by flowers with a deep, black background, forcing the color of the florals to jump out at the eye. Obviously a sales piece, Crow helped himself to one, folding it carefully and tucking it in his inside jacket pocket. He'd get his assistant, Peggy, to send her a note of thanks or something.

A machine answered the line. He looked at his watch, realizing it was perhaps a bit early for anyone to be in Robert's office with the one-hour difference in time zones. He re-dialed, only this time to Robert's home. Still no answer. *Must 'ave stayed the night at his new girlfriend's house,* he thought. *Now, laddie, try to remember her name*

and where he said she lived! He paced; a habitual pattern that surfaced
when solving riddles. Raising his forefinger in the air, he declared,
"Got it! Susan Therandon! Thounds like Susan Sarandon with a lisp.
Right. And Thuthan Therandon lives thumwhere in—Laguna!" He
laughed aloud at his own silliness.

He couldn't remember the area code for Laguna and not wanting an information charge to appear on Nikki's phone bill, began
searching for a phone book. The desk drawers held only supplies,
the cabinets, only books. An armoire facing the desk contained a
small television and stereo and other files and supplies.

The kitchen seemed the next most likely location, so there he
returned.Verde green cupboards gave the appearance of some storybook Italian or French country place. The cooking space opened
into a seating area with large, soft leather couches adorned with
tapestry pillows. A thick area rug with an East Indian design sat
atop a wall-to-wall carpet. The ancient, well-used stone fireplace
faced the room, flanked by two doorways.

Large windows opposed each other and through the one on
his right he saw another part of the building, indicating the cabin
was much larger than it appeared from the front. A round wood-
en painting portraying hanging grapes was bolted to an exterior
wall. The whole effect seemed rather Hansel and Grettel-ish. As he
ventured further, he beheld a grand tree with sweeping branches
cradling the house. On the lowest branch sat a large male peacock,
whose very presence in the desert setting seemed so unlikely, it
took him back a little. The bird's long, bright blue neck caught the
sun, and its tail feathers hung a full five feet beneath the branch.
His imperial beauty seemed surreal.

Beyond the tree he saw a swimming pool and some sort of
structure to its right, though the foliage somewhat impaired his
vision and he could not quite make out what purpose it served.

The window to his left exposed a patio area, also adjoining more building. Gardens of vinca surrounded the edges. The patio held a surface hot tub and another large tree whose trunk grew straight out of the stone and concrete. A small wrought-iron table set was topped with a pot of geraniums. Beyond the patio, the property appeared to fall away to the stream and the pastures on the other side where he could see Pegasus lazily grazing. He felt as if he'd stumbled into a magical realm.

The room held an oversized television along with all the latest electronic media equipment. On either side of the room two matching cinnabar sideboards were topped with striated yellow marble. Original oil paintings graced the old log walls; paintings of flowers, landscapes, still-lifes, and a few portraits. Over the seating area hung a sizeable old wagon-wheel, appointed with propane lights. A more eclectic collection of furniture and treasures he had never seen, and yet everything seemed complementary and nothing seemed out of place. The room welcomed him. It felt relaxing to be in a place that invited you to sit comfortably without concern for the monetary value of its surroundings. Quality, without ostentatious pretense, was evidenced everywhere.

Turning back to the kitchen, his eyes were drawn to something in the dining alcove; an oil painting of an old cowboy wearing glasses and a straw hat. The eyes of the cowboy looked back at him with a definite mischievous twinkle while the mouth twisted in an ironic smile—the kind you see on the face of someone who just got the better of you. It wasn't framed. In fact, of the eight or so oils in the room, only a few were framed. The portrait did not hang on the wall like the others in her home, but instead sat angled on the rack as if on purpose so the old man could keep an eye on things. *Probably a portrait of her father,* he thought.

Opening the antique European armoire in the corner of the

kitchen, he searched for a phone book. Unexpectedly, he found elegant china and crystal of the highest quality. He rummaged through the room, drawer by drawer, until he found a phone book, feeling somewhat ashamed for having invaded Nikki's privacy.

He obtained the area code for Laguna, but realized he'd still have to call information for the listing. *What a bloody supreme waste of time, ye idiot!*

"Hey, mate!" Dylan tried to cheer his agent with his own enthusiasm, as Thuthan Therandon made it clear his call had awakened them.

"Dylan, aren't you in Utah? Is there a problem?" Robert inquired with an equal measure of concern and irritation. He hadn't had his morning coffee or a cigarette and very much resented being roused from a peaceful sleep.

"Caught mi foot in the dunny, mate. Need ye'r help." Dylan laughed at the standing private joke between them.

"When are you going to trade in that dumb *Crocodile Dundee* humor? What's the problem?"

"I got here a few days early to take advantage of the scenery and to get into the character of it, ya know? Anyway, borrowed a damn Celica from one of the crew who said, 'Go over to Zion …not the part where the tourists are…go to the west side. It's really beautiful and ye can hike without anyone seeing ye or knowing who ye are.' 'Right,' says I, and I'm off at five a.m. I drove an hour to get to the right road, and then, five miles from the main highway, in the middle of nowhere, the car stopped cold. I mean, bloody cold. Mi cell wouldn't work so I hitched a ride on the back of a horse with a local rancher. I'm using her phone now, and I can't remember any crew numbers to call for help. Can ye locate them and call me back?"

"Sure, Dylan, but Brenda has access to that stuff and she's

undoubtedly stuck on the freeway for about an hour. Can you just sit tight? Maybe you can borrow a horse from the rancher and go riding instead of hiking and I'll leave you a message."

"I'll work something out. Ta, man. Here's the number in 'Yee-ha,' Utah. The rancher's name is Nikki, in case I'm not here," he said, thinking the day might not be wasted if he took his agent's advice.

He hung up the phone and turned, surprised to see her standing at the doorway. "'Yee-ha,' Utah, huh? As opposed to 'Yee-ha,' Dublin?" She winked, unoffended, accustomed to others seeming snobbish about their culture-fied, high-powered lives in the city and looking down on her—actually feeling sorry for her out in the middle of nowhere. Few people knew she came from their lifestyle of high power, high finance, lavish, expensive homes, and moved to this sacred place just to get away from the illusions that make people feel so empty inside. Certain he would not find this personal information of interest, the temptation to flaunt it was disciplined into a sly smile to the right side of her face.

"I meant ye no disrespect. In fact, I have a sheep ranch miself in 'Yee-ha,' West Cork in Ireland." He hoped his repentant remark sounded sincere.

"You ever get there, or is it just a dream upon which you pay taxes?"

"Ouch!" He winced. "Ye cut right to the heart, don't ye? I try to get there at least twice a year. Mi parents are still alive and live there. Da's too old to actually do any work, so mi older brother, Mic, runs about two hundred fifty head of sheep for me. Just a humble lit'l place, kind o' like ye'rs; too beautiful for words, expensive to keep, but it's where I go to recharge and remember who I am." There was wistfulness in his voice as it trailed to a whisper when he said the last few words.

"Well, you're no different from the rest of mankind. We all want our cake and to eat it too. But, as the old adage goes, 'one cannot ride two horses at the same time.'"

She had changed into denim pants which hugged her graceful, little frame, and a slightly oversized gauze shirt with the sleeves rolled to mid-forearm. Except for her watch, the only jewelry on her hands was a very small gold ring, worn above the middle knuckle joint of her wedding finger. A chain hung around her neck, but the pendant seemed to be nestled between her breasts and he decided not to take his eyes there. Her hair, no longer in the braid, flowed softly around her face. The slightest bit of make-up could be detected on her eyes and her lips were covered with a soft, pinkish lipstick. Her matching eyes shone clear, bright, and intense, and though quite friendly and welcoming, seemed to look straight through him.

"Any luck?" she asked, as she headed toward the kitchen.

"It's going to take a bit o' time for them to get back to me. Where can I be out of ye'r way so ye don't feel obliged to cater to the movie star?"

"Well, you mentioned you'd come over here to get into the character of the place, right? Want me to take you to any secret places; places where the gods of Zion allow only people from exclusive circles?" Her hushed voice implied a secret, but her eyes were laughing at him.

"Ye wouldn't be making fun of me, now, would ye?" He purposely used the old Irish, "ye" whenever he felt the need to charm someone. Due to his work in the States, however, he often used the word "you" in the very same sentence. Though it was an error often made by those learning a new language, he seemed to do it on purpose. "I try mi best to really give it mi all with each character I play—to know what his surroundings make him feel like—

what gives rise to his character in the first place." He stood directly before her, challenging her with his eyes, even though the corners of his mouth were turned up in a smile, indicating his willingness to engage in this playful banter.

"I'm serious," she said with a sparkle in her eye. Then her voice softened to the point of reverence and her demeanor changed, signifying she was, in fact, serious. "There are places here very few people know about that I personally hold sacred. I've never offered to take anyone to them before, but somehow I feel quite comfortable offering it to you. This is a very special place on this planet, and I promised myself and the mountain gods to keep it holy."

"Now, ye're scaring me. Are ye one of those *New-Age* wackos who holds crystals to her head and talks to angels and stuff? I think that stuff's a load o'—excuse the expression—shite!"

"All things in their own time, Mr. Crow." She dropped the subject, hiding her disappointment. "Why don't you just wander around the ranch, then. It's over six hundred acres and maybe that can give you a feel for Zion. I'll take any messages for you. Just close any gates you open so my horses and cows don't go dancing off to some stranger's party," she said, turning to look out the window. She didn't want him to see her eyes, to see how he'd just insulted her.

"Well–right. Ok, then," he said, a little confused about how quickly the conversation had turned from light, comical banter to her apparent desire for distance. He didn't actually mind, however, because he had hoped to be *alone* in Zion today. He headed for the door to make his "exit, stage left." "I thank 'e for ye'r help, Nikki. So... I'll just explore a bit and be back in a while."

The old screen door slapped behind him, and he actually looked forward to being alone in that wonderful garden. He looked at every stone piled one upon another in the little rock walls, filled with the usual autumn varieties, including one type of flower with the deepest indigo coloring he had ever seen. The unusual paintings on large round pieces of wood adorning the exterior walls of her home attracted his closer inspection. The vegetable garden, so free of weeds, convinced him the gardening gnomes must be maintaining it. The whole little kingdom proved more than a charming site. It elicited a charming feeling, or truthfully, more the feeling of being enchanted.

He crossed the lawns to the back of the old home, discovering the building next to the pool to be a covered, open area for eating out of doors. Two very long redwood tables looked as if they could seat fifty or more people. The water in the pool tested a tad frigid for his taste, seeming less than inviting. The picnic area looked ancient with a sagging roofline, as if its entire foundation had sunk a foot or two since its erection. He had to duck his head just to gain entry under the edge of the pitched roof. A miniature Viking ship, about six feet long, complete with oar lights and a dragon's head at the helm, hung in the apex of the ceiling, and though wildly out of place in the desert setting, fit perfectly in her little magical kingdom. The extraordinary ship was certainly as interesting as everything else he viewed.

Trophy horns and an elephant's tusk were mounted throughout the picnic area. He opened a door into a covered and screened room. A stone water fountain gurgled in the corner and brightly colored furniture made for a hospitable retreat. The pole-and-screen construction formed two and one-half walls of the room; the other walls were covered with cupboards. Oil paintings hung on both the solid and the pole-and-screen walls. Bright yellow canvas curtains hung open along the entire screened area. As he entered further into the room, a hutch caught his eye. The open shelving displayed small sculptures of stone, clay, and wood. In the corner of the room sat a tall, narrow, sculpting table made from two-by-fours with an unfinished piece on top; a white stone with three figures---the largest embracing the two beneath it, the next largest, embracing the smaller one. The hands of the largest figure rested on the head of the small one, while the middle figure's hands rested over the heart of the small one. Though quite unusual and still a work in progress, it appealed to him. A leather tool case lay open on the counter, exposing chisels and files with a mallet positioned near. *So, the lady's an artist,* he pondered as he fingered the tools.

He thought himself thoroughly accustomed to the catered luxury of his lifestyle, the feel of leather and cold steel, the hard, angular lines of the furniture in his apartments, the complete lack of plants due to his inability to stay in any one place for long. He'd finally grown comfortable with the modern art he had chosen (or rather, his decorators had chosen for him): modern art, with no meaning and all meaning. An insight struck as he realized he had done nothing more than nod his approval for the purchase of the items in his various abodes, having chosen none personally. Though many beautiful objects adorned his places, he had attempted to make everything useful, even if its only use was to impress others.

Most of his dwellings represented temporary stopping platforms. Nothing in them held any particular sentimental attachment. Even if they were considered elite masterpieces in architectural and design circles, he could easily sell them with no regrets. The only place that spoke to his heart was his home on the ranch in Schull. There he had surrounded himself with things, animals, and people he loved. Every picture on the wall, every stick of furniture represented some valued part of his life. His ranch held his dreams and his memories. He had purposely chosen not to let a decorator or anyone else help him put it together.

This little haven now before his eyes demonstrated beauty and charm born of devotion and love, with its beauty and magic as useful as anything useful. The structures appeared old, but charming, and unique. Everything possessed character, as if someone loved each square foot and had made it a sanctuary of sorts. He appreciated that deep within his soul.

It had been two years since he had been home for more than a few days. He had adapted to elevators and doormen, bodyguards and hangers-on—each wanting a piece of him, his life, talent, money, or whatever. *It's a game,* he reminded himself often, *and ye have to play it to be in mi chosen vocation.* Consciously aware that every profession has its aspirants who make up the courtly retinue of those who are at the summit, he knew his little universe was no different. The very thing that allowed him to keep order in his life was using the services of those who watched over his smile. No power is without its worshipers, and Crow definitely rode in a seat of power at this juncture in his life.

Who is this strange woman, looking back at me with mi own eyes, who created this little piece of heaven on earth? he wondered silently.

Reverie gave way to curiosity and impatience, so he directed his feet down the main road. At a fork he chose to go left. The pastures filled with mares and foals induced a sense of rural peace. He could hear every bird's song, every squirrel's chirp. A snake slithered in front of him: a big black and white snake, which eyed him warily and then, with indifference, glided past him into the tall brush.

He strolled down a wooded road toward some buildings evidenced in the distance. As the road turned, a small cottage with window flower boxes and an English garden entry came into view. It also had one of the unique round wooden paintings adorning it. Assuming someone lived there, he kept his distance.

In the fork of the drive, a sizable volcanic boulder supported a sculpture of a large, kneeling woman, holding what looked like a broken bowl full of stars. Her eyes gazed toward heaven with a large tear rolling down her cheek. At the base of the sculpture, almost hidden by the tall flowers that surrounded the boulder, a plaque read:

> *Whenever life hands you experiences of disappointment or betrayal and you feel your heart is broken beyond repair, turn your attention to God. He will fill your broken heart with the illumination of his Divine Love, Intelligence, and Wisdom. Then will this world appear to you as the illusion it truly is, and all experience will serve only to teach and enlighten you.*

Studying the piece more closely, what he had thought a bowl now appeared as a broken heart filled with stars. *I wonder if Nikki sculpted this?* He read the plaque again and again. *I wonder if she wrote that? If she did, I hope her heart is full now.* If he had pen and paper, he would have written it down for future reference. He had experienced his share of disappointment and betrayal in life.

Within a hundred yards two more houses could be seen: one small cabin with a tennis court next to it, and a larger log home, which seemed relatively new. *Maybe I'm trespassing,* he thought, hurrying past them to an old gate that hung on rusted antique hinges. He gained entry, and then closed it per his hostess' instructions. Ancient walls of stacked rock lined the dirt road, behind which, berry bushes grew as high as his head. Following the path to a stream, he removed his shoes and waded through to the other side.

A large boulder served as a seat while he allowed his feet to dry. Nearby, a cattle path running adjacent to the stream begged him to explore. He came to a section of the stream, adjacent to a towering sheer wall which rose a full eighty feet above him. Water plants with long draping tendrils hung lazily down the entire surface. The stream babbled gently. It reminded him of some hanging gardens he had once seen in Italy. "What an odd, but wonderful, sight in the middle of the desert—a veritable oasis," he declared out loud.

The welcoming shade under the trees beckoned, so he decided to lie upon the riverbank and bask in the serenity for a few minutes. The sun shone on his face every time the leaves blew slightly. They danced magically and hypnotically until he gave way to the sleepy movement of the shadows and closed his eyes.

How long he stayed, he did not know. He knew only that he dreamed of Nikki in this place with her hand outstretched, softly whispering, "If you'll just relax and trust me, I'll take you safely home." The dream, so serene and loving, made him long to stay lost in sleep, but once awakened, he could only be comforted by its memory.

Funny how mi subconscious works, he thought as he took off his shoes for the return trip over the stream. He had intentionally left his Rolex back in his room at the inn, not knowing whom he might come up against in the wilderness of Zion. Because he had lost track of time, he decided he'd better return to see if Robert had called.

As he approached her home, he saw Nikki leaning over her walled garden, deadheading some of the mums and singing softly to the indigo flowers. The tune, though hauntingly familiar, he could not name.

Her long hair, now hanging freely, reflected the sun and he wondered about her age. She said her husband had died, but she seemed too young for such tragedy. *Is she alone? She said she had a* son…maybe he's at school today. *How does she provide for herself?* These and a thousand other questions ran simultaneously through his mind.

She hadn't noticed him, so he stood still, slightly camouflaged by a tree, listening and watching. The scene embraced him with a sense of profound peace, and though he also felt that same peace in her presence, she awakened in him confusion and anxiety. It felt as if she expected nothing and yet everything from him—this unexplainably familiar stranger who had rescued him on a horse. Now, his ephemeral dream revealed that she would keep him safe and bring him home, if only he would trust her. *Of course,* he thought, *that could just be m' subconscious combining the events o' the morning.* The moment could have lasted forever as far as he was concerned. He didn't care about the impending phone calls or that he had work to do. He cared for nothing save standing there as a silent observer in her world.

Bear suddenly gave a warning bark that brought her head up. While waiving her acknowledgement of his presence, her lips broke into a smile of greeting. "All the numbers you asked for await your attention, sire," she said while bowing low, pretending royal respect.

They entered the kitchen and with a gesture of her hand, directed him to her tiny office yet again. This time she closed the door, which he assumed an act of courteousy to provide him with privacy. In truth, it had been done so she couldn't hear him say anything cruel about her or her beloved home.

"They'll be out to pick me up in about an hour and a half," he announced as he stepped back into her kitchen.

"Well, I guess I'll just have to put up with you for a while longer. How about a cup of coffee or some food?"

"Sure, I'd love a cup. No food though…still trying to maintain a slight weight for the film," he said, patting his belly.

A phone rang in another part of the house. She excused herself and ran lightly a good distance before he at last heard her
answer. *"Oh, Bonjour, mon ami!"* The conversation continued in
French for a few minutes and then switched to English. "Jacqueline,
my dear, I convinced Jean-Claude I would take such good care of
you since you're coming alone! I've booked the place for January
18th and I've cleared my schedule. We'll have a ball." There was
silence as she listened to the caller, and then he heard her say, "I'm
so sad to hear you sold the place in Nice. I assume you're keeping
the Paris apartment?" More silence, and then, "I'll call you when
you get back to Tahiti next week and give you the particulars. I'm
a little busy right now. Besides, I know it's late there and you two
need your sleep."

He half expected to hear her blurt out that a famous movie
star sat in her kitchen, but she made no mention either in French
or English. It surprised, but delighted, him to hear this woman
rancher from 'Yee-ha,' Utah, speak French.

She summoned him from his perch in the kitchen and he followed her voice. Unexpectedly, he entered a large room of about
sixty-by-thirty feet. It dropped down several steps to a seating area
that held white canvas furniture in heavy wicker frames. The beautiful fireplace rose about twenty feet to the apex of the pitched
ceiling. Large game heads mounted on the walls were highlighted
with individual spotlights concentrated on the most pronounced
features. Many of them looked African. On one of the massive log
beams supporting the ceiling crouched a cougar. A large caribou
stared down from over the fireplace, and an elk peered at him
from above a piano. Small African cats, a fox, a funny ferret-look-
ing creature, an owl, and oddly, a turkey peered curiously from
their appointed places. In addition to the mounted trophies, large

wooden sculptures of cranes, swans, and a life-size fawn tastefully joined the wild array.

The entire space, created from darkly stained rough cedar, required the full artificial lighting of the area just to see in the middle of the morning. The central light fixture, which hung from the ceiling by a thick chain, consisted of a three-tiered candelabra created from deer antlers, at the tip of which small, yellow flame-shaped globes shone eerily.

Past the initial seating area sat a stately billiard table. Beyond that, three stairs led to a large office, complete with desk, credenza, copier, and computer. Adjacent to the desk a square burlwood table surrounded by four large wicker chairs nearly implied card playing as opposed to business deals. The office offered the only window in the room. Cantilevered out from bottom to top and tinted light blue, it looked somewhat like the helm of a ship. An unusual room, to be sure, and while heavily populated with game trophies, still did not feel like a museum.

"Thought you'd like to see this crazy room," she said encouraging him to enter further. "The two previous owners of the ranch were both big game hunters. Their escapades and trophies were both famous and infamous, and people still love to drop in to see what remains. Actually, when we bought the place twelve years ago, thirty heads were removed from this room alone. Prize elephant tusks reached from floor to ceiling, weighing close to two hundred fifty pounds each."

Crow whistled in awe.

She droned on in a monotone, like the practiced tour guide she had become over the years. "Every cross support (she pointed to the heavy logs above their heads,) had a large cat of some sort positioned as if about to leap through the air and pounce on its victim. Some of the trophies were both illegal to hunt or own, and

I heard that silver crossed a lot of palms to get them out of Africa.

"A lion-skin rug, complete with the head, filled the lower seating area, and the biggest Alaskan polar bear skin I've ever seen covered most of the floor up here." She pointed to the office.

"After the old hunter died, his estranged son collected most of the trophies and stored them in a lean-to in his backyard. Unfortunately, the rodents had a heyday and he lost half a million dollars worth of beauties. I never could figure out why he didn't just put 'em in a museum until he could build a proper space. It's almost as if his careless act of destroying his father's dreams provided a subliminal way of 'getting back at daddy' for his lack of attention throughout the years."

She turned her guest's concentration toward the fireplace. "This beautiful masterpiece is created of full rounds of petrified wood which were mined here on the ranch. Because of the weight, a bearing wall had to be built in the basement just to support it."

She took his arm and led him up the three steps. "I always called this area my husband's 'command center.'" Looking tenderly around at his things, she gestured her hand back toward the game room. "Scott always said he'd never worked in such a large office before we moved here. The room is so depressingly dark that I never spend much time in here—so, for the most part, the entire room became his office. Personally, I thrive on light!

"This crazy window was copied from the bow of a ship the old hunter had seen in New Orleans. You see, natural light on the trophies destroys the skins and their value."

They looked through the window to a lawn surrounded by shrubbery. A small stone building, whose roof sat at the same elevation as the lawn, caught his eye. In answer to his raised brow she explained, "That's the skeet shoot house. There's still equipment in there for throwing clay pigeons. You just bring out a foot pedal to practice shooting. I let the boy scouts come up a couple of times each year to use it."

"Hunt ye'rself?" He seemed slightly baffled at the unexpected surroundings.

"Don't kill any animals," she almost whispered. "In fact, I've been a vegetarian for the most part of my life. It's just that the place and this room had such historical lore I couldn't bring myself to alter it much. We moved here when our son was small and I made up voices for each trophy to convince him they weren't menacing beasts hovering outside his bedroom, waiting to devour him." They both laughed easily.

"Ye raise cattle, but ye don't eat meat?"

"I keep barely enough livestock to maintain my greenbelt tax status. Scott used to tease me by saying we had the only herd of cows with names! I sell off the calves each autumn to the 4-H club so children can have the opportunity to raise them."

Just as people don't want to defend their desire to eat meat, she did not want to defend her desire not to use animals as food.

The tour being over, she ushered him gently toward the kitchen area again. With an unidentifiable longing, he wished he could see the rest of her space, but she didn't offer, and he didn't ask.

He watched while she heated some milk and filled the automatic coffee maker. After shaving a bar of Mexican chocolate and dropping the slivers into a big mug, she poured the hot coffee and milk over the chocolate, topping it with a splash of heavy whipping cream, a dash of cinnamon, and a drop of vanilla. "This is my specialty—similar to a bitter latté, but rich and full of flavor. It reminds me of my life: always wanting and enjoying the sweet, good, and beautiful things, but finding each treasure comes with a slightly bitter price tag."

"Have ye had a hard life, then?" he queried, avoiding direct contact with her eyes; a technique he had mastered to make people feel comfortable enough to open up.

"In retrospect, I'd have to say I've led a charmed life. I guess with age one learns to love and embrace each experience, happy and sad, for what it teaches. Some things I would choose never to experience again, but I don't believe in coincidence, so I know each experience has served me in some way."

He was pretty certain now that she had composed the words on the plaque by the sculpture.

Nikki pushed the steaming mug toward him. Concerned it would offend if he refused, he accepted the offering and sipped cautiously. Ambrosia excited his taste buds with a taste both sweet and bitter, rich and full of life, just as she had described.

Who is this woman? he thought again. *She seems so familiar. Must be her eyes. She's beautiful in her own sort o' way, but she's not glamorous—at least not what I usually have around. Yet, there's a unique beauty to her.* Then again, he found most women had their own unique beauty. He had made a habit of finding it in each one he met. *Stop it, ye git! Ye get plenty of female attention from some of the brightest, most beautiful women in the world. Don't ye be doin' something ye'll regret!*

He leaned backward, reached into his leather jacket and retrieved a pack of cigarettes.

"Would you mind not smoking in here? We can take our coffee out by the pool," she suggested politely. Her voice did not reflect judgment or unkindness. She simply stood with her coffee, opened the door and steered him out with a pleasant smile on her face.

"Crushin' habit, I know. Been smoking since I was twelve," he said apologetically. "Mi uncle owned a pub when I was a nipper, and I decided I would try every single brand of cigarette he carried. I thought it made me look 'cool'. By the time I'd achieved mi goal I was hooked. Tried to quit a time or two, 'cause I know it's bad for mi health. Guess I'll just be one of those guys who lives hard and fast and dies ugly."

As they walked through her garden toward the pool, she spoke as if reflecting on a past memory. "All addictions come from something infinitely deeper than a physiological need. It doesn't matter whether the addiction comes in the form of chemicals, tobacco, alcohol, food, sex, lying, pornography, work, or whatever. I don't think there's a soul on this planet who hasn't had to wrestle *that* alligator on some level."

"Ye?" he asked as they sat on the wooden bench beneath the Viking ship.

"Oh, indeed, yes. My addictions disguised themselves as sweets and salty, greasy foods. Funny, though, as soon as I looked for the root of the problem, I still ate the same things. Extra weight hung on my backside for a long time, but when I made an effort to discover and eliminate the *true* cause instead of battling the effect, the weight just fell off! Every challenge a body faces originates in spirit by misdirection of thought and feelings. Opposition comes veiled in many forms, but each is an opportunity to rise to the next level of consciousness. I've come to understand just how powerful my thinking and feelings are in relation to all I create."

"Just like acting, eh?" It was more a statement than a question. He took a long drag of his cigarette, blew a ring and watched it float upward, away from her.

She narrowed her eyes, weighing her next words. "I've always thought of actors as people who need to experience a great many things in their short lifetimes, and acting out so many different roles provides a sort of fast-track pathway of learning. The rest of us experience the same things you do, vicariously, by watching and identifying with your characters. We seem to have the free will to accept or reject the story, but you have to live the emotion of the story, which makes it a part of your permanent record. Maybe actors are on their last round." She laughed like an old wise woman while sipping her coffee and peeking over the rim of her cup to see his reaction.

"What do ye mean?"

"Reincarnation."

Oh, God, he thought, *we're entering a territory I don't want to get into. Do the fast switch, laddie.*

He gestured toward her left hand. "So, I notice ye don't wear a wedding ring...or would that be one ye wear above ye'r middle knuckle?"

She looked down at her fingers. "Actually, I wear this little band on the middle of my finger to remind me I am not yet complete."

"Because ye'r husband died?"

"No. I knew I wasn't complete many years before he changed domains." She realized he had purposely altered the course of the conversation. "I make you uncomfortable, don't I?"

"No, no, not at all. In fact, ye seem really familiar to me." He shifted nervously, his body objecting to the candidness of his comment. "It's just that I'm kind of sick of all the New-Age crap that's been floatin' 'round for a few decades. I looked into it a few years back with a girlfriend who was really into metaphysics. Somehow, it seemed to me that those involved were people who were so unhappy with this life that they created a fictitious la-la land. Didn't seem to make 'em any better people, however. By God, a fair lot of 'em made some big bucks out of it, ye know? It's kind o' like they just turned it into another organized religion."

"Wow! Most people don't figure that much out in thirty years.

I'd say you're right on track, dear."

His face gave away his thoughts, which she read like lightening. Her broad use of "dear" had been interpreted as intimacy. "Sorry," she apologized. "Just a habit I got into when my son was in elementary. Helping out at the school, I found it easier to call all the children 'dear' or 'sweetie' or 'honey'. That way they could tell I had affection for them even if I couldn't remember their names. Just kind of carried over into the rest of my life and it's been part of my M.O. ever since." She engaged him with a mischievous wink. "For an actor, you don't have a very good poker face!"

He gave a slight laugh and changed the subject yet again. "Ye'r son live with ye?"

"No, he's at Stanford." She felt sure he had no sincere interest in her life, and she didn't feel like making it a part of this small talk.

"Only one child?" he persisted.

"I have six, counting my late husband's, and seventeen grandchildren. However, I only bore one child of my own."

"Ye look sort of young for the likes of all that."

She shrugged her shoulders. "I guess some people are just ageless." Nikki did not want to talk about age because she knew it would lead her down a conversational path about no time and space, and quite obviously, this man was neither in the mood nor ready for it.

He took out another cigarette and looked toward a rocking chair. "Ye mind if I shift?"

"Feel free. So, tell me about the movie production in which you're involved."

"Ever read the book, *The Teaching of Little Crow?*"

Her face lit up with recognition. "Fabulous book! I adored it. It was written so long ago, I didn't know many people knew about it."

"Well, I play the role of Little Crow as an adult. They had a hard time finding someone to play Little Crow as a youngun', due to the cleft in mi chin, so they decided to keep me bearded. That's why I'm wearin' this rather ragged mop on mi face. I hate to wear a false beard, so I grew this one specially," he said while smothering the cigarette on the sole of his shoe. He had seen his uncle do this on many occasions and because he had revered him since childhood, he learned early to mimick the maneuver. Seeing a garbage pail in the corner, he rose to eliminate the stub.

"A situation arose with the studio, however, where they're not certain whether to use the ending given in the book or to create another that will be more Hollywood acceptable. Actually, we are filming two possible endings; one being that I teach mi people to be peaceful and lay down their arms at the cost of mi own life, as written in the book, and the other; that I use mi gifts to protect and defend them at all costs. The editors and producers will determine which one'll sell best.

"The whole native American thing has piqued mi curiosity since I was a lad," he confessed.

"For a guy out looking to get into character with the land, playing the part of a white shaman, your blantant avoidance of the subject of metaphysics surprises me." She hadn't phrased it as a question, which left him free to respond, or not, as he chose.

He shifted nervously in his chair and his eyes were downcast as he spoke. "To be honest, as much as I don't like to talk about things like past lives and other dimensions, I think the character I'm playing in this show was me, somewhere. I feel the need to play it over again and do the right thing this time. I know it sounds daft, but it's as if I need to make mi peace before I'm booked straight for hell." He looked up, directly into her eyes, almost as if seeking approval.

"Maybe it's no coincidence that you're starring in a film called *The Teaching of Little <u>Crow</u>.*" She emphasized "Crow" in reference to him rather than a fictional character. Her inflection seemed to go over his head, however, or maybe he just wasn't listening, for he showed no signs of response.

"I see you're uncomfortable with this subject, but I may be able to shed some light on your situation, if you'll allow." She waited for his nod of consent.

"Well, a long time ago," she continued, "I had terrible dreams every night—so horrible that many nights the thought of going to bed had me shivering with fear. Many nights I awoke screaming. This went on for about three months. I looked haggard every morning and my family started to suffer because I was tired and cross during the day.

"At the time I was involved with a healing group who worked directly with angels." She could see him start to squirm and roll his eyes. "Oh please don't roll your eyes," she said sternly. "They're just as real as you or I! Anyway, one night we gathered for a healing session for the people involved in a big quake in Turkey. While in meditation, the lucid vision of the quake's devastation made me feel as if I my nightmares had become reality.

"I called upon a magnificent angel friend, Aurora, to enlighten me on the subject. Quite honestly, I hoped she would magically make my nightmares go away. I know when the voice in my head is hers, both by the way she communicates and the delicious scent that pervades the atmosphere when I work with her. Although she's helpful, she's also very direct and *always* points out my responsibility for *all* my creations."

His attention span for her story matched that of a two-year old, so she hurried the story slightly before he actually yawned or something equally horrifying.

"Well, she simply said, 'Nikki, you know how to heal situations in the world by consciously holding them in a state of perfection, so, what is it you don't understand about how to heal your nightmares?'

"Then she explained several things, which combined, eliminated my sleepless nights.

"First: never go to bed without replaying the day and correcting everything in your 'movie' that doesn't *feel* right, including words which were spoken unkindly or in any way, shape, or form, hurt another or yourself.

"Second: stop watching television or reading material that contains experiences or emotions you do not wish to establish in your world. For me that included a majority of movies and the daily news. The computer we call the brain stores input every twenty-four hours. If the garbage is not corrected, then the input is just that—garbage. The brain mixes the garbage together with other input during the sleep stage and sorts it into its proper 'file' for later retrieval. That's why dreams get so mixed up sometimes. This garbage now becomes part of your reality and is naturally retrieved and acted upon in given situations. You literally give it permission to act in your world. What you *allow* into your vision and hearing *becomes* a part of you. If you cannot avoid exposure, you do have the power to immediately negate or re-script the event. Knowing what's going on in the world and acting upon it to bring things into balance is entirely different than allowing the junk to *become* your reality.

"Third: prior to sleep, project, by visualization and feeling, those things you desire to work on during the sleep state. She told me our consciousness (and it's all consciousness) never sleeps. Only the body rests."

Finally taking a breath, Nikki wrapped up the lesson by toying with his Irish accent. "To sum up, mi dearie, 'playing it over again' actually corrects what's stored in the archives. All you have to do is *feel* it while you playact. You see—if you remove the destructive tendencies from your consciousness, the creative law expands the reality of God's perfection into the framework of things. It automatically corrects the otherwise imperfect image in your cellular memory. I don't think it eliminates the responsibility of your karma, but at least you no longer drag the excess baggage with you, affecting everything you do."

He rocked backwards in his chair. "Do ye think there's such a thing as karma?"

"Personally, I think it would be impossible to untangle every thread of mis-creation from every lifetime. I believe we're held responsible for the way we create—the way we use God's light, whether that be through thought, feeling, word, or deed. We're in a school of sorts, learning how to use this energy in a constructive way. Unfortunately, it's the lessons of destruction—the school of hard knocks, so to speak, by which most people learn. I may not be able to directly undo every harm I've done in every lifetime, but I can use the Law of Forgiveness to eliminate the energy forms that hold both my memory, and the memory of those involved, in bondage. Once those forms are recycled back into pure energy, I can use that energy, that light, anew, for constructive, useful purposes that inure to the benefit of all. I think when you 'get it,' you graduate from this school, or the wheel of reincarnation.

"Karma is just another way of saying that you're responsible for your creations. If they're unpleasant, destructive, or inharmonious, it's also your responsibility to 'uncreate' them."

Thoughtfully shaking his head, he asked, "How can ye be responsible for somethin' ye can't even remember?"

"Make no mistake—you remember! Your physical body holds cellular memory from your own experiences and that of group consciousness. You also have several energy fields that surround your physical body. They've been called 'minds' and 'energy bodies' and many other names. But, the fact remains, you have a thought, feeling, and memory body, in addition to your physical body. They hold every single energy form you have ever created. It's just that your conscious mind is like a computer—using that which is needed at the time and storing the remainder in files for later retrieval.

"Usually, the things that are needed for the progress of one's soul will be triggered by something that provides an opportunity to 'replay' an experience that wasn't constructive the last time around. Most people describe a *feeling* that surfaces rather than a conscious memory of a particular event. It's an uncomfortable feeling that gnaws at you until you act upon it. There are some who actually remember past life circumstances, but the memory usually appears as a fleeting moment, recalling the 'essence' or 'emotion' associated with the event."

He said nothing, just inhaling his cigarette smoke deeply. She waited for him to blow it out, but it didn't come. His lungs seemed to have taken all the smoke directly to his brain.

"I hate that ye make sense and I hate even more the fact that ye told me these instructions came from an angel." His flippant remark belied the measure of understanding revealed in his voice.

"Say," he said, obviously trying to redirect the conversation, "may we wander down past ye'r barn? I didn't get a chance to explore in that direction."

Oops, I did it again, she thought apprehensively. *Scott hated it when I let my thoughts come spilling out without editing them for the person or people with whom we were speaking. Probably concerned they would judge him by me,* she remembered. Though often a sage, she sometimes thoughtlessly allowed words to escape her.

Reaching for his coffee cup, she led the way up her cobbled path, back to the kitchen. She extended no invitation for him to enter her space this time as she merely reached through the screen door, placed the cups on the counter, then turned and silently headed toward the barn. Crow and the Lab followed just as quietly.

They took the steep hill instead of the stairs and his foot slid on a small group of twigs. As he slipped, Nikki grabbed his upper arm to steady him, for she had once injured her tailbone sliding down the hill and didn't want him hurt. His biceps were huge and hard under his jacket, and though she was strong, she couldn't put her small hand around them. Luckily, the leather jacket was well in her grip and he recovered.

He laughed nervously, slightly embarrassed at his lack of grace. "That's twice today ye've rescued me!"

"Just relax and trust me and I'll take you safely there."

He stopped dead in his tracks and faced her, looking deep into her eyes. Now, three times in less than two hours, she had used these words, though once in his dream. She wore a knowing smile as if she understood something he did not and had no intention of sharing or explaining. *God, I want to kiss her and shake her at the same time. What kind of game is she playing with mi head?* He controlled himself, regained his composure, and edged his feet ahead more steadily.

"Ye have a nice barn facility—that's totally empty! Why don't ye keep ye'r horses down here?"

"I think it's cruel. Most of them just want to play and run in the pastures and along the stream. They're harder to catch when we want to ride them, but they're much more content. I keep Pegasus here three days of the week so I don't have to miss the sunrise for trying to find him in the dark. Stalls and paddocks are for the convenience of humans, not the well-being of animals. It's easier to huck the feed into twelve stalls standing in a row, but my horses thrive on the pasture grasses during the summer season. I don't supplement until winter. If the temperature drops below freezing, I put them in here for the warmth."

She seemed to him a gentle soul with gentle manners.

They walked toward the gate where she had set Pegasus free and to her joy, there he stood as if expecting her arrival. She kissed his muzzle. "Don't you just love the feel of a muzzle on your lips? It's soft like a newborn's head."

"Never actually kissed one."

"A newborn's head or a horse's muzzle?" she said, poking a bit of fun at him. "Try it. Pegasus won't mind."

He stroked the strong jaw line, looked into the creature's eyes, leaned forward, and kissed his nose. Surprisingly, Pegasus did not jerk his head as he was wont to do at the approach of most strangers. After all, a kiss is a very intimate gesture. Nikki winked at Pegasus.

"Ye're right," Crow said, turning to face her. "Hope his snout's clean."

She wrinkled her nose and smiled an impish grin. "Didn't lick any snot, did you?"

Chuckling at her slightly off-colored comment, he asked, "Ye like horses, then?"

"Was terrified of them until a year ago. Let's just say I have a tremendous amount of respect for their size and power. Pegasus is more than a horse, however. He's sort of like a guardian angel that rescued me after my husband died—helped me find my strengths again, so to speak. Scott named him Pegasus because his gait is so smooth it feels like he has wings." She spoke almost dreamily as she stroked his muzzle.

Except when he gets a pebble under hoof, Crow remembered, thinking again about the urge he had to hold her so tightly to him after the horse slipped on the steep entrance road.

He didn't trust his emotions just now—perhaps because he'd spent two solid years away from home and reality, filming one blockbuster after another. Riding the crest of the wave of fame, he found it necessary for his career. Even though he had fully committed to his decision, he felt something inside exploding. Tired of catered food, tired of all the people and their demands on his energy and time, and tired of wearing a mask, he longed to be just Dylan—doing something that reminded him of his true identity. *Oh well, if all goes well, I'll not be here long—then I'm headed for mi own 'Yee-ha,' Cork to connect to mi roots,* he thought. He planned to take a year off to regroup.

Since his widely publicized break-up with a famous actress three years prior, he had leapt from one meaningless relationship to another. Crow felt requiring a partner to join his wild ride of fame would be truly unfair. He knew it wouldn't last forever. In his industry the standing joke was "fame has a half-life of fifteen minutes." Those adoring fans would no doubt find another object to worship as soon as something promising appeared on the horizon.

Known to be quite a private person, there, nonetheless, existed within him a true and committed passion for performing. Aggressively seeking fame, even as a youth, Dylan learned early that he derived his personal power from his audience. The goal of his career aimed toward being the best in the business, for he considered himself a consummate artist of the highest caliber. He had paid his dues long enough to select the roles he actually *wished* to play, at last finding himself in a position where Hollywood came to him and not the other way around.

Though his reputation commanded an obscenely ridiculous salary, he viewed it only as a measure of his contribution to the industry. Certainly, the word "greedy" could not be applied to his soul. Even when he didn't have two pieces of brass to rub together, he had possessed an immeasurable depth of generosity.

Composing and performing music provided yet another outlet for his unlimited creativity. He had an Irish version of a rock-'n'-roll/Celtic band he and some friends created when they were in prep school: *The Rollovers.* Never expecting their work to sell, nor ever to go on tour, they still enjoyed the process of their joined harmony and inspiration. Their original melodies and lyrics revealed their deepest feelings rather than just copying another's commercially viable style. Not until he had won his first Oscar had anyone paid attention to the band. When Crow's personal assets improved as a result of acting, he financed their first CD, reeling with shock when it actually showed a profit. *The Rollovers* went on tour with a dozen performances, which sold out, not for the band's "gotta havit beat," but because Crow was the lead singer. None of the lads gave up their day jobs, however. Goes to show what can happen if you get your foot in the door. He knew there were a lot of talented people in film and music who never get seen or heard.

He began thinking how things had gone awry this morning. It had taken meticulous planning to slip away from the bodyguards, press, and everyone else he knew would want a piece of him today. Known for rising late, sneaking out at five a.m. would be unexpected by everyone. Luckily, one of the crew had offered the use of the Celica. *Piece of shite car,* he thought.

A quick glance at his eyes lost in thought warned Nikki not to break the silence. She cooed softly to her horse hoping to quell her racing thoughts. *Mighty I AM Presence,* she whispered as prayer in her mind, *I know this man. I know his soul. I recognized him the moment I saw his eyes. How may I best serve him for his highest and best good? I know there are no coincidences, and that you, or his higher self brought him here this day for a reason. Hold complete dominion over my lower self, Mighty I AM, that I bring to his life what he requires and not frighten him away again.*

The dogs barked their warning as a horn honked from Nikki's home above them.

This can't be it, God! Please don't let him just drive out of my life—there's so much he needs to know. Please, please, do something!

Crow jogged up the steep road so quickly, that she thought he might not even say "good-by," or "thank you," or "great cup of coffe," or anything. Climbing the stairs slowly, she prayed harder with each step. By the time she reached the top, the car was edging the steep hill leading down to the barn. Rolling down the window, Dylan shouted, "Oh, just coming down to say mi thanks and farewell. I'm truly sorry to have disrupted ye'r day."

As Nikki approached the car he noticed tears in her eyes—those eyes that looked just like his. She quickly averted them, regained her poise and leaned through the open window, over Dylan, to shake the young driver's hand.

"Hi, I'm Nikki. So, they sent you to rescue Warner Brother's sacred cargo, eh? Have you called a tow truck for the Celica yet?"

The driver appeared to be about eighteen years old. His long red hair was tied in a ponytail. Turning down the volume on the radio in order to be heard, he declared, "Its owner is coming after the shoot today. Says it's simple and *he* can fix it himself. You think it's safe up on that road?"

"Sure—slow season right now—only a dozen or so cars a day."

Nikki turned her attention to Dylan, realizing their faces were only inches apart. "Well, Mr. Crow, it's been real. Good luck with the film. I'll look forward to seeing you at the Cinema 8."

Her scent was deliciously fresh, like air, wind, rain, and spring violets. Her breath in his face smelled sweet as he inhaled it— quite the opposite of his, which reeked of tobacco. Close enough to kiss her on the cheek, he leaned slowly forward to do so. She didn't move, but hesitated, closing her eyes for the slightest second as if trying to memorize or remember something.

As Nikki withdrew from the car the pendant around her neck caught on Dylan's jacket. The talisman consisted of a double-terminated quartz crystal anchored to a gold disk by a slender band of gold. "Wait! Don't drive off just yet," she said, untangling the chain. "I have something I'd like to give you."

Running toward the house, she quickly picked one of the unusual indigo flowers he had watched her serenade and disappeared inside. She returned bearing a small blue velvet bag with a tie-string top, through which she inserted the stem of the flower. As she offered the gift, she enfolded his hand within hers and gently squeezed. "Keep the flower by your bedside until it wilts and dies. The other is just a little something I want you to have. You'll know when to use it."

The moment felt slightly embarrassing with the driver next to him. It was everything Dylan could do to refrain from telling the lackey to beat it so he could spend the rest of the day with her. The driver unintentionally grazed the gas pedal with his foot, however, and the magic of the moment evaporated. Reality set in.

She watched them drive away, down around the barn, around the lower paddocks beneath her house, and then up the side road a hundred feet from where she stood. The car appeared to be going in slow motion---or maybe it was her deep desire holding it back, willing it to return. The engine finally won, however, as it turned the big bend, out of sight. Gone. He had breezed into her life for a few brief hours and now he vanished like some ephemeral specter. She felt as if part of her heart had been ripped from her breast. It felt hollow inside, like a hunger that must be fed.

Dylan had no intention of diluting his morning's experience by sharing it with the young driver. Though curious to see what the bag held, he placed it on the floor by his feet as if disinterested and feigned sleep on the journey back. The whole incident seemed like a dream. He tried to relive some of the feelings he experienced that morning; feelings that were totally alien.

Chapter 3

The ducks stood at attention near the edge of the pond—their morning ritual while waiting for Nikki to toss them some cracked corn. She acknowledged them by opening the creaking door to the feed shed. An ugly clapboard lean-to had been transformed with paint and design to appear as a miniature cottage. Upon its exterior wall hung a concrete relief of a rabbit and over the door, a small sculpture of a kitten with wings. Inside, her sleeping cats stretched upon the signal of the squeak, knowing that breakfast was coming. The dogs stood patiently at the door waiting their turn. As soon as the dogs had their share, the peacocks and ducks stood in line at their bowl hoping for a nibble. They always preferred the dog food to their own. Even in the animal kingdom, the other creature's grass is always greener!

She wanted to spend time savoring every remarkable minute she had experienced that morning. Instead, she felt compelled to head for her bedroom and meditate.

Two hours later she emerged, went straight to her office and started flipping through her Rolodex. *There it is! Janice Stringham.* Janice: the backbone of the filming infrastructure in southern Utah. They had become fast friends during the filming of *Coyote Summer* at Nikki's ranch in the spring of 1994. Every time a film company used her ranch, Janice stood ready to see to the details. Nikki suspected they paid her extra to keep the location owner happy—which she always did.

Her fingers trembled while dialing. Janice answered the phone herself.

"Janice, Nikki James speaking," she announced into the phone.

"Oh, girl, I'd love to talk, but I'm just heading out the door to Kanab. Got a big feature going on over there!"

"I know. That's why I'm calling. Who handled local casting and details?" Nikki asked nonchalantly.

"Actually, it was such an important account, I did it myself."

"Who's the consulting shaman? Anyone local?" Nikki reached for a pencil and paper.

"They insisted on the genuine article from this area. I got Grace Moon to do it, though she was quite reticent. She doesn't go for the glitzy thing—had to consider it for a long time. Then she called out of the blue and declared her participation actually critical to the success of the movie. She's a real mystery to me, that one!"

"Grace and I go way back, Janice. Is she carrying a cell over there by chance?" She scribbled Grace's name on the paper, followed by a happy face.

"Whatcha up to, girl?" Janice asked suspiciously. "Want to meet the big star? You know it's Dylan Crow, don't you?"

"Already met him this morning. I've just got a real strong impression to talk to the 'shaman' for the movie. I think she can really influence him in a constructive way. Honestly, Janice, I'm not trying to interfere, but this could make or break his performance." Nikki's voice took on an air of authority.

Janice hesitated long enough to consider the weight of her decision. "I gave Grace one of our phones. You know, she won't hardly answer the phone at her own home unless she intuits the reason for your call."

"I'll take the risk, Janice. Please, give me the number!" She sounded serious and Janice knew her well enough to know she wouldn't take no for an answer.

"Ok, 653-7423," Janice responded hesitantly. "Keep it discreet, Nik, or I could lose my standing with these guys."

"Thanks. This may be the most important thing you'll ever do for me. I owe you big time!" Nikki pushed the button down before Janice even said good-bye.

653-7423, she dialed. It rang five times before Grace answered a whispered, "Hello."

"Grace, this is Nikki James. I know you're involved in a shoot over there today. Can you get to a place where no one can hear you and call me back?"

Nikki and she hadn't worked together for years, but they remained social friends and held each other in high esteem. They had previously collaborated in vibratory healings with gemstones. Though each approached the science from different angles, they learned a great deal from each other and a permanent bond had been established.

"Sounds ominous. Are you alright?" Grace put her hand over the speaker and spoke to someone in the background.

"Yeah, but this is important and relates to your work over there. Here's the number. Call as soon as you can, OK?"

Nikki sat motionless next to the phone for forty-five minutes, waiting for the call, willing the call. Finally it rang and she grasped for the receiver like a last chance. She called upon her higher self to maintain her harmony and calm conduct while silently calling Grace's higher self to assist in the call.

"Grace, I heard you're the shamanic consultant for *Little Crow,* and I felt compelled to speak to you about the star."

"Go on," replied Grace with a seeming lack of curiosity.

"There are no coincidences. He showed up at my ranch this morning. I recognized him, but not as Dylan Crow. Do you understand?"

Grace remained silent, but Nikki trusted her friend's deeper comprehension and wisdom.

"Could you offer to do a stone-laying on him so he could

experience it first-hand?" Her stomach gave a sickly lurch, realizing she was begging.

"If it feels right, I could."

"Please ask, both your guides and his, if it would serve a higher purpose. If your answer's positive, try to convince him to have it done on the grid I built at the Green Valley Spa eighteen years ago." Then she stammered. "Oh crud…it just occurred to me it might not exist any more."

Grace's calm reply assured her of the grid's survival. "It's the only place I offer services at the spa when they ask me to consult with their clients. It's missing the central power crystal though, Nik—remember the one in the copper pyramid?"

"I still have it, Grace. In fact, I think it's important for you to use it over his heart chakra. No one, other than myself, ever used it after my husband got so sick under its influence. It took me years to understand what I'd done to his energy field that day by letting him sleep on the grid for two hours. You know, he had side effects like radiation poisoning that lasted for a week!" Nikki confessed. "Look, if Crow agrees, call me and I'll get the central stone to you."

Some eighteen years earlier, Nikki had very technical dreams about a twelve-pointed, star-shaped energy grid made of copper tubes, copper wires, and large quartz crystals. The dream repeated three times a night for a week until she finally told Scott about it. He suggested she write the material down next time so they could both get some sleep.

The details of its construction were meticulously accurate in terms of the physics requirements. She understood from her dreams that no one should remain on the grid for more than fifteen minutes if the central stone was in place.

Curiosity led Nikki to get up each night after she received this information and write down the particulars.

She shared the knowledge with her friend, Carole Light, who had recently opened a mind/body/spirit spa on one of the mesas in Green Valley near St. George. Carole suggested they construct the grid in one of the outdoor gardens adjoining the treatment center. Nikki arranged to purchase the large crystals she'd seen in her dreams at the spring Tucson gem show. They were costly, and she thought she must be out of her mind. The copper structures were pre-welded in the privacy of her garage. With the insistence of Carole's business partner, the full grid installation took place at night when none of the spa guests could ask prying questions neither Carole nor Nikki could truly answer.

Setting the exact angle of the stones proved very difficult with the modest equipment Nikki possessed, so she guessed a little on some. Finishing at two in the morning, she covered the grid with a foot of dirt and, absolutely exhausted, headed home. At four a.m., after dreaming she had set the angle incorrectly on two of the stones, she rose from her bed, drove to the spa, dug them up, and started over on those two points.

The next night, she, Carole and Grace, who at the time was employed by the spa as a massage therapist, joined to *dedicate* the sacred geometry grid to the wholeness of any person who used it.

Grace, a shaman in the Hopi tribe, seemed to be absolute innocence incarnate. Nikki loved her from the moment they met. Grace smudged the boundaries and drummed and chanted things Nikki didn't understand, but everything felt right. They called forth the God within and summoned the Angels of Light, the Ascended Masters, the Elohim, and the Archangel Michael. Suddenly, the entire sky seemed littered with hundreds of shooting stars, and the three women wondered aloud at the coincidence.

Afterwards, they took turns lying beneath the great center

stone: a large, perfectly clear, eight inch quartz crystal with all six sides terminating in a point. The distance across the base of the stone measured over five inches. Due to its pointed termination, the stone held a positive, masculine energy. Copper wire wound around the base of the crystal thirty three times before it attached to the center apex of the copper pyramid from which it hung. An extra length of wire dangled long enough from the pyramid for a person to hold in his hand as a grounding wire. Because Nikki had been instructed in her dreams to allow the participant to remain beneath the center stone for only fifteen minutes, their encounter was brief. None of the women had life-altering experiences; they just felt good.

With faith, but a marked lack of understanding of either how it should be used or its purpose, they joyfully dedicated the newly constructed energy field as a sacred space. With their little ritual complete, they tearfully embraced each other and departed.

Greatly excited, Nikki woke Scott to tell him about the stars.

She convinced him to go first thing in the morning and lie over the grid upon a massage table. As a dyed-in-the-wool Mormon, Scott thought most of her "woo woo stuff," as he called it, represented foolhardy nonsense. Nonetheless, either from sheer exhaustion or curiosity, he agreed to go.

The moment he lay upon the table with his hand clutching the copper wire, he fell into a deep sleep—no doubt because she had kept him up all night with her enthusiasm. Thrilled to have him actually participate, she allowed him to remain asleep *for two hours*---not the prescribed fifteen minutes. Upon awakening, he experienced immediate nausea and instability. For five days he suffered symptoms akin to radiation poisoning.

Nikki chided herself for allowing something or someone "out there" to put this information in her head and then blindly constructing it, while not understanding or even having asked about its ramifications. She took the center power stone to her home and stored it. The foundational grid remained intact, but she determined to obtain a thorough education about crystals, grids, and sacred geometry before she ever allowed anyone to use the full grid again.

A privacy fence surrounded the area where the grid was buried, and plantings were made to ensure a beautiful, harmonious spirit. Carole reported only her truly authentic healers and best therapists desired the use of the grid. Most of them were unaware of its presence, but were intuitively drawn to the energy of the space. The grid garden had matured into a rare and stunning site. Many people treated on the grid described amazing physical and emotional healing. Nikki was one of them.

After years of intensive research she understood she had constructed an electromagnetic field that created a perfect energy balance with the original vibratory structures of the human physical and light bodies. She learned that when an object of low frequency is introduced into a field of a higher frequency than its own, it will begin to resonate at the higher rate. If the object's rate of vibration is too low to accept the frequency and remains very long within the higher field, it will shatter; much like an opera singer hitting a particular note and shattering a glass.

Responsibility for creating the grid at the spa weighed heavily upon her, for she wanted to harm no one, even inadervtantly. Carole's long-term experience with thousands of clients who used the grid convinced Nikki that, though the frequency of the partial field remained strong, no one experienced deleterious effects.

Once again, Nikki lay upon the grid and hung the power stone over her own heart chakra. Grace performed a special stone-laying upon her body in the early morning *soular rays:* the first rays of the sun that peek over the mesas. The shaman was an absolute adept with the use of stones, or her "dearies," as she called them. She knew spiritual magic on the deepest levels and yet claimed relatively little formal education. As the sun hit the power crystal it felt as if a bright light had been switched on somewhere inside of Nikki. She failed at her attempt to describe the incident to Grace, for there were no words or familiar points of reference from which to draw a comparison.

That day marked a turning point in her attention. Though a staunch supporter of modern medicine, psychology, and technology, she found herself drawn inexorably toward esoteric teachings and alternative healing methods. Her entire background, for the most part, had been intellectually, scientifically, and logically oriented—with only the five senses used to define reality. Now, however, she felt ready to embark upon a spiritual journey through a leap of faith that took her from attempting to control everything in her life to releasing everything to a higher power.

Chapter 4

The production group lodged Dylan in the Kokopeli Inn's only suite. Although it lacked uptown luxury and privacy, he had lived in worse conditions for other location shots. He preferred a small inn to a trailer, any time. All eight rooms were rented for the duration of the shoot to accommodate those with VIP status.

Mrs. Walsh, the owner and sole employee of the inn, proved to be an elderly English woman who took great pride in her clean and tidy establishment. Dylan loathed having his belongings moved or rearranged without his permission, but had long since aborted the habit of cleaning his space. A maid, therefore, equaled a necessary evil. Unfortunately, the owner routinely reorganized her guest's things to create an uncluttered appearance. Sometimes she would even throw away notes and other things that *looked* unimportant.

He brought a wooden box full of *lucky charms* to each film engagement; talismans given to him by loved ones and devoted fans. While considered by some a funny bit of superstition, he saw no difference between his idiosyncrasy and that of a basketball player who prayed a certain way before each free throw. His friend, Marco, played professional soccer and wore the same "lucky" socks to every game during the season! To curious, uninvited eyes, they may have appeared as junky trinkets, but to Crow, they were of inestimable value. So, when he had strange little things lying about his space, he didn't want someone to move or throw them away.

☯

When the driver dropped him at his temporary digs, Crow retrieved Nikki's gift and headed straight for his private suite. The flower had not yet wilted, even though the temperature in the car had been uncomfortably warm. He carefully placed it on his bedside table.

The suite had not only been cleaned, but his personal belongings had been unpacked and organized. Dylan supposed the maid had performed the chore as an act of courtesy, but was nonetheless perturbed by the invasion of his privacy.

Sitting on the edge of the bed, he lit a cigarette and opened the velvet bag, tipping it upside down in his large hand. Out spilled a golden disk with a double terminated quartz crystal upon it. *Must have taken it off her necklace,* he thought. No chain loop, however, led him to believe it a duplicate. *Maybe she makes them or something.*

He examined the piece closely, marveling at how something that grows naturally in the earth could possess such clarity and geometric perfection. One end of the crystal came to a point, and the other had a flat edge across the top, with one of the facets being larger than the others. There were no markings on the disk and no beveling at the edges. "Hmmmm," he said aloud. "Well, a nice gesture anyway. I wonder what she meant when she said I'd know when to use it?"

Although his hike in Zion had been prevented by the car glitch, he felt his precious time had not been wasted. The experience appealed to both his senses and spirit. Nikki had sparked feelings of personal familiarity, yet at the same time, triggered foreign, previously untapped emotions about his soul. A part of him knew internal changes were stirring, but his ego screamed, *I haven't got time for this—not now!* Even so, her gift represented an omen of good fortune prior to the shoot and would be added to his sacred *lucky charms.* He placed it next to the flower.

Because several days were free before filming his parts, the time would be used to better prepare his character. He pored over the script while smoking and drinking wine. Famous for his uncanny ability to concentrate, he worked straight through the dinner hour until late in the evening.

Crow detested his first few nights in a different bed. Historically, he either sought female companionship for distraction or consumed enough alcohol to deaden the experience. Sometimes he used both. During the last year, however, his interest in sleeping with *just anyone* was non-existent. Though he found sex quite pleasurable, it usually had too many strings attached. Even his overdeveloped ego no longer felt it necessary to prove himself a virile, appealing buck. Wanting to concentrate on his job right now, he opted for alcohol alone, polishing off the bottle of Merlot he'd opened earlier.

As he reached to turn off the light, he noticed the flower on the bed stand looked as fresh and beautiful as the moment Nikki handed it to him. He studied it with awe, rolling the stem several times between his massive fingers, then laid it carefully back on the nightstand.

Crow stared blankly at the faint shadows around the room when he woke at three a.m. Obsessed with thoughts about his morning with Nikki, he tossed and turned for twenty minutes before deciding sleep no longer appeared an option. An old saying attributed to Thomas Edison came to mind: "If you're going to sleep, sleep. If you can't sleep, then make a good job of it." He turned on the light, lit a cigarette, and sat on the edge of the bed.

"You just have to replay it and *feel* it the way you want it corrected," Nikki had said. As he pondered the message from Nikki's angel friend, he shook his head and grinned. The odd events and coincidences of the day were replaying on the screen of his conciousness—the car stalling just above her ranch; Nikki, out on horseback at that hour of the morning; how easily she lifted him to the horse's back; how several times he'd had the strangest desire to reach out and embrace her; the repetition of a promise to bring him safely home if he would trust her; the profound peace he felt at the ranch; his sense of long-term familiarity with her; how, in a few short hours, she challenged things inside of him he really didn't want to look at right now.

He reached for the crystal pendant, turning it over a number of times in his hand. "Just nonsense," he whispered. Standing and stretching, he ambled over to his *lucky charms* box, opened the lid, and tossed the disk inside.

Next to the box sat the book, *The Teaching of Little Crow*. He decided to read. Piling the pillows high behind him on the bed, he settled in and proceeded where he'd left off in the plane.

Knowing Crow was returning from the sacred canyon where he had spent a full cycle of the moon receiving instructions from the spirit world for his people. The horse knew well the pathway, for Knowing Crow had made this journey many times. He had seen the man with the mules and deliberately held his distance, not trusting the white men who were beginning to come in larger numbers to his land.

In a small clearing by the stream, signs of someone's camp still lingered—probably the white man's. He saw horse and mule tracks, a spent fire, and disturbingly, blood on the ground.

Knowing Crow followed the trail of blood until he came upon a dying mule. There were no signs of coyotes, but the night and the scent of blood would surely bring them. He could not bear to see the creature suffer, so he asked the mule if he wished his spirit to be freed. With consent, Crow cut the great artery on the mule's neck and chanted his spirit to the skies.

Nature would take its course with the carcass, which, after all, merely served as a house for the spirit, and the old man felt no remorse at leaving it behind. He regretted only that the beast had suffered—or more so, that the white man had left it to suffer.

He led his horse to the stream for a good long drink before they began their journey again. On the beach of the stream he found more blood in the tracks of an adult and two cougar cubs. Upstream, in a small heap, partially in the water, partially on the sandy shore, he saw the body of a young white man, flesh torn asunder and bloodied from head to toe.

Knowing Crow knelt down, placing his ear close to the boy's lips. He could hear no breathing. No doubt the boy's companion left believing him dead. The old man raised the palms of his hands over the body to detect whether any life force remained. Blood had clotted on the boy's neck and he knew he would have to work quickly for the spirit to linger. He carefully dragged the boy by his feet a short distance from the water, concerned that moving him very far could prove disastrous.

His devoted horse stood guard over the boy while the old Indian moved through the low-lying grasses, gathering sticky webs from the spiders. He collected leaves from the desert lilies and then dug deep on the shore until he obtained a mound of clay. With two hands full of his desert medicine, he went back to treat the boy's wounds. The leaves were laid carefully over the webs and plastered into place with the wet clay.

Knowing Crow tore off a piece of the boy's legging, soaked it in the stream, and tenderly washed the dried blood from the boy's arms, legs, and face. He built a small fire a few feet away and sat next to the boy, stroking his head and speaking softly in his native tongue.

At sunset Knowing Crow dozed. He dreamed that a great

spirit bade him "keep the boy alive," foretelling that if he would teach the child all he knew, the boy would become a great blessing to his people for generations to come. When Crow awoke, he again held his hands above the heart of the boy, detecting the energy that rose from the body into his old palms. The life force was stronger than when he first found him. Crow positioned himself comfortably at the boy's head, placing his hands over the crown, and chanted and sang for six more hours.

They stayed in the beautiful spot by the stream for three weeks while the Indian nursed the boy back to health. Angel was too weak to be frightened. He realized the others had left him for dead and wondered why he had been abandoned so many times in his short life.

Knowing Crow began to teach the boy his language by showing him an object, saying its name, and encouraging the boy to repeat it. Angel learned quickly and enjoyed the game they'd made of it. The Indian pointed to a crow flying through the sky, then to himself, so the boy would understand what his name meant. Six months would pass before Angel understood the meaning of both the first part of Crow's name, and that the crow symbolized a revered messenger from God.

When, at last, the child had recovered enough to travel, Knowing Crow pulled him up on his horse and the two departed the magical place for a yet unknown destiny for Angel.

Arriving at the tribe's camp, many curiously came to see the young man riding with their shaman. Knowing Crow had always helped his people with humility born of pure wisdom. They were good and kindly people who accepted the boy, even though white skinned, without hesitation. Because Knowing

Crow never had a family of his own, the tribal elders decided the boy would become his responsibility. From that day forth, the boy, once named Angel, was known as "Little Crow."

Chapter 5

Knock, knock, knock, knock, knock.

"Mr. Crow," a soft, half-terrified, but insistent voice called. It was Peggy Bloomfield, his assigned personal assistant. "Mr. Crow, are you awake? You have a meeting with Hal Hannigan and Peter Laslow in fifteen minutes."

Silence.

"Mr. Crow!" she called louder. Peggy had heard, although Mr. Crow was usually considerate with cast and crew, he had a reputation for eating people whole in the early hours of the morning. In fact, behind his back some of the Hollywood grunts used the epithet, "His Royal Heinous," to describe him. Even though an admirer of his work, she hoped not to have to grovel too much during the upcoming six weeks.

"Mr. Crow!" She rapped harder. Still, no answer came. Peggy's mind raced, trying to decide the best course of action. Her job lay on the line for she had to tap dance for the producers as well as Crow. In a panic, she set off to find the owner of the small B & B.

A lilting, feminine voice could be heard singing from the direction of the kitchen.

"Mr. Crow has a meeting and I can't seem to wake him. Would it be possible to get a key to his room, please?" Peggy pleaded in a frenzied tone, as if her life depended upon the woman's participation.

Mrs. Walsh, stirring something on the stove, turned, smiled, and calmly replied, "Oh, good morning, dearie. Mr. Crow was up with the roosters—or perhaps I should say with the crows." The old lady read serious frustration on Peggy's face and tried to put things into perspective. "Just a little humor, dearie. Couldn't have gone far, luv, with all those security fellows hanging about. Why don't you ask one of them?"

"Didn't say where he was headed, then?"

"No, luv. Drank a cup of coffee about five and went out the back door."

Peggy pushed open the screen door and stepped outside. Perhaps she would find him on one of the porches or wandering around the little town looking for a newspaper. The drivers weren't scheduled to take anyone to the set for another hour, so she couldn't figure out where he could be.

Peggy thrilled at having landed her first big production assignment and certainly didn't want to blow it the first few days. After being unemployed for six months, she desperately needed this job. *Maybe I could hook a signal button to Crow and connect him to a GPS!* The passing thought brought a giggle. Inner childlike thoughts always surfaced when her grown-up self took things too seriously.

The porch door swung open behind her and Crow stepped out. "Mrs. Walsh says ye're somewhat frantic to find me."

"Oh, yes, Mr. Crow. You have a meeting in…" she checked her watch, "three minutes. They're anxious for you to meet Mr. Joe Chatauk, who is playing the part of the old shaman, and they're bringing a real shaman with him in case you have any technical questions." Then, as if she were giving advice to the new kid on the block, she added, "Also, Mr. Hannigan and Mr. Laslow are real sticklers for schedules."

"Right," he said. "Where are we meeting?"

"Luckily, in Mrs. Walsh's sitting room!" She took his arm and ushered him like a small child.

They entered a rather Victorian room with décor incredibly contrary to the name of the establishment. Apparently the inn had, at one time, been Mrs. Walsh's home. Her son named the inn *Kokopeli*, thinking it would draw people to the mystery of the area.

Dylan had worked with Laslow before, but it was his first

meeting with the co-producer and director. Hal Hannigan, though a handsome man with an immaculately trimmed white beard, appeared about fifty pounds overweight. Beneath his designer glasses, suspicious gray eyes darted around the room assessing those in attendance. Atop his head a black baseball cap sported a red circle with a slanted line through it, under which appeared the bright yellow word "bullshit." His belly hung well over his Levis and his shoes were unlaced. While checking his watch for the third time, he nodded as if pleased when Crow and Peggy entered.

Hal held a prestigious standing in the business and Crow felt honored to meet him.

"Morning Dylan," Laslow greeted, rising from his chair to shake his hand. "I'd like you to meet your other taskmaster for the next six weeks—Hal Hannigan."

Dylan turned to Hannigan and extended his hand. With dignified composure and unerring charm, Crow flashed his famous smile as they shook. "I'm a great admirer of ye'r work, mate. Ye're a shockin'-fab' artist." He made it clear it was a privilege to work under his tutelage, though he realized his comment sounded a little over the *fan-club* edge.

Scoring points already, are you, sonny? thought Hal. *You think you've got my number, but I'll definitely make you earn your stripes.* Hannigan had protested offering Crow the lead in the film because of his well-earned reputation for being highly opinionated, explosive, and interfering with both the director's and producer's judgment.

"I'd like you to meet Joe Chatauk, your co-star," and turning towards a woman sitting in a rocking chair, Peter said, "and Grace Moon, who is here to advise us about the shamanic traditions of her people." After the obligatory handshakes, all were seated.

"As you know, Dylan, we'll be filming two different endings to this show to see which plays best for public acceptance in a preview situation. We're just not sure which will sell better at the box office." Laslow continued, "The finale represents two different roads and your character has to make a decision to follow one or the other, the outcome of which entirely alters the history of his adopted people. Now, I have to get you to feel and portray the character from both sides of the mirror, and that's going to take a lot out of you emotionally."

Crow nodded his understanding.

"Grace, here, will be glad to tip you off about the details of rituals and insights as much as she can," *(or is willing,)* thought Laslow, "but, she's spent most of her time with our researchers and writers, who have now corrected any errors in the script. She'll be on the set every day and available twenty-four hours a day" (he winked at Grace timidly) "for any questions you may have. Grace is not staying in Kanab, however, and has a life of her own, so, I'm sure you'll extend the courtesy of reviewing the details of the story well and getting your questions answered during reasonable hours. She and Joe have worked closely for the last three weeks and now she'll avail herself primarily to you, Dylan.

"Well—you've got forty-eight hours 'til we push all your buttons. Peggy will bring you what we've filmed so far to help you get into character. By the way, Paul Weislow has done a superb job as the younger Crow. You'll especially want to pay attention to the mannerisms he's created—might help if we carried some into the later life stuff."

Once again, Crow nodded silently, allowing Peter to finish his speech uninterrupted.

"Why don't you spend a little time with Grace this morning to clear up any questions you may already have? I also thought you might want to see your first location today to get the lay of the land." Laslow, obviously hurrying through the interview, finally took a breath, allowing Crow to respond.

"Fair well ye know me, Peter. I'd appreciate it. What time?"

"How about three?"

"Fine. I'll be ready."

"I'll send a driver to pick you up then." Laslow clapped his hands together as he stood, summarily concluding the meeting.

Crow was a hard worker. According to all the experts, and as per his deepest desire, he *had* become one of the best in the business. He repeatedly reached deep inside, striving to pull more from himself and his performance with each film. Though somewhat burned out from the two straight years of filming and in desperate need of solitude to recharge his batteries, he felt compelled to accept this movie. He wasn't ready to share the reason with the producers, however, and laughed at himself for having so easily shared it with the "rescue lady" he'd met the day before. *Funny how most people can share something with a total stranger and feel safe*, he thought. *Unfortunately, I always have to assume everyone is out to sell mi soul to the media. I've had enough cloutin's from those self-servin' parasites.* He had purposely cultivated an over-developed sense of privacy during his career.

Joe stood and stretched. "Any chance we could get acquainted with each other a little later tonight, Dylan? I have something important to get done before my driver hauls me back to the canyons."

"I'll be about."

"Well, dear woman," Joe said, kissing Grace on the cheek, "don't be too hard on the greenhorn. I have a feeling he's not used to magic as powerful as yours." He winked at Crow.

Grace chuckled. Her gentle and kind mannerisms immediately

put Crow at ease. He presumed Joe's comment merely a playful attempt to daunt him.

Chapter 6

Grace was an unusual looking woman. Dylan guessed her to be in her late fifties or early sixties. Standing regally at five-foot, ten-inches, her flowing white gauze outfit gave her a mystical air. Long salt and pepper colored hair hung in a braid down the side of her right breast. Crow had observed that older women rarely wore their hair long and found hers somewhat disarming. However, it added a flavor of authenticity to her ethnicity. She had a lovely tanned face etched with small lines. Her brilliant blue eyes with permanent corner wrinkles gave the impression of a smile even when her mouth did not participate. Then she smiled.

Her buckteeth shattered Dylan's Hollywood vision. *Oh, well,* he thought, *she's the real McCoy and not the actress.*

"Miss Moon," he said softly, guiding her back to the seating area, "I do have a question or two." He proceeded to ask intelligent questions, the depth of which intrigued her. She responded with innocence and gentleness; characteristics that sometimes led people to believe she was a doormat. Nothing could have proven further from the truth.

After several hours of questions and answers specific to the show, he seemed to switch characters on her. He pulled out a cigarette and asked if she minded.

"You know, it's quite stuffy in here. Why don't we go out and sit on that lovely swing on the porch?" she suggested.

He caught her drift, and since he intensely craved a cigarette, stood and politely led the way.

She did not sit on the swing with him, but rather, sat opposite in a wicker rocking chair. Grace wanted to look into his eyes; so much could be read from someone's eyes.

He laughed mischievously as he tried to bait her. "So, how

does a real, live Indian shaman end up on a Hollywood production?"

"Actually, Mr. Crow, I was told you needed my help. *You.* Not the show," she replied, with no additional input.

"I guess that would be Hannigan. I heard he thinks I'm a bastard. Probably thinks I can't handle the part. Well, to be honest, I haven't been able to do mi homework properly on this one, which means mi work with ye will be critical to the outcome, eh?" He crossed his leg and stubbed out his cigarette on the bottom of his shoe.

"Mr. Crow," she began in a businesslike tone, "I believe in being honest with people, even if it makes them uncomfortable. When first approached about this project eight months ago, I didn't even consider it. My purpose is not to obtain money, though they are paying me quite a lot. Nor is it to attain a reputation for possible future gain. I live in a trailer park with a modest income. I don't even own a television and I've never seen any of your work."

His brow furrowed in puzzlement. "So, why'd ye lower ye'r personal standards?"

"I just told you. I was told *you* needed my help." She paused, her eyes raised as if looking at an object above and to her right, as if hearing instructions from an invisible source. "This information didn't come from Warner Bros. They could have replaced me in a heartbeat. Let me back up a minute because I really do want you to understand."

With his curiosity piqued, he leaned forward as if about to hear a hushed secret.

"During a sweat lodge ceremony about two months ago I had a vision in which *YOU*, or I should say, your higher self, asked me if I would be willing to help guide you. You told me if your lower self accepted this guidance, your performance would affect millions of lives." Her gaze penetrated his soul through his eyes, observing his reaction to her words.

He held absolutely still as though someone had shot him with a stun gun. A slight lull filled the conversation as he considered her words. His heart longed for her to be telling the truth, but he had been exposed to so many weirdos pretending to be something they weren't that he had begun to believe they were all frauds. He reached for some humor to bring them both back to reality, laughing heartily and slapping his knee. "It pays to be a movie god, doesn't it? Not everyone gets assigned a real shaman to show him the way!"

"The choice is yours, Mr. Crow. Spirit never coerces, it only nudges." Grace showed no hint of offense. She continued to watch his eyes to see if he would make contact or look away as he spoke. He passed her test, the test of a sincere questioning heart, when he looked directly at her. Anything less would have demonstrated he was not yet ready to graduate to a higher level of understanding.

Suddenly Crow felt enveloped in an old, familiar sense of comfort and protection: a good sign. As a young child, when asking spirit-oriented questions, his mother told him to find a private space, close his eyes and pray. She swore the angels would cradle his body while they answered his questions directly. Always disappointed that some magnificent angel with wings never appeared to tell him what he wanted to know, he nonetheless never forgot the feeling that surrounded him when the angels "cradled" his body. He wasn't sure he actually believed in angels, but he did believe in a higher power of sorts. How could he deny the many times it felt as if either someone or something outside of himself shifted gears for him?

Dylan leaned forward in his chair and lowered his voice. "Do ye believe in past lives?"

"No. I *know* about other lives. Past, present, and future are all happening at once, and yet each choice affects the activity in the others." She rocked gently in her chair and waited for the next question.

He hesitated, not quite trusting the situation. He had heard the quantum physics theory that supported her statement, so he ventured further. "What I'm about to tell ye, I say in confidence. I don't want to see it splashed on the tabloids tomorrow—understand? I've got enough crashin' busybodies interfering with mi life." He felt he had driven his point home with his terse, *"understand?"*.

"Mr. Crow, do you somehow intuit that I'm the type who sells gossip to the media?"

"If I did, I wouldn't be about to spill mi soul to ye, now would I?" he answered, softening a little.

"I guess your question was moot, then!"

"OK! OK!" *What have ye got to lose, lad—I mean—really?* he wondered silently. He took a breath and jumped into the deep end. "The reason I accepted this role is because I think I may have experienced something similar—somewhere—sometime, and that it affected many lives. I had two choices; just like the ones mi character has in our separate finales. I believe the reason we're filming both has something to do with me personally—on some other level of consciousness. On the other hand, since I have no voice in determining which ending goes public, I can't help but feel I'm imagining m' involvement could make any difference anyway. They hired me to make a believable character out of this guy, regardless of the ending. At any rate, I have this lingering hope I can somehow correct this past error by doing this show and doing it right." He looked to her for a sign of empathy.

"How will you know which ending is right for you?"

"I don't have the answer to that question right now. I trust I'll know before we shoot them toward the end of the month. So, guru Moon, what is it ye think ye can do to 'guide' me?"

"Insight!" she said flatly.

Cool! he thought. *The studio hires someone to handle mi spiritual dilemmas!*

She spoke again in the absence of any audible response. "Your insight, not mine. I'm neither a guru nor a prognosticator."

Blast. This may take more work and time than I'm prepared to give. Yet, he knew deep inside this opportunity would not be presented again.

"What would ye have me do to obtain this insight?" he asked, pushing off with his foot so the swing would rock to and fro.

"Let's start with the basics, Mr. Crow. Do you think you can trust me—trust me with the parts of yourself you don't show to the world?"

"I won't bullshit ye, Grace. I don't really know if I can. I've spent so much energy trying to safeguard mi privacy, I may have lost touch with the ability to trust anyone." He looked out across the lawns, seeing everything and yet nothing.

"If you'll just relax and trust me, I'll take you safely to the door of your understanding. The rest is up to you." Grace smiled innocently.

What? What? he thought incredulously. *What are the chances those exact words would come out of this lady's mouth... 'If you'll just relax and trust me, I'll take you safely...' Is it some southern Utah phrase or something?* His foot stopped the swing and he took a noticeable breath. Staring directly into her eyes without speaking a word, his heart raced wildly with both anticipation and apprehension. The whole situation reminded him of looking at the crazy mirrors in an amusement park, trying to find the true image. They all looked sort of bona fide, but each mirror distorted the picture slightly.

He'd been in total control of his career now for more than seven years, no longer having to play inane roles just to get in front of a camera. Questionable advice from agents or publicists no longer affected his status. An intelligent man, he made his way in life with undeviating purpose: marching straight to his objective without changing direction. He had arrived at that heady position where one is free to call the shots. Yet, the experience to which he was agreeing to participate would require trusting someone else to guide him. That could mean only one thing: giving up control.

"Let's take a wee stroll," he said, rising and stretching, pointing toward the garden. He could usually hide his nervousness if he did something physical. Grace stood and, without a word, tagged behind him as he descended the four steps to the ground level. Annoyed by the presence of eavesdropping security agents posted around the vicinity, he led her to a more private area behind the inn.

Holding his hands behind his back in a thoughtful pose, he stopped and faced her deliberately. He cocked his head slightly to the right and took a deep breath. "Do ye believe in coincidence?"

"There are none, Dylan. What you need to understand is that you are writing your own story. The only real person in the story is you. The rest are character actors and props whose jobs are to create circumstances that force you to draw the conclusions necessary for your spiritual development. Your higher self directs the show. Each circumstance or 'coincidence,' as you called it, is prepared for you. *NOTHING* in your life, from the important to the mundane, is coincidence."

She walked on, assuming he would follow. "You are not a body with a spirit, Dylan. You are a spirit with a body experiencing this dimension! Reality is your spirit. This—"(she directed her arm to all around her) "—is the illusion: the Maya. Your purpose in life is spiritual progress; it is not fame, not money, not accolades, not possessions. That is why all men, under all circumstances, have the ability to grow—different stories to develop what is required for their spirit. You've changed your character a hundred times in this lifetime alone, not only in your personal life, but also by agreeing to act stories out for others to watch, to accept or reject according to their will."

Something inside obliged Crow to listen, even though the conversation was getting uncomfortable. "I may have a different point of reference about God and spirit than ye, Grace, but I'm curious to hear anything ye wish to share with me—either from ye'r own observations or from ye'r ethnic traditions." He attempted to ensure conversational maneuverability in the event she directed any of her thoughts at him personally.

Grace stopped, picked up a small stick, and strode to a fallow area of the garden, signaling him to draw near. "I'd like to repeat a legend which has been handed down through many spiritual belief systems. If you don't mind, it's my nature to use the old oral story tradition to relay information."

He nodded his consent.

In the dirt she drew a circle. "Let's say this is God. This represents not some 'guy,' but the whole of God: All That Is. God had so much love that he could not contain it and wished to create something upon which to lavish his love; something that could reflect his beauty and perfection back to him. So, drawing divine energy and substance forth from his own heart, he created 'The Other.' Some spiritual traditions call this the 'Mother.'" She drew a second circle directly beside the first.

"The Mother," she continued, "although a part of God, had

taken so much of the quality of his heart that she had a vast, void space in her own heart capable of unlimited energy in motion. The Father now lacked the intensity of this 'e-motion.' God could no longer experience some things without all of his heart and only when he merged with the Mother could he experience the fullness of his magnificent ecstasy in limitless creation. He could only experience the depths of e-motion vicariously through her.

"God the Father and God the Mother were so filled with Divine love that they wished to have another upon which to lavish this energy, something that would reflect their beauty and perfection back to them. In joining their two flames they believed their creation would have the Father's pure light of intelligence and the Mother's pure heart. When the new white fire body formed, the polarities of the feminine and masculine aspect were created, each having the same blueprint, so to speak. This blueprint is unique only to the two created thusly, though the Father/Mother God created them without number."

Grace drew a circle beneath the other two, drawing within the circle the sign of the oriental yin and yang. Connecting the three circles with equidistant lines, there now appeared a triangle: a trinity.

"So, the first children of God were created; half of which were filled with their father's light and intelligence, while the other half possessed their mother's heart. Yet, the seed of the positive male energy appeared in the negative, and the seed of the negative female energy, in the positive." She drew a distinct dot within each of the yin and yang halves. "These are twin flames, Dylan—beings who must, in fact, join together to be complete and whole. They do not oppose, but are complementary, always fulfilling the Law of One: the Divine Whole. They unveil in flesh the faces of Alpha and Omega. You have, no doubt, heard them referred to by many names; Twin Flames, Soul Mates, Twin Souls, Split-Aparts, Divine

Lovers, True Lovers, etc.

"The children lived with the Father/Mother God in unlimited experience, joy, and bliss for eons and eons of time.

"Then one day, a child of God asked the Mother why she was not as beautiful as the Father. She went to the Father and asked the same question. God the Father told God the Mother that if she would trust him in all things and promise to be obedient in all things, he could show her how to be as beautiful as he. Pensively she considered his comment. Finally, she replied, 'How can I make a promise about something that I have yet to experience?' From that day, the Mother chose to gain intelligence and beauty through experience. She began by lowering her frequency until her form became first gaseous, then liquid in nature—moving more and more into density.

"The Father loved the Mother, and called upon his servant the wind to bid him take a gift to the Mother for her sojourn. He wove a fabric of golden threads and made a sack that drew together at the top. God stuck his finger in the sack and filled the golden threads with his luminous substance and then withdrew his finger. He gave the sack to the wind to deliver to the Mother.

"The spirit of the Mother emerged from the liquid state and accepted the gift from the wind. When she opened the sack, millions of golden threads burst forth and spread across the water. These threads contained many of the children of God who wanted to experience intelligence first hand with the Mother.

"Those children who expressed a desire to descend were allowed to go by their own free will. Before they left their estate, however, the Father explained that the density experience would be an education of the soul based in duality consciousness. He also explained that the only way his children would not be tempted to rush back to his perfection would be by creating some sort of barrier or veil of

forgetfulness. Lovingly, he assured them they would remember
home and their true heritage if they connected with their hearts.

"'That which I AM,' said the Father, 'is eternal and pure spirit and I have individualized myself in each of you. My light is too
bright, my energy too strong, my frequency too rapid to descend
into density. You will, therefore, have to transduce my light—step
it down, in order to have the experience and still maintain your
contact with that which is true.'

"He showed them how to send only a fraction of themselves to
the density experience. He commanded the individualized God self,
the Great I AM Presence in each child, to create from themselves yet
two more bodies; creating a trinity. The first body created was the
Christ-self. Though it was composed of Divine intelligence, wisdom,
and love, it was created to be the vehicle through which the I AM
Presence could receive information about the third part of himself,
which was to experience density. This Christ body would act to step
down energy and light from the God self, but would also be completely aware of all things that happened in the material world to the
lower self. This transducer also had the ability to communicate and
'step-up' the information received from the lower body in order to
communicate it to the I AM Presence.

"This intercessor has been called many names by many spiritual belief systems: the 'Christ-self,' the 'higher mental body,' the
'higher self,' 'one's guardian angel,' etc."

Grace looked up from her drawings to read the comprehension
level on Dylan's face. "Do you understand this concept, Dylan?" she
asked. Without waiting for his answer, she drew a simile. "It works
in the same way that a crystal does with electricity or information
contained in wave form. It's also like going to a foreign country and
having a razor that is equipped to handle 110 volts of electricity, but
the foreign country offers only 220. You use a transducer to safely

reduce the voltage so your equipment won't blow up. Right?"

She drew yet another group of circles. The children, as shown by the yin and yang circle under the Mother and the Father, now had two circles directly beneath them. Grace referred to the yin and yang circle as the "Divine I AM Presence, individualized." The second she termed the "higher mental body," and the lowest circle she titled "lower self."

"Before the children left his presence, God the Father told them they would not be allowed to return until they had learned to co-create with the purity of his Divine Wisdom, Love, and Intelligence.

"Now," explained Grace, "I could have told this tale through the modern voice of physics, but I prefer the story instead. The point is, you have the divine spark of God individualized within you, above you, and around you, Dylan. The unfed flame of God is anchored right within your physical heart. Your Christ, or higher self, is physically located above you and your I AM Presence, above your higher self. The energy for your life force is sent from your I AM Presence to the higher self, which then transduces the frequency to one your lower self can use without consuming your density. The energy is channeled through the top of your head at the crown chakra and then to all the energy centers in your four lower bodies. The perfection of your God self, your I AM Presence, would flow uninterrupted, creating that same perfection in every aspect of your life if the energy was not otherwise re-qualified."

Crow sucked a stilted, frustrated breath, and reached in his pocket for another cigarette. "So, if this God self, or I AM Presence, or whatever ye call it, is so perfect, and it's a part of what we are, why is mankind so hopelessly flawed?"

"Because, little brother, mankind's heart is frozen for lack of love. He has forgotten how to connect in his heart and remember his heritage. Through survival strategies in duality consciousness, man has re-clothed his creative energy to appear as many things that have neither been desirable, nor harmonious. His creations have brought little joy to himself or others. The lower self, through personality and ego, has, over the eons, claimed dominion and has taken the position that it is separate from God. In the majority of mankind, it abuses its co-creative powers with God because it is too blind to see that it is part of All That Is and is responsible for its own creations.

"On the other hand, one has to applaud the courage it takes for a soul to incarnate at this juncture where the density of the heart is so thick. Man's indominatable soul seeks its true heritage in spite of the insurmountable odds it has created for itself."

Grace was acutely aware of the battle waging within Dylan. No one likes his belief system challenged, and having challenged his, she knew he ached to debate with her. Because she had promised to act as his guide, however, remaining in the professor's seat was imperative. "Your I AM Presence has been merciful and compassionate. It has permitted your chosen pathway without judgment, but has also allowed you to experience the consequences of your choices, knowing that this, too, is a pathway of learning.

"Your I AM Presence is the producer of your show and the director is your higher self; your Christ-self. The energy, which is light, is transmitted from these higher dimensions to your physical being, which includes your physical, emotional, thought, and memory bodies. Each body, (or field, as it is termed in physics,) is part of the whole picture and what happens in one, affects all.

"Because you are a sentient being of free will, you have the ability to *clothe* this energy and create anything you want. This unmanifest light cares neither who uses it, nor what is created. It has no discerning capability in and of itself. That's your role. Think of it sort of like electricity. You can use it constructively or destructively, but, of itself, it has no powers of discernment. There is nothing to stop you from creating heaven or hell.

"The great fiat is 'CREATE'! But God intends for you to create with his wisdom, intelligence, and love, held in perfect balance, the same way he creates. Every single lesson of every life is to bring you to recognize and accept that you are One with All things—One with God—and that every creation you issue forth affects the whole. Learning to master your thoughts and feelings in a sustained, harmonious way allows your I AM Presence to move through you to create in an unobstructed fashion. Do you understand?"

She terminated the discourse abruptly with her elementary question.

He had been listening intently, but wished he could have written down what she had said to him. He understood conceptually, but didn't know if the information could make it from his head to his heart—or perhaps, it was from his heart to his head. This simple woman, in a few minutes, shared her version of creation and where mankind stood in relation to the same. Something within him recognized some truth in what she offered, even though presented in a different version than the one he learned in Sunday school as a child.

"Forgive me," he said. "I want to hear more of ye'r perception of reality, Grace, but just this moment I think I need to digest what ye've said. I'm not certain that what ye've shared has leant any 'insight' regarding mi role in the show."

She stood, and with a look of deep understanding in her eyes, reached into her skirt pocket and pulled out a business card, printed with her name and home phone number and her cell number penciled on the back. After she pressed it into his hand, they continued walking side by side with the space of silence between them.

When they reached the front of the inn, she spoke softly, assuming his soul a bit tender from having been exposed to a new paradigm. "The 'insight' will be yours, Dylan—not mine. I just reminded you of the basics, that's all. If you desire the fullness of the gift I have to offer, I'm sure I'll hear from you." Grace put her hand gently on his back as they walked, like one friend comforting the other. "All gifts must be *accepted* in order to be useful and the choice is yours—alone."

"Do ye have some sort of shamanic knowledge or ritual that can help me access that part of m'self that feels like I've been down mi character's road before?" he asked in hopeful hesitation.

"I do—but you're the one who takes the journey. I'm but a way-shower. You'll have to commit to the journey because I can't drag you. That's what free will is all about."

Dylan felt overwhelmed. "Can I think about it and call ye later?"

"You heard the man. Right now, you own all of my time." Grace looked toward the sun to determine the time of day. She wore no watch and had long ago learned to read nature's clock. "Speaking of which, it's getting late. If you have no further need of me right now, I think I'll scoot over to the set."

They said their adieus and though she embraced him like an old friend, he was caught off guard and did not embrace her in return. The embarrassment of the moment passed and she smiled and waved good-bye while heading toward an old heap of a car in front of the inn.

Wow, he thought, *she really doesn't care about material things.*

☯

Crow opened the screened porch door to the entry hall and ran up the stairs to his suite. He found Mrs. Walsh in his room making the bed. The indigo flower had disappeared from the bed stand. "Mrs. Walsh," he said softly, so as not to alarm her, "did ye throw away the flower I put on the nightstand?"

"I figured you picked it this morning, luv, and it would be dead in a few minutes anyway."

"Where is it?" He began frantically searching the garbage cans. They were all empty, for she had already removed the empty bottles, smelly ashtrays, and bathroom trash.

"I took the bag downstairs to the ash bin just moments ago." She couldn't understand why he attached such importance to a flower. "I'm sorry, Mr. Crow—I'm sure it's quite ruined by now. I'll just go out in the garden and pick another for you. Will that make you happy?"

"No, no, that won't be necessary." He stared out the window into the yard, his thoughts racing.

While she continued to clean the suite he slipped quietly down the stairs to find the "ash bin," as she had called it. About twenty feet from the inn he found a small fenced area, camouflaged by shrubbery. *A likely place,* he thought. He half ran to it. "Voila," emerged from his lips. He assumed the topmost garbage bag would hold his treasure, so he ripped it open. *Yep, it will surely be ruined.* Then, as he dug through the debris, he saw a hint of indigo and reached past a mess of ashes and cigarette butts to retrieve the flower. He was shocked to find it still in perfect condition, save for the need to blow off some ashes. He gently blew them away and guardedly carried it back to his room.

"Mrs. Walsh," he said, "I think I'd like to keep this flower as a good luck piece during the show, even if it fades and withers. I retrieved it from the bin and I wonder if ye'd be good enough to allow me to keep it on the bed stand, undisturbed."

She looked at him quizzically. After all, she had a whole bush full outside and could bring a fresh bouquet of them daily in a vase, if he liked. He seemed intent on this particular one, however. *Crazy Irishman!* she thought, but smiled and said a little sarcastically, "Sure, dearie. I'll stand as sentry and protect it with my life if you want. Shall I bring a lit'l vase with some water for it?"

"Thank 'e. That won't be necessary." He had no intention of explaining his fascination with whatever phenomenon kept it alive even though it had been severed from its source for quite some time. Nikki specifically instructed him to keep it by his bed until it died. *Did she do something special to it? She couldn't have. She didn't have time. I watched her pick it and she stepped into her her home for only a few brief moments,* he thought.

After an approving appraisal of her work, the innkeeper left the room, closing the door behind her.

Crow sat on the edge of the bed and stared at the flower, smelling it over and over again. He had not noticed its intoxicating fragrance the day before. *M'be somethin' in the ash bin added the new bouquet,* he thought, laughing. *I must remember to ask Mrs. Walsh the name of this flower.*

Lighting a cigarette, he pondered all that Grace had shared with him. *She could be just some crazy fan who's willin' to do anythin' to get close to me. No television?* he thought. *Everyone owns a bloody television!*

He dropped to his knees to pray---something he hadn't done since his childhood in Sunday school. Unaccustomed to this activity, he just spoke as he would to a trusted friend: "God, Great Essence, whatever name ye'd like—I don't know if there is something larger than m'self out there that controls the destinies of men. Maybe I'm at a fork in the road; maybe I'm just imagining things, but I *feel* something different than I've felt before. I simply want to do the right thing. I never have much believed the things

I learned as a kid, but I still have faith ye exist and somehow ye care about me. If this is something that will bring me enlightenment, please show me the way. Amen." Out of habit, he scanned his space to ensure there were no listening ears.

Crow looked aghast at his watch which read 2:52 p.m. *How could so much of mi day have slipped through mi fingers unnoticed?* he wondered. He realized he'd had no breakfast or lunch and rushed down to the kitchen to ask Mrs. Walsh if he could take a piece of fruit with him.

A knock at the front door interrupted their conversation. It brought her automatic reply of, "Right with you, dearie." She pointed toward the larder in approval of Dylan's request as she headed down the hall.

"Mr. Crow," she sang, "it's a young man to fetch you."

Chapter 7

The driver introduced himself as "Chuck" and explained they would be going to a place that required some hiking. Glancing at Crow's feet, he suggested changing the Gucci loafers to something a little more appropriate. Crow agreed and hustled back up the stairs to change. "I'll not be long. Get the engine runnin'."

The Jeep Wrangler handled the twenty some-odd miles of bumpy dirt roads pretty well, but the interminable scenery of juniper and sage wore thin on the star. Without warning they came to a precipice that overlooked Zion. The view was absolutely extraordinary by comparison to that on the journey. "This reminds me of the Grand Canyon." Dylan jumped out and walked to the edge to get a better look.

"Zion is far more spectacular than the Grand! You know what Zion means, don't you?" asked Chuck.

"Read somewhere the Mormons named it. I just assumed they named after something in their religion." Crow slipped his sunglasses down his nose and turned to his guide, giving him the appearance of an old, wise, curious owl.

"Indeed, the name did come from the Mormons, but the name itself means, 'the place where God dwells.'" Chuck walked around the back of the jeep and pulled out a backpack, rope, and some climbing equipment.

"Would we be rappellin', now?" Dylan's tone signaled mild curiosity, but alarm was written all over his face.

"Shouldn't have to, but some spots might be easier for you if we have some gear. You should see what we've gone through to get all the equipment down there. We had to send a team of pack mules from Kolob on the west of Zion. It was the only route accessible for the big stuff. Couldn't even get quads through, so we took horses and mules. From here, however, it'll only take us about thirty minutes to get down." Chuck's air of confidence put Dylan at ease.

Crow offered to carry some of the equipment, but Chuck, in his twenties, burly and muscled, had obviously been instructed to make the trek as easy as possible for his charge.

They followed a steep deer trail for about three hundred yards to the edge of the red sandstone cliffs. Chuck looped the rope through an existing cleat, driven well into the sheer edge of the mountainside. "Just for safety," he said, throwing a harness to Crow. Dylan had done a little climbing for another show and had no trouble sliding into it correctly. Chuck secured the rope to Crow's harness. "You won't have to rappel, but you should hold on tightly and allow the rope to help you descend. It's only about two hundred feet 'til you hit a flatter area and we can hike without the rope from there."

"Sure... 'n'...how do we get back up?" posed the now concerned star.

"Well, I'll go up first and use a little of my 'Jack LaLanne's to make it easier for you," Chuck said, teasingly referring to his abundant muscles and the old fitness guru.

"Right, then." Crow cautiously established his footing on the steep, downward ride, gliding effortlessly to the two hundred foot level. He waited while Chuck followed suit.

The path led to a very narrow gorge. Green, almost glacial looking water from the Virgin River ran through the canyon, nearly touching both sides in most places. It appeared as if they were coming to a small box canyon. Dylan noticed, however, the river wasn't damming and assumed there must be an entrance to another part of Zion's hidden world just around the bend.

Climbing around a large sandstone outcropping, they crossed

a threshold into an ethereal landscape that seemed to belong to some other world. Spirally twisted stone sculptures surrounded them. They formed a natural art of such rare beauty in structure and flow that it took Dylan's breath away. Their exquisite magnificence rose above him hundreds of feet, occasionally allowing little streamers of sunlight through. Crow felt as if he'd been delivered to another planet, bereft of life as he understood it, but filled with a kind of energy that was more alive than anything he'd ever experienced. He touched Chuck's arm to stop him for a moment just to absorb the awe and wonder of it all. The guide seemed to understand without a word being spoken.

Crow promised himself to bring his Nikon next time so he could capture the extraordinary vision and send it to his family. Sending photographs of his location was his way of keeping his loved ones abreast of his life since time and space often kept them apart.

They hiked on a dry sandy streambed that snaked through the maze of sculpture. Wind, water, and time were obviously the three great artists here. "The old streambed must have connected to the Virgin at some time," Crow thought out loud.

"Still does," replied Chuck. "This ain't no place to be in a storm, 'cause there's no place to run for safety. Flash floods have killed more than a few determined tourists, I'll tell you! The water can rise fifteen feet in a few seconds, and I'm not exaggerating."

Winking with feigned timidity, Dylan stammered, "So— heard the weather report for the coming days?"

The brawny guide chuckled and let the comment vanish in the arid atmosphere that surrounded them.

Upon arriving at base camp, a cold beer was offerd to Crow. Spring water sufficed for his escort.

"What did it take to get permission to film in the park?" Crow asked the location manager.

"Months of hard-core negotiating, the payment of a sizable fee, and inconvenient promises such as having to pack out everything, including our bodily eliminations, when the shoot is over! So, if you have any business to do, we've set up some privacy screens and portable toilets about three hundred yards downstream. OK?"

Not wanting to be diverted by the crew's preparations, Dylan asked if he could wander about to get a feel for things without supervision. The crew, only too happy to send him on his way unattended, had a good deal to do in a relatively short time.

Crow hiked further up the streambed and found the location of the scene marked with red plastic ribbon. The sand had been freshly raked and the crew warned not to step beyond the temporary border. He wanted to *feel* his scene, however, and casually made his way over it.

In their first shot, his character, Little Crow, would be taking his adopted father to the sacred heart of the canyon. A warring tribe to the south has mortally wounded Knowing Crow. To oblige the old man's last wish, Little Crow brings the dying shaman here to free his spirit. After great effort, they arrive at the entrance to the sacred canyon, but the old shaman will not allow his white son to go further. He believes his adopted son is not yet worthy to step into this holy place.

Crow had been studying the scene in his room, but it took on new meaning in the presence of the scenery—"the heart of the place where God dwells: a place so sacred that only the pure in heart may enter."

☯

In the first shot, Little Crow is filled with grief at the inevitable loss of the man whom he has called "Father," and feels only anger and vengefulness toward his warring neighbors. His heart is anything but pure at this moment. Still, he must convince his father he will be prudent with the use of sacred wisdom in hopes the dying man will endow him with his last treasure: his knowledge about the use of a legendary crystal. The old shaman then reveals his most valuable secret to his white son, entreating him to use the magic wisely, for its misuse would surely haunt him through eternity.

His noble character has tears in his eyes, tears welling up from the depths of his wailing heart that cannot, and will not, be denied their outburst. "Father, send me not away, but let me stay until I know the spirits have carried you with the eagles." He cradles the head of his beloved father in his great hands.

A younger version of himself would be playing the white shaman through the first part of the show. This would not be Crow's opening scene as movies are not made in contiguous parts, but pieced together later. His entrée would be shot in about two weeks. However, Crow believes this scene is a critical point in the show because it leaves two pathways open to his character. He knows the action must leave his audience with a sense of profound anticipation and an absolute, sure knowledge of the dichotomy between the spirit and mortal pathway.

Dylan sat, pretending to cradle his father's head in his arms and looked around to see if the magic of the natural scenery could be captured. The scene would require the kind of close-ups necessary for a whispered conversation and he wondered just how the producers would work it out. *Surely they would not have gone to all this effort only to let the scenery get lost,* he thought. He had to trust they were the best in the business and would pull it all together.

☯

He stilled himself to listen to the canyon. The bawdy sounds of the crew in the distance distracted him immensely. Crow knew he would have to memorize this incredible place and feel his character in the privacy of his room in order to construct the emotional journey on which he hoped to take the audience. He imagined what it would sound, feel, smell, and taste like, had he been alone. A slight breeze ran through the sculptured halls and left a cool gentleness in the atmosphere. The subtle scent of sage filled the air. *The feeling*... he had thought as he entered the canyon with Chuck, *was one of holiness—as if a great, silent mass was being held and one dare not speak, nor even think, for fear the mountain gods would notice the interruption.*

Absorbed in his silent reverie, he failed to notice the large black crow that had landed on the boulder just above his head. Its earsplitting shriek alerted him to the approach of human footsteps. The crow did not take to flight, but sat regally with the sun shining off its blue-black feathers. Piercing eyes met Dylan's gaze as their souls greeted one another.

The clock sped on as if a time-warp had taken place. Chuck's face peeked around the corner. "Hey, boss, gotta get goin' if we're gonna make that climb in the light. OK?"

The bird hopped from its perch and with a loud swoosh, grazed Crow's head with its wing as it departed.

Gathering his senses, Dylan stood, and walked in an attitude of reverence and silence. In fact, he said nothing all the way back. His guide didn't pry or encourage conversation except for the few commands given to help the star back up the steep section of the canyon.

Chapter 8

Crow's stomach growled ravenously. He'd forgotten to take the herbal diet pills that curbed his appetite. The part called for him to look lean, but genuinely strong. It seemed as if he'd been doing roadwork, lifting weights, and taking diet pills for four straight years. They gave him a little extra energy without making him nervous, however, and he'd gotten quite used to them. He hoped he wouldn't be on them for the rest of his life.

By the time they arrived at the inn the catered dinner service had been cleaned up. Crow querried a security guard to determine where a bar could be located. "Hey, haven't they told you you're in Utah yet?" The cocky young fellow laughed at his own joke. "Just kiddin'. They serve beer and wine in most of the restaurants—but no hard liquor."

"Anyplace good to eat where I won't get mobbed?" Crow lit a cigarette as he surveyed the main street.

"Sure. You'll find the locals are pretty used to movie stars, though. They won't be clamoring for autographs or anything. Sometimes they stare a little, but they don't actually try to intrude. It's the tourists you gotta watch out for. You can usually spot them by their sunburns." The guard attempted a serious tone as he removed his James Bond-like sunglasses. He pointed to a building kitty-corner from where they stood. "If you just want to stay in town, try over there—authentic Mexican with molé sauces and everything. Got a nice selection of brews too."

"I take it ye've tilted a few there, then, eh, mate?"

"That I have. I'll be glad to escort you, Mr. Crow. Haven't eaten yet this evening myself. You can dine with me or on your own as long as I'm close by. OK?"

Dylan wanted to fill his belly, but had no desire for the young man's company. He said he'd get someone from security when he decided to eat. A car drove up and when the occupants sidetracked the young man with questions, Dylan crossed the street and headed for the restaurant. With his beard and the rim of his baseball cap shadowing his eyes, he really didn't think anyone would notice him. Not too many people knew he was in town yet.

His waitress appeared to be of native-American descent and he wondered if the tribal connection remained strong in the region.

"You're quite lovely," he flattered her. "Are you from here?" He carefully spoke in his Americanized voice, eliminating the "ye's" and "mi's."

She blushed. "I was raised on the Moapa reservation, but I've lived in Kanab since '96."

"You still tribal?" Crow realized he sounded like a stupid tourist.

Suspicious, fidgeting with her pencil, she answered, "What do you mean by 'tribal'?"

"Do you still participate in your tribe's rituals or ceremonies?"

"Look, friend," she spoke softly, "people are always curious about the Indians around here. There's a nice exposé printed and available in all the tourist shops in town. In fact, if you'd like one, I'll step next door and get a copy for you."

"Sorry, ma'am, I meant no offense," he offered apologetically. "Just wanted to know something about someone in the tribe."

"You a cop?"

"No—just here with the film crew. I met a local shaman named Grace Moon today and wondered if she's for real." Crow slugged down half a glass of water indifferently, hoping he had tripped her trigger.

"As real as they get, brother. She's one of the old ones, though. Knows stuff the young ones don't and doesn't seem remotely interested in teaching the old ways to anyone." She tried to change the conversation. "You ready to order yet?"

"Yeah…" he said, staring intently at the menu, "I'll have a Pacifico and the sour cream and molé chimichanga with rice, please."

When the food arrived he inhaled the slightly cinnamon and chocolate fragrance of the molé sauce. He wolfed the meal down quickly and made a mental point to put his diet pills in his pocket so he wouldn't feel this way again.

Hailing his waitress to order another beer, he noticed she seemed a little friendlier. *I'd wager someone identified me and told her,* he thought.

"I didn't mean to brush you off or anything earlier, sir. It's just that sometimes people twist things a little and word gets 'round that you're talking trash behind their backs, ya know? As for Grace, I hold the highest respect for her. As far as I know she's brought only good things to this planet." She straightened her apron and gently placed his bill on the edge of the table. "Anything else I can get you, sir?"

Deciding to forego the calories of a second beer, he pulled out some cash, including a generous tip for her. As he stood to leave, the young security guard entered with a female in tow. He saw Crow immediately and nodded to him rather brusquely, as if he'd been slighted by Crow's apparent disregard for his offered services.

Dylan wandered back to the Kokopeli Inn and headed for his suite. The bed had been turned down and next to the chocolate on his pillow his indigo flower had been arranged with a sprig of mint and a little note: *See, I didn't throw it away this time!* signed, M. Walsh. He chuckled at her quirky sense of humor and reached for the flower. Still as fresh and beautiful as the moment Nikki presented it to him, its fragrance seemed to permeate the room.

Oddly, however, the smell did not overwhelm the senses. It was more like walking through violets in the early spring; the intoxicating scent you perceive for a moment and then, no matter how hard you try, can't smell again until you re-enter the garden; a fragrance you wish would linger, but once having made its way to the limbic system, deposits its message, and disappears.

A nicotine impulse surged through his veins. He remembered the package in the pocket of the leather jacket he wore the day before. While retrieving the cigarettes, the pamphlet he had secreted away while in Nikki's office came with it. He carefully removed the beautiful business card, placed it on the desk, and traced her name with his index finger. Then he perused the advertisement: *vacation cottage rentals...away from the maddening tourist traps and crowds: a unique place for those who desire a private interlude with Zion.* "So that's what those little houses were," he said aloud. Photographs of the cottages, equestrian facility, pool, and the tennis court had been superimposed over an image of The Great White Throne. A brief list of "things to do" appeared in one corner, opposed by a map to the ranch. Terms of the rental were outlined, including a specific request for *non-smokers only, please.*

The pamphlet further described the facility as a working horse and cattle ranch. A picture of a young blonde woman training horses in the arena caught his attention. He quickly flipped through the rest of the brochure looking for pictures of Nikki. To his disappointment, no photos of her appeared at all.

Knowing he had only one day left before they shot his first scene, Crow settled in to study the script. In spite of well-intended efforts, however, the powers of concentration failed him.

Surrendering to the unconscious mind, he contemplated both Grace's discourse and her offer to lead him to the door of insight. *Can I trust her?* He truly wanted to have the experience of working with a real shaman, if only to tell stories about it later. *The Rollovers would really get off on that. So what if she's some kooky old Indian who thinks I came to her in a dream and said I wanted her help? Maybe I did! Stranger things have been known to happen on this ol' planet!* he thought.

Lately, Crow had been painfully analyzing his life as a whole. He lived in dedication to his careers as both an actor and musician, and spent every free minute playing as hard as he worked.

Scrutinous observation of others allowed him to see the world as if watching a play while loving every character—hero and villain, sinner and saint. Often he mimicked the behavior of others in order to better understand their character. Because he could thoroughly imagine wearing their skin, he became a master of inoffensively teasing people; providing a humorous perspective of their eccentricities.

There were no complaints as to his creativity and careers. Even though he needed a break, he thoroughly enjoyed his work. Success, wealth, and fame suited him.

His drinking could very well be considered borderline alcoholism, but his occasional bouts with drugs had not taken him over the edge. Justifying his behavior by stating, "I'm a sensitive artist," had become increasingly transparent and certainly fooled no one—least of all, him.

Relationship-wise, he got on well with others. Love, however, eluded him. Having amorously known an unlimited supply of women, it never failed to both amuse and disappoint him that true love had been nearly nonexistent.

Now, riding the high tide of his career, he felt something missing he couldn't quite put his finger on.

A strong inner knowing silently promised a change in his life—or at least the direction of his attention. He couldn't help but wonder if everything that had been happening had something to do with it. Having consistently trusted his gut reaction, he simply could not ignore that his gut told him to call Grace.

Dylan located Grace's card. He turned it over and over in his hand, questioning the wisdom of calling her, feeling as nervous as the first time he'd ever called a girl. This wasn't romantic nervousness, however, but rather an anxiousness of unknown origins. He felt like Alice in Wonderland about to jump into the rabbit hole; knowing that once he did, his ability to control his destiny may no longer be in his hands. "Damn it, man, just call her!" he chided himself harshly. He had to admit the possible development of all good human virtues in a belief system different than his own, so he dialed.

The phone rang only once before the very gentle, calm voice of Grace Moon answered. "Hello, Mr. Crow. I expected your call."

"I didn't know I would call, miself, until just now when I dialed!" he retorted somewhat suspiciously. "Oh, right—the caller ID read 'Kokopeli Inn.'"

"I don't have caller ID, Mr. Crow. Now, what did you want to ask me?"

Crow found himself pacing about the room as he spoke over the remote handset. "Ye said ye could take me on a journey to help me better connect with mi character, Little Crow."

"No, Mr. Crow. I said I could take you safely to the doorway of your insight. From there, you must journey alone. Do you have the courage to take the journey alone?" She had said it without encouragement, without judgment, without sentiment of any kind—just a simple question. Silently she awaited his reply.

A very pregnant pause ensued before he willed his voice to respond. "Aye, yeah, I've courage enough! Bring it on!" he snapped as if he'd been challenged to a fight in a bar.

"Mr. Crow," Grace replied evenly, "I've agreed to help you *if* you desire my help—only *if* you desire it. Now, step away from your ego, 'Little Crow,' and ask me again."

Batabang, bataboom! —"Little Crow"—she used his character's name to refer to his ego. He understood loud and clear, remembering Nikki had done the same.

"Ms. Moon," he said with sincerity dripping from every word, "I would consider it a great honor if ye would willingly lead me where I must go to understand what I must learn. How was that?"

"That's better." She smiled at her end of the line. "So, would you be interested in a stone-laying tomorrow?"

He didn't want to appear uneducated, merely guessing it was some tribal voodoo reading or something. "Sure. Can ye come to mi room about eleven in the morning?"

"No, Dylan," she said as if explaining to a small child. "You'll have to make more effort than that. You can drive through Zion and pick me up in Hurricane at six in the morning. From there we'll go to the Green Valley Spa where I'll do a stone-laying in the morning sunrays. The spa services section is closed until eleven, but I have my own keys. I'll handle all your services myself and no one will know you're there—at least no one on this domain."

When her last words sent a shiver down his spine, Crow wondered if he should back out before it was too late. His macho ego wouldn't allow her to spook him, however, so he asked for directions.

Now he had to find a car without a driver, plan his escape without being noticed by security, and let Peggy know he'd be gone for the day so no alarm would be sounded.

☯

"Peggy—" he said apologetically, having awakened her with his call. "Listen, I want to see some of the sights for miself tomorrow, but I don't want security taggin' along. Can ye get me a car and cover for me so the hounds will stay at bay?"

Still in a daze, the voice on the line did not register immediately. She blinked hard, squinted and tried to make out the time on the clock next to her bed. "Mr. Crow?" she asked sleepily.

"Aye, 'tis I—the royal pain in the butt!" He thought his humor would rouse her a little more.

"I guess I can handle that. You can take my Hyundai if you like. Not exactly a limo, but no one would notice you, if that's what you're hoping for." She stifled a yawn. "I'll bring the keys over in the morning. OK?"

"Well—I hoped to get out of here early—like around five a.m. Could I come to ye'r room and get the keys tonight?"

Her motel was within walking distance, so he raced down the stairs and out the back door of the Kokopeli within seconds. The rear of the inn had little exterior illumination as compared to the street side. He could easily play dodge-ems with the shadows and get past the guards. *Bloody Hell!* he thought. *Anyone could circumvent these clowns. The security personnel are little more than window dressing. Oh, well...I guess that serves a purpose too.*

Crow tapped lightly on Peggy's door. She had pulled a sweatshirt over her nightgown and her hair was tousled and flat on the back with a distinct cowlick poking up. Peggy stood in the doorway and whispered a few directions about her Hyundai and its gas requirements. Pointing to the dark blue car parked close to the doorway, she tossed him the keys with a promise to handle the "big boys." He thanked her profusely before departing on foot, thinking it best to return in the morning for the car so as not to arouse suspicion tonight.

"Hello, Nikki. It's Grace. Did I wake you?"

"No, not at all, dear. What did you two decide?" Nikki did not wish to prolong the conversation with small talk.

"Tomorrow morning with the *soular rays*. You feel like bringing the stone down tonight or waking up with the roosters?" Grace laughed gently, knowing full well that either option would keep Nikki from her bed.

"You get to sleep, Grace. I'll bring it down now and leave it on your porch. Will your dog make a fuss?"

"Butch sleeps on my bedroom floor these days and, unfortunately, he's a little hard of hearing, so I doubt he'll even notice you. Can you put it in a box or something so it won't get scratched?"

"Sure. I'll clear it and everything. Remember—only leave it over him for fifteen minutes! Thanks, Grace. Thank you with *all* my heart and soul!" she whispered.

Nikki stared thoughtfully into empty space as she hung up the phone.

Chapter 9

Exhaustion overtook Crow for lack of sleep the previous night. After sneaking back into the inn and setting his alarm, he lay upon the bed, still clothed and shod. He slipped into a deep, dreamless sleep from which he awoke at four thirty a.m., completely refreshed, but chagrined he had fallen asleep fully attired. Rushing through his morning toiletries, Crow then grabbed both the keys to the Hyundai and Grace's directions and headed out the door at four fifty five. No security guards were in sight.

Grace really did live in a small trailer house—smaller than the ones he used on his sets. Although the neighborhood appeared pretty rustic, her diminutive lot was immaculate. The entry consisted of a petite flower garden with wind chimes hanging from a dwarf apricot tree. Approaching the door he noticed a large cardboard box from which protruded a pyramid of copper tubes centered over a large quartz crystal.

Grace turned and bid her dog good day before stepping onto the porch. After they exchanged kind pleasantries, she picked up the box holding the contraption. "Well, then, all things in order, let's head for St. George."

For the most part, the town still slept for the early hour. Dylan searched the main street for a coffee shop, hoping they'd have time for a quick cup. He hadn't even had a cigarette in Peggy's car and the jitters were setting in.

"We can't afford a delay, Dylan. I'm sure you'd like a wake-up infusion, but I've got to catch the first morning rays for this work. Anyway, it's best to avoid caffeine before a stone-laying. I'll arrange for a drink at the spa."

Her ability to read his mind unnerved him.

They drove into an area known as Green Valley. As they

reached the top of a large mesa the spa came into view. For all the courts evidenced, Crow assumed it to be a tennis resort.

A five-foot red marble sculpture of an Indian woman greeted them. They entered a large hall decorated with gorgeous area rugs atop alabaster flooring, white furniture arranged in conversational seating, and extraordinary art at every turn of the eye. Life-sized, carved wooden angels were displayed in raised alcoves similar to ones seen in cathedrals. The combination of native-American and angelic influences created an unusual harmony. Passing through the entry hall, they arrived in front of a large, round interior window. On the other side of the glass a life-sized sculpture of an angel, with finger to lips, directed all who enter to do so quietly. Grace unlocked the door and switched on the lights.

A lovely reception desk lacked an attendant. The shelves were stocked with metaphysical, spiritual, inspirational, and self-healing books. Bath products, jewelry, accessories, and scents were professionally displayed in an adjoining room. He followed her through several corridors, each with walls hand-painted with charming scenery. She led him into a room with an oversized Jacuzzi bath and turned the knobs for the faucet. After testing the temperature of the water, Grace added a fizzy bath powder that turned the water an iridescent indigo color and filled the air with a luscious scent. Tinted lights within the tub accented the bluish-purple hue and the water swirled and sparkled with a life force of its own. Striking a match, Grace lit several candles throughout the room.

"Wait here a second, Dylan." After several minutes she returned with a tall indigo glass filled with floral scented water. "Sip it while you bathe." Pointing to a terrycloth robe to don after his soak, she announced, "You can wear that when you're through and I'll come back to get you in fifteen minutes."

Hell's bells, he thought. *Do I have to get naked to get a stone-laying? Maybe it means I get laid on stones or something.* He chuckled at his thought while testing the sweet liquid. Removing his clothing, he hung them on the provided pegs and slipped into the bath. Soft, lilting music issued forth from some invisible source. He tried to relax, but wished he had asked more about Grace's intent before participating so blindly. Dylan closed his eyes, listening to the music for a minute or two, then opened them and stared into the colored, effervescent swirling water. The candle's aroma layered the same scent as the bath. Lovely floral murals had been painted on the walls and live vines grew from pots up wooden trellises, attaching themselves to the ceiling stucco with their miniature tendrils. Fresh cut blue and indigo flowers rested in camouflaged vases, giving them the appearance of growing from the vines. All in all, he found the carefully orchestrated sensory experience quite agreeable.

A soft knock at the door signaled it was time to dry off and put on his robe. Crow peeked out the door to find Grace ready to escort him to an unknown destination. "Ye're sure no one's here?"

"Just leave your clothing," she instructed. "No one will disturb them or your valuables. Could I get you to remove your jewelry as well?"

He did so, though with a little suspicion. *Hey ol' chap,* he thought, *ye told her ye'd trust her, so just do it!*

She led him down the corridor, through a small kitchen, and out a door into a walled garden area. Beautiful flowers still flaunted their heady late summer display. Statuary of Indian maidens and angels had been placed throughout. It reminded him of Nikki's magical patch. Vines draped every wall and a large tree hung its shadowy leaves like a grand canopy.

They entered yet another garden, equally beautiful. A canvas drape tied to the side of the fencing served as a doorway to the private space. Grace closed it, encasing them in privacy. A massage table had been centered over a wooden dodecahedron platform. At the edge of the dais stood Grace's crystal contraption, now hanging from a large hook at the end of a tall copper pole rising from a heavy base. "What is that thing?" he asked, pointing.

Apparently, she had no intention of satisfying his intellectual curiosity and quietly asked him to lie down with his head in a northern position.

Crow laughed shyly. "Am I clothed for this operation, doc?"

"No, save for this towel placed across your privates. I'll be laying stones in sacred geometrical designs upon your chakra centers, including the one at that area of your body. I promise not to be familiar with you. However, you will feel some things being placed over your towel," she said matter-of-factly.

"It's bloody cool out here. Can I have a wee blanket or somethin'?"

"Trust me, in a few minutes the *soular rays* will hit you and you won't even notice." Grace stepped out so he could disrobe, lie on the table, and put the towel over its designated area.

A small table next to his head displayed an open leather pouch filled with a variety of small stones; some precious, some cut, some ordinary, like pebbles from the beach. "Dylan," she began, "I don't have time to explain everything now, so please refrain from asking questions until we're through. The *soular rays* last only the first fifteen minutes after sunrise and I've got work to do to prepare for them.

"Firstly, will you pray for help and guidance from your I AM Presence, your higher mental body, guides, and angels." She looked at him for a response. A bit of an uncomfortable silence passed before he spoke.

"Grace, I don't know how. I want to. I just don't know how!"

"It's OK, Dylan. There's no one special way to do it," she said compassionately. "I'll be glad to call in the troops, but you must follow my words with conscious intent. Do you understand?"

He merely nodded and closed his eyes.

"Beloved Mighty I AM Presence within me, I AM here and I AM there, and through and in thy name, I call upon the I AM Presence of this soul, Dylan Crow, upon his higher mental body, his guides and angels, the Beloved Ascended Master, St. Germain, Mr. Crow's ancestors, and my own guides and angels. Surround us individually with thy protective light and see to it that only that which is for the highest and best good of this soul enters this sacred space. We ask for guidance and insight into that which Mr. Crow most needs at this time, and thy service and light are invited and welcomed with our deepest gratitude." Grace stood, not with her hands clasped and head bowed, but with arms stretched wide with welcome embrace for the spirits, her head turned skyward. It had been a prayer of supplication, but also one of declaration and gratitude.

She took a deep breath, holding her hands at his crown chakra on top of his head. Her touch felt light and comforting as her breathing became heavy and rhythmic. Then she removed her hands and seemed to be doing something above him. Energy swirled at each area where her hands moved across his body. Sensing the small stones laid upon him one chakra at a time, Crow thought, *God, I'd like to hover above miself and see the patterns and stones.* Dragging the contraption closer to the table and positioning it over his heart, Grace placed the grounding wire over the palm of his right hand and gently closed the fingers.

Within seconds the sun hit the table upon which he lay, clad in nothing but a small towel and stones from Mother Nature. The

shaman moved to the space above his head again, but this time
reached down and touched his shoulders. He immediately relaxed,
deeper and deeper still, until no sensation of being in a physical body
existed. The influence caused him to believe he floated weightless
with the sun dancing on his skin, sensing its warmth and light penetrating within. No longer thinking logically or asking questions in
his mind, Crow consciously merged with the light and his only
remaining desire was to *be*.

He lay there quietly for fifteen minutes, after which Grace
removed the center stone from over his heart. Easily sliding the
wire from his hand, she removed the pyramid from its hook and
departed, closing the canvas drape noiselessly.

Crow dreamed.

Standing at his side, a young, handsome, bearded man with
violet eyes gazed fixedly ahead. Crow touched his companion's
arm and the man pointed. As if an observer and an actor in a play,
Dylan saw himself, slightly different in appearance, walk into a
great and beautiful temple with columns of intricately carved marble. Wearing a long garment secured by a jeweled belt with long
beaded strands dangling two feet from an ornate clasp, he strode
with determination through the large, empty halls. Arriving at a
heavily decorated door fashioned from gold and inlaid precious
gems in geometric designs, he quietly entered. The walls of the
room were burnished gold and the floor, a violet stone. In the center of the room an unusual flame rose from an elaborate altar: a
tripartite flame, dancing with equal plumes resembling ostrich
feathers---one blue, one yellow, and the other, pink.

A young, elegant woman entered with such grace, it appeared
as if she floated. Her long, dark hair was braided and tied with a
thin leather strap, at the end of which dangled a single malachite
bead. Upon her forehead rested a thin gold band with a double

terminated crystal mounted on a small gold disk centered between her brows. Deep green eyes, rimmed with a circle of violet blue engaged the matching eyes of the young man. A large dark mole in front of her left ear looked more like a beauty mark than a blemish. Although slight, an air of supreme dignity surrounded the woman. Both she and the flowing, violet, silk robe she wore, seemed to be lit from within.

"Brother," her clarion voice pleaded, "I pray you, do not take this action. I know your heart is heavy with sadness for all our losses, but this is *not* the higher law our father taught us. If you use the crystal the way you intend, it will surely bring ruin, not only to your enemies, but ultimately, to all you love."

"I can see no other way to defend and protect our people, Amala. You must trust my judgment. We've been attacked and it's our only defense. The council agrees we have no alternative. If the great central crystal comes under the dominion of our enemies, they *will* use it to control everything from our energy sources to our economy and it is we who shall be enslaved. It must be destroyed!"

"You know not the power with which you are dealing. I entreat you—I beg you—choose another pathway." She spoke with mingled desperation and tears.

"My mind and hand are set, Amala. I only came to say goodbye, for I know you will leave." He reached for her hand, pulling her close to his breast, and embraced her small frame.

She looked into his eyes and softly spoke. "Heart of my heart, soul of my soul, flame of my flame, I pledge to return and find you and remind you we cannot return home without each other. Without you, I AM not complete and cannot continue the full journey. I will chase you through eternity until I wear down your stubbornness and turn your eyes homeward, even if it takes forever! I love you with the most Divine love another soul can give and all other love created by man will leave you hungry until we unite again." With these words, spoken as her eyes held his like an irresistible magnet, she removed the golden band from her forehead and pressed it into his hands. "Remember always, my dear, dear brother, how you can find me."

She turned and walked slowly to the flame, her head tilted heavenward. Looking back at him one last time, she disappeared from sight as her body drew its light to a single point.

The man lowered his head and eyes with the agony of complete loss. There he remained for several minutes. With a mournful moan, he turned and left the room.

In a swirl of light the scene changed and Crow saw himself among distinguished looking men all clad in shifts and glorious, long colored robes. They entered a chamber deep beneath the earth, hundreds of feet high. In the center of the hall, an enormous, radiant, clear crystal nearly reached the domed ceiling. It sat upon a large disk of gold that extended around its perimeter by a hundred feet.

Encircling the great stone, the men intoned a sound so discordant that the stone took on a milky appearance and began to fracture. At the sight of the fractures the intonations stopped, but the crystal continued to break apart. With their faces reflecting alarm they gave wing to their feet, escaping the chamber with haste. The crystal exploded with such force that the earth and all upon it shook and rocked to and fro. Structures began to crumble and people were crushed beneath their enormous weight. Waters of the ocean rose in great waves of utter destruction and swallowed their beloved city whole.

Crow, the observer, watched, so moved, that tears filled his eyes and heartache consumed his soul. He turned to the man with violet eyes to beg his removal, but the man simply pointed ahead again.

An aged woman with long, white braided hair, tied with a slender leather strand with one malachite bead, lay in a bed. Her face was lined with age and the front of her left ear dotted with a dark, raised mole. Bright green eyes rimmed in violet shone clear with alertness. About her neck hung a chain with a golden disk pendant, upon which was anchored a double terminated crystal.

As a young man entered the room, Crow recognized himself, though he appeared, once again, slightly different. "Mum, I've come to say good-bye. I'm taking my men to the north to defend the border. We may die in the effort, but I cannot, in good conscience and honor, follow your advice to lay down my arms. We must protect all we love from our enemies."

Speaking evenly, the ancient one looked out the window near her bed. Her eyes were fixed on a truth as if it were a tangible object in her view. "Your actions will only provoke them further. The enemy is not the men you seek to slay. It is but a force, an energy that moves through them, and can only be conquered by love. By seeking more destruction you only bind yourself longer to the wheel of reincarnation."

She reached for his hand and drew him close. "You are the heart of my heart, the soul of my soul, the flame of my flame, son. I cannot stop you from taking this pathway, but I can tell you that someday it will come full circle and all you truly cherish will be lost. Take this," the old woman said, as she removed her pendant, "and use it as I showed you as a child. I will know when you need me again. I love you with a love so Divine that no space or time can ever change. No earthly love can take its place and though you now leave me of your own accord, I will find you again and remind you of the truths I taught you as a child." With her last words she hung the pendant around his neck and kissed him on the cheek.

Tears were in his eyes as he departed.

The scene changed to one of warring enemies, clashing swords, spewing blood, and body parts slashed and torn asunder. The young man, deeply wounded in his shoulder and neck, bled beyond control, knowing his own death imminent. Drawing the pendant from beneath his blood stained jersey, he placed it over his third eye. "Mother, you were right. I *have* brought our destruction. Forgive me, for I leave you defenseless." These were his last words before his eyes grew fixed and clouded. The warring mob raged forward like an uncontrolled fire, destroying everything of beauty and grace in the village, including the boy's mother.

Next, he saw himself a knight in England riding full gallop toward a village engulfed in smoke. The gates admitted him to hell, with signs of carnage everywhere he turned. He leapt from his giant steed and ran to the door of his dwelling, still in flame. There he found his daughter and wife, both with their throats slit and their skirts lifted, exposing their bare bodies stained with multiple bloodied handprints. His horror at the sight was overwhelming and no air could be sucked into his lungs. Hearing a noise, he turned to discover his father in a heap in the corner of the room, badly beaten and nigh to death.

Anger renewed his breath. "This is what comes of your way, Father!" he spat at the dying man. With rage on his face, he lifted the old man and dragged him out of the burning cottage, dumping him unceremoniously by a watering trough. Tears and blood spilled down the deeply creased face as the old one signaled his boy to come close enough to hear him. The knight approached and looked into his father's eyes. His own eyes reflected back at him.

"Heart of my heart, soul of my soul, flame of my flame, know that I love you with a Divine love far deeper than any that mankind can create. There is no death, only a change. If you avenge the deaths of those you love, the cycle will never end…for the great law commands that all things move in a circle and that which you send into the world comes back with more of its own to the creator. If you live by the sword, you will die by the sword. Hatred cannot heal hatred. Cruelty cannot heal cruelty. Everything you do affects the whole and no amount of anger or revenge can change the cosmic law. Be responsible only for your own creations and you will draw unto you that upon which your attention is held." The dying man struggled as he tried to remove a thin leather strap, clasped together with a malachite bead, which he wore around his neck. The son helped him pull it over his head.

Into his son's hand the old man pressed a talisman he had worn most of his life: a golden disk with a double terminated crystal anchored by a thin gold band. "I AM not so far away as you fear, my son, and though you've chosen a different path than mine, you can always call upon me for wisdom when your heart yearns for truth. I will find you again, for neither heaven nor hell can keep my heart from yours. I love you with a Divine love that cannot be compared to any love which man hath made."

With his last words the bloodied man slumped to the ground in death. The knight, angry, but moved, stroked the old man's hair. As he pulled it backward, Crow noticed a dark raised mole in front of the dead man's left ear.

Crow turned to the man with violet eyes. "The sorrow of these scenes is more than I can bear. Must I look further into this misery?"

"No, dear one," said the peaceful man. "I respect your wishes and if you will remember, you will have the guidance for which you asked printed upon your heart for eternity." The peace surrounding the man saturated the space all around Crow as he softly spoke. "Dylan, remember yourself without judgment, that you may learn.

It takes great mettle to look into the mirrors of your experiences, especially when the same choices have been repeated over and over again, leading you only down the same road. In your world is it not said, 'If you always do what you've always done, you'll always get what you've always got'? Brute force is inevitably returned with brute force, my son. What one puts out into the world must, by law, travel the great circle of life collecting more of its kind and return to its creator."

The man with violet eyes reached forth and pressed his thumb to Crow's third eye with his fingers spread over his forehead. The peace which had permeated the atmosphere now filled him as his eyes opened to see the sun a third of the way into the sky.

How long did I sleep? Dylan wondered. Then he realized the small stones were still on his body. "Grace, are ye about?"

"Good day, sir," Grace said quietly as she entered the private garden. "You've been on a long journey. Lie still for a moment while I check something." She stood over him with a pendulum and moved it from chakra to chakra. Upon coming to his heart, she reached her hand to his chest and laid it gently upon him. Dylan began to weep uncontrollably and though embarrassed to be doing so in her presence, found he could not withhold the cry that came from his heart in deep, painful sobs. He wiped away the flood. For several minutes longer he cried inaudibly. Finally, willing control, he closed his eyes, allowing himself to be embraced by the calm silence that surrounded the space. He had unexpectedly experienced a catharsis of his soul.

"I'm going to remove my 'dearies' from your body now," said Grace faintly as she stroked his head. With swift hand the stones were lifted with the same dexterity with which they had been laid. "Your robe, mi lord," she said draping it across his chest. She turned on her heels and removed herself from the room, carefully securing the canvas drape behind her.

Blimey! What just happened to me? he wondered. His mind raced trying to determine if it had only been a dream since it was obvious he'd been sleeping. Crow could not identify what made him sob so and now felt embarrassed to face the shaman.

Slipping into the robe, he padded barefoot back into the building, having failed to notice the slippers left for his use. The sound of voices and the clatter of dishes could be heard fairly near. Grace led him swiftly to the bathing room. "You were out a little longer than I expected. The staff is arriving and we need to leave quickly through the back exit if you wish to remain unidentified."

His belongings lay exactly where he'd left them. As the dreams haunted his consciousness, he haphazardly buttoned his red flannel shirt, leaving one side an inch lower than the other. *Were these visions of past lives?* he wondered. Though convinced he had played the main character in each of the scenes, an understanding of the meanings behind each tale remained fuzzy. *If these were past lives, it's no wonder I've sought so many roles as protector and defender. Could there be karma involved here?* Looking down, he realized his error and rebuttoned the shirt.

What about mi opposing character? Each had a similar appearance to the woman who rescued me the other day---somethin' about the eyes, I think. And, what about the pendant and the leather lace with the bead? Mi subconscious probably just mixed mi experience with Nikki into the dreams. But...the mole? Who do I know with a mark like that? Unable to think of anyone, he forced himself to apply speed to his task so his departure would be undetected.

Driving back to Hurricane, Grace thought him oddly silent for one so full of questions, but respected his quiet reverie until they pulled into her driveway. "Just need to get the crystal out of the back seat and then I'll leave you to yourself."

"What is that thing?"

"It's like a generator. I used it to *power-up* the grid over which you were lying in order to magnify the frequency of the electromagnetic field you were in."

"Ye mean I was on some sort of machine?"

Already out of the car, Grace opened the back door and retrieved the box that held the power stone. She put it on the ground and sat back in the front seat with the door open. "A very long time ago a friend of mine created a force field of sorts which is buried in the earth just beneath the garden where we did the stone-laying. This field is created from highly charged electron movement achieved by the combination of the sun's rays, sacred geometry, and quartz crystals. The grid is constructed of copper tubing that conducts the electrons—just like copper wire conducts electricity. Crystals act as receptors, storage units, magnifiers, and transmitters of this light energy. Positioning the power stone above your body completed the instructions to the field.

"The woman who created this has only allowed the use of the power stone with four other people in eighteen years: herself, her husband, the owner of this spa, myself—and now, you. I've promised to return the stone today that she may safeguard it still."

"How did ye talk her into letting ye use it on me?"

"She just knew it would be right for you. There are ways of asking and knowing that go beyond logic and reason, Dylan," Grace nearly whispered.

"OK, OK..." He paused, and with eyes staring forward out the windshield, blurted out his thoughts. "I have a million questions, Grace, but I'm so embarrassed about what happened to me with all that bloody, childish sobbing, I'm having a wee bit o' difficulty even looking ye directly in the eyes. So, this is me, swallowing a hell of a lot of pride. Can we just drive around while I try to assimilate everything before we talk?"

"Dylan, I've given my promise to your employers that I'd be available to you twenty-four hours a day. I've given my promise to your higher self that I'd guide you any way I could. I think driving around until your mind can begin to grasp things is an excellent idea. Perhaps we could head toward Kolob and return the crystal to my friend."

He gratefully accepted when she offered to replace him behind the wheel. Before he got in the passenger seat, however, he pulled a cigarette from his pocket.

"Hey," she said, leaning over and catching his attention outside the door, "the last thing you *need* right now is that cigarette. If you honestly want to comprehend what just happened, *don't put up a smokescreen!*"

Looking hard at the cigarette, he debated her words with his own thoughts. Somewhat disappointedly, he tucked the fag back in with the others and returned the package to his pocket while sliding into the passenger seat.

They passed through the city of Hurricane, then to the LaVerkin junction that led back toward Zion. He remembered from his little misadventure two days prior, the little village of Virgin signaled the turnoff for Kolob. Grace drove another five miles and to his astonishment, pulled right into the Red Rock Canyon Ranch. Seeing the closed gate, Grace shifted the gear into park, jumped out, and hit some buttons on a keypad mounted on a nearby cedar post. A huge grin came over her face while she laughed and danced in a circle as the gate swung out. Both her behavior and the fact that they were headed back to Nikki's ranch, mystified Crow.

Grace sidled back into the driver's seat with obvious glee dripping from her smile. "I remembered it! Haven't been here for a long time, but I remember how my friend used the same code for everything! She always said it was her destiny number for this lifetime—and it worked! Good luck too, I'll tell ya, 'cause it's a long walk down to her home!"

"Wait!" Crow said with suspicion in his voice. "Ye mean to tell me the lady who lives here arranged for this 'stone-laying'?"

"Look, Dylan, I told you I like to be honest with people, even if it makes them uncomfortable. Nikki called me on the set and told me she'd helped you the other day and had a strong impression you needed a stone-laying. I told her flatly that unless I received my own confirmation, I would in no way suggest such a powerful tool for you. When I asked, however, your higher self sanctioned the idea. Nikki also felt it should take place over the grid along with the use of the great central crystal, both of which were imperative to the success of your deepest needs. In fact, she drove to my home in the middle of the night and delivered it especially for you."

This feels like a set-up, Crow thought, frowning. His face assumed an expression of distrust. Silently he wondered if there were some sort of magic or witchcraft, or some other foolishness going on. *Why did they each use the same words with me; 'If you'll just relax and trust me, I'll take you safely…'? Isn't it just a little beyond coincidence that my dreams on the table included little parts of Nikki in them?* He didn't really understand anything about mind control, but suddenly all his red flags went up and every possible doubt and fear that could exist in the soul of a man surfaced.

His heartfelt interest in receiving guidance through this supposed shaman had turned to something that made him eye her warily. "Say, I'd really just like to stay up here while ye deliver that thing. OK?" "…*That thing,*" spoken with disdain, as if it had been a tool of violation.

Grace made eye contact with him, took a deep breath, then said,

"Dylan, you have a soul connection with this woman—one I'm certain even she's only beginning to comprehend, and one you'll have to ask your own heart about. There are no coincidences. *There are no coincidences!* Don't let fear be your guide, Dylan. Let your heart be your guide. There is only one tyrant in this world, and it is ignorance and the fear that comes with it!"

The imprint of absolute calmness relaxed the skin around her eyes.

Crow breathed deeply, consciously trying to quell his own fears. "Grace, what do the words 'heart of my heart, soul of my soul, flame of my flame' mean to ye?" His heart raced, afraid to hear her answer; afraid he could not buy into this concept of reality and did not have it within him to do something about it if he did.

"Why do you ask?"

"I dreamed it several times while upon the table. Several people spoke those words to me. They seemed to be the same person— yet not. One appeared as an old man; one, an old woman; another, a young woman. They had similar attributes, but for certain, these words were spoken to me by each," he said thoughtfully.

"You've had the privilege of seeing your twin flame, Dylan," Grace began to explain, "…at least the privilege of seeing your twin flame in relation to past lives. Do you remember my explanation of twin flames when I drew the circles in the garden? Most people don't meet their twin flame until each has developed far enough along their individual spiritual pathways to begin to merge again. There are some, however, that have such love between them as to draw them together lifetime after lifetime.

"A twin flame doesn't necessarily mean 'soul mate' as you may have understood it on the romantic level. Very often twin flames are drawn together because they cannot complete their earthly purpose without each other. It could well have been seen as a relative, friend, or lover. Twin flames who do join as lovers on this plane, however, generally have bliss untold in their reunion, for it is the ultimate union of the Divine Feminine and the Divine Masculine. This Divine Love between twin flames originates in the heart flame: the unfed flame of the I AM Presence, which is anchored in the heart and breathes the very spirit of life into matter to animate it. Divine love does not begin at the lower chakras—the energy centers of the human or lower self.

"Of course, you know the energy at the sexual center of one's being often misleads a person, causing them to believe they possess Divine Love for another. Though twin flames may experience this level of connection, it will be the orgasm of the heart that tells them the truth."

Dylan's eyes widened. "The orgasm of the heart? Like a flaming ball of energy that magnifies in the heart and reaches a crescendo, then spreads throughout every nerve and cell in the body?"

"You're asking me something you've experienced, n'est-ce pas?" she asked. "Sometimes the experience is as physical as you describe. Sometimes it's just a profound peace in all the higher centers—a knowingness that rises above the conscious level of being and reverberates in the heart.

"You and your twin flame agreed to bring God's love to this world by descending into density. You agreed to participate in multiple incarnations in both the feminine and masculine energies so both halves of the whole could learn to be the divine instrument of God. As I mentioned yesterday, you spent eons of time in blissful harmony with your divine cosmic lover, but then mankind began to fall in consciousness, believing himself to be separate from God and began to misuse God's energy. When that harmony was lost—when distrust, fear, and belief of separation took hold—mankind began a journey in which he became the recipient of his negative karma.

"Most twin flames became vibrationally separated and, no longer preferring one another, became entangled in complex associations with other souls, experiencing lifetime after lifetime of trying to untangle the karmic mis-creations between them. People are drawn to these alliances like great magnets because their souls know they have karma to release with one another before they can return home and to their twin flames. Everyone's soul cries out for his return to that perfect state and that perfect union.

"So—many times, when one is magnetically drawn to another, they may be but soul mates or part of a soul group trying to work out their mis-creations. Soul mates are different than twin flames. They are those who echo your same desires in mastering similar karma and developing the energies of the same chakra center. Deep love can exist between these soul mates and soul groups. Then there is the Karmic relationship—one to which you are drawn to work out negative karma. These are usually the toughest, because they are absolutely binding. They're extremely important, however, in mastering one's spiritual pathway.

"Every incarnation since this *fall in consciousness* has been spent in creating negative karma or trying to undo or balance that karma in an attempt to return to your wholeness and your reunion with your twin flame.

"Twin flames don't always have a smooth go of it either, though, Dylan. Because they have lived through so many incarnations in personality, they have acquired traits that will sometimes bring even the most divine lovers to loggerheads. Twin flames don't always recognize each other right away, either. Awareness seems to precede love."

Crow opened the car door and started pacing like a tiger with mind and heart reeling with a pitch so steep as to upend his craft. He felt something so profoundly true that it could not be denied, even though his logic kept screaming to discount and distrust everything he had experienced over the last few days.

Stopping in his tracks, he turned and strode toward Grace, who watched him with absolute amusement. "Does she know?" he nearly demanded.

"I think somewhere inside she knows. However, when Nik spoke to me she referred not to any connection between you two, but rather your personal need to 'relive' something so you could clear your understanding prior to your performance in this movie. She, as did your higher self, seemed to think it would affect millions of lives."

"Oh, mi God," he whispered. "I told her, as I told you, mi character felt like one I'd played in real life somewhere—that I had two choices similar to those we're goin' to film. Told her I wanted to get it *right* this time. Could she care so much about a total *stranger* to go to that much effort?"

"Can't answer that one. To be honest, you'll have to find your own way regarding Nikki, Dylan. I wasn't called in to make some sort of match for you, only to help direct you to those insights and memories held at a cellular level that affect your current behavior. If you recognize her as your twin flame, and this feeling goes beyond your loins, you'd be casting a sacred opportunity away to let her slip out of your life—even if she doesn't know. And, Dylan, it's not something you should just blurt out to another soul because I assure you if she doesn't know, fear and doubt could easily push her from you."

"Can I confront her about having called ye for mi benefit?"

"Wisdom might direct otherwise, I think. Besides, she's not here, or the gate wouldn't be locked. As I said—there are no coincidences."

They drove down the steep entry hill, then along the winding road to Nikki's magical kingdom. He wished Grace could drop him off and let him stay, but time would not allow. They deposited the box at the front door and neither Bear nor the Lab did anything more than wag their tails at them. As the car scaled the steep entry hill he asked if he could shut the gate. "Sure. The code is twelve-twelve," she instructed, knowing full well he wanted to memorize "her number."

Chapter 10

Joe Chatauk caught Crow's attention as he walked down the hall of the inn. "Ho there, Dylan. You wanna talk about tomorrow's scene for a minute?"

After the surreal experiences of his morning, Dylan ached to be doing *anything* he actually understood and over which he had control. "Sure, mate. In fact, I was just wondering how to find ye to ask the same thing." A twinge of guilt twisted his gut for having lied.

They strolled down the hallway to Mrs. Walsh's sitting room. "Will it offend ye if I smoke?" Joe shook his head so Crow lit a cigarette before he sat down. "I got out to the location yesterday. It's fantastic. I believe it will provide the needed impetus to put us both in perfect character. The feeling is one of a space between worlds. Have ye seen it yet?"

Joe's lips widened to a self-satisfied grin. "I introduced the spot to the location manager. The producers thought it would be too much trouble to get the equipment there, but I convinced them it would be worth their time and money."

"So, ye want to rehearse it a few times tonight?" The smoke from Dylan's cigarette stung his eyes as if it were being held in a vacuum around his head. *Must be the circulation of the air in the room,* he thought. He leaned over and prematurely stubbed out the butt in an ashtray.

Chatauk tilted his head slightly to the right, almost as if craning to hear something. Then he put his finger to his lips, more to stop words from spilling forth than in contemplation. He gazed downward, remaining quiet and still for what seemed a long time. The odd action caught Crow off guard as he silently observed him.

"Just had a brilliant insight," Joe offered finally. "Why don't we both meditate about it tonight and cut it first run right on location tomorrow?"

"Ye're kidding, right?"

"I think this one calls for it, son."

Crow studied the old man's face. "Ye're dead earnest, aren't ye?"

Chatauk nodded.

Dylan's natural response would have been to blow the suggestion away with a puff of smoke, but his gut reaction said "pay attention!" "Look, Joe, to be perfectly honest, I don't know how to meditate. I can contemplate. I can analyze. I can try to feel and visualize the part. I can pick apart each inflection of mi voice, each lift of mi brow, or grimace of mi face, but I don't know how to meditate into a part."

Joe's expression softened, like the face of a grandfather about to offer sage advice to a beloved child. "The role you play in this movie's just a vision quest for you, son. You're going to have to connect with the dichotomies within your own life that equal those presented to your character before you can *play* it right. That ain't somethin' that comes from your head. You got to connect here," Joe whispered softly while touching Dylan's chest.

Had it not been for the experiences of the previous seventy-two hours, Crow might have told this stranger to get his part, or his jollies, any way he thought fit, and he'd get his part his own way—thank you very much. But he suddenly felt like a child in the presence of this man and didn't even feel slighted or annoyed by Joe's term of intimacy: "son."

"Ever pray?" asked Chatauk.

"Not much." His uttered prayer on bended knee the preceding day flashed before his eyes. "Something like hitting a brick wall for me when I use the semantics I learned as a kid in Sunday

school, ye know? I just always felt like men try to make God in
their own image instead of the other way around. Ye've heard that
quote, 'he who has nothing else, has religion.' Well, I think I
believe something like that; like it was myth made up to control
the masses. I'm just a spiritual rebel, I guess."

"Sounds more like someone who's rebelled against the concept
of organized religion. That's not the same thing as a spiritual rebellion."

Wow! Crow had never thought of it that way before. He silently thanked Joe for acknowledging this out loud for him. "So, ye of
the 'brilliant ideas,' got any to get me on first base?"

"Yeah, but we'll need more privacy," Joe suggested. "My room
or yours?" Then Joe repeated the crazy thing with his head and his
finger again. "On second thought, let's use yours. The suite should
be bigger and we need a little room."

They climbed the stairs and entered Crow's nest. Mrs. Walsh
had already been in to clean and everything appeared neatly organized. Joe immediately noticed the beautiful indigo flower on Dylan's
pillow. "They don't put one of those on *my* bed!"

"Actually, it's kind of a joke between the ol' lady and me. A few
days ago mi car broke down and it was a gift from the woman who
rescued me."

"A few days ago?" Joe moved to the bed for a closer inspection. "May I?"

Dylan could think of no reason to refuse the request, so he
nodded.

Chatauk gently lifted the flower and held it before his eyes.
Then, as he inhaled its fragrance, seemed visibly transported by its
scent to some form of ecstasy. He held the stem in his right hand
with the palm of his left a few inches above the flower.

Fascinated with the man's behavior, Crow surveyed him curiously without interruption.

"You ever met this lady before?"

Crow shook his head. "Ye think it's poisoned or something?" Dylan asked, chuckling under his breath.

"This ain't no ordinary flower, son. This beauty's been charged with life force beyond that of its original source."

"Sorry—no comprende."

"Some folks—usually those educated in a higher spiritual capacity—know how to draw the life force from the very atmosphere around them and infuse it into an object by their focus. Remember in the Bible how Christ made the dead fig tree live again? Same thing. The energy can be qualified to hold the life force in the object for as long as they command it to be there. Could be forever self-sustained or just until its task is completed. Whoever charged this is a true adept. I'd like to meet her. Did you get her name or anything?"

Crow felt as if he were drowning in a sea of information that had risen wave upon wave, upon wave, through circumstances over which he seemed to have no control. The foreign content of these relentless waters overwhelmed him, and yet, something inside begged to know more. Every fiber of his being confirmed that he stood on the precipice of a great event in his life. Still, his head shouted things like "too right!" and "no way!" He honestly didn't know if he could take the leap of faith required to explore the hidden depths of his soul.

"Aye," he said as he walked to the desk and picked up her lovely business card. He handed it to Chatauk, hoping he could divine something just from looking at it. If he did, he made no mention.

Joe smiled sweetly. "Yep, I'd sure like to meet this one." He started to put the card in his pocket, but Crow offered to copy the address for him on another piece of paper. Chatauk grinned knowingly as he read the look on Dylan's face and handed the card back.

"Well, to the valuable necessities then, shall we?" asked Joe. "I'm just going to show you a pathway I take. It's not the only one out there, but one with which I personally derive my own inner hearing."

He began to move the furniture out of the way to make a space on the floor large enough for someone to lie down. Crow thought how uncomfortable the hard floor looked, and glanced hopefully toward the bed. "Nope," said the old man. "I'd like to help you and I can't maneuver around your body on that bed." He instructed Crow to lie down with his head to the north.

"Can't I at least use a pillow?"

"Sorry," Joe answered. "Got to have your spine straight for this one. Don't want any kinks in the energy flow."

Chatauk knelt above Crow's head. "Now, just relax while I sing you through this one. Next time you can do it for yourself."

*Twice now, in one day, I've been placed in a prone position and assisted by an Indian to connect to mi inner self. This is getting way kooky. Oh, well...what's the worst that can happen,*Crow thought silently, *I get a nap or somethin'?*

Joe held both hands over Crow's forehead. Dylan could feel energy bouncing back and forth between the man's hands and his third eye area. The force, at first, felt sporadic, then settled to a constant rate of exchange. Still holding one hand over his forehead, the old man moved nimbly around to Dylan's side and raised the other over his heart. The same sensation began again, but the vibration reverberated deep inside Crow's chest. Uneven at first, then as with the forehead, it settled into a relaxing, constant rhythm. Then both head and heart began to beat in sync. As soon as the sensation stabilized, Chatauk returned to the head of his *patient*, knelt down and stretched his arms out to his sides with the palms of his hands facing up.

The old Indian began to intone repeatedly a sound much like the "aum" Dylan had heard in oriental films. As he concentrated more closely on the sound, however, he realized Joe chanted the words, "I AM." The sound started high in the man's head, then sank deep into his chest, rising again to be held on the "M" in his sinuses. Dylan tried silently mimicking the same sound, thinking it might help the process. After about five minutes the distinct impression of weightlessness surrounded him. Consciously, he allowed the sensation to engulf his physical body until only the sound of "I AM" engaged his full awareness. His mind went blank, like an empty screen. How long Chatauk chanted, he could not tell, alert only to the throbbing rhythm of his third eye and heart beating in unison. They were now vibrating to the sound of "I AM."

Softly, calmly, the old man spoke. "You are both Little Crow and Dylan Crow. Ask your higher self to reveal to you, through hearing and vision, that which you need to know."

As if hearing the instructions from some far off place, Crow silently requested assistance from God and his higher self.

The scenes of his earlier dreams replayed on the screen of his mind. Nothing could hinder the visions, as he saw them clearly, one scene after the other. Even though he tried to *will* his attention back to silence in order to hear or see something from his higher self, the morning's dreams would not disappear.

He heard Joe calling from far away. Then his voice sounded closer and closer, until finally, the words were directly above him. Feeling returned to Dylan's arms and legs as he became fully aware of his body once again. Opening his eyes and blinking a few times, he pushed himself up to a cross-legged, sitting position.

"Well?" Chatauk queried.

"Weird, man. It felt like I was just floating and somewhere inside of me pounded a rhythm like a heartbeat—only not just in mi chest. Then, somehow I got distracted and started thinking 'bout some stuff that happened this morning and I couldn't get back to the silence. Sorry. Guess I'm just a bad student."

Joe stood, stretched his legs and helped Crow to his feet. "Well, I wasn't in your head, son, but I'd say you better pay attention to what happened to you this morning!" The old man smiled in a wizened sort of way and Crow swallowed hard. "Read your lines only once tonight before you go to bed and see what insight your dreams bring you."

Sauntering over to the bed, Joe raised the flower to his nose one last time, inhaled its fragrance, then gently put it down. "You're pretty courageous to try this tack with me, son."

Tack, hell! thought Crow. He fully intended to practice his lines, movements, and facial expressions in the mirror the minute the old man left.

"Wanna get something to eat?" Joe asked.

Crow looked at his watch, shocked to discover they'd been at it for some two-odd hours. He could have sworn he'd only lain there a few minutes. Joe's eyes were laughing at him. "Yea- ea-eah," he finally spit out, with distinct space between each sound.

They decided to take the meal offered in the catering tent. Joe deliberately chose a table far from the crew members where their conversation could not be overheard. While eating, Dylan confessed he had never seen any of Chatauk's work.

"From what tribe do ye hail?" Crow asked curiously.

Joe snapped a raw carrot with his teeth. "Actually, my mother's Blackfoot and my pa's Apache. But I guess I look enough like the Hopi to play the part—though most people wouldn't notice the difference anyway—kind of like all blacks look the same to most caucasians."

"What ye did up there just now—is that something ye'r people do?"

"I assume you're referring to my ethnicity?"

Crow nodded.

"My people are just the same as everyone else on the planet at this point in time. Some of the old ones maintain the true traditions, but the middle and younger generations are pretty much distracted by survival and possessions, alcohol and drugs. They're so busy frantically living the illusion, that for the most part, they're steeped in spiritual apathy. I'm not putting 'em down; it's just the way with most of the world. People have forgotten why they're here in this great school and as a result they have a hard time graduating because they won't pay attention."

Joe swallowed a large mouthful of mashed potatoes and continued. "My own insights haven't been easily earned. My pa was a mean alcoholic and my poor mother spent her life cowering in terror of him all of the time because he used to beat her. Took his fair share of swings at my sister and me too. By sixteen I had become an alcoholic as well. As a kid I was too afraid of my dad to interfere with his drinking and violence, but I *became* him, all the same. Dumb, huh?" He looked at Crow, not like a man ashamed of his confession, but as though observing to see if his audience truly listened. "At twenty-three, they imprisoned me for manslaughter after I ran over a little girl while stoned out of my mind. Did a fiver. Prison only turned me to drugs 'cause they're easier to get than alcohol."

Joe ceased speaking, noticing the judgment behind Crow's eyes.

Dylan had lit a cigarette, pretending to be hearing the information nonchalantly. Although he had known people who drank, took drugs, or did other self-destructive things and had certainly done his share, somehow the story spilling from Joe's lips seemed contrary to the spirit he felt with him.

The smoke from Dylan's cigarette suddenly engulfed his face, especially irritating his eyes. He couldn't figure out why this phenomenon happened twice in the presence of Joe Chatauk. Obviously perturbed by the interference, he crossed his leg and ground the butt on the bottom of his shoe.

Grace's words blazed through Crow's mind. "If you really want to understand what you've just experienced, don't put up a SMOKE-SCREEN." *Is it possible for somethin' like that to get in one's subconscious mind and manifest literally?* he wondered.

"What?" he said, when he saw Chatauk laughing.

"Nothing."

"So, how'd ye end up in this profession?" The sincerity in Crow's voice opened the door of communication again.

Joe leaned forward and lowered his voice. "I came out of prison as hard as a man can be: mean, stoned, bored, indifferent to everything. All I could think of was my next fix. Blacked out one day and woke up on a streambed, nearly drowning. To this day I have no memory of how I got there. Everything in my life seemed completely empty and out of control. As I pulled myself to the bank of the stream, there stood a young man just staring at me. He didn't say a word—merely walked over and extended his hand to help me to my feet. His eyes were a remarkable, intense shade of blue and a feeling of profound serenity permeated the very atmosphere around him. He'd built a little fire and motioned me to sit near it, which I did—gratefully, 'cause I was soaking wet and chilled to the bone. When the man finally spoke, he said, 'You've forgotten it's only a play. What you truly are is magnificence, glory, and nobility. I AM all there is. I AM here and I AM there, and I AM you.' I had been looking at the fire 'cause I didn't want him to see the tears in my eyes. When I looked up he was gone.

"For days I thought I'd dreamed the whole thing. Deep in my soul there existed such a hunger for his words that maybe I invented him or something. Anyway, it made me want to get straight, so I talked to an old padre who had a little mission on the reservation. He got me into something like today's version of AA: kind of a spiritual approach to my addictions. Can't say my recovery ran too smoothly. I remember the days I'd just sit clasping my hands together so I wouldn't reach for another drink. Well, to make a really long story a bit shorter, that began a spiritual pathway that's gone on for fifty-some-odd years now. Just like AA, I have to do the spiritual work. No one can do it for me. No one can do it for *you!*" he added, looking directly into Crow's eyes.

Quickly averting his thoughtful gaze, Crow didn't respond.

"As to your question," Joe continued, "when the man said I had forgotten it was only a play, it got me to thinking if that was true, I wanted to play the parts of magnificence, glory, and nobility.

"I had no particular aspirations past that of regaining my sanity at the time. One day I met a man in a restaurant who needed some change. Turned out to be a casting director who just *happened* to be looking for an Indian. I don't know if he felt obliged after I had helped him, but he asked me to come in for a reading. I got the part and started working two days later. Funny thing, though, the character I played had to demonstrate utter nobility. There are no coincidences. I've been in the *play* ever since that day, but I never accept a role that places me as a man without those three virtues. It's true, like you, not everyone knows my name, but the price I'd have to pay to meet the seducements of my lower nature is too high."

Crow chuckled. "What do ye mean—the seducements of ye'r lower nature?"

Joe's eyes looked down rather than at his companion. He spoke quietly, as if being gentle with himself. "People who attain great fame or fortune sometimes get to feeling totally irresponsible and calmly go about consuming everything in their path. They accept honors, power, and wealth—rightly or wrongly obtained—and often misuse or abuse them. Lost in the fearful ego, they find themselves involved in useful betrayals, usually of the things that matter most, or the people that matter most. Too easily, they assume authority received from that which is false.

"It'd be far too easy for me to have a complete lapse of conscience if I rose to a position like the one you now hold. I have to daily remind myself it is not my ego, but God moving through me, performing the roles I play. I try to behave with the conscience of God and that keeps me on a path that serves me well.

"Even though I consider my work a calling, I know ambition sometimes disguises itself under the name of a 'calling,' and in all good faith, it could easily be misconstrued and deceptive. If I stay clear about things I won't end up in some sort of sanctimonious confusion. I'm just not willing to succeed by infidelity to my own truths and understanding. The mantle of self-importance, appetite, and lust *could* gratify my material desires, but it would definitely starve my spiritual aspirations."

Crow had listened and heard.

Joe stood, suggesting they go to their respective rooms and "dream a little dream."

Chapter 11

Turning to the page where the storyline would begin for the next day's shoot, Dylan stood before the mirror in the bathroom to practice his few lines and facial expressions. He had become an absolute master of the slightest facial movement to express his feelings in front of the camera. So much is said by the subtleties of a physical expression and the nearly whispered voice.

Reading the scene layout, Crow looked past Joe's to his first line and tried it on for size. He spoke in character to the mirror. However, each time he tried another line the reflection of his eyes in the mirror distracted him. Surrendering, Dylan leaned over the vanity with both hands supporting his upper body and began to talk to himself. "Ye're not going to let me do it this way this time, are ye? Ye're going to sit there and tell me to travel the unfamiliar road for a change. Well, mi lad, according to Grace and Joe, there are no coincidences, so just prop ye'rself up on the bed, read the script, and hand the rest over to God."

Stripping for his shower, he glanced twice at the mirror. The light hit his body at an angle that outlined the image of very pale, petite, geometric designs on his forehead, throat, chest, and stomach. "I guess ye got a little sun while those stones were on ye this morning, boy!" He couldn't quite tell what each represented. They almost looked like flowers, but the one on his chest definitely resembled a twelve-pointed star! "God, they'll get a kick out of this in make-up tomorrow!"

Crow piled the pillows high and turned back the covers so he could read his script before sleeping. Out of sheer habit, he reached for a cigarette, then looked hard at them. Although mind and body genuinely craved one, he *willed* himself to forego the pleasure after Grace's words had hit their mark.

Scanning the pages proved futile for no words registered in his brain as thoughts of the day's events prevented any true focus. His head ached as if he'd been cramming for a final.

After two hours of non-stop reviewing the day's events, he tossed the script on the bed stand where it knocked his flower to the floor. Scrambling to rescue his prize, he hoped it had suffered no damage—but not so much as a bruise or scratch appeared. While inhaling its fragrance he contemplated Joe's comments about an adept charging the flower with additional life force. *The ol' man must be nuts, he thought. No one can do stuff like that. Can they? I'll just pick one of Mrs. Walsh's and see how long it lasts for miself!*

Dylan adjusted the script on the nightstand, laid the flower on top of it, and turned off the light. Perhaps he could concentrate on the script in the morning before they left for the canyon.

Lying on his pillow staring at the ceiling, he whispered reverently, "God—ye got me into this—ye'd better see this through tomorrow, 'cause it's obvious I'm going to bloody well stink—big time! By the way, if ye could be so good as to provide any insight as to *how* and *why* I'm playing this part, I'd be obliged. Over and out." With a chuckle, he rolled to his side and closed his eyes.

Relentlessly, the dreams of the morning replayed in his mind, prohibiting sleep. In each vision his character opted for fear in the form of attack in order to defend the things and people he cherished. His opposing character begged him to choose another pathway. Every time, however, he stubbornly chose the first, which resulted in disaster upon disaster until all he loved was annihilated.

In the morning he would play the part of the young shaman who had followed his father's teachings of peace only to find all he holds dear had been threatened under the attack of a neighboring tribe. His character desperately hopes to wrench the secret of the great crystal from his father's lips. He intended to use its unearthly power against his enemies to save his own people. How could he follow the pathway of peace when all his heart demanded was vengeance? Part of his soul respects, honors, and loves all the principles the shaman taught him. But as his adopted father lies dying, he is overcome with fear; fear that approaching the attacks with forgiveness and peace will only enslave his people. In the dreams, he faced the same dilemma. It had been doubt and fear that moved his character to act—not love—not loving his enemy as himself.

With this last thought he finally slipped into a deep, calm sleep.

☯

"And action," announced the director.

The chalkboard clicked. "Scene 85, take 1," declared a crew member.

Knowing Crow, bloodied and weak, is carried in the arms of his adopted son. Little Crow's eyes are steely, beyond pain of heart and soul. His strong arms carry his father weightlessly, effortlessly as he crosses the river. The old man is nearly unconscious.

"And cut," came the next instruction. The producers hit the rewind button and viewed the scene. "Perfect, gentlemen. No need to re-shoot that one," Laslow said with a big smile. "A good omen, that! Things always fare well when the first shot is right on target."

☯

They shot the next scene where Dylan had crossed the red tape only days before. Laslow insisted they use the natural ethereal light, arguing with his co-director that the sound of the generator detracted from the native harmonies of the insects, birds, and wind. Hannigan finally agreed.

Knowing Crow is cradled in his son's arms as he leans against a boulder. Behind them is a large opening to what in reality is a cave, but from the camera's eye appears as a narrow entrance to the sacred canyon.

The crew and director played their parts and the film began to roll.

Crow is sobbing great silent tears of absolute abandonment. His father, his teacher, is leaving him. Worse still, he feels part of himself forsaking his father's pathway. Crow cradles Joe's blood-streaked head in his lap while the camera catches the image of him weeping without voice and face grimacing in ultimate spiritual pain as he looks to the heavens.

Joe opens his eyes slowly, speaking almost in a whisper. "You cannot go into the place of beginning with me, my son. You are not yet worthy. Leave my body here."

Crow, with real tears washing his father's face, replies, "I will stay with you until your spirit soars with the eagles, my father." The tenderness Crow expresses through his stroking hands and melodic voice are beyond the belief of the crew, who stare in awe at his ability to move so quickly into character.

Knowing Crow speaks again with eyes looking not at his son, but to a vision in his heart. "I know you now hope for me to reveal the secret of the great crystal that you may use it to harm our enemies, but ponder well these last words I give to you. This is the treasure of all my knowledge: my son, if you watch the abuse of others and react with equal or greater abuse of your God Power, you, by the law of all the universe, invite the consequences. All Life is One, my son. An abuse of power by any part of the whole has an effect on all. But if power is used wisely by any one part, all are blessed. Do you understand?"

"I think I do, Father," Little Crow replies with furrowed brow.

Joe winces with his character preparing to separate spirit from matter and closes his eyes. After a few seconds he opens them again and looks to Crow pleadingly. "If you draw forth the light of the Great Father by your thoughts and direct it into the crystal, it will become greater and greater and you can use it to send love and forgiveness to your enemies. If you focus that light with intent to harm, it will harm not only your enemies, but everything you love as well, and your debt to the whole will be long in the settling. You have within you the power to focus your intent into its great womb and that intent will multiply as the sands upon the beach. Use wisdom, my son, not knowledge. You must, of your own free will, through your heart and mind, clothe your God Power with *Divine intent.* Seek not revenge, for it is not your enemy, but a force that has been imperfectly clothed that must be challenged. Love is the energy that changes the nature of all situations to harmony." Joe spasms his body as the sound of death rattles from his chest.

Little Crow, deserted by the spirit of his father, is left holding only his carcass. "Fly swiftly with the gods of the sacred canyon my beloved father," he whispers, closing the old man's eyes with his fingers. Rocking back and forth with the lifeless body as if with a small child, Little Crow's eyes narrow as the blood from his father's wounds drips freely down his own arm. His facial expression transforms from one of tenderness to one of rage. Clutching his father to his breast with eyes pressed hard shut, he screams to the heavens a howl so forlorn that every creature near and far stops in its tracks.

Many of the observers were sobbing. The moment had been so touching that the director forgot to yell, "Cut."

Crow broke character and smiled over to the camera. "It doesn't get any better than that, mate!"

"God, yes, yeah, yeah…cut!" Laslow ordered as he flung his arm over his head to the cameraman. They rewound the film and played the scene back. They did it again, and yet again a third time. Laslow turned to Hannigan and proclaimed, "He's right. It couldn't get any better than that!"

The entire shoot took less than an hour; record time for a scene of this intensity in any movie either producer had the pleasure of filming. Crow and Chatauk were climbing the steep section of the mesa before eleven a.m. The next sequence wasn't to be filmed until the next morning, which left Crow with an entire afternoon and evening for himself.

"Simply amazing," said Chatauk as they hiked toward the Wranglers.

Crow stopped a moment, placed his hands on his hips and turned back to stare behind him. Pausing, he placed his forefinger thoughtfully to his lips. Then he turned back to his companion. "I know. It's like the whole scene just spilled out of both of us and flowed out into the world, wasn't it?"

Chatauk winked at Dylan. "Maybe the *spirits of the sacred canyon* entered us and played it out so perfectly the first time."

"To be honest," confessed Crow, "I couldn't remember mi lines. In fact, I probably missed a few. But it was weird—like I just became Little Crow and felt his every emotion!"

Joe put his arm around the younger actor. "Well done, son."

"Which ending are they filming first, Joe? Do ye know?" Crow asked, as they waited for their drivers to collect the ropes and throw them in the tiny storage space behind the tailgates.

"I heard they're doing the original ending of the book first."

"Good," Crow said more to himself than Joe.

Mrs. Walsh, tidying up in Dylan's suite, acted surprised to see them arrive back so soon. With an amiable grin she said, "Why, hello, dearies. You boys through already, or did the equipment break down?"

"Actually, I had a bet with Mr. Chatauk that ye'd clean mi room before his and we raced back to see who won!" Crow guffawed, wondering why he felt so light and happy. He hadn't taken any breakfast and offered to leave Mrs. Walsh alone while he ate lunch with the proviso she would leave his favorite flower on his pillow. "What's the name of this variety, anyway?" he asked while he held it to his nose.

"I don't know its genetic name, dearie, but around here we call them heaven's bells. Can't figure for my life how this one remains alive. Can barely get mine cut and to the kitchen before they die, they're so fragile!"

Could Joe be right about the life force thing? he wondered. *Maybe that Nikki babe is a voodoo queen or something. Or maybe...she could be the highly evolved soul Joe claims, who, by the way, just happens to be mi twin flame.* Get a grip man, he said to himself. It almost seemed too funny to be thinking about. *Wholly illogical...and yet...*the thought dripped off to nothingness.

He really did spend the afternoon learning his lines for the next day.

☯

During the following weeks most of the shots represented the older shaman teaching the younger, especially capturing their camaraderie and love for one another. For Crow, they caused no undue emotional strain for he felt like a duck in water during what he referred to as "joy" scenes. He swam effortlessly in happiness, both on and off screen.

Chapter 12

Three weeks into the shoot they began preparations for the final scenes. Laslow figured a week for his segment, the story's original ending. Hannigan, however, itched to get to his genius in the bloodthirsty revenge battle that would be shot during the scheduled final two weeks of filming. Hal just loved the ending where all hell breaks loose and Crow uses the power of the crystal to destroy his enemies. Of course, that ending would be very bloody and Crow would appear as an avenging angel of God, come to the rescue of all that is innocence and purity. In fact, Hannigan had been responsible for selling the studio on the idea of trying the other ending. Since the book wasn't all that well known and its author dead, who cared anyway? Any story could be altered—right? And he loved a story where nobility smacked of power and strength used to defend the righteous.

Joe had finished his work and began preparing to head back to Montana to enjoy the autumn before he and his wife wintered in Florida. He bragged to all who would listen, "There is nothing more seductive than autumn in the mountains of Montana." Before he left, however, he felt compelled to see Crow one last time.

Dylan and Laslow were on the set discussing the previous day's shots when Joe tapped him on the shoulder. "Hey, old man! Are ye away, then?" Crow asked, slapping Chatauk on the shoulder, rubbing it back and forth like he would his dog. He had truly come to respect and admire this old Indian in their few weeks together and committed to watch Joe's entire repertoire when he took some time off after this film.

"Got a minute?" Joe asked, looking intently into Dylan's eyes.

They shook hands with Laslow—Joe, for the last time—and turned to take a stroll out of earshot. "You've got an important decision to make, son," began Chatauk. "You need to decide which pathway you'll take. Once *you've* decided, you need to be willing to face heaven or hell to see they print the pathway *you* decide upon. Do you understand?"

"Has Grace been talking to ye?"

"I may seem like an stupid old Indian, son, but I have my own insights."

"I haven't got much voice in the matter, Joe," Dylan said, stunned by Chatauk's intrusion into his soul's dilemma. "I mean, I may want them to do it mi way, but ye see how they cringe when I make even the slightest suggestion that may dent their egos. Hannigan's just waitin' for the opportunity to chew mi butt!"

Joe spoke in absolute earnest. "Trust your guidance on this one, son, and *make* the time to seek it. It worked pretty well the night I serenaded you, didn't it? Remember, this is *your* vision quest—*your* play—and it must be played out the way *your* heart tells you to. I like you, kid. How can this old man convince you to lay all your fears aside and do what's right for you?"

"I appreciate ye'r advice, Joe. I'll try out the meditation gig again before I get into it…I promise."

"Well, got to get goin'. I'm making an extra stop on the way to Vegas today." The mischievous Indian had a twinkle in his eye. "There's a little lady I want to meet at the Red Rock Canyon Ranch."

"No kidding? Ye called her, huh?"

"In a way, I think she called me."

"Nikki called here to talk to ye?" Crow asked in disbelief.

"No, not by telephone, sonny. The lady just sent a little soul light to the set and I made contact with it. But since you don't believe any of that…what do you call it…'shite'…what do you care?" Joe smiled as he ruffled Dylan's hair and turned on his heels.

"Take care and God be with you," he shouted backwards as he walked away.

"And with ye, mi friend."

Nikki, the rescue lady. He hadn't thought about her for several days now. Wrapped up in his work, he hadn't even had time to pay much attention to the heaven's bell. Crow wondered what Chatauk and Nikki could possibly have to talk about. A vision of the old man strolling up to her front door and inviting himself in for a cup of something made him smile. *She'd probably take him in too!* he thought.

That night, as promised, Dylan cleared a space on the floor, but this time used a pillow. With his head to the north, he began to intone the sound "I AM" as he remembered Chatauk doing. At first he spoke aloud, but after a few minutes found himself chanting the mantra in his mind. He tried to focus his attention on his third eye to see if he could sense the same rhythmic energy he had experienced with Joe. It was subtler, but present, nonetheless. Then he moved his attention to his heart until he could feel it there as well. When the two were in sync he stopped chanting and lay motionless in body and thought. At two a.m. he awoke with understanding in his eyes and great anticipation for the next day's shoot.

The scene opens with Crow returning to his village after leaving his father in the sacred canyon. The village shows all the stomach wrenching signs of pillage, rape, and plunder. As Little Crow's eyes survey the horror, he runs through the village in panic searching for his beloved Chensauhi, the woman he intends to take as wife. He discovers her body, ill-used and brutally murdered. Wailing is heard throughout the village as the survivors mourn their unthinkable losses. The brother of Chensauhi steps to Little Crow and with a vengeance thick with malice asks if the old one told Little Crow the secret of the great crystal.

Little Crow is too shocked to even hear the question.

Truthfully, the vision created by the cast and crew appeared so authentic, his soul took the bait. He *was* too shocked to hear the question! Crow never watched advance preparations for a scene so it could elicit from him the intended response.

Falling in a heap over Chensauhi, he weeps and weeps, though it is not written in the script.

When the director called, "Cut," the entire cast and crew give him a standing ovation. They didn't know he was *not* acting. His reaction had been truly heartfelt as if his soul had experienced a similar scene in another life.

"I've never seen him meet this quality in a performance before," Laslow whispered to Hannigan. "I didn't think he could top his performance in *Marrakech*, but I feel another Oscar coming." Just as the scene from the sacred canyon, the *discovery* scene required only one take.

That afternoon the filming took place in a makeshift kiva: the underground ceremonial cave where father and son had spent so many hours in communion with the spirit world. With a fire in the center, Little Crow would be holding the great crystal in his hands, contemplating its possible use. The entire scene had to be portrayed without words, depicting his struggle with facial and body expressions alone. The film captured the image of a broken man, too numb of spirit to seek guidance from higher sources. Both the last words of Knowing Crow and the words of the brother of Chensauhi, whispering plans for retaliation, would be dubbed in later.

Crow stands deliberately erect with the great crystal in his right hand and with his left hand, tosses his sword to the earth in disgust. He stands beneath the entry hole where the light of the sun enters, raising the crystal to the light. Then, drawing it down to his forehead, his lips move in silent prayer.

"God, he's good!" repeated Laslow for the umpteenth time, knowing this scene, also, would involve only the one take. Perfection imbued everything from the lighting to the slightest movement of Crow's eyes. Notorious for shooting everything six to fifteen times for all the camera angles, the director counted the whole affair as a mystery.

☯

Crow found no need to prepare for his most important scene the next morning, for he had surrendered the whole thing to a higher power. Sleeping like a content infant throughout the night, he hadn't the slightest concern for his performance. The only conscious effort he made involved avoiding cigarettes.

☯

"And action," the monotone voice drawled.

After the chalkboard snap the scene delivers Little Crow in a position facing his enemies with the great crystal in hand. His enemies appear fierce, but somewhat afraid of the crystal for a great legend has arisen regarding its unearthly powers. The leaders of the enemies murmur amongst themselves, some of them desiring bloodshed and others wanting to flee for fear of the crystal.

Little Crow turns to look at the faces of his remaining tribe, now alight with drunken pride, assuming he will use the crystal to destroy those who took so much from them. "Lay down your weapons," he instructs his tribe, "and take them up no more! These," (he points to their enemies,) "are our brothers gone astray in their hearts and we must teach them the ways of peace. Seek not, dear ones, to heap destruction upon destruction until all is lost, but give yourselves gladly to the bringing of truth to these, our family. For All is One Life and if we destroy them, we destroy a part of ourselves, and no grace shall set us free until light claims dominion over the darkness. Seek to heal the hatred and sickness of your own hearts and we will live in peace with one another."

One among the angry enemies draws his arrow and shoots Little Crow through his heart. Stunned, Crow falls to his knees with the great crystal in his hands and gently places it before him on the ground before falling backwards to his death.

The chief of the enemy tribe is quick to give the signal not to fight and reprimands the shootist. All gaze at the dead shaman with shame in their hearts, seeing clearly that, even though he had the power to destroy them, he sought to love and unite with the very people who had taken from him all he cherished. The warring tribes drop their weapons and surround the dead man in absolute humility. Members of both tribes carry his body and the great crystal away.

"And cut. And PRINT! I don't even want to review it, Dylan. You had me convinced to lay down my sword," Laslow confessed.

While the crew prepared for the epilogue scene, Grace approached Peter Laslow and quietly asked for a moment of his time.

"Sure, Grace, give me about three minutes."

Removing herself from the crowd, but remaining in Peter's sight, Grace stepped to a wooded area in which a single ray of sunshine broke through a clearing. The bright halo of light surrounding her body made it appear as if she would shortly be ascending through its brilliance into another domain. As Laslow approached, the scene literally took his breath away.

"God, I wish I had a camera in my hand just now. You can't believe how magical you look in that light!"

Grace smiled her knowing smile and then quietly addressed her employer. "Mr. Laslow, the next scene will portray the last of your genius in this film. May I be so bold as to suggest that you prepare to allow for some synchronicity in the shot?"

"Synchronicity, Grace? Anything in particular you have in mind?"

"Sometimes the spirits ask for free reign with subject matter as valuable as this. Just be alert for anything out of the ordinary and flow with it. I generally don't watch movies or television, Mr. Laslow, so I'm no authority on this subject. I want you to know, however, that I believe that you have not only created a poetic, beautiful piece of art—but also that you will offer a gift of inestimable value to all who see it. Thank you for letting me work with you. I have come to both honor and respect you as a soul."

"Thank you, Grace. That means a lot to me. But, you talk as if you're leaving the production. We still have to film the other ending, you know."

Grace's eyes assumed a look of wisdom as she smiled graciously. Taking him by the arm, she led him back toward the cameras.

The epilogue scene depicted the combined tribes taking Little Crow to the mouth of the sacred canyon where they deposited his body and the great crystal so none could learn and misuse its power. When the crowd dispersed and only Crow's body remained, a large crow landed on the boulder just above his head.

Peter took a quick sideways glance at Grace, who smiled and nodded. He quietly instructed the cameraman to pan out just far enough to catch the bird studiously examining the human body beneath him. Silence reigned while all present were drawn into the magical moment.

Suddenly above them came the squawk of the crow's mate and the bird stretched its enormous wings and took to flight. The cameraman followed with his lens, focusing as best he could. When the two birds joined company they circled the group three times and then flew away.

Crow, obviously playing dead with his eyes closed, lay wondering when "Cut" would be called.

"God, that was fantastic!" yelled Laslow leaping around like a child. "Cut!" He ran to Grace and kissed her on the cheek and twirled her around in a little jig.

The applause rose from the cast and crew as they excitedly exchanged views about the crow's coincidental appearance.

"I don't know what you're all going nuts about," said Hannigan glumly. "Crows are the harbinger of death."

Grace quietly interrupted before his fears could be spread to the crew. "One could look at it that way, Mr. Hannigan. The truth of the matter is that they *always herald change*. Haven't you had time to read the story you're producing?"

Embarassed to admit he'd not read the original novel, he dismissed her comment with a shrug.

When Crow dusted off his backside and joined the throng, the story thrilled him to the core. After Laslow told him Grace had forewarned him of an impending spiritual event, he couldn't wait to speak with her.

Separating the shaman from the crowd, Dylan asked, "Did ye arrange that?"

"No, but I was made aware of its coming."

"Grace, we haven't had too much time to talk off set, but I want to thank ye for the early work we did together. M'experience durin' the stone-layin' played a substantial, influential role in the way I handled things."

"I know."

"I never told ye what I experienced. How could ye know?"

"Come, now, Little Crow...I thought you dropped all your defenses."

Dylan knew without knowing and gently embraced her with a peck to the cheek.

"This is the last time I'll be seeing you, Dylan. I'm proud of you, proud of your choices. When the final work hits the big screen, the hearts of the whole world will cheer. Your courage is remarkable."

"Mi courage?"

"Yes, little brother. Your courage. You changed history. But you're not quite through."

"Yeah...we've got to film the other endin' now."

Grace sidled closer and whispered in his ear. "Your true test of courage is yet to come."

"Won't ye be here during the re-shoot to help me through?"

"You don't *need* me anymore, Little Crow. You've found your heart."

☯

"Can I get to the screening room and see all mi shots before the end of the day?" Crow requested of Laslow.

"Sure. You can head over right now and see the pieced together version right up to today's work. Hannigan's going to meet me after dinner for a review and you're welcome to join us then as well, if you'd like."

"Right. I'd like that."

He watched the entire production, including the scenes shot by his younger version. Though all the rigors of editing and the soundtrack were yet to be completed, he felt very satisfied both with his own performance and the quality of the show itself. After his supper he would join Laslow and Hannigan to see what the day's work produced on film.

☯

"Hey, Chuck." Crow smiled at the husky young crewman. He

rather liked the way the *rescue lady* had said "hey" instead of "hello" and had found himself mimicking her several times over the last few weeks.

"Evenin', Mr. Crow. You might want to give those two a few minutes, unless, of course, you relish the idea of standing in the middle of an active battlefield."

Accustomed to co-producers who engaged in animated emotional debate over the way things *should* be, Crow walked past Chuck into the viewing room. He overheard Laslow telling Hannigan how he considered this ending the right one to use— defending the ending as given in the book as the authentic and true version that *should* be represented on the big screen. The overheard conversation influenced him a bit, but when he saw the day's completed work, he absolutely agreed with Laslow. BANG! Like a bolt of electricity passing through his veins, *he knew this was the right finale.* He turned to Hannigan and said, "PRINT!"

"What did you say, sonny?" snapped Hannigan.

This time Crow did resent hearing someone refer to him as "sonny." Straightening his back, he summoned all his strength of character and with a dead calm tone, deliberately stated, "*A.* I am *not* ye'r son, and *B.* I won't be doing the other version." He saw Laslow laugh silently, but did not give him away.

Hannigan already had enough pressure built up from his heated debate with Laslow and erupted like a volcano. "You little son of a bitch! Who the hell do you think you are? You think just because you got a big name out there that you're sitting in the producer's seat on this one? Well, you're not! You're just an overpaid glamour boy with a great press agent. The real genius is the detail *I* bring to this production and between me, and your contract, *I* say you have your ass on the set at eight a.m. mañana. Do you read me, kid?"

Crow stood and, with great restraint and utter dignity, shook Laslow's hand. "Ye do great work, mate. It's been a privilege and an honor to work with ye." Then he turned to the fuming Hannigan, red with rage, and evenly affirmed, "Sometimes ye just gotta do the right thing." With strength and boldness, he strode out of the screening room and went looking for Peggy.

Chapter 13

"Peggy," Crow said as he ushered her away from some of the crew members, "I need a little time with ye. OK?"

His voice sounded quite serious and butterflies began winging their way from her stomach to her throat. *Did I forget to do something he asked?* she wondered. Without further word he guided her back to the Inn, located only a few buildings away from the catering tent where he found her. Guiding her up the stairs to his suite, he unlocked the door and held it open like a gentleman.

"I just lit off a bomb and I need a getaway accomplice. Are ye game?"

Her brow pinched in anxiety. "Wait—sir. Could you define what type of bomb you mean?"

After frantically dragging his luggage out of the large closet, Crow began stuffing them with clothes. "I told 'em I *wouldn't* participate in the second ending they've chosen. I just know the one we finished today is the one this piece needs, ye know?" he nearly asked while looking to her for some kind of confirmation.

"Can you do that? I mean, can't they sue you or something?"

He moved to the bathroom to gather his toiletries and toss them in a small, leather duffel bag. "Hell, yes. Ye know how much brass they've got tied up in this production? On top of that, everyone is union and they're gonna insist on full contract time, which is, at minimum, another two weeks. So I just arranged for the cast and crew to go on a free vacation, and I can tell ye, it's gonna get bloody ugly around this inn in about an hour. So what I need ye to do is find some sort of vehicle that can handle mi luggage and sneak me out of here, pendin' the coolin' of Hannigan's fury."

"Where will you go? Want me to make a hotel reservation or something?"

Moving to the desk to pick up all his little papers and his *lucky charms* box, he looked down to see the brochure for the Red Rock Canyon Ranch. *Perfect!* he thought. *No phones in the rental units, in the middle of nowhere where no one will know who I am. Sure, 'n, what would be the harm in getting to know Nikki a little better? After all, she is mi twin flame,* he thought in jest, not quite fully believing all he'd experienced in his early days in Utah.

"Aye, Peggy—call this number and see if they can book one of their units for me tonight. The lady's name is Nikkol."

Peggy drew the brochure from his hand and located the number. Crow reached down and clicked the speaker button on the phone.

A soft, feminine voice answered. "Red Rock Canyon Ranch."

"Hello, I'm calling about your rental units," said Peggy.

"Yes, how may I assist you?"

"My name is Peggy Bloomfield. I'm the personal assistant to Mr. Dylan Crow and he has requested that I book a reservation for him at your facility."

There was a pause. "Out of curiosity, how did Mr. Crow know we had rental units?"

"Well, he gave me a brochure he must have picked up somewhere. Now, as to his possible reservation…" and then Peggy was interrupted.

"Peggy—that's your name, dear, right?" said Nikki. "Peggy, would you be good enough to give Mr. Crow a message for me? Will you tell him when he can come down off his pedestal and gather enough courage to call me himself, I'd be glad to talk with him about a possible stay at the ranch?"

Flabbergasted, Peggy looked at Mr. Crow in horror. She'd never seen anything but people tripping over themselves, fawning over him to meet his every need—and this woman had the audacity to say such a thing!

Crow laughed as he signaled her to hand him the receiver and reached for the button to take the phone off the speaker. "Sorry it took so bloody long to get to the phone," he quipped. "These pedestals these days are so high, it's hard to get down without breaking ye'r neck!" His face shone with light and laughter, so Peggy breathed a sigh of relief. "Can you hold just a second, Nikki?" he asked, not waiting for her reply. Holding his hand over the receiver, he turned to his assistant. "Peggy, can ye get to work on a suburban, or a van, or *somethin'* right away?"

"Sure, boss. I'm on it!"

With her efficient comment, Peggy departed and he found himself alone with Nikki—or at least her voice. "I'd sure like to come and stay at ye'r lit'l piece of heaven for a bit—that is, if ye'd be willing to lower ye'r standards."

"I don't know—we don't normally cater down to the likes of movie stars." Nikki laughed. "You must know, since you stole a brochure, that these units are only about eight hundred square feet. How big's your entourage?" she queried.

"Just me."

"What? No assistant? No girlfriend? No groupies?" she inquired teasingly.

"Just me."

"Who's going to wipe your nose, and cook, and clean, and do your laundry?"

He hadn't thought about that. He hadn't had time to do anything but try to figure out how to get out unseen. "Guess I'll have to play that one by ear."

"I don't accept smokers, Mr. Crow. Prejudice, perhaps, but why should I ruin one of my units for someone else's stinky habit?"

He could tell she was toying with him, so he bantered back with her. "If I make ye a solemn vow only to smoke outside, may I stay?"

"OK, OK, OK! You've twisted my arm." She rolled her eyes, chuckling quietly.

"So, when are you planning to grace us with your presence and I'll check the booking schedule?" He heard her turning pages in a book.

"Aaaaah, I was hoping ye could take me tonight," he said tentatively.

"OOOOO, no can do brother. Both units are filled and my guests don't leave until tomorrow around four."

An audible sigh sounded on his end of the line, followed by an uncomfortable pause. He decided to confess his situation to her.

Nikki listened attentively and then whispered, "Bravo! I am so proud of you!"

Not knowing exactly why, he felt grateful. His back straightened as if he'd been complimented by an esteemed peer.

An offer followed that surprised even her. "You could bunk at my home in my son's old room until they leave, if you aren't afraid of me."

Desperate not to be noticed at any hotels or airports, Dylan agreed to her proposition. "So, I'll get someone to deliver me tonight then, alright?"

"How long you planning this hideout program, Mr. Crow?" she asked.

"About two weeks, 'til all the dust settles down. Can ye keep me that long?"

She looked at her schedule, which she had purposely left open for a month while her ranch manager was out of town. She had only allowed her current guests to come because they had booked a year in advance. Nikki didn't much like having strangers on the ranch when there alone. *Coincidence, having both units empty right now?* she thought. Silently she turned her head upwards and mouthed the words, "Thank you, God."

"It just so happens I can. So, how will you be paying for your stay, sir?"

Her request caught him off guard. No one questioned his ability to pay for anything for years. "Ye serious?" he asked. "Can't ye trust that I'll pay ye when mi stay is over?"

"Could I have your credit card number to hold the reservation, Mr. Crow?" she insisted, though he heard her laughing. He thoroughly enjoyed their comical banter and the way she had of putting him in his place with a smile. Reaching to his pocket for his wallet he actually recited his Visa number.

"This is the deal, Little Crow..." Nikki began, "you pay me for two weeks rental, whether or not you stay the full two weeks—OK?"

"Just how much will that be, ma'am? I like to know the cost of things before I spend mi hard earned brass!" His eyes winced in mock pain.

"I'll be charging your Visa two thousand dollars, plus ten per cent tax—so your total will be two thousand two hundred dollars, sir."

"Pretty steep for this neck of the woods isn't it?"

"It's not the Plaza, but it's clean, cozy, and private, and hey, dearie—it appears I'm the only game in town tonight, right?" she shot back.

"Deal! I'll get there just as soon as I can."

With a gentle knock on the door, his co-conspirator made her entrance. "I found a Tahoe. You think we can fit all this luggage in if we fold down the seats?" she asked, noticing the suite half full of his expensive, matched luggage.

"No worries!"

Peggy glanced around the room to see if he had forgotten anything. "Will that crotchety lady let you stay at her place?"

"She was just playing with me. Maybe she doesn't know how important I am!" They both laughed at his ability to poke fun at himself. "So, where's the big powwow happening?"

"I think they're going to rename the screening room, 'the screaming room.' I do believe Laslow is stalling, hoping you're trying to escape. We can get you out the back way here. Chuck's waiting downstairs to help with your luggage. He heard what you did and, Mr. Crow, you're not the only one on the set who thinks you made the right decision!" It was her way of saying "bravo" too.

He blushed a little as he began searching for something. There it lay on the pillow---a beautiful, indigo flower.

As Dylan headed down the stairs with his treasures in hand, Chuck took the cue, darting up to carry the luggage. "Gees," he whispered under his breath, "the guy must have thought he'd be staying a year or so!" After five trips, Chuck had loaded the Tahoe, which he personally lent to the secret mission. "Want me to drive you, sir?"

"Do ye mind if Peggy takes me and returns ye'r buggy later tonight?" Crow posed, already knowing what Chuck's response would be.

"No problem. I'll just go out front and distract that security guy. Now," instructed Chuck, "if you'll just hunker down there a bit, they'll think it's Peggy driving out alone in my car." According to the wisdom of his command, Crow bent over his legs so he wouldn't be seen in the car as they left.

BOOK II

Chapter 1

As they drove through Zion in the dark Peggy yearned to ask him a thousand questions. Because of her training as a personal assistant, however, she remained discreetly quiet.

Crow sensed her nervousness about losing her position with the studio. "Ye're taking quite a risk here, aren't ye?" he asked softly in a deep and concerned tone, just that moment realizing the part she played in his departure may jeopardize her career.

"Oh, what the hell?" she voiced tenuously with a quick sideways glance. "There's always *another* big star who needs my assistance—*somewhere*. I don't know if Hannigan will fire me or not, but sometimes you've just got to do what you know in your heart is right! Right?"

When they approached the town of Virgin he instructed her to slow down so they wouldn't miss the road to Kolob. As the green street sign came into view, they turned and proceeded east on a long, winding road. Peggy drove slowly to avoid the numerous deer traveling in small herds. Because of the heavy cloud cover, the lights of the Tahoe seemed the only sign of human life in the inky blackness of the night. Even the shadows of the mesas were barely visible. "You sure you're going to be alright out here in the middle of nowhere?" Peggy asked nervously as a prickly sensation of eeriness engulfed her.

"Hey, I'm a tough guy! Haven't ye seen any of mi pictures?" Humorously, he offered his flexed muscles for examination.

The Red Rock Canyon Ranch sign loomed before them, but the gate beneath it was closed. Crow jumped out of the passenger seat, strode directly to the keypad on the inside of the left cedar post and pushed the numbers twelve-twelve. The gate beeped and swung open while he dashed back to the car. As they began their descent, Peggy muttered, "Sweet Jesus, this is one steep road!"

"Aye," Crow agreed. "And if ye're not anxious to be shipped home in a ziplock bag, I advise huggin' the left side."

At the bottom of the hill the road forked and Peggy wondered which road to take. There were no streetlights of any kind to indicate where to go, but lights were evidenced in the distance in both directions. Before she could ask, Crow directed her to stay to the left.

Headlights appeared in front of them. Nikki pulled up next to the Tahoe and rolled down her window. "Just coming up to open the gate. I could swear I closed it when I came in earlier...must not have hit the button hard enough!" she said, a little confused.

Peggy began to relay that Mr. Crow knew the code, but he jolted her arm to prevent the disclosure.

"Head up to the main house, Mr. Crow, and I'll turn around and meet you there. By the way, I'm Nikki James," she added, leaning out the window to shake the hand of the pretty, little blonde driving the car. "I'll lay odds you're Little Crow's right arm, Peggy. Correct?"

"Yes, that's right. We spoke earlier." Because of their alarming phone conversation, Peggy had been terrified this woman, to whom she now entrusted her charge, would be some horrible troll. One look at Nikki's smile convinced her she simply had a sense of humor, and the weight lifted from her shoulders.

Nikki pulled around them, heading further down the road where she could safely turn her car while Dylan directed Peggy to her house. "You've been here before, haven't you?" she asked.

"Twice, but it's a long story."

She didn't push him on the subject and obediently parked the car in front of a little cabin. A peaceful, blazing fire brightened the windows, welcoming them. Peggy popped the latch for the hatchback and Dylan commenced removing his sizable array of luggage. After parking her car, Nikki leaned against it while watching him struggle with the bags. Looking slightly perturbed, he asked, "Ye got someone who can tend to these for me?"

"Sure! I'll just holler for him. He's around here somewhere." She put her hands to the sides of her mouth to make a megaphone and yelled, "Hey, Little Crow—got some real man's work for you. Get your lazy arse up here and drag in all this movie star's belongings."

Peggy pretended to be getting something from her purse in order to avoid letting Mr. Crow see her chuckling.

Winking at Crow, Nikki waltzed to the entry and anchored both the outer and inner doors. She made no offer to help carry the luggage, but leaned over the kitchen island, counting each time Crow brought in a load. "You pack light for a two week trip to the desert!"

"Alright, already!" he said in sweaty exasperation. "That's the lot!" Then he pointed his forefinger at Nikki as if she were a naughty child. "And *ye*, young lady... thanks for all *ye'*r help!"

"I learned a long time ago it's best to allow people to be responsible for their *own* baggage, in their *own* particular fashion."

Her dual intent whacked him between the eyes. He inclined his head slightly, wondering if she meant what he thought, or truly referred only to his luggage.

Completely taken aback by the charm of the old cabin, Peggy scanned the room and enthusiastically offered, "What a cool place!"

"Pretty rustic for the likes of Little Crow, I suspect." Nikki said, handing her a glass of mineral water.

"Thanks. I was a bit parched." Peggy seemed a little agitated as she turned her attention to Dylan. "Well, I better get back to Kanab before they suspect my part in this charade. Here's my number at home." Peggy handed him her card. "You can leave a message on my machine when you're ready to adios. I'll find a way to get you to an airport or something. I'll check it periodically during the day while we're still in Kanab— that way we won't get caught communicating over the cell. Just give me a ring when you think it's safe to surface."

"That won't be necessary. I'll be his chauffeur—if I can rent a U-Haul or something for all this stuff!" Nikki teased, jerking her head toward the luggage.

Dylan embraced Peggy, gratefully kissing her on the cheek. "Ye've been an angel and I really appreciate it. I truly hope ye're not sacked over this."

"Me too," she whispered under her breath.

"I'll just follow you up and close that darn gate behind you!"

Nikki stepped out behind Peggy, leaving Crow to find his own way around. As the headlights disappeared he took time to survey the room and reacquaint himself. The luggage did take up the entire kitchen and he laughingly mused over Nikki's teasing about it. Having lived out of suitcases for so long, he actually hauled a full wardrobe everywhere he went. It did seem a bit much under the circumstances.

A few soft lights illuminated the great room and the fire's

lapping tongues of flames ignited gas pockets within the logs, emitting little hissing and popping sounds. He'd never really needed to use any of the fireplaces in his apartments except for atmosphere. They were all gas and he'd nearly forgotten how nice a real fire felt. It reminded him of home: his ranch in Schull. He extended his hands to absorb its warmth.

Glancing at his Rolex, he felt ashamed to see that it read eleven thirty. It had taken them longer to get out and over to the ranch than he had thought. Crow really was expecting a lot from this lady who just *rescued* him, yet again. A guilty twinge twisted his stomach as he realized he had neglected to send so much as a note of thanks to Nikki for the first time she'd rescued him.

The lights from the car signaled her return. He didn't dare to tell her he knew the combination to her gate, or that he had been there with Grace Moon only a month before. He decided to let her think she had not hit the remote button hard enough.

Entering her home quietly, Nikki gently tugged the door closed behind her and slipped the funky old latch in place. Even though a bolt was mounted on the door, he noticed she did not lock it.

"Alrighty, then!" she said, clapping her hands together. "Let's get you settled for the night so *I* can go to bed." She smiled graciously while assessing his belongings. "Tell me, *please*, that one of these bags contains something with which you can survive the night so we don't have to haul all of them back to my son's room!"

"Since I'm the designated porter on the ranch, I'll see to it miself." Rummaging through the numerous bags, he located the small leather duffel that held his toiletries and a gym size bag with comfort clothes stashed inside.

He followed her back through the game room, turning again to the right to enter his temporary quarters. The soft lighting of the space welcomed him. The bed covers had been drawn and a fluffy down comforter lay upon the top. Several pillows had been thoughtfully stacked, ready to cradle his head.

An oil painting of an Indian woman hung over a chest of drawers. Her face portrayed an odd combination of peace and watchfulness. The room's colors were strong with the lower third of the walls dark blue and a yellow stucco wall treatment on the upper two thirds. The windows were framed in the dark blue as well. Large closet doors on either side of a door that led to the bathroom had been painted in a deep, rich red. Above the petrified wood fireplace hung a picture of a soaring eagle.

A small corner oak desk and credenza took up one whole wall. Along with a computer and phone, an electric drum set sat upon the desktop. Conga drums were wedged between the credenza and a file cabinet and a classical guitar hung from a brace on the wall. Framed posters hung here and there; surely her son's idea of decorating, tastefully woven into the design of the rest of the room. An Indian rug, with colors as strong as the walls, had been laid on an angle over the wall-to-wall carpet. Tennis trophies lined a high bookshelf.

He took it all in silently.

Concerned her humble home looked paltry by comparison to Crow's accustomed surroundings, Nik broke the silence. *Oh well,* she thought, *beggars can't be choosers.* "Your bathroom is through this door," she said, pushing open the one between the closets.

He followed behind her into an unusually large bathroom, given the approximate age of the cabin. Oil paintings of seascapes and boats hung on the walls. This pleased him, as he loved the water and spent a great deal of time on it. Thoughtfully examining each, he felt some were breathtaking.

Pointing to a light blue cast iron tub reminiscent of the fifties,

Nikki said, "There's your shower and here's the door where you go *outside* to smoke." She took his arm, guiding him to a frosted glass sliding door, which opened to the pool side of the house. "I've taken the liberty of providing a small metal trash can so you can dispose of your butts where the animals won't get to them. OK?"

Dylan smiled down at her pretty little face which seemed entirely too serious about the smoking issue. Her furrowed brow amused him. "I promise not to burn down the place or let any of mi nasty smoke into ye'r precious home!" He said it with neither wittiness nor malice; only a promise given with a smile.

"Well, what else can I do to help you get comfortable?" she asked attentively while walking back into the house and closing the doors. "By the way, this is how you lock this door," she showed, "if you're afraid of the boogie man. I haven't locked a door in this house since we moved here, however, so if you need protection, you'll have to yell real loud."

"Don't ye ever worry about intruders?" he asked.

"If God isn't watching over me, then no one is." Though she had a humorous grin on her face, she looked straight into his eyes with absolute sincerity. "Thieves and murderers are only superficial dangers, Mr. Crow. I've discovered the greatest threat to my security lies in *my own* thoughts and feelings. The greatest dangers come from within, not without."

With a knowing laugh she turned to lead him back to his sleeping quarters. His lingering gaze indicated that her comment had been thought provoking.

She exposed a television, DVD player, and VHS equipment in the closet opposite the bed. "There's no satellite connection for this room, so if you want news, sports, network, or HBO, you'll have to use the set in the kitchen. I presume, however, the emotional expense of your day has wearied you somewhat and I'd wager you'd just like to get to bed. Am I right?"

"Shows that much, eh? Maybe I'm not such a good actor after all."

She left him to his assigned space and tossed a comment behind her as she headed through the hall outside his room. "There's food in the fridge and the drinking water comes from the cooler just inside my office where you were on your last visit. Feel free to rummage around the kitchen for what you need."

As Nikki passed directly across the game room and entered her bedroom through an opposing doorway, he noticed she didn't close her door. Nonetheless, he gently closed his so he could change into something more comfortable.

Twenty minutes later he emerged from his room clad in sweat pants and a T-shirt. The lower half of her bed could be viewed through the open door, revealing Nikki sitting in her bed, knees bent to her chest. The house was dark except for the kitchen fire-light casting phantom shadows on the walls. He made his way through the darkened game room, up the three stairs to the kitchen, and turned on a lamp by the couch. Opening various cupboards and the refrigerator, he hoped to find some alcohol. His search came up empty, but he marveled at Nikki's sense of organization. Everything seemed to have its place. She had even sculpted her drawers!

Crow quietly headed back toward his quarters, then decided to ask Nikki if she had some booze hidden somewhere. He stepped noiselessly to her door, entering the small hallway before her room. Though she had a book in her hand, her head tilted back as if she had fallen asleep reading. Her long hair had been piled and clipped on top of her head. The covers were drawn up under her arms and her shoulders were bare. *Oops—may have overstepped mi boundary a wee bit*, he thought.

It startled him when she suddenly spoke without opening her eyes or moving her head from its resting position. "Mr. Crow, are you lost, or do you need something?"

He cleared his throat. "Ahem…I'm sorry to intrude on ye'r privacy, but I wondered if ye might have something a wee bit harder than this drinking water?" he asked apologetically.

"Sure. Try the tap water—it's harder than a hammer!" She laughed with her eyes still shut. Slowly, she opened them and gazed at him.

"It's just that I sometimes have a rough go of it the first night in a new bed. A lit'l drink takes the edge off—makes it a little more comfortable, that's all."

She motioned for him to turn around so she could step out of her bed and don the silk robe that lay on the couch a few feet away. As she tied the belt she said, "Come on, I've got a cure for that!"

Turning on the lights in the game room, she headed back toward the kitchen. He followed and sat down on a barstool at the island. Nikki filled an electric teakettle with water, turned it on, and selected a tea. After spooning some honey into a large, brightly colored terra cotta mug, she opened the fridge to retrieve a gallon jug of whole milk.

"No milk, please" he requested politely.

"Milk!" she demanded. "Unless, of course, you have an allergy or something. The calcium helps you to sleep and all your smoking diminishes your body's ability to absorb calcium. I'm pretty sure it's screaming for this milk—OK?" With the concoction thoroughly blended, she pushed the mug across the counter and waited for him to sip. Once again, she offered him a comfort drink that delighted his senses.

"Hey there, Butch Cassidy, what are you going to do with

yourself while you hide out in *these here* canyons?" she asked, refer-ring to the famed legend of the area.

"I dunno! Thought maybe I could hire ye to take me around to see the sights or somethin'." While swallowing, he looked over the rim of his mug to see her response.

"Well, first thing tomorrow, you can take my car to the gro-cery store and get some provisions. If you want alcohol you'll have to go to St. George. You can only get beer at the food store."

"Aaaaah," he stammered, "I'm hoping not to starve during the next few weeks and I really don't know how to cook, save a can of soup. I noticed in ye'r brochure the nearest restaurant is fifteen miles away. Any chance I could join ye for one meal a day?" he asked, tentatively testing the waters.

"Hold on there, buckaroo!" She stood with hands on hips, pretending to be put-out. "You mean you want me to be your chauffeur, your tour guide, security guard, and cook? What's next—laundress? That's asking a bit much, isn't it?"

"I'd make it worth ye'r while. It's not like I think ye don't have a life or anythin', it's just that, well…well, never mind. I was just hoping…" he said, looking into his cup pathetically. He waited to see if she took the *poor me, I need someone to take care of me*, bait.

Her smile surprised him for her mouth grinned only on the right side. Leaning across the counter as if it were a clandestine meeting, in a low, sultry voice she said, "I have terms, and you'll have to pay—big time!"

Works like a charm, he thought, mentally patting himself on the back for his years of experience in manipulating women.

"Here's the deal:

A. My ranch manager has taken some of our horses to California for a month of racing. I am, therefore, the only grunt on the ranch and I want your help with the chores every day…that's feeding animals, irrigating pastures, cleaning the pool and hot tub, landscape maintenance, mending fences, chasing cattle, mucking the occasional stall, and cleaning the cottage where you'll be staying. I cannot abide a man who will not roll up his sleeves and work!

B. I'll feed you once a day with the proviso that you participate in the preparation and clean-up of said meals—which doesn't mean sitting over on *that* side of the counter and watching me work while making idle conversation.

C. As for your laundry, I'll show you how to work your washing machine and dryer and you can wash your own underwear.

D. As tour guide, I can arrange to take you where you'd like to go, as long as it doesn't interfere with my schedule, and as long as you pay for the gas."

Her audacity delighted him. Aside from his family, no one dared that type of boldness with him. He couldn't help but smile. Spitting on his right hand, he extended it to her to seal the deal. He fully expected her to reel with disgust, but she spit on her own, and they shook. "So what's the schedule for morning, *boss?*" he mocked.

"I like to ride early in the morning. Greeting the sun as it tops the mesas is quite magical. You're welcome to join me for this early inspiration, *or*, I can let you sleep until I return around eight. Then, there'll be some irrigating and animal feeding. After that, we can go to town together and you can show me what you want to eat at the store. I have to go to Intermountain Farmers and WalMart for some animal feed. You can dress incognito and slum with me for a few hours and carry all the heavy stuff!

"Upon our return, we'll wait for my guests to check out. You can remain in your room so they don't see you, but quite frankly, they're a group of really old Germans on holiday and I doubt they'll ask you for your autograph. Then we'll head to the cottage to clean it up and you can transport all *that* (she pointed) to your own little house! We can cook dinner *together* tomorrow night, then you can veg, or read, or watch a movie, or whatever your little heart desires," she finished.

Bloody Hell, he thought. He hadn't quite planned on this, but was curious to see if she'd make him stick to the bargain. "So, what time do we ride?"

"Out of bed by six, catching horses and strapping tack by six twenty. OK?"

"Have ye a reasonably trained mount I could use?" Crow stood and took his cup to the sink, washed it with soap, dried, and returned it to the spot from which she took it.

"You can ride Jake. He's a tad spunky, but then again, so are you!" She smiled somewhat mischievously. Turning off the lights, she put her hand in the small of his back, directing him toward his room. "You sleep in sweats, or do you dress a little lighter?"

"Getting personal, now, are we?" he retorted.

"I was merely going to step out while you stripped down if you sleep lighter, that's all. I haven't finished with you yet."

Oh, jackpot! he thought,—*a woman in mi bed to distract me from mi first night woes!* "Well, then, turn around or something," he suggested. He pulled off his clothes and got into his bed.

She turned when the cover settled and noticed by his discarded clothing that he slept in his skivvies. Walking to the window, she raised the shade, and opened it. A cool breeze filtered in.

"Bit nippy for that, isn't it?"

"Oh don't be such a baby! The fresh air's good for you and the sound of the stream and crickets will lull you to sleep. Now…you sleep on your back, side, or stomach?"

Far too curious to see what would happen next, he rolled onto his stomach with no verbal response.

Turning off the light, she instructed him to move over a few inches.

He obliged.

Sitting on the edge of the bed and placing her hands on his neck, Nikki began a gentle massage, moving her little fingers into his hair and scalp, rubbing his head lightly and pulling his long hair through her fingers. Carefully kneading his shoulders, she gradually decreased the pressure until her hands were barely touching the little hairs on his back. Her very touch felt so familiar, so welcome, he completely relaxed and gave way to the comfort of it. Soon he breathed heavily. She quietly stood, leaned over his head and planted the slightest kiss on his hair. "Now you stay put this time," she whispered. She left his door open and made her way back to her own bed.

Chapter 2

"Hey, sleeping beauty…" Nikki whispered, "daylight's wastin'."
Dylan turned in his bed, sleepily acknowledging that he heard her.
"There's hot coffee in the kitchen and I'm heading out to find Jake.
I'll meet you at the barn in twenty minutes. OK?" She half expect-
ed him to say he'd rather stay in bed after all, but he didn't, so she
snatched her jacket and headed out the door.

He had a little trouble finding something to wear for all his hurried packing. Fifteen minutes had passed and he moved quickly to
the kitchen for a cup of coffee. Nothing sounded better than a cigarette, but he figured an opportunity to smoke could be seized while
at the barn.

Dylan took the stairs with the handrail as no one would be
available to break his fall should he slip again.

In the prep area stood a tall, sorrel quarter horse with a white
diamond on his forehead. Nikki tended to Pegasus in the breezeway, draping a blanket on his back. "Tack's in this room behind
me. Just roll the door back and you can choose for yourself. Jake's
kind of partial to the small bit hanging on the north wall, but you
can decide." Gathering the reins of the Hackamore and a wad of
the mane, she leapt to the horse's back.

With effort he rolled back a large, heavy wooden door and
entered a well-stocked tack room in which one English riding saddle hung among the westerns. While familiar only with English,
he decided to try western for a change. Dylan possessed a sincere
soft spot for animals and searched diligently for a nice thick blanket to ride beneath the saddle to ensure the horse's comfort.

"Hello, Jake," he said softly as he cinched the saddle strap. The
sorrel expanded his stomach to see just how far he could push this
new guy, but Crow knew that trick and gave his belly a little

nudge with his knee. When Jake exhaled Dylan cinched the strap one more notch. "We'll get along just fine, won't we, fella?"

They mounted and walked their horses down the long driveway. Arriving at the bottom of the steep entrance road, Nikki hopped down and suggested Crow do the same so they could lead their horses to the top without additional weight. As soon as they crossed the Byway she mounted and led Pegasus in a dash to the *Stairway to Heaven*. Crow took the challenge and with a "Hee-ah" and a brusque kick, he was off. Jake had been retired from the race track for only a year and Dylan nearly fell off when the horse bolted. Crow had no intention of allowing this little gal take the lead on everything, so he heeled Jake on until they passed Pegasus. Raising his arm with a fist at the end, he declared himself "the winner."

Nik had only run her horse to get to the mesa top before the sun's rays hit. Crow had taken a little too long saddling his horse and she had not wanted to distract him. Lightly amused, she realized he thought she had challeged him to a race.

The sky appeared a molten gray, just waiting for the kiss of the sun before it would share its intense blue colors. They began the ascent up the carved mountain, wending around and through eighty foot ponderosas. With his horse sweating and panting, Crow walked him slowly up the steep trail. The view from the top encompassed beauty of such astounding grandeur as to arrest the heart. Red and white sandstone mesas intricately carved by wind and rain were bathed in the early rays of the sun. Their supreme dignity and nobility struck an awesome chord inside of him. Beneath the mesa, a stream meandered through a lush green valley hidden from the sight of the world. It looked like a scene from *The Hobbit*.

Nikki dismounted, allowing Pegasus to roam freely. Assuming

he should do the same with Jake, Crow looked up in alarm as his horse took off running down the mountain. It all happened so quickly, it didn't occur to him to grab Pegasus and he chased the errant horse on foot.

Nearly splitting her side laughing, Nikki silently wished she could capture *that scene* on film. She approached Pegasus and whispered, "I bet you two scallywags arranged that, didn't you?"

☯

The sun had risen to the edge of the mesa and induced her early morning trance. Meanwhile, Crow hiked back up and watched her from behind a large tree. With head tilted back and arms extending out from her sides, Nikki embraced the light. Swaying in the golden rays, she danced as gently as a soft breeze while in deep meditation. After completing her silent prayer she walked to the edge of the mesa and began to sing.

"Oh Mio Babbino Caro…" the words and notes came soft, but clear. The song sounded vaguely familiar and Dylan wanted to get closer to hear it better. He sneaked up behind her, certain she could not detect his footsteps upon the sandstone. The song rose to its crescendo as his own heart joined in the power of the moment. She sang from some opera and danced in the morning light as he stood motionless, allowing the full spectrum of the scene to fill his soul. Then, surprisingly, she reached her hand backward, turned to him and asked, "Do *you* have a song to offer the canyon spirits?" She had known he stood there all along and yet showed no intimidation by his presence.

"What's the name of that lovely tune?" he asked quietly, so as not to break the ethereal spell of the moment.

"It's Puccini— 'Oh Mio Babbino Caro'—a song sung from daughter to father, telling him of her deep love for her lover." The import of the song sung to the golden rays of the new day, her thanking God her father for bringing *him* back into her life, sailed over Crow's head. She had expected no less.

"Aye…I'll sing a little ditty to appease the gods," he said, smiling. Never embarrassed or afraid to perform under any circumstance, his beautiful voice issued forth a sweet old Gaelic tune.

Nikki swelled with delight beyond his comprehension, not for his performance, but for his willingness to sing to the spirits of the canyon. She had never shared this experience with another human and his willing participation colored the event with a certain sacredness.

"I take it you couldn't find Jake?" she said, laughing at the memory of seeing him run down the mountain chasing a racehorse three times his size.

"Ye think Pegasus can take us both, or am I hiking home?"

She liked that he said "home," not "the ranch." "Why don't you ask *him*?" she asked, gesturing to her friend.

Crow smiled and casually sauntered over to the grazing horse. "What do ye say to that, fella?" Pegasus raised his head and looked at Nikki, then back to him and whinnied. "And I'll be takin' that as a 'yes' then, ol' boy?"

She stepped to her friend, stroked his mane, pulled off her backpack and offered him the ritualistic apple. Pegasus took it gratefully. Retrieving two small bottles of water, she threw one to Dylan. "Let's lighten this load a little and you can carry it on your back—unless of course, you want the front seat this time," she said, winking.

"Tell ye what, I'll take the back seat if ye'll let *me* drive!" He flashed his famous smile, punctuated by a small dimple on the left cheek. "Deal?"

"Deal!"

Nikki held a wad of the mane in her hands, pulling herself up to Pegasus's back with ease. When she offered her bent foot once again, he knew she had the strength to raise him safely into position. His arms encircled her as she handed him the reins, knowing full well that Pegasus could do just fine without anyone "driving."

She loved the way Crow's arms felt around her: like they were two puzzle pieces that fit perfectly.

He noticed the same thing, but neither made comment about it. Dylan spoke easily and freely, with his chin just above her right shoulder. Her scent smelled exactly as he remembered: fresh and subtle, like rain, wind, and air. His beard tickled her ear and she reached up to push it back.

"I guess I won't be needing this scruffy thing any more. Want to help me cut it off?" he asked.

Turning in his arms, the situation begged for a kiss, though neither offered it. "You mean you'll expose that famous cleft to me *privately?*" she teased.

"Be my honor, ma'am!" he replied in his best John Wayne imitation.

Pegasus plodded slowly, rhythmically, as their bodies joined in a dance of sorts. The morning birds provided the music while the golden rays of the sun looked like dazzling streamers hung around a great ballroom. He closed his eyes as he realized he was becoming aroused by the experience and knew, unmistakably, that she knew too. They sat much too close physically to miss this one. He did not try to adjust himself away from her, nor did she attempt to pull away from him. If anything, she leaned into his frame a little more. He could feel her heart beating frantically against his chest and hear her shallow breathing. Both silence and full communication passed between them—though neither knew what to do with it. The feeling grew intensely and rapidly until Crow sensed the electricity so strongly he could bear it no longer.

"Let's give Pegasus a wee break, shall we?" he said, sliding off the blanket to the earth. He raised his arms to help her down, but pulled her close to his chest, catching her between the mass of the horse and the mass of his body.

The slightest hesitation shifted between them while each tried to decide if they should follow their natural instincts. Regaining control, however, each deliberately reined in their feelings.

"Ye live in quite a splendid place, Nikkol," he said, attempting to ease the tension.

"The world is filled with so many beautiful places, isn't it?" she remarked softly, distractedly. The blood that had rushed to her southern hemisphere began to stabilize and redistribute. Consciously clearing her mind, she determined not to allow any physical longing to cloud her mission with him. When they remounted, she sat behind Crow and set up her own defenses.

Arriving at the barn, they found Jake in the tack room where Crow had left the door open. The naughty little devil had pushed the top from a grain bin and had been helping himself for quite a while. "Looks like you'll have to walk him so he won't founder," she directed.

"*I?*"

"Well, let's recap the events of the morning, shall we? *Your* mount, the door *you* left open, and the horse *you* neglected to tie on the mountain. You think *I* ought to do it? Give it about an hour, would you? Then put him on the stream with Pegasus," she said, laughing at him.

She brushed Pegasus down and thanked him for his hidden agenda of the day. He ambled behind her to the pasture gate, entered and turned, waiting expectantly for her kiss on his muzzle.

Dylan led the sorrel down the road, muttering something gruffly under his breath. Nikki giggled and ran up the stairs to take her morning shower. By the time he had finished his chore she had showered, dressed, and had breakfast cooking on the stove.

"Is this a freebie, or will I be doin' double-time on the next meal?" he asked. She smiled mischievously, saying nothing, and turned to load the dishwasher.

"Well, then…I'll just clean up a bit, then we can go *slummin'*," he said, rising from the counter.

"You got any slumming clothes in that sumptuous wardrobe of yours, Little Crow?"

"Levi's do?"

"OK…a pair of Levi's and that T-shirt you had on last night. I'll find the pièce de résistance of a jacket and you can wear your sunglasses and baseball hat."

When he emerged he found her offering him the most unattractive plaid shirt-jacket he'd ever laid eyes on. "I can't wear that!"

"Sure you can! It's the Virgin style, and I promise no one will even look at you twice." What he didn't know was that she would place a cloak of invisibility around both of them so they would be seen, but not noticed. Even though she would use the vibratory law she had learned while working with force fields, she felt certain he would not be ready to hear about it at this juncture.

When they got in the car, he looked oddly out of place in the passenger seat. "You wanna drive?" she asked, reading his thoughts.

"Ye mind?"

"Not at all. I'll just navigate for you. OK?" she offered.

His disguise worked! No matter where they went, no one even noticed him. Even after he boldly removed his sunglasses, still, no one noticed him. He looked a checkout clerk directly in the eyes while buying a tabloid with his picture on the front, yet there wasn't a spark of recognition.

They actually played in WalMart. He had never been comfortable enough before this to be seen in such a public place---especially a discount house. While he looked at the endless stock and held things up to share with her, Nikki wondered if he had ever been in a store in his entire life! After trying on twenty pairs of ten-dollar sunglasses, he actually chose three to purchase. Along with a new baseball cap, he threw some funky boxer shorts in the basket, stating, "Ye never know when the washerwoman will quit." He spent an hour in the automotive department. In the electronics/video section, brazenly holding up a DVD of *Marrakech,* Crow asked in a loud hickish voice, "Honey, didn't yew tell me this guy is the hottest babe in Hollywood? Should we buy it just to keep yew satisfied?"

While they had originally come for twenty-three dollars worth of dog and cat food, they left with a bill of two hundred eighty three dollars. Nikki allowed him to pay cash for his purchases. She knew he would not dare offer a credit card with his name on it and laughed as he struggled to meet the bill in cash. "Need some help, *honey?*" she mocked. Seeing him a few bucks short, she handed him a fifty-dollar bill.

"That was the greatest!" he said as they left the building and rolled their full cart toward her car. He hadn't been that entertained doing something so simple in a very long time.

"I don't want to burst your bubble, Dylan, but have you noticed people look past each other rather than *at* each other most of the time?"

"Ye know, *Babe,*" he said, continuing their frolicking familiarity from WalMart, "people look *at* me all the time. I can't say that I look at them, but I sure know they look *at* me."

When he chose two cases of wine at the liquor store, she paid for them. "Feel like stopping at an ATM?" she asked.

"Right," he said. "Now that's something I *do* know how to do, 'cause I never go into the bank."

As they drove toward Hurricane he handed her two hundred fifty dollars. "OK—we're even—or close, right?"

She laughed silently, knowing they would never be even. He had provided her with more joy and amusement than money could ever have purchased.

They arrived back at the ranch at two thirty and his stomach complained loudly for lack of lunch. "Ye hungry?" he posed, putting a grocery bag on the counter.

"Not really. I don't usually eat in the morning and breakfast kind of filled me up."

Blast, he thought, and reached for a banana. He'd have to wait for her, or rather, for *them*, to cook dinner this evening. He settled for a beer.

The dogs barked. Through the window she saw her tenants pulling in front of her house. "Wanna vamoose?" she asked.

"No, I think this trashy jacket really does the trick!"

Dylan sat at the counter while she introduced them, actually stating his real name, but the elderly people didn't even blink an eye. *Maybe I am getting to think a bit much of miself, after all*, he thought.

The travelers seemed mystified by the kitchen filled to the brim with luggage, but made no comment.

After settling their account, the Germans drove away and Nikki turned to Dylan, raising her right eyebrow in a teasingly authoritative gesture. "Get to work, slave!"

The morning had tired him, but he began loading his suitcases into the bed of a white Tundra truck.

Nikki took him to the cottage by the statue and he asked if she had sculpted the kneeling lady.

"Yeah, I did. She helped me make a major transition in my life," she confessed.

"And whose thoughts would those be on the plaque beneath it?"

"Mine."

She maneuvered around him on the walkway and pulled open and anchored the door for passage of his cargo. The tourists had left the place rather tidy. He had not expected the cottage to be so utterly charming. The entry room consisted of sitting and dining areas combined. A large, heavy wicker couch opposed matching chairs with purple chintz upholstered cushions. Two striped ottomans sat atop an authentic, brightly colored Indian rug. A huge sand painting of a pot hung over the couch and an Indian headdress, framed inside a lucite box, hung on the dining room wall. The television was stationed across from the seating area. Four wicker chairs, upholstered in a soft salmon colored fabric, surrounded the glass and wicker dining table. A tall, oddly shaped, Mayan looking armoire spanned half the wall of the dining room. The stone fireplace looked promising for the cooler evenings.

The master bedroom had been furnished with a queen-size poster bed, covered with a down comforter and pillows encased in fabric matching the upholstery from the corner posts. Upon a lacquered, off-white bureau sat a large, white clay lamp and a bronze cache in the shape of a duck. A small Indian headdress, also framed in lucite, hung over the bureau.

"Are these things real?" he asked, pointing to the headdresses.

"They are!" she revealed with pride.

Atop a mirrored desk sat an old record player with albums stacked next to it. He eyed it with curiosity. "Does this antique work?"

"Antique? I'll have you know I spent a lot of time listening to those old albums and I'm not exactly an antique! In fact, there are about a hundred in the bottom of the armoire in the dining room if you're interested in oldies but goodies."

The kitchen was small, yet adequate. She showed him how to lift and secure a large cutting board she had built to increase the working space in the kitchen.

Wow...on top of her many artistic talents she's a carpenter!

She stowed the food and alcohol he had purchased, neatly putting each thing in its own place. He marveled at how quickly she could organize things.

The second bedroom held another queen-size bed with a sage green coverlet. A stunning oil painting of a bouquet of roses adorned the wall. The room measured only ten feet square, yet it held a clothing armoire. She opened the closet in the second room to expose a washer and dryer. "When you're ready, I'll show you how," she explained.

He walked through the kitchen to the bathroom, which also had a separate door to the master bedroom. Though petite, it had been charmingly decorated and would suit his needs. Out of the corner of his eye he saw an enormous, brown, hairy thing scurry around the bottom of the tub. As Dylan attempted to kill it, Nikki eyed him sternly, then obtained a tissue, gently collected the ugly creature, and carried it outside to the lawn. "It's only a wolf spider that got in the house by mistake," she said. Crow shook his head in mild amusement.

Actually asking him to scrub the toilet, Nikki hid her amused smile while she cleaned the bathtub. They changed sheets, vacuumed floors, dusted furniture, wiped out the fridge, and cleaned off the stove. After windows were washed, logs stacked in the fireplace, window boxes watered, and the garden weeded, she nodded in approval.

Nikki asked him to load the big garbage can on the back of her truck so she could drive it five miles to the dump. Through the window of the cottage she saw him start to lift the can, which he dropped quickly, putting his hand to his lower back. He tried again and this time succeeded. Looking distracted and massaging his back, he entered the cottage again.

"Let's take inventory of this *baggage* thing," she said, raising her brow. "Do you want to open these up and choose a bunch of stuff to handle your life while you're here? We can store the remainder of the suitcases in that second bedroom." He appeared visibly tired, so she assisted him, carrying more than half the heavy load to the extra room. She helped him arrange his things in the drawers and closet.

He kept rubbing his lower back.

"That the area where they operated?"

"How did ye know that?" he asked, wondering just how much she already knew about him.

"Is there anything about your life that hasn't been spread over the front page of every magazine known to man?"

"Aye, well I think lifting mi booty so many times really got to it today." He plopped down on the bench at the end of his bed.

"You want me to work on it?"

"Sure! Where do ye want me?"

Motioning to the bed she instructed him to remove his shirt and lie on his back. "Now, I'm not getting fresh here. OK? I'm just going to roll with you for a minute to loosen the muscles." She lay down at his side and took his arm and hung it loosely over her shoulder. Placing her hand under his waist to get a gentle grip on his *owie,* she began to rock back and forth. He closed his eyes, trying to ignore the pain. Nikki threw her leg over his tummy and continued to rock him so only his upper torso would move. Next, rolling him on his stomach, she straddled his body. After sharply clapping her hands and rubbing them together quickly, she applied the kinetic heat to his lower back. When the muscle relaxed under her hands, she pulled his arms down to his sides and held his wrists while rocking him again.

Her body rhythmically rocking upon his buttocks created undeniably acute sensual awareness. Gratefully, he lay face down so she couldn't see.

Nikki had learned this method of massage from one of the alternative therapy masters at the Green Valley Spa. Though she had used this therapy to help many people before, it was the first time she had personally become sexually aroused. Looking at his muscular frame she examined the moles, freckles, and surgical scar on his back. She moved her hands to the base of his spine and began a gentle massage, allowing him to move his arms back over his head. Continuing the massage in circular motions, she worked from bottom to top, and gradually to both shoulders.

Completely exhausted and relaxed by the massage, Crow fell into a peaceful sleep.

As she slid her fingers over his shoulders and down his arms to his hands, he fiercely grasped her right wrist. Recognizing that deep, deep sleep of a weary person, Nikki wasn't certain what to do. She tried to free her arm, but he clenched it tighter in his massive hand. Sliding off his back to his right side, she lay motionless only inches away from his body, waiting for him to relax his grip and dozed off by his side.

Half an hour later he awoke trying to identify his surroundings. Turning his head to the right he found her lying asleep next to him with his fingers clenched tightly around her wrist. She looked like an angel in that unstudied attitude of sleep with mouth turned up in a slight smile and cheeks blushing a soft pink. Her face seemed lit with a vague expression of contentment and happiness. Crow's eyes followed the line of her exposed neck down to her breasts, which were gently rising with each deep breath. She emitted the slightest purring sound, which he found very comforting. Her hair flowed back from her face and as she turned her head slightly, he noticed it ---*a mole in front of her left ear, about two centimeters in size!*

His movement stirred her dreams and she regained consciousness, blinking and staring at him. Lying still, he gazed into her eyes, once again noticing their resemblance to his own. Raising on his elbow, he asked in his best Rhett Butler voice, "Why Miss Scarlett, to what do I owe the pleasure?"

"A death grip!" she replied, chortling as she pulled her numb arm from under the pillow to reveal his indented and red fingerprints. "Is that how you capture your victims?"

"Victims? Babe, they come to me like bees to the flower. I don't need to *capture* them!" he teased in mock vanity.

She wondered if he'd come to the habit of calling women "Babe" just as she had come to the habit of calling people "Dear" or "Darling."

"It's getting late. I'll bet you're hungry, huh?" she asked. He was, indeed, hungry—hungry for something for which he dare not ask. Crow didn't trust himself right now and was completely unaware that Nikki felt the same way.

He knew he could have any woman he wanted in his bed and didn't want this to be just another one of those flings. Distance would prove the best policy. "Ye know, I think that helped mi back. I'm kind of worn out from all mi slave-driver's orders today, so I think I'll just grab somethin' here. Then neither of us will have to spend time in the kitchen tonight."

Grateful he wasn't hungry and desired privacy, Nikki internal-
ly sighed with relief. Every part of her ached to reach out and hold
him. *Why did I let myself get this physical with him?* she thought.

Caught in limbo between her spiritual devotion and the
desires of her physical body, she felt as if she'd betrayed all her
training. Years had been spent disciplining the energy to rise from
her lower chakras to her heart. Now, she found herself looking at
her twin flame with the opportunity of millenniums, but her
lower self was truly putting her to the test, providing a seduction
she feared she could not resist.

*If I can just remove myself from his body, his voice, I'm sure I can
do the right thing*, she thought. "Mighty I AM Presence within
me," she silently uttered, "take dominion of my lower self and see
to it that I offer my beloved what he truly needs for his highest
and best good."

She turned on the heat and acquainted him with the cottage
and its contents before she departed.

☯

Foraging through the food they had bought earlier, Crow
found some bread and pastrami and made a sandwich. He poured
his favorite Merlot, lit the fire, and sat down at the dining table.

What am I doing? he wondered. He felt things in her presence
he had not felt with any other person in his life. Having enjoyed
their foolish banter, he wondered if all "highly developed souls"
were this much fun. She wouldn't let him wear his usual masks; a
relief and yet a concern at the same time. He had used them so
well over the years to hide the pain he'd felt in unfulfilled relationships.

Staring at the flames of the fire, he chuckled, knowing Nikki
would make him clean out the ashes in the morning and set
another.

He felt anxious, not about quitting the show, but from the disturbing, uncontrollable urges he had with this woman. He searched for a cigarette to settle his nerves. Since he'd promised to smoke outside, he decided to take a walk to clear his head. Finding the flashlight exactly where Nikki said it would be, he donned his leather jacket and began to wander around in the dark.

His feet led him back up the quarter mile to her home. Bear barked, but only once. As he stood on the dock in front of her place staring through the lit windows from a distance, she stepped before one in the kitchen with a phone at her ear. He wanted to knock at the door with some excuse for having walked up, but he truly didn't have any—he just wanted to be near her. The door opened and Nikki called to her dogs, who came running for some sort of treat she had in her hands. Though he stood motionless, she saw him anyway.

"Change your mind?" she hollered.

"Actually, took a wee stroll so I could smoke. Guess where this road leads?"

"I've got to go switch the irrigation water. You want to walk with me?" she asked, while the dogs licked her hands clean of the last traces of crumbs from a cookie.

He truly felt in this dark place she might require his protection and answered gallantly, "I'd be honored to watch over ye."

His words took her back a little. *Always the protector and defender*, she thought. Grabbing a jacket and a pair of gloves she headed out to join him. The Lab tagged along as they walked back down the road to the pasture just above his cottage.

"I'm going to give you the white truck to use as you please while you're here so I can use your hard muscles for better tasks than walking to my home."

"Ta," he said sincerely. He hated feeling like a captive due to lack of transportation.

They looked to the skies and a billion stars shone above them. The lack of ambient light stretched the night skies into eternity. The moon had not yet risen, but she knew it would rise over the mesa soon and cast a light so beautiful upon things that it would take his breath away. Nikki wanted to see his face as the moon kissed her ranch, just as she had seen it when the sun kissed the earth earlier that day.

"Worlds without end have I made," she quoted from scripture, "...and all this and more shall ye do." She paused as she looked to the sky. "What do those words mean to you?"

"I dunno," he said after a minute. "I can't imagine we exist alone in the universe and yet, God and heaven and all that stuff seem so elusive to me. I've seen enough to convince me *we* are the masters of our destiny. I don't think anything's written in stone or preordained and I don't know if I believe that life goes on after death the way most religions preach. Did ye ever see the movie, *Groundhog Day?*" he asked.

"Uh huh," she answered softly while kicking a stick to the side of the road.

"Well, I think that's about as close to the way I believe as anythin'. Ye know—the guy just wakes up to the same tripe every day—playing out hundreds of scenarios, experiencing every option of one day's events until he learns to behave in a constructive fashion that expands his own knowledge, talents, and consciousness, harms none, and benefits anyone who crosses his path." The words spilling from his lips were more a confession of his soul than a light topic of conversation.

Quietly he thought for a few minutes about how confessing is always easier in the dark when you can't see the seeds of judgment in someone's eyes. "Maybe that's what our idea of reincarnation is about. I don't think ye die, then head off for some cloud or end up before some judgment seat where St. Peter says ye get past the gates or not."

She didn't want to interrupt his reverie, but they had arrived at the gate for the irrigation and she knelt down and gave it a few twists.

"That was simple," he commented.

"Yeah, this one's easy. It's the ones you have to do with a shovel and a dam that are hard. It's a muddy job!" She stood erect again. "There's one more further down this little lane."

Shining the flashlight ahead of them, he followed.

The Lab barked as it chased after a night creature.

"What kind o' wildlife ye got around here? Anything that might eat me?" he asked.

"Well, you've met the horses, cows, dogs, cats, ducks, and peacocks, but you've yet to meet the cougars, coyotes, deer, bobcats, squirrels, rabbits, herons, rattlesnakes, and tarantulas." Just then the Lab chased a skunk right in front of them, who, though not yet defending himself with his only weapon, still left a malodorous waft of air. "Oh yes, and did I mention the skunks?"

"Heavens, what a smell!" he croaked, pinching his nose.

"It used to make me sick when I first moved here. Now I'm so used to it that I just think, *MMMMMM, home!*" she said, grinning to one side of her face. "Funny how a certain scent elicits feelings related to its repeated exposure in your life—you know—like the smell of bread cooking in the oven makes you feel loved and welcome."

"Speaking of scents, Nikki, would ye tell me about that flower ye gave me the day we met...why its scent becomes more divine every day and why it doesn't die?"

She slowed her step until she came to a complete halt. He

reduced his pace to match hers until she turned and looked up into his eyes. "To be honest, Little Crow," she whispered, "I didn't think I'd ever see you again. I had hoped it would compel you to think it through for yourself." She said nothing more, but took a few steps forward.

Watching her walk away, a sense of anxious sadness overwhelmed him as though he had watched her leave this same way before. *I beg you...please don't leave me here in the dark again*, echoed an oddly familiar voice in his head as he quickly caught up with her.

"I get the distinct impression that ye've no intention of explaining further."

They had arrived at the next gate, so she climbed down into the sunken area to complete her task. Offering only the silence of the night in answer to his question, she hoped the chore of turning the valve would distract him.

"Say, did a man named Joe Chatauk ever come by to see ye?" he asked, lending his arm to brace her while she twisted the regulator.

"He left his card on my gate." Nikki brushed the mud off her gloves. "I would like to have met him though. I've admired the characters he's played over the years. Always had a sneaking hunch he only plays himself. Did you send him?"

"Nay...in fact he told me *ye* sent some 'soul light' to the set and he connected with it. Kooky, huh?"

She knew they might be entering dangerous territory too soon and didn't want to drive him away, so she moved back into her playful banter with him. "Oh yeah, I shine this twenty gigawatt spotlight from the highest mesa every night and anyone who sees it can come visit me," she said, sappily. "I usually only get those pesky UFO's, however!"

Recognizing her thinly veiled dodge immediately, he chuckled. "There's something 'bout ye I can't quite understand and it's clear ye have some safeguards 'round it. Forgive me for letting mi curiosity invade ye'r private life."

He reached for her hand to help her out of the hole in which she stood, now shin deep, in water. Jerking just a little too hard, the force pulled her right to his chest. They stood motionless, breathing heavily in anticipation. He didn't want to push her too fast, but this constant surge of sexual energy between them could not be denied.

"Well, it's getting late,"she said awkwardly. "I guess I should let you get back to your bed. You should sleep well tonight."

"Doubtful…" he returned, feigning self pity, "for as well ye know, I changed beds again and I've no one to brew special tea or rub mi back for me. Guess it's just me and the wine."

As they drew near the main road again the moon began to peek over the blackened mesa. The leaves on the trees interfered with their view. Nikki took his elbow, turning him back around. "Hey, walk up the entrance road with me and see some magic first."

Crow had to hustle to keep up with her, so she reached back her hand and grabbed for his to pull him up the steep hill. He *knew* the comfort of her touch, recognizing it deep inside somewhere. Other hands he'd held hadn't inspired this sense of belongingness.

Half way up the road they found a large boulder to sit upon while the moon made its debut. It spread its soft rays of light over the surrounding hills, dancing and reflecting on the pastures beneath them, bouncing off the irrigation water that flowed flood style across the earth. It appeared unusually huge, inspiring tales about the man in the moon, which they shared with gentle laughter.

To Crow, Nikki seemed utterly composed, tranquil, and serene. Looking into the night skies was the same as looking into her heart.

When they stood to leave, Dylan's foot slipped on some loose gravel and slid into a cactus. "Blast!" he growled.

"Got a little prick?" Suddenly realizing by the look on his face that a double entendre had just escaped her lips, her cheeks blushed from embarrassment.

"I have no intention of dignifying that comment with a response!" He chuckled, surprised at her slip of the tongue—wondering in fact, if it was. "However, I may need a surgeon to remove the things poking in mi socks."

She offered her shoulders for his arm to use as support as he limped all the way back to her house. Even though in pain, he noticed how well she fit him with her shoulder tucked perfectly beneath his arm.

Nikki led him into the kitchen and gently removed his shoe and stocking. Hundreds of miniscule cactus spines protruded from his quickly swelling ankle. "OOOOO Baby!" she exclaimed. "You've done 'er up brown, Mr. Jones. I guess the brightest light for surgery would be the one next to my bed."

☯

Helping him to the back end of the house, she invited him into her inner sanctum. The large bedroom appeared spotless. A deep blue chenille coverlet rimmed in gold braid, hung over a tapestry skirt on the king-size bed. Pillows of tapestry and salmon-colored fabric covered the top third of the bed. The night tables were unique dressers covered in a lacquered grass cloth and topped with brass-based lamps which did throw a lot of good light. Above the bed hung an original oil of a seaside view from a small patio overlooking the Cote d'Azure. The colors of the room consisted of mottled golden yellow and off-white, creating a calming atmosphere. Positioned beneath a window, a burlwood desk provided a private work space. Mementos and books covered an old-fashioned French bread rack. Sandwiched between attractive end tables sat an eight-foot silk and down couch, adorned with tapestry pillows. A beautiful hand carved armoire occupied the northeast corner. Crow assumed it held electronic equipment.

Opposite the bed, in a petrified wood fireplace, logs had been stacked, ready to be lit. The whole effect gave the impression of comfort and dignity. Dylan always believed you could tell a lot about a woman just by seeing the non-public spaces within her home.

He noticed a dozen or so books on the dresser closest to them. *Her preferred side of the bed,* he thought.

Handing him a pillow, she positioned him face down with his head at the foot of her bed and carefully angled his injured limb under the bright light. Disappearing for a moment, she returned with a towel and some tweezers. She lifted his leg gingerly, placing the towel beneath it to catch all the hair-like needles as she removed them. "I hope I can get these all out for you. They'll dissolve by themselves in a week or so, but they can hurt like a bugger under socks or pants."

Opening the armoire, she revealed a television and other electronic equipment, as he had guessed.

"I'm going to create a little distraction for you, if you don't mind," she said handing the remote to him. The movie channels are the three hundreds, sports in the fours, and news in the sevens."

He scanned the news channels. After listening to a number of true, live, horror stories, he sensed Nikki's discomfort and flipped to the movie section. To his chagrin, *Present Tense,* a movie he had made four years earlier with Anne-Marie Hawthorne, was being

aired on HBO West. He had fallen madly in love with her and
their affair extended through almost a year. Anne-Marie had been
in the middle of a complicated divorce that ultimately proved
detrimental to her children and opted to stay with her husband
after their messy and painful affair. Crow had grieved the loss of
her deeply. It had been the closest he'd ever come to even asking
someone to marry him. Following that fatal event, he maintained
his relationships on a superficial level, never wanting to feel that
kind of pain again. After all, they were only women.

"You sure you want to watch this?" Nikki asked. "Shall I just
go get a little salt to throw in that wound in the middle of your
chest—or has it scarred over yet?"

"Right," he said glumly. "Sometimes ye just gotta close the
door on impossible dreams." He clicked through the other channels disinterestedly, until the soft, relaxing melody of a music station caught his attention. Burying his face in the pillow, he surrounded his head with his arms, not wanting Nikki to see the
heartache he was unable to hide. *Jasus, Mary, and Joseph! This is a
lousy time for the ghosts of unfulfilled love to haunt me,* he thought.

Quietly, Nikki went about the business of plucking needles.
Her hands were gentle and adept at her surgical skill and he hardly noticed any pain while she worked.

There were so many needles she reckoned it would take about
another half-hour or so to finish the job.

Her hands and eyes shifted into autopilot while her mind
focused on Crow. She could tell he was reminiscing about Anne-
Marie and decided to draw him out, knowing unresolved pain just
festers until a wickedly untreatable manifestation assumes control
of both heart and mind. "What have you discovered about love
during your life?" she inquired softly.

He twisted his head and looked at her, allowing the space of a few moments before he decided to answer. "I think I'm the king of unreturned love," he confessed as he turned his face away from her again. *Good Lord, is she a mind reader too? How did she know I was thinking 'bout diggin' up old, emotional garbage? I think I've dealt with it, then something triggers feelings I thought had died a natural death. Guess I haven't quite come to terms with these emotions I buried... 'cause here they are, rearing their ugly heads at a most inconvenient time.*

Temporarily suspending her work, Nikki stepped to the end of the bed and kneeled down in front of him. Cupping his chin in her hand, she gently pulled his face so his eyes would meet hers.

"It appears you've experienced your share of pain in this life, Dylan. Maybe you've built a wall around your heart to try to protect you from that kind of hurt again. But—one can have a lonely heart, even if he's with people he loves. I think the whole human race feels that way, Little Crow. We *all* have issues of abandonment, worthlessness, and unrequited love, the origin of which stems from a loss so grand, it goes far beyond intimate or tribal relationships. There's a relentless hunger in our souls that's associated with our *perceived* separation from God and from a part of ourselves that some refer to as our 'other half'."

Despondently he responded, "I'm shockin' thick-headed sometimes, Nikki. Maybe what ye're sayin' is so, but it's a wee bit difficult for me to connect mi *perceived* relationship with God to mi terminated relationship with Anne-Marie."

As if jolted with a cattle prod, Nikki felt certain *now* was a good time to entertain ideas of the higher laws of relating. Without skipping a beat, she began again. "We have four 'lower' bodies: the physical," she touched his arm, "the emotional, the mental, and the etheric, or memory, body. Each receives, stores, and transmits information. The etheric body, which interpenetrates the other three, contains information from every lifetime.

"The memory of our Oneness with God and our Divine Other Half is still held in our etheric body. However—we've experienced hundreds, or perhaps thousands, of lifetimes of forgetfulness of both. That lingering *memory*, both on an energetic and cellular level, caus-es an unexplained longing for something more—*a divine discontent*, so to speak, that can be relieved only by *consciously remembering*. The fact is, you couldn't separate yourself from God or your other half, but, *we have forgotten* our relation to both."

"Ye talkin' 'bout soul mate memory?" he asked with polite interest, still hoarding what he had learned with Grace. Although the shaman had explained the difference between soul mates, karmic relationships, and twin flames, he wasn't sure that he bought the whole idea. He wondered just how much Nikki knew about the subject, and if she, like Grace, believed, or intuited *they* were twin flames. Grace's words echoed subconsciously: "*Don't just blurt it out, 'cause if she doesn't know, fear may drive her away.*" He continued, "Anne-Marie told me *we* were soul mates. So much for love eternal, eh?"

Nikki hesitated, looking deep into the reflection of her own eyes staring back at her. "The term 'soul mates' has been loosely used to describe certain liaisons in which one feels truly connect-ed to another soul. I believe relationships exist with souls magnet-ically attracted to one another who have similar attributes or who are, perhaps, learning similar lessons…as a support of sorts, help-ing one another through this earthly education."

Nikki's eyes assumed a distant thoughtfulness as though con-necting to a sacred personal memory. "What I'm speaking about is the origin, the fabric, of one's soul. When God created mankind from his own heart cells it was for the purpose of experiencing himself through relationship, having a vehicle that could *reflect* back all his attributes and beauty, while continuing to expand God's perfection through their individual creations. God gave his children this same opportunity by splitting each cell into two halves. One has a positive charge and the other a negative charge which, in reflecting their perfection to one another, create their wholeness. Together, they are the perfect reflection of God. Separate, they can become aligned with the highest within themselves, remembering their at-one-ment with God…but *only* when they are joined together do they become the fullness of the reflection of God and his unlimited creative attributes.

"Repeatedly, throughout the legends, myths, and spiritual beliefs of mankind, the story's been told of this sacred duo and how, through consciously and deliberately turning their attention away from God, not only did they *fall in consciousness*, but also, the two were separated by disparity. It's Adam and Eve leaving the Garden of Eden. A world of history's passed while these two parts have explored all manner of *relationship,* but they always *long* for one another, for only in this holiest of unions is God's reflection complete.

"Anyway, didn't mean to bore you with *my* belief system. I just thought I'd cast a new light on your experiences to help you gain some cosmic perspective. It might just be that your relationship with Anne-Marie existed for the sole purpose of jump-starting your search for *true love.* True love never hurts, Dylan. True love is seeing your perfection reflected through another's eyes, knowing the other's eyes are, in reality, yours. True love is *given* and must, by the nature of cosmic law, be returned multiplied."

He turned his head away, laying his face on his arm again. "Blah, blah, blah. Maybe, but sometimes a fella just wants what he wants. He doesn't want to have to defend or analyze the reason for his desire…he just wants it."

She tousled his hair gently, stood, and went back to her work.

The music from the television played softly in the background until she heard the distinct, heavy breathing reminiscent of that afternoon and knew he had fallen asleep. Her sharp eyes located and nimble fingers plucked the hair-like cactus spines for another ten minutes. Wanting to inspect every angle to see if she missed any, she ran her fingers lightly across the surface. Because of the hair on his legs, the really small ones were impossible to detect. Had he been awake, she could have asked if he felt any pain as her fingers stroked his skin. Since he slept, however, she decided to use the sensitivity of her lips to discover any more of the diminutive devils.

Lifting the injured limb slightly, she began a gentle caressing with her lips and could feel no more spines. Unconsciously she kissed his leg, moving light energy from the top of her head through her mouth, willing each affected cell in his leg to return to its perfect form with her love.

Crow lay absolutely still, hiding his awareness of her behavior. He had been filled with reminded emotional pain for the last hour. Now, this sweet creature healed his injury with the balm of her kisses.

Thinking him asleep, Nikki stood over him and prayed for her beloved twin flame. Raising her arms toward heaven, she declared in the slightest whisper:

"Mighty I AM Presence, through thee and in thy name, I call upon my higher mental body and the higher mental body of Dylan Crow. I call upon our guides, angels, and those masters, angelic, and cosmic beings whose light may best be utilized for both of us at this time. I AM here and I AM there. I AM the self-illumined, self-sustained activity of Divine Intelligence, Wisdom, and Love, forming an impenetrable, invincible, invisible field of light around his body, which repels all discordant mis-creation from without, and corrects all within. I AM holding complete and self-sustained dominion over his every word, every deed, every thought and feeling, intention and attention. I AM holding complete dominion over his conscious waking day and his conscious dreaming nights, that both may serve to enlighten him."

She envisioned him being held within a great field of white light and lowered her arms as if directing that light to encircle his body.

"I AM the self-sustained, perfect pattern and form of every cell, every organ, every aspect of his physical body, as given forth from his higher mental body to the intelligences within this temple of his divine spirit. I AM his perfect health, beauty, youth, vitality, strength, agility, and energy, forever and ever self-sustained.

"I AM unlimited abundance, prosperity, and wealth of every good thing he desires, brought forth and poured into his hands from our Father's unlimited treasure house, every hour, every minute of every day. Pour forth thine unlimited truth, thine unlimited at-one-ment, thine unlimited joy, thine unlimited divine and earthly love, thine unlimited perfection, thine unlimited creativity, and thine unlimited wealth. See to it that I AM the Divine Wisdom, Intelligence, and Love within him to utilize these gifts of the Father to bless, heal, enlighten, illumine, prosper, unify, and beautify all within his reach. Thy Divine Will be done through him, as him, on earth, as it is in heaven.

"I AM the Law of Love drawn forth from the Ascended Master's Octave with the Violet Consuming Flame of Forgiveness flaring up through his four lower bodies with the magnification of the light and power of a trillion suns—breaking apart, melting, annihilating, and consuming all cause, effect, and memory of every destructive creation from every lifetime—past, present, and future—self-sustained, self-sustained, self-sustained, until such time as every discordant quality and entity mis-creation has been dissolved and consumed therefrom and replaced by the cosmic light of the Cosmic Christ and he has ascended into mastership."

She envisioned him standing with feet upon the earth and the great and powerful tongues of violet flames blasting from the earth, up through his feet and around and through his physical, emotional, mental, and etheric bodies; engulfing him in a circle of flame as wide as his arms could stretch and the full height of his body twice over.

"I AM the electronic blue belt of protection which surrounds this great field of light, holding all within in complete protection, on all levels of his being, until such time as it is no longer required."

She raised her arms yet again, envisioning and surrounding the entire circle of light with yet another field of blue light.

Having prayed so fervently, she moved closer to the bed and held her hands over his back at the heart chakra. There she consciously directed light from her I AM Presence into his heart. She then stepped back and began again:

"With all my being, I thank you God, that I AM here and I AM there. I extend my deepest love and gratitude to the I AM PRESENCE within both of us, our higher mental bodies, our guides, our angels, the Ascended Masters, the unlimited legions of the Violet Consuming Flame, the Great White Brotherhood, the Great Divine Director, Beloved Victory, the Angelic Kingdom, the Archangels, the Great Cosmic Beings, the Elohim, the Kumaras, and the God of the Great Central Sun, which I AM individualized. I thank you for love and light and for holding thy sustained vibration within all mankind eternally and victoriously."

❧

Although Crow feigned sleep, he craned to hear every word she whispered. He visualized that which she commanded and could physically feel the energy she directed in and around his body. The area around his heart filled with a powerful energy, an electrical charge, which seemed to be building momentum, expanding and expanding until it exploded and radiated through and beyond his physical body, out into the room. Thinking back to the first day he met her, he remembered how this same feeling had overtaken his body in a paralyzed spasm of bliss. A *heart orgasm,* he thought, remembering Grace's explanation.

Nikki noticed he'd begun to physically tremble. Thinking him asleep, she lifted the down comforter from the other side of the bed and gently draped it over him.

Stepping through her dressing room to the bathroom, she quietly closed the door, took a long shower, and prepared for bed.

Crow lay perfectly still, head spinning, overwhelmed by the sensation of profound peace that seemed to pulse through every nerve and cell of his body and beyond. He yearned to know more. Part of him, however, feared this may only be wishful thinking on his part and he didn't want to be drawn into yet another hugely disappointing experience. His inner dialogue shouted, *Get out while you can!* Nonetheless, he lay there pretending to sleep because he didn't want to move or do anything that would disturb the feeling that surrounded him.

Nikki quietly stepped around the bed, listening for his heavy breathing. She leaned over and kissed the top of his head so lightly he hardly felt it. Mouthing the words, "Sweet dreams, my dearest, dearest love," she turned off the light.

Silently, Nikki crossed the hall to Sam's bedroom and climbed between the sheets where Crow had slept the night before. His scent remained on the pillow and she buried her face into it as if she could, by osmosis, bring that part of him inside of her.

Chapter 3

As usual, Nikki rose early. She silently opened her bedroom door to find Dylan in the same position as the night before. After collecting her riding clothes, she backed out of the room and closed the door with timorous care.

She dressed, brushed and braided her hair, topped it with a baseball cap and headed down to the pasture to find Pegasus. When she gave the horse free reign to lead the adventure, he took her by the stream where her eyes and mind wandered through the beauty and wonder of the place she loved so well. Nikki thrilled at the idea of sharing it with the man, who by any number of miraculous coincidences, now slept on her bed.

"Pegasus," she said reflectively, "you seem to recognize my guest. Tell me what you think I should do." She leaned forward and rested her upper body on his great neck, wrapping her arms around it. The horse paused beneath a tree where its shade hung over them like a great cloche of comfort. She stroked his flesh and sighed heavily. So many mixed emotions were vying for her attention, and yet, she recognized that in some way the experience was taking her somewhere she needed to go. *Maybe this isn't just about Crow. Maybe this is about me, too,* she thought.

Returning to the barn, she brushed and grained her friend, then allowed him to follow her back to his pasture gate. As she shut it, Pegasus turned to look at her, bringing his head close to nuzzle her face. "Thank you dear one," she whispered. "How I love you."

As Crow still slept, her morning's toilette took place in her son's bathroom, sans make-up, curlers, or hairspray.

Nikki brewed a cup of her special coffee—the one with the bitter Mexican chocolate—symbolically reminding herself about life. She took it to the table outside her bathroom by the hot tub, but arrived there by walking from the front door rather than through her bedroom. She had no desire to wake Dylan or disturb his dreams.

The morning sun danced on her skin as Nikki allowed its light to fill her. She never thought of the sun's rays as damaging, never wore sunscreen. She accepted it as light from God. By raising her own frequencies through constructive thoughts and feelings, she sent this light, qualified by love through her own heart, out into the world. It had become a habit throughout the years. To her, light, in any form, *was* God.

To his chagrin, Dylan awoke to find himself still upon her bed with the door to the bedroom closed. He wondered if she had slept next to him.

Entering the bathroom, he gazed into the mirror. "Hey mate. Where do ye think the road will take ye on this fine morning?" He smiled and his reflection smiled back. Having slept so deeply, so peacefully, his entire body felt enlivened, healthy and anxious to move. Stretching for his toes, he realized he had full range of motion for the first time in years, with no hint of pain or strain. He lifted his pant leg to inspect his ankle, yet no sign of injury, redness, or tenderness remained.

His clothes were rumpled and his hair had been redefined as if a party of wild fairies had danced in it all night long.

He decided to freshen up in her shower. There were no curtains or sliding doors: just a large, sunken, open, tiled space with a corner seat. Slipping out of his clothes, he walked down the four steps to the cold tile floor and quickly put his feet on the soft mat positioned just beneath the showerhead. Tepid water poured over his head and body for a long time as he enjoyed its silky sensuality. Along with the usual array of shower toiletries, seashells lined a tiled ledge. He wondered if she loved the sea as much as he.

While drying off he inspected the room more closely. Live ivy, growing from large pots, had climbed up the walls and onto the ceiling. A soft yellow tile covered the lower two-thirds of the walls, with the upper walls finished in a mottled verde colored stucco. Several oil paintings hung throughout the room; two of charming cottages with colorful gardens and the other, a fabulous landscape of a streambed in winter. Above an upholstered bench hung a small poster with a quote attributed to Benjamin Franklin: *He, who is good for making excuses, is seldom good for anything else.* A frosted glass door to the right of the double sinks led to the hot tub terrace.

Crow dressed in his rumpled clothes and headed for the kitchen through the very quiet house. Stepping into the great room, he could see Nikki through the window with her head tilted back and eyes closed. A smile of contentment brightened her face. Dylan stood motionless, wishing he were inside of her, feeling, experiencing whatever it was that induced her state of obvious bliss. Her countenance exuded a tangible radiance as if a mysterious exchange were taking place between her soul and the universe.

His nose led him to the coffee where he found a cup, filled it up, and walked around to join her. "Good day, mi lady. 'Tis a beautiful morn', isn't it?"

She glanced at her watch. "Good morning. I hope you slept well."

"Can't remember!" he joked.

As she perceived his jest, her lips widened to a big smile.

"May I join ye?"

"Please," she said, motioning to a chair. "And, how's my patient this morning?"

"Ah, grand, just grand." He lit a cigarette and blew the smoke away from her. "Mi leg doesn't hurt at all this morning, doc. Ye made a fine job of it! Ta."

"We do our best to please," she insisted in a Julia Child voice.

"What's the agenda today, madam tour guide…or is it madam boss today?"

"Well—after we irrigate a bit on the lower ranch I thought I'd take you over the Kolob Mountain to Cedar City. It's quite a rise in elevation, however. Have any problems with high altitude?"

"Nay."

"The leaves have turned up there and this is my favorite time of year to make the drive. Kind of excited to have your company. Beautiful things should always be shared.

"Want a bite before we get to it?" she asked, standing to stretch. Wearing a white V-neck sweater over a pair of black, cotton slacks seemed somewhat incongruous with her bare feet on the cool morning. She answered his accusing smile when he looked at her feet. "Sometimes you've just got to touch the earth—you know, just skin to Mother Nature." With a sweet, innocent smile, she led him toward the front of the house.

"I'm sorry I fell asleep on ye'r bed last night," he lied, for it had been the best night's sleep he'd had in years.

"You are, for certain, the only guest I've ever had who's done so, Mr. Crow," she stated shyly.

"So, where did ye sleep?" Subconsciously he hoped she would say next to him.

"I slept in Sam's room on *your* dirty sheets!"

Once in the kitchen, he pulled some bread out of a bag, tossed it in the toaster and opened the fridge looking for butter and jam. She made orange juice and sliced an apple for them to share.

They sat informally at the counter chatting about animals.

Crow's favorite *person* in the animal kingdom was his Great Dane, whom he missed dearly. His brother, Mic, had been entrusted to provide loving care of him at the ranch in Cork. "I find animals nonjudgmental and always willing to love unconditionally. It's a real pleasure to be with them, isn't it?"

"As you've seen, they're a *very* big part of my life, Little Crow. They have been some of my greatest teachers."

He felt so comfortable in her presence, as if he had known her for eternity. They moved easily around each other while cleaning the kitchen, like an old experienced couple. Completely at ease in her home and among her things, he felt bold enough to open drawers and doors without permission. Silently, he wondered if this related to the atmosphere or just her.

"I'm going to run out and pull a few weeds in my gardens and my mind while you change clothes. OK?"

"Ye'r mind?" he asked, raising one of his thick eyebrows.

"Yeah…I'm probably the only person in the world who *enjoys* weeding the garden. It reminds me to pluck by the roots, all the thoughts and feelings I don't want in my head and heart. Funny little tradition, but it works for me." Always indulgent and gentle when trying to educate someone, she used examples to teach whenever possible. When an example wouldn't work, she just invented a metaphor.

He drove her white Tundra to the cottage where he turned off the lights that had been left on the night before. After he changed clothing and brushed his teeth he headed back up to her home.

Nikki wore a sizable, heavy pack and though he offered to carry it, she politely refused his assistance. They walked around the north end of the pond and up a small footpath leading to her manager's home, which had been built on the mesa just above hers. In front of the home sat two well-used quadrunners.

"You know how to drive one of these?" she asked, pointing to the vehicles.

"Sure."

"Take your pick, then, and let's get going!"

He took the Polaris, she the Kawasaki, and they drove down the manager's driveway, connecting into the main road just before the pond. Nikki led the way to the closed entry gate and steered close to the keypad, leaned over, typed in her number, and the gate swung out. Passing through, she turned back to Dylan with instructions. "Hit the number twelve-twelve, then drive through quickly before the gate closes again. I don't like to leave it open when I'm not there."

Relief flooded through him when she freely offered the code. Another faux pas with the gate would surely reveal his experience with Grace and he did not feel ready to share the shaman's revelations with his hostess and trusted that Grace would never disclose their private conversations to anyone.

Distracted by the extraordinary scenery as they drove down the Byway, he realized she had turned right on a dirt road. He had to pull the brake hard to make the turn with her. Nikki led the way down a hill into an area where an old barn appeared ready to collapse. A few outbuildings and stalls remained, but the roofs were dilapidated and it looked as if no one had maintained anything for thirty or so years.

She gestured to the structures. "We never decided what to do with this lower ranch, except to graze the cattle here. Just couldn't get my husband to pull these pieces of junk down. He used to have the men stack hay and wood under the shelter of the old things."

At the end of a narrow dirt road she stopped and turned off her engine. Crow did likewise and followed her on foot. Ahead of them frantically barking dogs signaled their approach and he wondered if a wild pack roamed free on her ranch.

"Hello!" she shouted. "Hello, Andy? Are you home?" Turning a corner, they were accosted by three furiously yapping dogs tied in front of makeshift shelters. Precariously perched on columns of cinder block sat a small, pathetic trailer house looking to fall into pieces with the next stiff breeze. Behind it, another dozen or so canines were tethered next to small, rustic, wooden structures.

A somewhat ragged, long-bearded man opened the door to the trailer. "Nik, is that you?" he hollered.

"It is, Andy. Could you reel in the troops?"

At his command every single dog sat and silenced its voice as if a well-trained platoon obeyed a tough drill sergeant who had earned their respect. Andy eyed Dylan up and down before turning his attention to Nikki, offering her a big smile with a mouthful of discolored and rotting teeth. His hands, face, and clothing were covered in a layer of dirt that looked as if he wore it as a second skin. The stench that permeated the very air around him smelled as if he'd been sleeping with the dogs for a year. But his bright, clear, blue eyes, which spoke of wisdom, contradicted his primitive appearance.

"I thought the *kids* would like a little treat today," she said, removing her heavy backpack. She unzipped it and offered twenty some odd pounds of frozen beef to him. "I've been cleaning out the freezers and I still have quite a bit of that last cow we slaughtered," she fibbed. "I know you've no place to store the meat, so I thought I'd bring some down a bit at a time." Nikki knew that Andy would share this meat with his "children," his sixteen dogs he considered his only family. She also knew, however, that it would be the first solid meal he would have eaten in a week or so. Nikki never *butchered* any of her cows, but had purchased the meat from a grocery store for the malnourished, homeless man.

Digging deeper into her bag, she offered him six large squash. "I just can't eat all that's in my garden, Andy. Can you take these off my hands too?" His dirty hands reached for her offering with trembling gratitude as he glanced at Dylan with eyes of suspicion, then back to Nikki in question.

"My apologies, Andy. This is my guest, Dylan, who's come to help me irrigate this morning."

Dylan extended his hand to shake Andy's, wishing he'd brought some gloves.

"Pleasure to make your acquaintance, Dylan," Andy said in a gentlemanly tone. Immediately he turned his shy attention back to the woman with whom he felt comfortable. "I'll be glad to do it for you Nik, if you'll just tell me which ones need to be done. By the way, you had some intruders last night about two in the morning. Just a couple of kids who wanted to get high and smooch, but I shooed them away."

"I'm so grateful to have you here, Andy. It's like having my own guardian angel of the lower ranch," she said sincerely. "Well, we've got a lot to do, so we'd better head out." She turned to the *kids,* blew them a kiss, and expressed her hope that they dine well. As they mounted the quadrunners, she waved good-bye and turned back toward the pastures.

The lower ranch, though perhaps a little more wild, appeared every bit as beautiful as the upper. Green pastures stretched for acres and acres, surrounded by the old, white, wooden fences. They drove toward the stream until they arrived at a locked gate. She grabbed a shovel that leaned against the fence and walked to a ditch where an orange plastic dam covered in dirt directed the water flow to the east. After shoveling out the dirt, Nikki used her gloved hand to remove the dam, allowing the water to flow to the west. She then crossed to a parallel ditch to lay the plastic and heave dirt upon it to direct the new course.

"May I haul that spade for ye?" he asked as they walked.

She tossed it to him with a satisfied smile on her lips. "Thanks."

"Who is that fella?" Dylan didn't want to appear nosy, but the situation seemed out of place with her life and his curiosity demanded an answer.

"He's a homeless soul who used to live in a cave upstream a bit. Had so many dogs that no one would let him live in any kind of development. Those dogs are his family. About six years ago he started getting occasional jobs in town and I'd see him walking, wet to his hips, down the road. He looked pretty scary, but one day I got the courage to stop and offer him a ride. It took a week to air his unique scent from my car! Anyway—he's a Vietnam vet who's been diagnosed as a paranoid schizophrenic and he's been receiving a small stipend from the government ever since the war. I think it's just enough to barely keep both himself and his dogs fed, however.

"When I asked him why he lived across the stream, he told me he just moved from spot to spot on BLM land so they wouldn't kick him off. There's a law that says a person can't camp for more than two weeks in one spot. I pointed out a section of land on this side of the stream that's on the border of the ranch and BLM land. It's kind of hidden and I don't think those guys know it's actually on their property because we've been taking our water from that point for eons. To make a long story short, he moved his campsite the next week and has been there ever since." She laughed softly, smiling back toward Andy's area. "I'm not certain, but I think he rearranged the survey markers so it appears he's on our land.

"He carries a gun around and scares off trespassers, unwanted fishermen, and swimmers down here, and I really *am* grateful to have

him. I've never paid him and he's never asked for pay. He's a very
proud and intelligent man. Andy won't accept any personal responsibility for his physical or psychological conditions, however, and
works only when all other options have been closed to him. He
spends a lot of energy blaming the government for his situation.

"I just like to take an occasional offering down to him. That's
all."

"Aren't ye ever worried he may bring that gun up and do ye
harm...*especially* if he's a *paranoid schizophrenic?*" Dylan asked
with concerned sincerity.

"No, I don't! I won't allow such thoughts into my consciousness, Dylan. Andy may be going through some important life lessons about his ability to create right now. I'm of the opinion that
our circumstances reveal the truth about the way we *believe* and
think. Sometimes the picture's so obvious, it's almost as if the universe hands you the lesson on a silver platter! Anyway, 'one never
knows when one is entertaining an angel, unawares.'" She winked
conspiratorially.

Dylan noticed she had spoken her assessment without criticism of the man's life. His lifestyle merely reflected his choices.
Nikki didn't try to change him, proselytize, or interfere with the
consequences of his choice of thoughts and feelings, which played
out in the meagerness of his existence. Nonetheless, she fed the
hungry and gave his spirit some joy when she could.

Crow looked at her beauty with new eyes, a beauty born of
goodness he suddenly recognized as more pronounced than any of
the glamorous women he had dated.

They drove to two more areas and repeated the procedure,
only this time he helped. She loved to have people around her
who, seeing that something needed to be done, did it. It

embarassed her to ask for assistance when help would obviously be appreciated. Leaning the shovel against the fence where they finished, she signaled him to follow her.

A lock secured an old metal gate, so they climbed over and headed for the stream. The red sand beach extended twenty or so feet on either side, and with bare feet and rolled up pants, they enjoyed its sensual softness between their toes before wading in the cold water. Like playful children, they splashed at one another. Nikki showed him the small trout hiding in the deep spots and the toads camouflaged by the stones. A water snake slithered within inches of Dylan's leg, startling him. He literally flew through the air as he leapt from the stream while Nikki squealed with laughter, highly entertained by his cowardice.

She pointed out the beautiful stones carried downstream from the mesas and mountains above. "I collected all the rocks for my garden walls from this streambed."

"Ye mean to tell me *ye* personally collected the stones and built all those walls ye'rself?" he asked in amazement.

"Well—I, and two brawny teenage boys. Took us a whole summer to do it, but I enjoyed every minute. My back had a few rough nights, though!"

He had seen his mother work alongside his father during his childhood. She was tough, in a soft sort of way, and Nikki reminded him of her. Crow, also, wanted to be with someone who would roll up her sleeves and work with him. Now, at age thirty-nine, he wondered if he'd ever settle down or have a family.

They dried their feet, put their shoes back on, and headed toward the quadrunners.

When they arrived back at her home she pointed toward the truck and gave him instructions. "Go back to your place and put on some walking shoes and a long sleeved shirt. Bring a warm

jacket and meet me back at my place in about twenty minutes or
so. OK? By the way, bring one of those bottles of red wine, will
you?"

He acknowledged her commands while starting the Tundra
and drove away.

☯

Rushing like a cartoon version of a tornado, she packed a
hamper for a picnic lunch, which included a beautiful, small lace
tablecloth, elegant china, crystal wine glasses, and silverware. She
pulled a vegetarian loaf from the freezer, quickly put together a
tossed salad, some sourdough bread, a block of cheese and fruit for
desert, and a large bottle of chilled Perrier. The supplies included
her largest picnic blanket, a portable CD player and CDs, including one she bought after they first met—The Rollovers, *By the Bye*.
She wanted to surprise him by letting him see she had ordered his
Irish CD, an item unavailable in U.S. music stores. He would
know she'd gone to great effort to obtain it. The objects were carefully loaded in the back section of her gold Lexus SUV. As soon as
he arrived, she stowed the wine with the other things.

Nikki took the driver's seat, though he protested with a raised
eyebrow, as he'd already established his desire to be in the *control*
position the day before. "The sights are so outstanding, I don't
want you to miss them for having to watch the ruts in the roads,"
she explained while opening the sunroof to let the gentle rays ride
with them.

They drove past Hop Valley, a place dotted with mounds of
layered red sandstone which resembled giant beehives. The vistas
of Zion were breathtaking as they traveled up the winding road
which took them past the high desert into a mountainous range
filled with massive pines and aspens. The aspen's leaves had turned
a brilliant yellow and glowed like Christmas lights as the sun

shone through them.

Once around the periphery of the Kolob Reservoir, they connected to a dirt road that lured them further up the mountain. Angled log fencing, restraining sheep and llamas within their pasture borders, stretched endlessly. When Nik spied a lovely area shaded by a thick grove of aspen, she declared, "This is a good place!" Crow helped her unload the heavy hamper. They found a flat spot where the sun danced slightly through the leaves and spread the large blanket. On top of this, she draped the linen and placed the fancy tableware, then served a delicious feast. He uncorked the wine and poured it in both the delicate glasses.

A CD filled with romantic soul melodies played in the background. Nikki loved music of all varieties, but realized she had unconsciously chosen a type that sounded very suggestive. The wine, which she rarely drank, made her feel a little too comfortable, and she began looking at him longingly. To check herself, she decided to change the disc.

"Would you dance with me to one of my favorite tunes?" she asked politely, with a deep, gallant bow.

Her request seemed a little odd, but he was willing for "impromptu" to be the guideword for his time with her. While he rose, she put on his CD, searching through the tracks for a Celtic romper called "Dancin' in Heaven." She clapped her hands and danced about with wild abandon like a teenager at a high school stomp. Recognizing his work, he sang along with his own voice blaring from the speakers. They looked like untamed children cavorting with no inhibition whatsoever. Laughing, smiling, and spinning each other around, they played through the entire tune. His schoolboy's laughter was contagious, as they fell in a tangled heap when the arrangement met its finale.

A sad, slow song followed as he held her quietly in his arms.

"I didn't know I had one of mi music fans leading the tour today! I love music. If I could have made it in that world, I would have, most likely, never begun acting."

"You have a lot of creative energy, Little Crow," she said, wriggling out of his arms and kissing him on the cheek like a mother.

She changed the CD back to the soul music, tidied up the dishes, and then lay upon her back on the blanket to watch the wispy clouds float in the sky.

While taking a smoke a little distance away and drinking in the beauty of the landscape, he thought about how nice it felt to hold her in his arms.

When she settled he decided to lie down too and placed his body juxtaposed with his head upon her stomach as if it looked like a comfortable place to rest. She didn't resist his uninvited familiarity. They chatted while she pulled some pine needles from his thick hair. Her hand rested on his head and stroked it while he spoke of his home in Ireland.

He described it like an excellent storyteller with all the details that encourage a mind to develop a clear and glorious picture. Nikki found herself longing to see this place he depicted as nestled between the foothills of Mount Gabriel and Schull Harbor in West Cork. His ranch of five hundred twenty acres spread to the sea where he could embrace both land and water. The sea held a special place in his heart and he took advantage of every opportunity to be upon it, whether sailing, boating, or fishing.

Crow's deep, melodious voice induced a trance as Nikki closed her eyes and took a mental journey to his homeland while falling into a light sleep.

Pulling himself into a natal position with his ear to her stomach, he listened to her heartbeat. With his arm stretched across her abdomen, he began to caress her body. The sensual music in the background and the feelings expanding in his groin led his hand to wander up and down from her hip to her breast. He pulled himself on top of her and began to kiss her face gently.

Now fully awakened and fully aroused, she complied as they kissed and rhythmically undulated their bodies together. Completely lost in his embrace, she could no longer tell where she ended and he began. With heart, mind, and body all increasing their vibrations to a frantic speed, she found her entire being shaking with an orgasm of the soul.

He felt it too---like nothing he'd ever felt before, and found he had loosed his seed within his clothing. He didn't care.

Nor did she.

Their embrace felt like the fierce grip of those holding onto something they fear losing. Neither said a word, just listening to the heavy breathing of the other and relishing the moment until the electricity in their bodies began to ebb.

All her caution had been thrown to the wind and though he had not entered her, she had experienced the most profound exchange of her lifetime. Even though she had given him ready access to her heart, fear and guilt began welling up from her stomach and making its way to her throat, damming up and preventing words. Tears surfaced and rolled down the sides of her face, spilling into her long hair.

The inconsistency of great souls will ultimately show. Each one journeying the pathway toward enlightenment must face his own dragons and either behead them or make peace with them. He had successfully demolished her interior defenses.

Crow felt the moisture on his skin and lifted his head up, looking into her deep green eyes. *Could that extraordinary moment have been unpleasant for her when it elevated me to heights I never knew existed?* he wondered. Then she pulled him to her and kissed him hard. *No,* he thought, *she felt it too. Those are not sad tears.*

They fell asleep in each other's arms. Upon waking, Nikki noticed how far the sun had moved as it shined directly in her face. "We better get going so we don't have to drive this dirt road in the dark," she said softly.

Afraid to break the connection, he did so unwillingly.

Crow had, during his lifetime, experienced sexual pleasures with a fair number of partners; some whose faces or names he could no longer remember. He had, during his lifetime, experienced what he had perceived as *love.* These were his only points of reference with which to view what had been happening with Nikki.

He'd only known her a few days. In spite of that, she seemed like a longtime beloved companion.

The definition of the word, *love,* was somehow transmuting into something new and unfamiliar. He felt something far beyond *love* as he had defined it previously, with his feelings including more than affection and passionate sexual desire, or the need to possess, provide for, or protect. Rather, he longed to have her *inside* of him, somehow. It seemed as though he'd been shipped off to a foreign planet and all the rules of physics had changed; new rules he had not yet learned.

They folded the blanket and packed up the car, each very quietly trying to bring some sense to what had happened during the afternoon. Nikki took the driver's seat once again, traversing the dirt road through another twenty miles of stunning sunset vistas until they reached the opposite side of the mountain.

"I know this sounds crazy after that big lunch we had, but I'm suddenly starved!" he said, as his stomach agreed loudly.

"Me too! Weird, huh? I know a great little steak house where you can beef up and I can get a potato. They even serve alcohol!"

❦

As they parked at Milt's Stage Stop, sixties music from a live band beckoned them. Eating would provide a superb distraction from the emotional turmoil that churned within each of their hearts. Nikki had suggested a steak for Dylan for she knew he needed grounding. She, however, ordered only a baked potato and they both sipped a glass of Merlot.

Though he wore no ugly clothes, no silly baseball cap, and no sunglasses, no one seemed to recognize him. Having no knowledge of the force field she consciously held around them, he thought perhaps the beard kept him anonymous,

As the band began to play, "Hello Stranger," Nikki stood and held out her hand, inviting Dylan to the dance floor where she held him close and sang the words in his ear:

"Hello, stranger…

It seems so good to see you back again

How long has it been?…"

While their bodies swayed slowly, intimately, she wished the dance would never end.

They took their wine glasses to a seating area, sinking into the deep couch in front of the hot blaze in the old fieldstone fireplace. She had drunk more wine that day than in the whole previous year and it produced a relaxed drowsy feeling.

Crow felt perfectly comfortable in their silence—not forcing idle conversation.

By the time they paid their bill and departed, the clock read nine-fifteen and she suggested they go home by circling through Cedar City to the freeway. It would take an hour, but she thought it safer than returning on the uneven dirt road of the mountain in the dark. This time, he drove. She had fallen asleep just after the turn from LaVerkin that headed toward Zion, but he knew his way from the junction.

"We're home, Nik," he said, softly squeezing her shoulder. He longed to ask her if he could stay the night in her home again, preferably in her bed, but as a gentleman, he decided he'd let her take the lead.

"Thanks for a great day, Dylan. I think I'll remember that one for eternity," she said, looking down instead of into his eyes. Letting herself out, she walked to the truck and opened the door for him.

I guess she missed her cue or somethin', he thought. He could sense she desired him, but saw her struggling with something else as well. *Perhaps it's for the best to give her some space.*

He thanked her, kissed her on the forehead, and asked what time to show up for work the next morning.

Although planning on riding at sunrise, Nikki extended no invitation to her guest. "My house at eight, boy," she demanded in an imperious tone. "We've got lawns to mow!"

"Oh, yippee! Can't wait!" Crow moaned while reluctantly climbing into the truck. He shut the door and drove the quarter mile to his cottage.

The bed felt comfortable, but empty. He reached over and pulled one of the large pillows to him and held it tight, dreaming of the afternoon. Just reminiscing made his body tingle all over as he experienced a mini version of the original incident.

Chapter 4

Nikki convinced herself that keeping occupied would avert the temptation to take him to her again. She assigned him the riding mower while she used the weed whacker and they started trimming at her house. An hour later, they moved to her manager's yard. After that, they headed for the rental cottages, followed by her mother's home. The sun had been wickedly hot, causing them to sweat profusely, and by one o'clock they were thirsty and tired, but done for the day.

"Wanna meet my mother?" she asked, wringing the water from her bandana.

"Sure, why not?"

Without knocking, they opened the door to the lovely log home, pulled off their grass-stained shoes, and wandered into the kitchen.

"Ma!" Nikki yelled.

"In here, honey," answered a gentle voice from the next room. Peg sat in her sewing room, hunched over a freestanding, lighted magnifying glass, doing needlework.

"Ma, I'd like you to meet a friend of mine," Nikki said, leading him into the room. "This is Dylan. Dylan, this is my mother, Peg."

"Pleasure to meet ye, ma'am," he said, extending his hand. He noticed Nikki had not offered his last name. Whether done for the purpose of safeguarding his privacy, he could not tell, for her mother's last name had not been offered either. Nik opened the refrigerator and brought out some iced tea. Only the lift of her right eyebrow asked if he'd like some refreshment. He smiled at her silent communication and nodded his grateful assent.

"I've heard the mowers going all morning! I'll bet you'll be glad when Don gets back, eh?" Peg shook her head, wishing she still possessed the limitless energy of youth. "This daughter of mine's a real worker!" Standing to stretch her legs, she took Dylan's arm and led him to a glass door that opened from her sewing room to a small porch. Gesturing outside to a small house (a petite duplicate of her own with raised, rock flower gardens on either side,) she commented, "See that little equipment cottage? Nikki built that a couple of years ago with her own two hands. Had never built anything in her life, but read all kinds of books so she could do it. She poured foundation, built the walls, roofed and tiled it, applied the log siding, did the rock work, and everything. The ornamental painting which hangs on it is mine, however," she said proudly.

"I'm blessed with work, Ma. It's no hardship," Nikki chirped in. "Besides, you worked right along side me doing the whole thing, Mum. So, who's the hard worker, eh?"

'I'm blessed with work'...what a wonderful attitude, he thought. He often felt like that because he *loved* his occupation.

They spoke of hummingbirds, flowers, and the natural beauty of the ranch. Unlike most first meetings, the conversation lacked any personal questions regarding him or even the reason for his visit. Crow observed, however, Peg's alertness to her daughter's eyes every time Nik looked *at* him.

"You need anything before we go, Ma?"

"No, dear, except, perhaps, to have you mail my bills when you go to the post office tomorrow." Nik took them, kissed her mother on the cheek, and headed to the entry to put her shoes back on.

"Thanks for the cool drink. Lovely to make ye'r acquaintance, Peg." Taken aback when Peg winked at him, he thought, *Maybe that's something she does to everyone. Or, maybe she's flirting with me...a seventy-eight year old flirt!* He chuckled to himself while he laced his shoes.

As they prepared lunch together, Crow mentioned he'd like to take a shower. "Do we have plans for this afternoon or evening?"

"Do you expect me to plan every minute of your day?"

He grinned like a spoiled child while rubbing the dirt off his face. "Well, ye did agree to show me 'round y' know—not just work me to death!"

"Actually, I thought it would be fun to head up to Zion to see a fabulous bit of eye candy called *Treasure of the Gods*. It's playing on one of those seven-story screens. An old neighbor of mine produced it and I think his work is excellent."

He left for his cottage with an agreement to return an hour later. Meanwhile, Nikki prepared vegetarian lasagna for their supper upon their return.

After showering, she dressed in white pants with a periwinkle knit top that highlighted the color that framed the irises of her eyes. Nikki slipped her crystal necklace over her head, tucking it inside her shirt rather than wearing it on the outside. "Listen God," she said, looking toward the ceiling, "I'm handing this one over to you, because my lower nature's very strong right now. Go before me with thy perfect energy and see to it that all is harmony and right action!"

They drove twenty miles to Springdale, the city adjoining the commercial entrance to Zion, where they parked before a building that contained the theater. Nikki knew exactly where to sit in the stadium seating for the most profound impact. The story included amazing photography of Zion, Kolob, Cedar Breaks, and Bryce Canyon. In fact, it included the very spot where they had filmed the the scene *the dying of Knowing Crow*. With the size of the screen and the closeness of the seats, one felt as if he personally soared in and out of the magical spaces like a bird.

"Ta, Nik. That really *was* worth seeing! Kind of frees the soul when ye become part of the scenery, doesn't it?" Crow wrapped his arm around her tiny waist to usher her out of the theater.

As they wandered through the tourist shops, Nikki admired an intricate silver bracelet crafted by a local Indian. When she wandered out of sight into the adjoining store, he purchased it.

Driving back to the ranch, she turned in her seat and enthusiastically informed him, "I've got a special treat for you tonight! How would you like to remain after supper and watch old, black and white Ronald Coleman movies?"

Though familiar with the old star, he had never seen either of the movies she mentioned: *Random Harvest* and *Lost Horizon*. Dylan had a weak recollection of the musical version of *Lost Horizon* that bombed in the late seventies, but he didn't care. If it pleased her to see them, he would gladly join her.

His contribution to dinner included chopping vegetables for a tossed salad while she toasted some sourdough bread topped with fresh garlic and butter. As the lasagna came from the oven the aroma filled the air with a tantalizing promise of a delicious meal.

Nikki had set a formal table rather than serving at the kitchen counter. To his amusement, she produced a funny looking bottle of wine, uncorked it with her teeth, and poured it in both of their glasses.

"What's this?" he said. "Ye told me ye didn't have any wine up here!"

"It's not exactly wine, but I think you'll enjoy it."

The dark purple liquid had a sweet smell to it and an effervescence, almost like champagne. She had charged it with life force to enliven and clear his senses instead of dulling them.

"Oy…it's fantastic!" he announced with his first sip. "What is it?"

"I make it myself from the wild Himalayan berries on the ranch."

"Ye ought to sell this stuff!"

Had he opened another bottle the effect would have been quite different.

Inclining his head toward the portrait of the old cowboy behind him, he asked, "Is this someone ye know personally?"

"That's my late husband. A delightful French friend, who also happens to be a wonderful artist, painted it. Though the portrait didn't thrill Scott, I adored it because Pierre had captured Scott's quirky mischievous smile. Even though *he* wouldn't purchase it, *I* did, and put it here so he'd have the opportunity to see the reflection of his *unique* character on a daily basis! Pierre also painted the picture of the magnificent Indian woman that hangs in Sam's bedroom."

Dylan wondered silently if Scott watched them now.

She took his plate and served his supper. Loaded with pecans, five kinds of cheeses, and a large array of vegetables swimming in a fabulous beefy tomato sauce, the flavor of the lasagna exploded in his mouth, exciting his taste buds. The pecans added a meaty texture. Crow smiled proudly when Nikki complimented his salad, even though she had made the dressing.

After cleaning up the dishes, they popped some kettle corn in preparation for their movie. Nikki inserted the old VHS tape of *Lost Horizon* into the player and they established themselves comfortably on the couch. Suddenly, a high pitched noise blasted from the equipment as it attempted to *eat* the celluloid, but Dylan's swift action saved the treasure.

"Consider ye'rself lucky, young lady. Guess we'll have to watch it in one of the bedrooms. We could snuggle on Sam's lit'l bed, if ye'd like?" he said suggestively.

Nikki recommended her room, stating they could sit on the couch or stack the pillows behind them on the larger bed.

Disappointed that she'd not responded to his invitation of intimacy, he soldiered on toward her room, carrying the large bowl of kettle corn.

Even though full, he couldn't stop sampling the sweet and salty treat which she purposely placed between them on the bed to create distance.

In the film, Coleman, a British Ambassador to China, and his brother board an airplane after evacuating the last of the Crown's subjects from a violent Chinese uprising. The flight, however, is diverted as they are mysteriously abducted and taken to a remarkable and secret place high in the Himalayas, called Shangri-la. The villagers show no signs of death, disease, or aging. Stored within a luxurious temple they find works of great art, music, literature, science, and ancient and modern philosophical writings collected from all over the world.

Coleman falls in love with a beautiful, highly intelligent young woman and experiences love in its purest form.

While tutoring Coleman, the High Lama, the wise old Belgian monk who created Shangri-la, informs him that he's actually hundreds of years old, but wishes to move on to the next dimension. Finally the monk reveals that he purposely *brought* Coleman there because both his political and philosophical views, and work as a world-renowned diplomat and philanthropist, prove him worthy to become the next guardian of Shangri-la.

Gold, precious gems, and other beautiful treasures of the earth are evidenced throughout the village. Initially, some of Coleman's abducted companions greedily plan to steal the precious valuables. As time passes, however, they become engaged in constructively participating in life in the magical valley: enjoying the roles they play to such a degree that they determine never to leave.

Coleman's brother, on the other hand, suspects foul play—

positive they're being held captive against their will. He falls in love with a young girl and convinces her to leave with him. Planning their escape, they use the nefarious tools of doubt and fear to persuade Coleman to go with them on the perilous adventure through the impassable snowy mountains. Within days of leaving Shangri-la, the girl ages rapidly and dies an old woman. Unhinged by her horrible death, Coleman's brother goes mad and jumps off a cliff. With the truth of Shangri-la revealed, Coleman spends the next several years trying to find his way back to both the magical kingdom and his true love.

Surprisingly, Crow enjoyed the story of a hidden place where the secrets of life are held and maintained by guardians until the rest of the world has evolved enough to share them responsibly. The idea of eternal youth and beauty appealed to him.

As Crow imitated Coleman's unique voice, Nikki listened with awe. "You're quite the parrot aren't you?"

He smiled proudly, for he had acquired the remarkable ability to mimic just about any voice he'd ever heard.

After popping the last kernel of corn in his mouth, Dylan rose from the bed and went to her bathroom to relieve himself, not bothering to shut the door.

It amused her to think he felt familiar enough to do so.

"May I get some more of ye'r homemade wine?" he asked, returning to the bedroom. He picked up the bowl and took it to the kitchen while she prepared the next movie: another Coleman plus Greer Garson; Nikki's favorite actress of the forties. She lit the fire so the room would feel cozy.

Crow returned with two glasses filled to the brim and handed one to her. The clock read nine when they plugged in the tape and half way through the movie, his head began to nod as he slumped until his head met her shoulder. Quietly, she lay watching the

movie while he slept. When it ended, her attempt to wake him
with gentle shaking failed. Even her voice could not spark a single
synapse in his brain. He was OUT!

While tenderly stroking his beautiful locks, she whispered,
"You missed the best part! Coleman awakens from his amnesia,
remembering his previous life with Greer and they are joyfully
reunited. I picked these two movies especially for us tonight, Little
Crow, in hopes you would wake from *your* amnesia. Heart of my
heart, soul of my soul, flame of my flame, I love you with a love
so Divine, it puts all human love to shame," she whispered, kissing the top of his head.

She carefully pulled her shoulder free, replacing it with a stack
of pillows before stepping to the bathroom to shower and prepare
for bed.

She knows! She knows! he screamed silently to himself. He had
a trick of pretending to be in a deep sleep from which he could
not be stirred; a trick used skillfully since childhood. Perhaps if he
were *out*, she'd just let him sleep on her bed again. He had been
very much awake and heard every word!

Dylan's heart raced wildly, not knowing what to do. Should he
just blurt it out? Did he believe such a thing as a Divine relationship could exist? Overflowing with both excitement and confusion
that could scarcely be contained, he wondered if he was he ready
to explore the depths of such a mysterious union when he knew
so little about it. Being the great actor, however, when she opened
the bathroom door, he continued to feign deep sleep.

Since they had been sitting on top of the bed, she found a coverlet and placed it gently over his body. After opening the window,
she turned off the lights and removed her robe. She wore nothing.
He opened his eyes at the moment she doused the lamp, knowing
the pillow shielded the light of the fire from revealing his

voyeurism. Her beauty took his breath away. He watched as she stood naked in the firelight, twisting her hair and securing it to the top of her head with a clip before she pulled back the sheets and climbed in.

Waiting to hear the even, quiet breathing of her sleep, he finally rose from the bed and walked into the bathroom and gently closed the door. He showered and borrowed her toothbrush to clean his teeth. Wearing nothing, he lifted the sheet and slid in beside her.

The firelight cast tall shadows in the room and he watched them play upon her sleeping face. Dylan lay on his side staring at her for another hour, wondering about the meaning of it all. Her arm slid along the bed, moving closer to him. She wore no nail polish, no phony nails—just what God had given her. Studying her slender fingers, he noticed, once again, the tiny little band above the middle knuckle of her wedding finger. *I wonder what she meant when she said she wore it to remind her she wasn't complete.* When he gently placed his hand over hers, she woke.

Nikki slowly opened her eyes to discover him gazing intently at her face. His torso was bare and his body lay beneath the covers.

"Nikki, may I stay?"

With a slight pause and moist eyes, she answered with a demure, "Yes."

When he pulled her closer and turned her back to his chest, she fit him like a glove. Every part, every curve connected them as one. Just as the previous day, the energy began to overwhelm him as he caressed her velvety breasts and kissed her neck. The excitement sent pounding energy not only to his groin, but screaming to every part of his body and mind. He became acutely aware of the smell of violets in the room, of the sound of her passionate breathing, of the tingling sensation from every hair on his body as it brushed against her soft skin. The world spun in slow motion as the firelight danced on their glistening naked bodies. Unwilling to postpone their union, his soul urgently demanded to be one with her the only way he knew how. He entered her from behind and nearly exploded for joy in the sharing of his body with hers. He never wanted to remove himself from within her. But, oh, how he wanted more!

As he held her tightly the crescendo moved up his spine into his heart and exploded all over again. Small, uncontrollable spasms shuddered through his body as the energy moved up his spine, right to the top of his head where it expanded and combusted, seeming to ignite everything around them. He embraced her so closely, as if he could pull her through his chest inside his heart, inside of him: all of her inside all of him! It seemed crazy and impossible, but he wished it more than life itself.

Born close to the water, he began to cry softly while he held her with delicate gentleness. There existed a knowing between them without any words, a knowing that *this was home*, that *this was right*, that *this was the most joyous moment of their lives*.

They repeated their lovemaking dance several more times until, in the early hours of morning, completely exhausted, they fell into a deep sleep enfolded in one another's arms.

Chapter 5

Slipping out of bed at eight, Nikki looked down at his sleeping face and adored it with all her heart. Before showering, she looked at her reflection in the long mirror. She hadn't made love with a man for what seemed like eternity. It wasn't that she found sex unpleasant—quite the contrary. But, she had followed a spiritual path for many years that required her to raise the energy from the lowest charkas to the higher ones in order to utilize the energy for purposes other than sensual satisfaction. Dylan sparked the flame, however, and it was the first time she had *desired* union with another in many, many years.

She looked into the reflection of her eyes and asked silently, *Have I done the wrong thing? God, never have I known such joy! How could this be the wrong thing? Please help me understand how to manage things for both of our highest and best good!*

The shower washed away her doubts as the water poured over her head in long, seamless rivulets of warmth.

Her eyes were closed and head tilted back when Dylan stepped into the room unnoticed. As he walked down the stairs of the sunken shower, the surprise made her jump. Gently, he pushed her back under the water and washed and inspected every inch of her beautiful little body in the morning light. Just beneath her pubic line he found a long thin scar that resembled a smile. He wondered if, like so many woman he knew in his profession, she'd had a tummy tuck. Running his finger lightly over it, he looked up for an explanation.

"I keep it to remind me how fragile and sacred life is. If not for a very adept and quick surgeon, both Sam and I would have passed to the next domain long ago."

Kneeling, he put his lips to the scar and kissed it, then turned his face to the side and pulled her to him with his head nestled in her belly. He wondered if her womb would ever bear his child. She washed his body in return and their passion flared again. With his arms around her, they swayed, dancing under the warm, running water. As he sang to her, she melted into him and before long they were making love in the shower. It seemed they had no end to their ability or willingness to share their bodies.

In spite of her insatiable greed for their constant amalgamation, Nikki winced and announced, "I'm not going to be able to walk for a week!"

"Me either!"

Aside from feeding the animals that morning, they spent the day in bed. Outside, dark purple clouds filled with rain, lightning, and thunder, provided an excuse to cuddle inside by the fire. They lay in each other's arms sharing little parts of their lives together.

He discovered that she, just as he, had only been through high school, though he dropped out early. Nikki had hoped to go to college, but married young and felt obligated to spend their money to obtain a degree for her husband first. She had audited many University courses and taken some by video and audio means. However, Nikki was a highly intelligent and very well read person who never stopped educating herself. Neither she nor Dylan felt the necessity for a degree in order to learn what they wanted to know.

She had moved away from home while still in high school—not because she didn't get along with her parents—but because she wanted to be Marlo Thomas of "That Girl," a sixties sitcom about an actress who moved to New York to be independent. Nikki just wanted her independence.

At the age of sixteen Nikki began working for an advertising firm. By utilizing the secretarial and accounting skills learned in high school, she ultimately became the manager of an office staff of eighteen people.

By nineteen she had married Joe, her high school sweetheart.

Opting for a change in careers at age twenty two, a brief stint in the music business ensued while working for the largest promoter in Salt Lake City. The drugs, groupie whores, and all the negative side of the business proved to be more than she could handle. It made her feel like a pimp. She participated in launching Billy Joel's first album at a small hall at the local university. By the time Joel returned the following season, she had to book the largest hall available. The last "biggie" she promoted was Seals and Crofts, for whom she held respect and gratitude when they requested only that she take them golfing before, and out for pancakes after, the show. They practiced the Baha'i faith and didn't drink, do drugs, or nail backstage groupies.

Her employer allowed her to book groups in local clubs as long as she split the proceeds with him. The music promoter's favorite expression was "fuck," and she learned to hate the word. Nikki discovered that people who used it constantly were either too lazy or too illiterate to come up with more descriptive language.

Even though some small careers were launched, she realized it was nothing short of a miracle to get her artists seen by the *right* people. Unfortunately, a great deal of her time passed in pubs while she drank a little, and sometimes, a lot.

Her husband, an athlete, wanted a cheerleader for a wife and had no interest in her life, or work, or any of *her* dreams. Like so many young men his ambitions toward becoming a professional athlete kept him pretty self-absorbed.

After her adventure promoting musicians, Nikki wrote a book on office management and went on the lecture tour, as well as providing private services to set up new firms just starting their offices. Not much money rolled in initially, but her husband assured her he'd be able to provide while she got her new business started.

Joe had been voted the youngest all American softball player in the U.S. one year and was invited to play in two big extravaganzas in New York and Philadelphia. Nikki had always wanted to go to Philadelphia, the birthplace of the Constitution and home to Benjamin Franklin—one of her heroes. They used their entire savings, which amounted to a whopping twenty five hundred dollars, to include Nikki on the tour. After drinking heavily on the return flight, Joe confessed he'd been fired and only pretended to go to work each day for the two previous months. They were dead broke.

When the plane landed she went straight to an employment agency and declared, "I need a job *today!*" The woman behind the desk stated unequivocally that her qualifications exceeded any job they had to offer. During their conversation, however, the woman mentioned they had just placed a secretary at a local advertising company the day before. Nikki caught the name of the firm and upon leaving the agency, drove directly to it, marched in, and asked to see the president.

While waiting to see him she observed the secretary chatting on the phone with her boyfriend for over fifteen minutes while filing her fingernails. When the president walked through the door and asked the secretary if she had finished typing the report he had left on her desk, she responded that she had been too busy. Nikki raised her eyebrow, but all guilt about attempting to replace the woman disappeared.

Kindly, the president of the firm allowed Nikki an audience, for he truly did not know *why* she requested one. The secretary, with a wink, had suggestively stated, "apparently she's here to see you for *personal* reasons."

Without revealing the new girl's inappropriate behavior, Nikki tried convincing him she would be a better secretary due to her experience in advertising.

"First of all, you're over qualified for the job and I can't pay you what you're worth," he told her through his laughter. "Besides, I can't fire her now—she's only been here one day!"

They started to chat about where they lived and found their homes were only a few blocks apart. Nikki mentioned she jogged past his house every day. Suddenly his ears perked up like a Doberman's because he, too, enjoyed running. The conversation led to other areas of similar interest and people they both knew. Before long it felt as if the two were old friends.

He had actually noticed that the new girl behaved like a bit of a bimbo, but attributed it to first day jitters. Feeling only slightly remorseful, he stepped out and let the other girl go. Nikki became the secretary/receptionist the next morning.

By her second week she assumed responsibility for handling all of the accounting for the firm. Within six months she had investigated every detail of the company's marketing research, discovering that due to poor management, a hideous mess had been made of the accumulated data. After three months of reorganizing the whole thing, the once failing department flew high and straight. She became Vice President of Research within the first year of her employment.

Things had gotten worse at home. Nikki considered Joe a decent fellow, but having realized she loved him like a brother, not a husband, she gathered the courage to leave so they could each pursue a life and partner that would meet both of their higher needs. Raised in a dysfunctional and broken home herself, she knew if she were to bear his children, the option of divorce would not sit well with her.

Her boss, the President and CEO of the firm, was Scott. She found him to be a brilliant businessman, capable of seeing the large picture, but noticed he lacked any true creative genius in advertising.

Nikki asked him if she could participate in the creative side of the business instead of being confined only to market research. Perhaps *because* she lacked any formal education in the area, she brought a new slant to the creative department. Determined to help their clients with a shoestring approach, she quickly became well known in the industry for her verve and ingenuity. Unsolicited clients with start-up companies began seeking her advice and her novel and economic approach. Most were not interested in working with the firm, but wanted only to pay her to consult with them.

After divorcing Joe, she survived the sexual revolution—miraculously, in retrospect—not creating unwanted life or disease in any form. Philosophically viewing those crazy years, she began to ask about the nature of the sex energy, which, somewhere deep inside, she knew had a different definition than the one she had experienced up to that point.

When Scott began having problems at home, Nikki became his close friend and confidant. Daily she felt herself slipping into that hazy place between friendship and love, though he was considerably older than she. Since she never had age issues, it didn't matter to her. When he and his wife determined their differences were irreconcilable, they divorced. His children still lived at home and were inclined towards treating him as a villain.

Nikki hadn't dared to believe Scott could also be in love with her, but as fate would have it, he was.

Sometimes, as in all long-term relationships, things seemed joyful and expansive. Other times it felt like the space of different worlds and cultures created a chasm between them and the line of trust and affection stretched dangerously thin. When things were tough she sought diligently to improve herself in order to secure

Scott's affection, but in the long run, learned all *self*-improvement is, in fact, for *self*—not another.

They loved to fly together, for they were both pilots. They owned a twin engine Beechcraft Barron and spent many hours crossing the U.S., Canada, the Bahamas, and Mexico. Flying, both privately and commercially, played an important role in their lives and work.

At age sixty-five Scott sold the advertising agency. A well known international firm had been wooing him for several years and he felt the deal would be lucrative for all the stockholders, as well as for the new firm. He wanted his investors to reap the rewards of their long-term devotion and initial courage in investing in him and his ideas.

Nikki went on to open her own small advertising firm.

During their marriage they lived in many places and owned a fair deal of real estate. She had lived longer at the ranch, however, than in any other location during her entire life.

Scott blessed her in many ways. He served not only as husband, but also father and advisor in many things. Sometimes he honestly felt inclined to support her ideas, but most of the time he reminded her of a kite string. She felt so free from other's beliefs that she would soar off, high into the sky, while Scott kept her grounded and safe from plummeting headlong to the earth by holding just enough tension on the string.

As she began her spiritual journey she continually asked for an understanding of Divine Love so she could apply it toward her loved ones. She realized the various pressures Scott and his ready-made family introduced into her life forced her into an understanding about personal peace.

Her husband never interfered with Nikki's approach to life or her less than orthodox philosophy, but he also never truly appreciated it. Every time he cut short any conversation in which she attempted to express how she felt in the depths of her soul, another brick found its way into the wall that separated them. Again, it only encouraged her into a place of growth where she could stand on her own two feet spiritually.

Many times during their marriage, in order to maintain peace, she gave away her power, bowing to patriarchal decisions with which she disagreed. Many times in their marriage Scott took advantage of his position. Luckily they came to a place of peace in their relationship as each reclaimed his own truth. Like many couples who spend long years together, they found a true and deep affection for one another, but more importantly, a true appreciation of each other's gifts and goodness. She felt her karma with Scott had been resolved before his untimely death.

Their son had been conceived five years after they were married. Sam's arrival introduced big changes in their lives, especially Scott's, as he'd already reared a family. Nonetheless, their son brought only joy to both of them. Nikki closed her advertising firm and spent his entire childhood as a dedicated mother, believing the maternal opportunity more important than any personal, materialistic goal.

Sam, now nineteen, earned a tennis scholarship to Stanford; one of her husband's Alma Maters. Scott had also attended Brigham Young University, the University of Utah, and the Sorbonne in Paris. He spent over seven years living in France and Switzerland, both serving his church and his country. The three of them made it a point to go to France and Switzerland a couple of times a year and had many friends in that part of the world. Sam and Scott had gone to the French Open when Sam was fourteen and the experience so influenced Sam that he set a goal to play in the Roland Garros Stadium five years later. He had a difficult time deciding whether to make big bucks as a tennis pro or take the scholarship and get a degree for his long dreamed-of profession. Nikki had let him make his own choice.

☯

Although born in the outskirts of Limerick, Dylan had been raised, for the most part, in Dublin. He lived with his parents and brother above a pub owned by his uncle. His father served as a prop master, and his mother, a costume designer, for the filming industry in Ireland.

His first taste of acting came at the age of ten. Maryssa, his beloved mum, encouraged his participation in the film industry. In fact, she was a major motivational influence in his life. When he turned eleven his parents gave him a kid-sized fiddle for his birthday, which he learned to play on his own, for they could afford no lessons. From the first day he touched the bow to the strings, he worshiped music.

A bit of rebel in high school, Dylan dropped out after deciding to pursue a career as a musician. He put together a group of friends that secured little gigs for school dances, small town fairs, and a couple of pubs. They cut a few CDs, but nothing they recorded actually sold much until he had made enough money and a name for himself in the film industry.

Dylan also sought his independence early. A scarcity of funds forced him to live in some pretty awful places in Dublin while trying to make ends meet as a young man. Odd jobs paid the rent, but he always explained his "temporary status" to his employers, hoping to take any acting job he could get. Never once, even when hungry, did he ask his parents to supplement his income.

Sometimes he and his best friend, Braydon, would busk in parks and near shopping and tourist centers, hoping their audience would throw change into their well-placed hats. Though surely a tough way to eke out an existence, they felt it gave them time to become both more skilled in their playing and also in their ability to move their audience. When one is but a few feet from his spectators, he can truly read their reactions honestly. They were many times chased away by the Bobbies and he had learned to keep a sharp eye open and his running shoes laced.

As a young actor he did everything possible to get in front of a camera. In retrospect, some of the work was pretty humiliating. Accepting parts in several truly appalling movies did not stop him from playing his character well. He had always believed that people had to pay their dues. Willing to pay the price for his dreams, he diligently persevered. Never having formally studied the art of acting, he was initially concerned he would be unacceptable in the industry. It didn't take long to figure out his natural abilities, however, and his confidence soared with each performance.

Monika, an actress from a British daytime soap opera, became his first lover. He spent many years with her, but when his career took off with U.S. films they severed their intimate relationship, though they still kept in touch. As his special, first love, Monika would always own a piece of his heart.

He was passionate about Ireland. Though he kept apartments in New York and L.A., he refused to live in the U.S., even though going home meant a zillion-mile trip. This prompted his title at the airlines; *the King of Frequent Flyer Miles*. He acquired the ranch in 1995—a two hundred ten hectare piece of land near Schull Harbour in West Cork. Just slightly smaller than Nikki's spread, it translated to approximately five hundred twenty acres. An ancient stone and thatched roof home that already existed on the ranch served as his parents' residence. Dylan had lived in a caravan for the first three years, with everything he owned left in boxes and terribly disorganized. Finally, with both the time and money, he built a place of his own, and though small, he adored everything about it. He designed it himself and adorned it only with things and furniture that meant something to him. Since he couldn't be around much to manage the place, his older brother, Mic, and his wife, Annie, and their kids, agreed to live on-site and take care of it. They lived in a trailer for a year until another house could be completed. Mic now ran about two hundred fifty head of sheep for him.

Julia Porter, a famous, rather racy, U.S. actress and wannabe producer, discovered him after she watched one of his early flicks from Ireland. He had appeared in the nude and also in several sex scenes, which he presumed to be the reason she cast him. His early characters were very often filled with fiery passion of either body or emotion. She wanted to produce her first action film, which proved to be truly a pathetic movie. The only good thing about it turned out to be Dylan's performance, but it got him seen in the U.S.

The most difficult part he ever played was that of a homosexual, for he and his mates pretty much looked upon "homos" as perverts. Just as with everything he agreed to do, he gave the role his all and it provided insight that changed his own tolerance level. Love is just love, no matter where or how one experiences it.

He played the part of a genius gone mad, and another of the town derelict, and once again, although he played the parts well, they were not the type of work he had hoped to do.

Several other relatively worthless movies followed until he was offered the opportunity to play opposite Mona Whittier in *LaBoheim* as an honest, tough, military officer who falls in love with an older lady of the night. The movie was nominated for several Academy Awards.

The following season he portrayed a big-wig in the oil industry; a man who opens up deep sea drilling in the Pacific. He had to gain fifty pounds for the part and dye his black hair red. Moreover, the show provided a chance to work with Hal Pace, someone whose talent he'd admired for years. The accolades rained down upon him like a summer storm.

Then came *Marrakech*, a part he truly relished playing. Though basically a bloody and violent movie, he played his character to absolute nobility and greatness. It won him his first Oscar.

Nikki interrupted, confessing she had not noticed him as an actor until she saw him in *Marrakech*.

Shortly after his Oscar debut, the producers of *Present Tense* decided to cast him in the lead opposite Anne-Marie Hawthorne and his life exploded. It had been a terrible roller coaster ride and he feared his heart would never mend, for he still felt deep affection for her.

He'd been scheduled to play a German naval admiral during WWII, but a fall during a scene damaged his lower back. The ensuing surgery indefinitely postponed that movie.

The opportunity to play the part of Albert Einstein in a film directed by the great Roland Zantman was offered next, and the role brought out Dylan's creative genius.

He pronounced *The Teaching of Little Crow* the best work he had ever done.

Nikki suspected if he chose the ending that served mankind, he would win yet another Oscar. She was glad he had not asked her opinion about the roles he'd played during his career, for she thought the majority of them beneath him. She considered him a brilliant actor—in fact, far more brilliant than any other "star" in the Hollywood sky. Recognizing from her own experience that ambition often makes one blind to the larger picture of the soul, she had great compassion for him. Even though his focus on worldly success domineered every aspect of his life, she loved the fact that the word "failure" did not exist in his vocabulary. His story continued.

A few CD's had been cut with his group, which he referred to as the "Overs." He could just walk in a room with them and pick up his fiddle and it felt like home, for there never seemed to be time or space that passed between them. Some concert tours had been performed, each of which sold out—mostly because he had fans that spilled over from the Hollywood side. Going on tour, though fun, was infinitely more tiring than he ever thought it would be. He never would make himself out to be *the* star and leave the band behind. In fact, he passed up four major contracts with the big recording studios over that very issue. He wouldn't even let them put his picture on any of the CD covers.

Nikki listened politely for hours, though she pretty much knew most of the story. He had been such a high profile figure that almost everyone knew about his life even before he did! She smiled deep in her heart recognizing how dedicated and loyal he felt toward those he loved. His willingness to share his bounty so generously with the people in his life to ensure their well-being touched her. From his description, it appeared his circle of loved ones supplied a major source of strength for him and he tried to provide the same in return.

From her brief personal experience with him, Nikki sensed his personality consisted of two different people. His professional self strutted with bluff and bluster, oozing with talent, self-confidence, and a deep desire to succeed and be acknowledged by accolades, fame, and wealth. As the majority of the world's population views success as how much one obtains in return for one's contribution, he felt it important to command the big bucks. She could see how, in his professional life, it would be easy for him to slip into the habit of saying one thing and doing another.

His private inner world required expansive spaces where he could touch the earth and appreciate nature and animals, where he could recharge his soul. His heart leaned toward people who were trustworthy, real and loyal; people who had a strong sense of self and a connection to reality. He needed to be near his animals and loved their simplicity. His family and extended family were his touchstone and the foundation of his character and world.

Both of these personalities were fully a part of him, and both fully valid. She admired his ability to stay connected to reality in the face of such opposing lifestyles.

She wanted to know what was going on inside of him, not outside. Though several attempts were made to subtly veer the conversation in that direction, she hit a brick wall. *I won't push,* she thought. *Today we merely watched the films of each other's incarnation this time around.*

Chapter 6

"Get up you lazy boy, we've got work to do! You think just because I let you sleep in the big house I'm going to let you off the hook?" Nikki straddled his back, tickling him, trying to make him turn over.

"What time is it?" he asked sleepily, noting the sun hitting the trees outside the window.

Nikki never closed the shades in her bedroom. She loved the moonlight as much as the sunlight.

"It's eight thirty. I never sleep until eight thirty! You're a terrible influence on me," she teased. Slapping him on the behind, she headed for the shower.

He decided to sleep until she finished. By the time he rose she'd made the rounds to feed the stock and small animals and he felt a little guilty. Nikki came through the door, bringing with her the freshness of the morning, with cheeks glowing from the chilly temperature.

"It's going to be a *beaut* today! I need to go upstream to the headwaters for my irrigation system. I think something's clogged, 'cause the pressure's a little low. We can take the horses just for fun. It'll make you feel like a cowboy!" She laughed as she stole a bite of the bagel he was eating for breakfast. "Want your own mount today, Tex?"

Grinning like a starry-eyed schoolboy, he said, "Ye think Pegasus would mind bearing both our weight again? I rather like riding with m' arms around ye."

"If it pleases me, Pegasus won't mind a bit—and the idea *pleases* me. Besides, it's less than a mile to get there."

Riding the stream in the mid-morning warmth of the sun was intoxicating. The sound of the gurgling water complemented the gentle feeling that embraced them as they walked the horse. His back swayed in a gentle dance, as the three mingled their energies together.

The "headwaters," as Nikki called it, turned out to be a wide section of the stream where a portion of the water had been diverted to a higher elevation in order to feed her ponds and the flood irrigation system that ran throughout her ranch. The silt had built up and a restricted flow was, indeed, the problem. Apparently, this happened not too infrequently, as Crow noticed three shovels stored in a cleft in the sandstone wall adjacent to the stream. She handed him one and they stood in the stream with their shoes on, digging out the silt until the water ran free again.

Dylan admired that she exhibited no hesitation about jumping in the cold water with her shoes and clothing on, getting muddy, and fixing something. He knew few women who weren't concerned with their fingernails, hair, clothing, or for that matter, doing anything that required getting dirty.

Their chore completed, they returned to their nestled seating arrangement on Nikki's friend's back. "I have a little something I'd like to share with you this morning," she said as she took the reins away from Crow. Instead of heading back to her home, she took the equivalent of a deer trail up a steep hill. Dylan leaned forward with her, hoping the blanket beneath them wouldn't slide and dump both of them down the cactus-laden mountainside.

He had to laugh when Nikki jumped off the horse and opened a green Park Service gate with a large sign indicating *no horses*. She motioned him to bring Pegasus through. They rode along a three-foot wide path on a hillside that dropped fifty feet straight down to an unforgiving rocky bottom. He had no choice save to trust the sure-footedness of Pegasus, for if the horse were not, they would all be dead before the adventure was over.

Ultimately the trail led them back down to the stream, which they crossed twice before they arrived at a beautiful waterfall. "It's pretty, isn't it?" she asked, anticipating his appreciation.

"Can we stay a while, boss?" He nuzzled her neck and kissed the lobe of her ear.

"Let's go swimming!" she suggested, slipping out of his arms and down off Pegasus before he could respond. She cast her clothes on the sandy beach to the side of the pool beneath the fall. It surprised and delighted him to see her uninhibited way of cavorting with nature.

"Would we be expecting any company, now, mi lass?" Crow asked, slightly concerned that hikers might be passing by, as the falls were obviously in Zion Park.

"Not likely this time of year!" Nikki gasped as her body became engulfed in the frigid water.

"Just let Pegasus roam free, Dylan." She knew he wouldn't stray too far from her.

Crow removed his clothes and stood by the side of the small pool, tentatively testing the waters. The temperature felt like the low fifties and, not being overly fond of frigid water, he thought twice about entering.

"Come on in, you masculine heartthrob of the female masses," she playfully teased while splashing at him.

His goose bumps had goose bumps. However, he wasn't about to let her make him look like a softy, so he gritted his teeth and dipped into the water, full up to his neck. "Why, it's practically a hot tub!" he protested between chattering teeth.

Their bodies became numb and accustomed to the cold as they played and swam in the shallow waters together, catching small fish with their hands. The curious creatures circled about and nipped at them.

"Oh, I forgot to tell you, there're weenie sharks in here that can take some pretty large chunks out of you." She winked.

Just then, something did bite his leg and he took her seriously, leaping out onto the bank. She followed suit, laughing with the deep throaty giggle of a small child.

Calling Pegasus to her, Nikki mounted bare, then held out a hand for Dylan to join her.

"Madame Godiva, just where do ye intend to ride in that state?" he asked raising his right eyebrow.

"Right up there." She pointed to the top of the falls.

He gathered their clothing and joined her for the short ride. Pegasus climbed the hillside and delivered them to a flattened area of the stream where enormous red sandstone boulders were reflecting the morning sun and heating up quickly. Nikki removed the blanket from the horse's back and laid it upon one of the great stones. "Let's warm up, shall we?"

They lay naked in the late morning rays, absorbing their freely offered light and warmth. Moments of absolute freedom are seldom experienced in people's lives because they fear one thing or another. This felt like the freedom of youth to Crow, who reveled in it.

He gazed at her face, with her eyes closed in sweetest repose as if in private conversation with the nature spirits. His eyes roamed down her beautiful petite body, which he felt was now a part of him. Her nipples were still hard and cold, so he leaned over and suckled one to warm her. Nikki reached down, stroking his head, and raised his face to hers. With such tenderness as he had never known, they made love to the music of nature. His thirst for her seemed quenchless and thoughts of keeping her with him forever were floating repeatedly through his head.

Exhausted, they lay in each other's arms for another hour.

Dylan half expected her to chide him for this lavish abuse of time, but not a word was spoken.

Upon their return they showered together, then went foraging for food. She showed him how to make a Waldorf salad and told him that her late brother-in-law had managed the Waldorf Astoria for thirty some-odd years. She spoke of her visits to the hotel, how so many dignitaries and celebrities could be found in the foyers, elevators, halls, and restaurants. "It was like the 'where to be, if you're a *wannabe*, temple,'" she remembered aloud.

He had stayed there twice in his life and agreed with her observation.

"Ye got any plans for the afternoon?" he asked.

"Say, Little Crow, I don't want to make you feel like I'm controlling every minute of your time. Surely, there are some things you have in mind too and I'd like to please you any way I can." Her eyes were pools of sincerity.

"Ye know, Babe," he began, "it seems like I'm always the one who's making things happen. I'm the guy arranging the parties, making rental reservations, planning the activities and fun. Have ye any idea how wonderful it feels to relax and let someone else do it for a change? Something 'bout ye makes me freely give up control."

OOOO, she thought, *that was a biggie for him.*

"OK, then…let's get my favorite toy out and we'll play with it this afternoon," she declared. She left him wondering what type of toy as she ran back to her bedroom and returned with a key, which she pressed into his palm. "It's the red one on the right side of the garage down by the barn. You go get it and bring it up to the house while I find some hats."

He hadn't ventured into the shop or the garages yet. There, nestled among hanging tires, cobwebs, and a thousand other

stored items, sat a beautiful deep cherry red, BMW Z8 convert-
ible. It purred like a sewing machine when he started it. Nikki
stood with a duster in hand as he pulled up the steep road to her
home. She deftly brushed away the accumulated layer of powdery
dirt, and showed him how to put down the top.

"Why do ye hide this beauty?"

"It's my wild thing. Once in a while I've just gotta put the top
down and fly around a little. I drive it when I'm feeling especially
free. Care to join me on a joy-ride?"

"May I drive?" he asked hopefully.

"I gave the key to you, didn't I?"

They headed toward the Springdale side of Zion. An old and
favorite tune of hers, "Cruisin' Together," by Smokey Robinson,
came through the speakers and she laughed at the amazing coincidence. Closing her eyes, she tilted her head back in gratitude and
sang along with Smokey.

Baby, let's cruise away from here…

She instructed Dylan to drive directly to the entrance gate. An
attendant with a vacuous expression stopped them to say they
would have to take the shuttle bus into the park. Nikki smiled
kindly and informed the man that Jenny Axton was expecting
them. Jenny, Nikki's close friend, served as the Park Director. The
bored attendant made a quick call, handed them a special pass,
and waved them through.

"It's who ye know, right?" Crow said, with a chortling snort.
"Are we paying someone a visit?"

"No—I just called Jenny before we left so we could drive
through with the top down. I wanted you to experience this magnificent place without any obstructions over your head, so I just
pulled a few strings!"

The term "magnificent" seemed paltry compared to the view. She took him to the place where the famous Narrows end and they hiked three miles upstream, finding a beautiful perch where they could enjoy the panorama uninterrupted.

"God's glory is everywhere when you open your eyes, isn't it?" she stated while inhaling deeply, breathing the majesty of the scenery into her soul. "These walls are a living trinity of Power, Wisdom, and Love made manifest in the material world to me. I like to come here to remind myself that even though I may seem small individually, I am part of something *infinitely* larger and *infinitely* more splendid. It's like I can feel myself filling up with the nobility of the place. Can you feel it too?" she asked, turning her head to face him.

Nikki seemed such a mixture of uninhibited, childlike joy and ageless wisdom that he found himself in awe of her. She was old and young at the same time; she danced with the sun and blessed the moon; she sang to nature and loved all creatures, great and small. She played in the earth's waters and sang to the flowers, enveloping everything that came within her presence in a welcome embrace of love and nurturing. Nikki didn't seem to study or analyze God; she merely seemed dazzled by God—awestruck by the union of atoms that give structure to nature. She spoke of the ability to *expose* forces by *recognizing* them, of individuality within unity, of the innumerable within the finite. Nikki *was* this same Power, this Intelligence, this Wisdom, this Love that she reflected upon in her surroundings. Every act, every word, every deed that came from her mirrored their perfect union. No somberness or any sense of preaching accompanied her expression of her beliefs: rather, one felt only a sense of her willingness to share her soul. She seemed to have an overflowing well of love that had to, by its very existence, find objects and people upon which to lavish itself.

"Ye used the word 'Power,'" he said, reaching for her hand. "What does 'Power' mean to ye?"

Nikki paused, searching his eyes to determine the sincerity of his question. "To me, *Power* is the very breath of God's Intelligence that animates all things, an energy, a pulsing, vibrating light that can be shaped into anything upon which the attention is held. It can be utilized to create beauty and perfection, but it can also be abused. I think it takes the other two parts of the formula—Wisdom and Love—to create the right balance in the use of that limitless energy."

"I believe we go through this school of life until we learn to manage that Power constructively, until, through our co-creative powers, we learn how to create with Wisdom and Love in such a way that with every thought, feeling, word, and action, we bless the whole. I think it's been the selfish concept of exclusivity that's held us from all we truly are and can be.

"When you chose the Power of Unity over the power of exclusivity and destruction in the ending of *Little Crow*, you set forth a vibration that will affect every single person who hears and sees the act of the principle. There is *never* a word, whether spoken, written, or sung, that does not go forth and affect and alter the course of the people's lives that receive it. Words with intent have power! You use this Power among the masses through your work and have a responsibility with that Power to bless, heal, illumine, and enlighten the millions of souls who watch or hear your creative act. If you abuse this Power by presenting material that does *not* lift the consciousness of man, you're also responsible for its consequences. The part you chose to play in this lifetime will force you to choose between your real, higher self and your ego."

Staring directly into his eyes, she offered her discourse, willing the truth of it into his consciousness.

Overwhelmed by her words and her vision of his Power, he sat silently, just glancing back and forth between her eyes with an intensity that studies rather than sees. When she finished, he could find no words. It hadn't been a conversation—it had been a tutorial, and he knew it. She never seemed to be at a loss for words that sent him reeling in thought.

Finally standing, she pulled him to his feet, embraced him, then led him by the hand back to the point of beginning. They walked in silence, for she understood the power of silence.

There were a few tourists, mostly foreigners, who smiled and greeted them in the friendly fashion of misplaced people seeking a sense of camaraderie among strangers. No one seemed to recognize him with his beard, sunglasses, and ball cap. "I think I'll shave this off tonight," he said, tugging at the hairs on his chin. "I don't think Hannigan's gonna find me and legally force me to finish the other endin' to *Little Crow.*"

"Oh, let me do it!" she begged enthusiastically. "It's been years since I've shaved a man. My stepfather always thought it funny to chase me around the house and catch me, rubbing his stubble on my face until I'd shave it off for him. He called it 'chin pie.' I used an old fashioned, single razor and strap with lots of foam. He'd sit on the porch in the morning sun every Saturday while I performed the ritual. During the week he seemed to manage just fine without me, however."

"Can I trust this famous face to a razor in ye'r hands?" He actually wondered about her ability to slide past the cleft in his chin and the raised moles without scarring his face.

"Darling, you could trust me with your life, if you'd only have a little faith!" she offered as she examined the work ahead.

As they drove the Kolob Road, the last rays dipped below the mesas and the clouds in the sky donned a brilliant pink fabric. Cougar Mountain, the largest landmark behind her ranch, assumed a radiant orange hue. The sky looked more indigo than blue and everything around them seemed electrified, brighter, and clearer somehow. By the time they reached the gate, the light had nearly disappeared. Dylan returned the ragtop to the garage until she felt the urge to fly again.

While they made a simple meal of toast with tomatoes and melted Jarlsberg cheese, he realized how much he enjoyed the simple act of preparing food with her. "Y' know, I've never even tried to help out in the kitchen before. I like it. It's fun to do it *together*, isn't it?"

"Too true. Most men don't realize that when *one* person has the *sole* responsibility for the welfare and maintenance of the others in their family, it feels like a form of slavery, inevitably ending in resentment. Surely any food prepared with resentment is charged negatively and can only poison those who feast upon it. I'm ashamed to admit I used to poison my family a lot!" she said, laughing at the memory.

"I tried to train Sam to be a contributing person to those around him. He's not only a gourmet cook, but can also handle his own housekeeping and laundry. I think his roommates are glad he had a *real* mommy. He's a good worker too—never afraid to get his hands dirty, or to try to fix something, or try something new. Smart little bugger, as well. His father taught him how to invest, and between his own investments and those his father made for him, he made enough money to pay for his own education. He's on a scholarship this year, but who knows how long that'll last?"

As she cleaned up the dishes Dylan found the remote to the television and began searching for CNBC. "Nik, this is the first time in years I haven't been glued to a news station or a newspaper, wanting to know what's happening in the world!"

He couldn't help but notice Nikki's humming over the news

broadcast. After the reporter covered a story on a political sex scandal that had held Dylan's interest for some time, he turned off the tele. He began tossing in his two bits worth of opinion about the scandal, criticizing the President of the United States for the role he played in the dilemma.

Nik seemed blatantly disinterested and busied herself in the kitchen while he droned on about the affair. When it was clear she wasn't listening, feeling slighted, he touched her arm and asked, "Don't ye even care what I have to say?"

"I care about everything that goes on in your head and heart, Dylan. Truly, I meant no personal offense. It's just that...well... I don't believe *your criticism* of the President or the situation actually does any good or in any way changes the circumstances. I don't want to be responsible for encouraging you to engage in *any* form of judgment, criticism, or condemnation—of *any* person, place, or thing!"

Shocked, his eyes widened in disbelief. "How can ye not be interested or have an opinion about world affairs? Are ye *purposely* as blind as that?"

"I'm very much interested in the state of this planet, my brothers, and the world at large, darling. I just have a different approach than you do, that's all. You see, when one participates, through thought, feeling, or word, in the process of criticizing, judging, or condemning something or someone, it starts an energy moving which affects the reality around us." She could see confusion in his eyes and decided to expound upon the theory a little further.

"We *create* with every single thought and feeling, with the power of our attention and intention, and with the power of our words and actions. If I judge or condemn another, where's that negative energy going to do its business first—in my personal energy field—right? Then it moves on to the subject or object of my criticism and creates both an unnecessary binding karmic connection between us, and a new reality for them. What may have been a temporary incident for their own learning now becomes a prison of opinion in which they're held in bondage! Then, that negative vibe continues on around the great circle of life, gathering more of its kind, and eventually makes its way back to me, *magnified*. BOOM! I just created hell in my *own* life under the guise of 'caring and having an opinion.'

"It's infinitely more powerful to affect change in the world and in the people around us in a constructive way. It's not that I'm blind to the injustices on our planet, it's just when I become aware of such activity, I do more to bless another, or a situation, and myself, by holding that person or situation in God's light of perfection. It frees them from the tyranny of the actions of their ego and comes back to bless my life. It's completely selfish in a way!"

He wanted to justify his viewpoint, demanding that we need to hold people responsible for their actions, but realized she was just trying to teach him how to manage energy. It had been a physics lesson. He sat silently absorbing and digesting both the dinner and her words.

☯

She obtained the barbering tools and set him upon a high backed stool that she pulled out of a large storage closet. Carefully draping a towel around his neck, she began to chop away his whiskers with some small scissors. When enough of the long hair had been removed, she stepped to the stove, collected the barber's foam from the hot water, and applied its warmth to his lower face, keeping his nostrils and lips free. Crow tilted his head back to rest on her breasts while her soft and swift hand movements sheared away the remaining stubble. It felt like a soft massage as she slid the razor easily over his chin and neck.

"Want some Elvis chops like you wore in that truly stupid

movie you did about the fifties rock 'n' roll group?"

He sat forward, realizing she'd seen an Irish flick he'd done when nineteen years old. "Truly stupid, so ye say? Ye'll pay for that bit o' cheek, lass!" he teased, leaning back again and closing his eyes. "On the other hand, it was a pretty ghastly movie, wasn't it?" he remembered aloud. "I'd hoped it got buried in the archives somewhere! No such luck, eh? Soon as a fella gets a wee bit of a reputation, they drag out every skeleton."

"With the possible exception of your Irish accented version of Elvis, the one redeeming value of the show was *your* performance!" she insisted. "Ye a'nt notin but a houuund dog…" she mocked, as he pulled her to his lap and lathered her face with the foam.

She didn't bother to tell him she'd viewed it, along with every movie in which he'd appeared, only after his first visit to her ranch.

"No, by the way, I don't want Elvis chops," he said sarcastically, placing a dollop of foam on her nose.

After she wiped the foam from her nose and the snowy goatee from her chin, she scraped the last hairs away and cleaned off his face. She didn't apply the usual stinging liquid to close his pores. Rather, she knelt before him and blessed his face with little butterfly kisses until he pulled her to him and insisted his lips needed attention too.

"Go jump in the shower and get those little hairs off, then we can sit in the hot tub under the stars for a while," she suggested.

He sauntered off to the shower while she vacuumed up the debris and sentimentally saved one lock from his chin, tucking it away in an envelope.

Nikki poured two glasses of his favorite Merlot and met him in the bathroom. She grabbed a towel and wrapped it around his still soggy body.

As he inspected his face in the mirror, he smiled at his reflection.

"Hey lad, haven't seen ye for a while. Looking good!" He gave himself the thumbs up, then turned and kissed her on the forehead. "Ta."

She remembered her English great-grandmother saying "Ta" for *thank you* all the time. It made her smile every time he used the *old* Irish.

She stripped, grabbed two dry towels, and they stepped out the bathroom door to the hot tub. The temperature registered one hundred seven degrees and it made him tingle all over. Its warmth felt welcome in the cool night breeze.

The moon had not yet risen, and as Nikki had turned off the house lights, the entire world seemed black. The sky, however, was lavishly alive and the stars sent their rays to bless the earth with the type of calmness and harmony that ensues from reflecting the vastness of the omniverse. They sipped his favorite juice while she nestled between his legs and leaned back against his chest.

"My, haven't the world and the heavens been generous in endowing us with their beauty today?" she commented. "Sometimes, I just like to sit out here at night and open my heart to the thoughts that fall from the splendor of the Milky Way."

He pointed out the formations of stars familiar to him and spoke of the importance of being able to navigate by them when upon the water. She pointed out the orbs that were strobing red, green, and white. At first he did not believe her, but then could see she had spoken the truth. "Must be gas belts around them?" he said. "Or… maybe we're not alone here in this ol' universe."

Rather than responding, she silently allowed him to wonder for himself.

Before a flickering fire, they made love until the early hours of the morning. He felt profoundly moved by the fact that each time they made love, his heart seemed to expand in an ecstasy all its own.

Chapter 7

At eight the next morning a man knocked at the door. Nikki wore sweats and Dylan's shirt, as they had barely emerged from the bedroom to get a cup of coffee. Not only did they both look pretty disheveled, but the house held all the signs of a man having dug in and made himself comfortable.

At the door stood Rick Snow, another rancher/B & B owner from the nearby city of Virgin. Rick's wife and Nikki's husband died within a month of each other, and he and Nik had become good friends while consoling one another. Knowing her manager was out of town, Rick dropped by to see if Nikki needed any help. Since she'd entrusted him with the security code to her gate and knew she rose early, he felt he would surely be welcome.

As Rick entered there was little question that Nikki and the man she introduced only as "Dylan" were involved. He'd never seen her so happy and radiant. As an act of respect, Rick removed his cowboy hat, and though he tried to converse nonchalantly, his eyes darted accusingly around the room, then back and forth between the lovers. When the phone rang in Scott's office, Nikki excused herself and told them to get acquainted while she answered the call.

Rick's demeanor unexpectedly and drastically altered. He forcefully stuck his hat back on his head and challenged Dylan with his eyes as he spoke sternly. "I may look like a 'born yesterday country bumpkin,' *Mr. Crow*, but I *do* know who *you* are and what kind of reputation you got. Now, I can see something's on 'tween you two, but I'm tellin' ya, if you're just *playing* with that woman and you hurt her in *any* way, you're going to have to face me later. You may be a big yahoo in Hollywood, but when it comes to Nikki, she's not one to be dazzled by glitter. She's out of your league, man. Understand? There isn't a man in a hundred mile radius who hasn't wished he were in your shoes right now…and that includes me. That's the kindest, smartest, dearest woman I've known in my life. I know she doesn't want me the way she wants you, but I'm telling you, she deserves the best life has to offer."

Dylan bristled at the unveiled threat, but controlled his urge to do something stupid when Nikki returned to the room.

"Rick, I do have a huge favor to ask of you. That was a friend of mine in Brighton who says it's supposed to hit the freezing point tonight up in those mountains. I haven't had time to winterize my cabin, and I'm going to have to run up. I won't be back for a couple days and I need someone to feed the critters and switch irrigation for me. Could I hire you or one of your men to do it for me?" she asked with enthusiastic sweetness.

She suddenly realized by the look on their faces there had been some tension between the two men while she had stepped so briefly away. Fully aware of Rick's deep affection for her, she became conscious that her appearance and the debris in the usually spotless room probably lit a fire under him. Nikki loved Rick as a friend, but had never led him to believe in the possibility of a romantic alliance. Stepping closer, she touched his arm and looked for his answer. Her tenderness seemed to calm him, though he kept glaring at Dylan, knowing she intended to take him with her.

"You can't hire me to do it, but I'll do it as a friend," he offered.

"I'll feed the animals and switch water this morning before I leave and tack a watering schedule on the door."

She tried to offer Rick a cup of coffee, but could see he literally wanted to bolt from the scene. Nikki escorted him to his truck and Dylan watched through the window as she stood on tiptoe and kissed the man's cheek. He felt sorry for him.

As Nikki pushed the screen open, she furrowed her forehead and raised an eyebrow. "Felt something kind of funny after my phone call—did he recognize you or something?"

"Not only that, he threatened to beat the shite out of me if I wasn't good to ye!"

She laughed, thinking Dylan might be teasing, for she'd never known anything less than the behavior of an absolute gentleman from Rick.

"Well, you heard my predicament. Want to take a trip north by car? We could stop by Bryce Canyon on the way home tomorrow for a few hours, or spend the night in a hotel before we come back. Or…" she said while winking mischievously, "if you'd rather stay here and be my stable boy, that would work too!"

"Who would feed me? Who would rub mi back and make tea for me? Who would make love with me all night long?" he asked with a little child's pout.

"I guess you're going, then!"

She told Crow what to bring to prevent him from hauling all his suitcases for a two-day trip. Nikki was a great traveler, whether it be to far-off destinations, or just a quickie to Las Vegas. She could always pack in less than fifteen minutes.

She allowed Dylan the control seat, of which he seemed so fond, and while he focused on the road she chatted about things she loved.

"Ye say ye 'love' this, ye 'love' that, 'bout a lot o' things!" he teased.

"Can one love too much, Dylan? Love, to me, is perfection made manifest."

"Love can be a bitch, Babe. It can take ye down for the count and leave ye so heartsick, ye can find little reason to rise from ye'r bed in the mornin'.'"

Nikki reached for his right hand and held it gently, as if nursing a wounded man. "No doubt, by the ego's definition of love, one can be mortally wounded. I'm referring, however, to *true love*, darlin'—something one *gives* to anyone or anything in all creation that magnifies and reflects its perfection. Obedience to the Law of Love can alter the course of any one life or that of all humanity."

Dylan caught a sideways glance at the intense expression on her face. The passion in her voice and eyes was undeniably sincere. "Nik, I can't say as I've ever experienced *any* definition of love that didn't ultimately hurt or disappoint me. Maybe I don't truly understand what ye're sayin'."

She sucked a halting breath, looked down at their joined hands and lured him further into unknown territories. "You know, most folks just choose the pathway of ego love because they've never been exposed to any other kind. They create discord upon discord and misery upon misery, which chases them through each incarnation until the great whip of life yanks them back to their knees—humbly begging an *understanding* of their misery. It's only the foolish person who won't learn by his mistakes. Ultimately, Dylan, I think all mankind will come to understand the only release from their continual suffering comes from obedience to the Law of *True* Love."

He listened without interruption or offering his opinion for he'd quickly learned to recognize when she was about to share something *truly important* to her—almost as if her very verbiage changed. She spoke more like a teacher than a participant in a conversation.

"True Love can only express peace and joy," she continued, "and pours out those feelings to all creation, unconditionally. It doesn't ask something in return or even remember what it's given in the past. It receives and maintains its joy by a continual outpouring of itself and is the foundation and proper use of all Life energy. When brought down to our human experience, it's the desire to give, and to give, and to give all of your own peace and harmony to the rest of the whole. Because it is a *giving*, it *cannot* hurt or disappoint.

"I learned a valuable lesson about love during a period when I felt desperately alone in my marriage. I didn't realize that Scott only reflected for me what I put out into the world. I *thought* I loved without limit, giving away every part of me, but I *demanded something in return*. My lesson not only taught me to love and honor myself, but also to understand the difference between Divine Love and my ego's expression of love—the one that left me with the inevitable feeling that love could never be returned to me full measure. When I changed my attention and just gave for the sake of giving, expecting nothing in return, love went out upon the waters and revisited me multiplied. It's the law of the great circle, you see. Whatever you put out must, by law, take the path of the circle, gathering more of its kind, and return to its creator."

He pondered her words silently. *The great circle. The same law that Knowing Crow talked about in the movie.* He marveled at how her humble soul loved, and though he'd never experienced what she described, that was enough to accept her message with an open heart.

So, lad, where does that leave ye in this formula o' hers? he wondered. "Ye have such a different perspective than I on so many things, Nik, it scares me a little."

"Have I made you uncomfortable?" she asked, sensing a new energy in the car.

Why are ye scared, lad? Are ye scared she'll see through ye? Scared she's so far above ye, she's completely out o' reach? Or...are ye scared she's off in la-la land—completely out o' touch with the real world?

"I just need a cigarette, Babe. Mind if we stop?" He did not wait for her answer, but immediately swerved onto the freeway exit at Fillmore.

It had been the first time she'd seen him smoke in several days. *Don't push him, Nik*, she thought apprehensively. *Don't push him away. If he wants to know, he'll ask you.*

She purchased some water, fruit, and a big sugar cookie slathered in pink frosting. Even though he laughed at her, they shared it greedily, like two small children hiding a sugary snack from their mother. As they stood nibbling in front of the quick stop, the mid-day light illumined her face. No signs of wrinkling or fading of beauty played upon her skin and he wondered about her age. He thought back to all she had told him on the day they spent in bed sharing their histories and started counting up the years. *She can't be that old!* he thought. *I must 'ave misunderstood some o' the sequence or something.* Rarely did he ask a woman about her age, but he decided to brave the question when they resumed their drive.

"When's ye'r birthday?" he asked nonchalantly, swallowing a large gulp of bottled water.

She paused, thinking momentarily. Though caught off guard, she answered, "We share the same, precise moment of birth!"

"No way! Ye mean ye know when mi birthday is?"

"Sure, doesn't everyone?"

Wow, exactly mi own age! he thought.

She hadn't lied. As his twin flame, they were created at the same moment. As the world counts, however, she was actually ten years his senior.

"Wouldn't it be great if we all lived in Shangri-la and never got old or ugly?" he mused.

"I love that story because it conveys some important elemental truths, Dylan. Eternal Youth is the Flame of God abiding in the temple of the body," she explained vivaciously. Nikki slipped off her shoes and turned in her seat, tucking one leg beneath her, before she went on. "It's like—God gave this amazing gift to himself and his creations. The gifts of youth and beauty of both one's body and mind can only be held permanently by he who's strong enough to shut out all the discord. *That* was the *simile* of the *hidden place* where no man could enter in Shangri-la. Without the permanent consciousness of peace, harmony, love, and light abiding within your thoughts and feelings, no amount of physical effort or plastic surgery will stop the body from aging and decaying. Every time some form of discord flashes through your thoughts or feelings, it impregnates within the flesh of your body. Eternal beauty and youth are *self-created, generated,* and *self-sustained* in the flame of God's Life in the human structure. True beauty comes from within and cannot be created by artifice. I believe it's God's plan for manifesting his perfection in the world of form and maintaining it."

"Whoa, lass!" Dylan laughed derisively. "Apparently, if ye'r thesis holds any water, no one on this planet understands it, 'cause there's a whole lot of *old 'n' ugly* out there!"

Nikki looked down at her hands. Certainly, through the eyes of the ego, what he proclaimed could be perceived as truth, but she knew that *reality* is perception and each man's perception is different than his neighbor's. She began to press her perspective again. "One can *learn* to utilize his energy in a constructive way that will inure to the benefit of maintaining his youth and beauty. On the other hand, nothing can stop him from using that energy destructively in fits of temper, rage, greed, appetite, and lust, thus destroying his own form and the harmony of the world around him."

He puffed the air between his lips, as if blowing off the incredulity of her words. "Do ye mean to be telling me if I sit on some mountaintop somewhere, seeking bliss and Nirvana, that I'll never get old and mi body will stay youthfully strong and 'and-some? I could be playing roles of young bucks at eighty, eh?"

"I'm in no way suggesting one remove himself from the society of his family or friends. I just believe if one *consciously* and *continually chooses* peace and harmony in his thoughts, feelings, words, and actions, he will, in fact, see the cells of the body reflect the balance that maintains the renewal of eternal youth and beauty."

Nikki squeezed his hand and softened the tone of her voice. "Little Crow, Shangri-la is a state of consciousness. It's a place within the depths of your very soul that knows the difference between illusion and reality."

"Well, bugger me! All this time I not only believed I lived in the *real* world, I thought the role I played contributed to how it wags!" he scoffed. *Blast her for calling me "Lit'l Crow" every time she thinks I'm needin' her sagacious insight! What was, initially, a charmin' and endearin' nickname is swiftly becoming a constant reminder that she thinks I'm not up to 'er spiritual standards!*

The volume of her voice reduced to a near whisper. It had been her experience that information that causes resistance is better delivered gently, rather than harshly. "You *do*, Dylan. That's my point! Your vision becomes other's vision. *You* are in a position to influence countless lives and you can *choose* to do it either through *love*, or by portraying the *illusion*. Either way provides a pathway of learning for your audience, but *you* are responsible for introducing or suggesting one pathway or the other by your example. And, let's face it, one of those pathways can be quite nasty. Unfortunately, illusory human perceptions have imposed such frightful limitations and destruction."

Oops, she thought, as she caught him visibly wincing. *Did it again.*

*Mighty I AM Presence...*Nikki prayed silently, *show me how to reveal to my beloved the ego's biggest lie of all? Show me how to expose*

the truth about the illusion created by the ego—how to help him
remember his inseparable connection with God, with love, with all,
and with me. I AM grateful that I AM truth and right action in this
situation. Thy will be done. So be it.

Suddenly, she vividly remembered what her angelic friend,
Aurora, had once advised about not imposing knowledge or
beliefs upon another unless they have expressed some form of consent. Aurora explained if she *lived* what she knew, people would
naturally ask her what made her world such a great place. It would
not be necessary to proselytize, rather, only to *be* the truth and to
hold a field of perfection and love around all that came within her
scope of consciousness. In this way, like a great magnet, she created a space in which God's perfection could be drawn into every
person, place, and condition.

Nikki abruptly switched the conversation to a history of Utah
and the Salt Lake Valley, hoping to distract him from the seething
vortex of frustration that had been building between them. Crow
found the story of the Mormon immigration and the trials they
had to bear interesting. It reminded him of Moses leading the exodus into the wilderness. She explained the division of different fac-
tions when one group held to polygamy and the other did not.
History, in all its forms, fascinated him.

"The Land o' the Mormons," he said, gesturing to the valley
ahead, as they passed the point of the mountain that divided
Provo from Salt Lake. Though he'd seen some of it on television,
the city's size and beauty seemed more impressive in daylight and
in person. He had passed through Salt Lake once before to attend
the Sundance Film Festival in Park City. His flight had landed in
the middle of the night and he'd been so pressed for time that he
hadn't bothered to notice much about the surroundings.

"Actually, the Mormons constitute less than half the population here. Salt Lake's a pretty cosmopolitan kind of place. They *do* have a tremendous influence however—spiritually, politically, and economically," she added. "They're an industrious, warm-hearted group, on the whole, and because of their missionary efforts, their influence is felt throughout the world. They're very family-oriented and work diligently to educate their children. The Mormons also have the largest genealogical research base on the planet because they believe their ancestors should be given the opportunity to accept their doctrine 'through the veil', so to speak. A large majority of their young men and a few young women agree to serve a two-year, self or family-funded, stint as a missionary. Most of them learn a foreign language in the process and the experience sets the pace for their lives of self-sufficiency and dedicated service."

"Sounds like quite a unique group o' people," he remarked.

"*Very* unique, as far as groups go. I respect both their spiritual beliefs and their organization."

"Given ye'r outlook, Nik, and since ye were married to a Mormon, why didn't ye become one?" Crow viewed her as a giant enigma and yet, he felt a desperate need to know all about her: to crawl beneath her skin to see what made her tick. How could he be so smitten with her, afraid to lose her, and then, at certain times, feel compelled to throttle her?

"I *was* baptized a Mormon at the age of eight. Spent my whole youth involved in the organization. As a young woman, however, I hungered for the kind of spiritual food that can't be offered by *any* organization—nor could it be learned second-hand. I guess you could say I sought the *source* directly. My search was not a criticism of Mormon doctrine, but rather, a need to be true to, and follow, my inner guidance for expansion of that which I had learned. You know, 'To thine own self, be true.'"

Nikki diverted his attention back to the tour, pointing out the direction in which the Great Salt Lake could be found and the different mountain ranges that ringed the valley. She hoped the distraction would soften his irritation with her.

"Oh, no ye don't! Ye can't get off the hook that easily, lass."

"Dylan," she said softly, "I'm a little confused. One minute you're anxious to explore spirit with me and the next you want to glue my mouth shut. I'd love to share my experiences and insights with you and have you share yours with me. When you choose to *argue* instead of discussing something, however, you basically negate what the other person has to say—which in essence, negates them. That's not necessary. It's through exposure to new ideas or paradigms and other's experiences of the world that we are offered the opportunity to grow. Spiritual growth is an inside job. You may belong to some organization and abide by their standards, but the only place you really connect is inside. I do have a story, just as you have one. When you really want to hear mine with an open heart and mind, I'll be only too happy to tell my tale."

He stared ahead while contemplating her words. Truth be known, he ached to drag her into a debate in order to belittle her beliefs. *She's right, however,* he thought. *I do want to know her— not compete with her. Until mi mood changes, I'd best hold mi tongue.*

They headed immediately to the ski resort, enjoying the difference in the scenery from the desert. The rugged mountains were twelve thousand feet high in places and thick with pines and aspen. The winding road took twenty minutes to traverse, until, at last, they reached the bowl of the canyon. Nikki directed Crow to a small side road and jumped out to unlock a purple metal gate. A steep road leading another quarter mile delivered them to a parking area just beneath her cabin. A three level wooden structure overlooking and adjoining the ski resort appeared before them. She mentioned that her husband had designed and built it in 1973.

They hiked some stairs and walked down a long deck lined with split wood, to a crimson door and stepped into a room that measured about thirty by thirty feet with a ceiling that peaked at twenty-five. A massive fireplace of heavy granite occupied fifteen feet of one wall and stretched all the way to the high apex.

Nikki immediately lifted all the blinds to let the light in. As Dylan opened a sliding glass door to access the porch swing he saw through the window, the view of the mountain bowl stunned him. He lit a cigarette and allowed the nicotine to settle his nerves. Joining him on the swing, she sensed she had pushed him too far during the trip, for when truly content, he seemed to have no need for the "stick."

Nikki reached for his free hand and pressed the most delicate kiss on his knuckles, whispering, "Thanks for driving up with me."

"Beats muckin' stalls," he teased.

They sat silently admiring the majesty of the surrounding peaks. After a few minutes she stood and excused herself so she could get about the business of preparing for their overnight stay.

Dylan stepped into the cabin again and took a good look around. The furniture in the great room was massive, but tasteful. A dozen lambskins had been sewn together to create a large area rug. It lay at the base of a corner couch which positioned its occupants to look out to the ski resort.

Certain the road would be impassible in snow, he asked how she got up the steep driveway in winter.

"I have a garage on the main road and use snowmobiles to make the trek. Frankly, I only come in winter if I'm entertaining someone who wishes to ski or to meet the kids. They ski while I clean, cook, and keep the hot chocolate on the stove!"

"Sounds like a blast to me."

"For the kids too. The resort's widely used by snowboarders and it's literally putting your life in the hands of uncontrolled teenagers to attempt alpine skiing. I love Nordic skiing, however, and the resort offers eighteen miles of prepared track out of avalanche danger. My favorite time to be in these high mountains is during the wildflower season of summer."

A long, wide, open staircase divided the great room from the kitchen and dining area. The height of the ceiling and the dimension of both rooms were expansive and liberating. So many homes were designed with immense height, without taking width and breadth into consideration. Usually small rooms with high ceilings made Crow feel as if he were starring in an Edgar Allen Poe story in which the walls mechanically squeezed in upon him.

The wooden walls were adorned with weavings, oil paintings, and wildlife trophies. Antique skis and snowshoes were mounted here and there throughout both rooms. Oversized baskets and old wooden farming tools hung on the kitchen walls and a thick, round wooden table filled the dining area. The freestanding, round, metal and glass fireplace with a red hood and flue created a visual separation between the kitchen and eating area. An island surrounded by four high stools stood in the middle of the kitchen. Pots and pans hung from a heavy metal rack in one corner and tools of a gourmet cook lined the countertops. Throughout the cabin, a red and black herringbone patterned wool carpet stretched from wall to wall, giving a feeling of warmth and coziness.

Nikki stepped from the kitchen down a hallway lined by at least two dozen pair of skis and poles held by pegs. At the end of the hallway a red door with a bell harp piqued Crow's curiosity, but she opened the door to the right instead. "Just got to turn on the electricity to the water heater," she explained.

"May I look about?" he asked.

"You're a curious one!" she declared teasingly. "But of course, señor. Mi casa es su casa."

He decided first to explore down the ski hall. Two identical bedrooms held king-size beds, with an additional fold down bed locked up against the wall. From the grass mat ceilings, the color and style of the carpets and furnishings, the rooms looked like something decorated in the seventies and never touched again.

Most interested in the red door with the bell harp, he pulled it open and the harp chimed. While he ascended the steep and unevenly shaped steps, Nikki silently stole behind him to see his reaction to *The Secret Playroom*. At the top of the stairs he opened the blind over the window to let the light in for his better viewing.

The banister around the stairwell had been cut to create a design akin to those he'd seen in Switzerland. They were creatively painted with a colorful floral pattern. The handrail had been painted a darker, steel blue, and the corner posts boasted the same red color as the door. The room's ceiling hung low on the sides, rising to a gable high and wide enough to span the room twelve feet in width and at least twenty in length.

A full-size foosball table was situated in one corner, followed by small red shelves at child level. Each shelf held baskets full of toys, dolls, cars, trains, books, paints, and crayons. A television sat on top of a blue cabinet that had a beautifully carved outer brace for securing the television in place. Its cupboard doors were also painted with a Bavarian design.

The king-size bed was magnificent. Its massive headboard had been painted in an elaborate floral design with certain lines carved through to provide interest. The foot-board matched its beauty. He could tell it had not been painted by the same hand as the other pieces of furniture around the room. A green satin down comforter covered the bed. Above the headboard hung an oil painting of an angel who placed a finger to her lips and looked down over her charges, whoever they may be.

On each side of the bed sat very small end tables, cut and painted with the same design as the headboard. They were topped with blue ceramic lamps and a variety of children's books. Centered on the sides of the bed were petite steps to take little feet to the large napping station. Next to each end table were child-sized upholstered chairs with ottomans.

A small, freestanding basketball hoop had been pushed to one corner of the room. A child-sized table, about three feet in diameter, had been painted bright red with a floral pattern encircling its edges. Three small folding chairs surrounded it. Upon the surface lay a partially completed puzzle with its scattered missing pieces.

A wee rocking chair sat opposing the television, as if anyone interested in watching would surely be alone. Another cabinet had been painted a soft green with Bavarian decor on its cupboard doors. *A child's clothing armoire?* he wondered.

The multicolored carpet stretched from end to end, but at the right side of the bed a small, longhair, Angora sheepskin had been thoughtfully placed so one would rise from the bed to place his feet into its deep, plush softness.

The large room had the same magical kingdom effect Crow experienced as he came to Nikki's ranch and explored her space the first time they met. He turned to find her observing him intently. "Wow!" he declared, "I wish I'd been ye'r lit'l un!"

Trust me, you have been, she thought.

"Ye must 'ave searched all over the place for miniature treasures like these," he said, gesturing toward the furniture.

"I made them," she said softly. "I got stuck up here one whole summer without a car when Sam was a baby, so I decided to do something constructive."

"Ye're fooling with me, right?" he stammered. "Ye mean to be telling me ye built those lit'l chairs and upholstered them, and ye built that bed and *all* the furniture?"

"All except the foosball table, the television, and the little rocker." She smiled proudly. Nikki always felt the excitement and wonder of a small child when she entered this room. "A dear, old friend, who happened to be a famous ecclesiastical artist, painted the bed for me."

"Does anyone ever use it?"

"Well, as I said, I built it when Sam was a baby and he and all the grandchildren loved it. Most of them are teenagers or older now, though I still have a few in elementary school. The older ones head for the basement to play ping-pong, pool, and video games. The little ones stay up here and create magic. I called it *The Secret Playroom* when they were small because it used to be an attic that could only be accessed by an old wooden ladder. I built those crazy stairs myself, and as you can see, I was none too good at the measuring program! Anyway, it has remained *The Secret Playroom* for any and all of my little ones who come to visit."

To Crow, it felt like the only room in the cabin that truly expressed her creativity.

Again he found himself wondering if she would ever bear his child. He hadn't even bothered to ask her if she wanted protection, nor had he asked if she used any form of birth control. Perhaps, subliminally, he hoped he would impregnate her. *If she's thirty-nine, however, she might be getting past interest in child bearing, both physically and mentally*, he thought sadly.

She led him up the open staircase that divided the great room and the kitchen to her bedroom. The expansive room had been furnished with a king-size bed, a lovely desk, an oversized leather chair and ottoman, a small couch, and a pine armoire that held the electronic equipment. There were a few nice paintings throughout the room, but he could see more of Scott's personality than hers in it.

"When did ye say he built this?" Crow asked.

"1973. This was always Scott's place. He designed and built it himself, hauling wood up behind snowmobiles with his oldest son in early winter. He lived here during his divorce and it came to mean something very special to him, like a cherished friend with whom he felt safe. I never changed much at the cabin because it seemed like his special place," she expressed gently while looking all about her.

"So, ye'r children and gran'children use it?"

"Absolutely! It's become a family tradition. They still converge on holidays and all the cousins think of it as the sacred family shrine. I just love to get them all together. It's pure chaos, but a lot of fun too."

"Did they inherit it from their da?"

"No. But, it's theirs to use whenever they want as long as I own it. We tried diligently to assist each of the kids financially while Scott was alive. I think they recognized how much we sacrificed to get them each started. There were a few times along the way they got a little confused about what they thought was due them, but as they matured and began raising families of their own, things came into focus."

"Money can be a real bitch sometimes, can't it?" he stated flatly.

"It's not the money. Money's just an exchange of energy. It's people's fear of lack and their fierce nature when they think they must take from another in order to *have*. Some folks have difficulty understanding the Law of Abundance."

"Law of Abundance?" he asked, laughing, as if the very mention of such a thing represented pure insanity.

"Yeah, Dylan. There are all manner of natural cosmic laws that affect every aspect of our experience. Everything is energy and exchange of energy. God's treasure house is unlimited and we were meant to live and enjoy life abundantly, but also with responsibility and wise use of that energy. You've read about great spiritual leaders like Sai Baba who literally precipitate all they require and desire directly from Universal Substance. If they can do it, so can we! Even though most people have yet to develop the concentrative powers to precipitate, they can, by their belief in boundless abundance and a belief in their own worthiness, draw to themselves, through infinite sources, all they desire! Since God's treasure house is unlimited, they're never depriving another by their own abundance. In accepting our Father's free gifts, however, we also have to accept the responsibility to *do no harm*, and to utilize this abundance in a way that blesses the whole."

He began to fidget like a schoolboy waiting for the bell to ring. He looked at his feet to avoid her eyes. "Well, boss, what's it take to winterize this place?" he asked, hoping to dodge the expanded version of her lesson.

Nikki sensed the day's various spiritual conversations were pushing him right off the edge of the cliff and moved swiftly to change directions. She located a printed list—one she left in the event one of Scott's children actually wanted to perform the ritual and save her the trip. Crow turned off valves and switched water lines and helped remove the hoses from the bibs, covering them with insulated plastic. The electric heaters on the walls were set to specific temperatures in the event the central propane heater went out. Nikki had called the propane truck en route and the driver arrived and filled the tank for the winter. Likewise, a man with a *honey truck* came about an hour later and emptied the sewage tank.

While inspecting the exterior planks she discovered a woodpecker had chipped a hole through to the double roof. Sealing the hole would be required before all manner of rodents made their way into the warm place for the winter. Since balancing the thirty-foot ladder took strength, she put Dylan in charge of the muscles while she climbed the height and performed the work. They carried porch furniture to the basement for storage and pushed line insulation around the window frames. She checked the function of the furnace and changed the filter, then turned it on, as a stiff, cold breeze began to blow, ushering in a frigid cold front from the north.

Only yesterday, we sunbathed in the nude in southern Utah and today we're facing snow in the northern territories. An interesting state, this, thought Crow.

Having finished their chores, Nikki suggested they walk down to the pub and have a bowl of soup or a sandwich and a glass of beer. He heartily accepted her offer.

A funky old log structure owned by friends, Don and Jolene Deseray, served as the pub. Don, a fifty-five year old, athletic mountaineer, had the appearance of a forty year old. In fact, he could have served as George Clooney's double. Jolene, on the other hand, seemed ageless. Crow would have taken her for eighteen, though he heard her say something about their son who had just graduated from college. Her slight figure, long auburn hair, and a truly happy face gave her the appearance of eternal youth. She laughed about everything and made everyone giggle with each exaggerated movement of her hands and eyes. They did not seem overly impressed that he, the famous Dylan Crow, sat across from them eating a hamburger. He enjoyed people who lacked affectation in his presence and could easily see why they were Nikki's friends.

The nighttime alpine winds were raw, cutting through his thin leather jacket as they climbed back up the steep road. At nine thousand feet Crow found himself actually panting.

"I made you walk this just so you would force air into your lungs. It'll help you acclimate for your sleep tonight," she explained while tugging him up the hill.

Nikki built and lit two fires: one in the massive granite fireplace, and another, in the central kitchen fireplace. They drank a little wine while watching a movie and cuddling under a camel-hair blanket. When the movie ended, Dylan stretched and sprawled out on the inviting lambskin rug while she located a romantic CD. She joined him on the lambskin and while the crackling fire played shadow games on their entwined naked bodies, it also gave new dimension to the depths of Nikki's eyes. At least a dozen faces seemed to be superimposed over her face, though each seemed to belong to her, and each seemed familiar. Once again, Crow felt overwhelmed with the desire to have her inside of him somehow.

"Would ye mind if we sleep in *The Secret Playroom* instead of Scott's bedroom?" he asked timidly.

She understood.

Oddly, he found he could fall asleep quite easily in her arms. Usually he found that after the initial night of making love with a woman, he desired a little space between himself and the lady in order to sleep peacefully. With Nikki, however, he wanted to wrap her up in a ball and tuck her inside his embrace for safekeeping, fearing he'd wake to find he had only dreamed of her.

When they rose she convinced him to take a bath in her round, deep soaking tub. She put bath salts within it, which while smelling different, reminded him of the effervescent bath he'd had at the Green Valley Spa that day with Grace. *That day with Grace,* he thought, ...*the dream within a dream that brought me back to Nikki's gate*. He silently blessed Grace for what she shared with him. A few minutes later Nik joined the soaking ritual.

Confident the cabin had been safely prepared for winter, they locked the door and drove down the road through a skiff of snow and headed back toward the warmth of southern Utah.

Chapter 8

When they reached the mouth of the canyon, Nikki inclined her head toward the city. "You want to see anything in Salt Lake before we split?"

"I'd rather get back where it's not so nippy, if ye don't mind," he said, eying her to determine if she desired to do something herself. She had once accused him of having a bad poker face: a mortal fault if you're an actor. But, it was *she* who owned the consistently honest face. Nikki always said what she meant and meant what she said. He'd spent his entire adult life reading between the lines attempting to understand what women *really* meant, for the majority he knew rarely spoke their truth. Most expected him to be a mind reader. Nikki was different—just straightforward, playing no games.

They stopped by Einstein Brothers to grab a bagel and coffee before they caught the freeway south.

"Let's check the conditions at Bryce," she said, tuning the radio to a weather station. Though straining to hear the report buried beneath the static, five minutes into the program they learned the cold front would remain in the extreme north while southern Utah would experience a lovely day in the mid-seventies. A huge smile crossed her face. "Yahoo! Wanna see another secret place Mother Nature's hiding? We can rent some mules in Bryce around noon and spend time in the bottom of the canyon. What d'ya say, Little Crow—want to be a real Indian for a few hours?"

He loved her enthusiastic energy, and knew that being alone with him in a picturesque place seemed to be part of the daily agenda. She understood his deep-seated need to connect to the earth. "I'd love to. Ye're not going to dock mi pay for missing a day of work, are ye?"

She dialed the trail ride establishment and before they reached the road that took them east of the freeway toward Richfield, she had arranged for two mules. As she had led a number of groups previously, Nikki knew the owners trusted her judgment and no longer insisted a guide accompany her. She asked if they would be good enough to put a saddlebag on Rascal, and said they'd be there between eleven-thirty and noon.

In a small city just prior to Bryce, they stopped at a liquor store to buy wine, and then a grocery store to get some cheese, bread, and apples.

The animals were saddled and ready, so they loaded their little bit of food and hit the trail. Mules were excellent for riding the sandstone for they were sure-footed, calm, and gentle. Rascal, the older mule, had a distinct light in his eyes that Nikki enjoyed, and she took him for herself. Dylan's mule, Joey, was a somewhat trail-sour, lazy thirteen-year-old.

Bryce's beauty staggered the imagination with millions of towering narrow monoliths standing like armies of stone. Viewing Bryce from above elicited an entirely different feeling than viewing it from the floor of the canyon.

They rode their mules into a little-known area which took most of the hiking tourists too much effort to get to. Once again, they had absolute privacy in yet another remarkable marvel of nature. Crow thought it an odd coincidence that they managed to have these extraordinary places all to themselves several times now.

They tied the animals to an ancient juniper, and while Nikki shared an apple with their transportation, Dylan prepared a little picnic on a nearby stone. "Hell fire!" he exclaimed brusquely. "We didn't bring a bloody corkscrew!"

"A girl scout is always prepared—ta ta ta da—magico, presto!" She lifted her jacket to expose a small Swiss army knife she had hanging from her belt.

"Does life ever catch ye unprepared?" he asked, a little annoyed at her seeming perfection.

With shy eyes cast downward she whispered softly, "The day you walked into my life."

He felt childishly proud to have caught her off guard a little. She always seemed a thousand miles ahead of him. He liked to hear her thoughts, but listening to the kind of things she was trying to teach him meant possibly having to understand and do them. He had a career in a field where everything appeared contrary to the type of cosmic responsibility she seemed to be thrusting toward him. *She'd probably never be happy in mi world*, he thought. *I've worked really hard to make it this far, and I won't let anything get in mi way.*

His sudden distance, evidenced by silence and lack of eye contact, confused her.

They hiked on foot until they entered a brush area just before a small pool of water where a rattling sound caught Dylan's attention. Perfectly coiled within twelve inches of their feet lay a diamondback. Wanting to jump, he stopped short when Nik touched his arm and spoke softly. "There is only God there. See only God there and don't make any sudden movement."

Nikki made eye contact with the reptile and in her mind, began a mantra: *I AM here and I AM there, I AM here and I AM there, I AM here and I AM there.* The snake's forked tongue smelled the air—smelled the fear around Crow. Though he held his head still, Crow's eyes searched to see if it would be possible for both of them to leap out of range. He knew he could push Nikki out of danger, but he'd be bitten. Then he heard her say her mantra out loud and observed that neither she, nor the serpent, would break eye contact with each other.

"Be still," she instructed in a calm whisper.

The three of them stood transfixed for a goodly three or four minutes, which felt more like three or four hours to Crow. Finally, the snake moved forward, slithering right over Nikki's foot and then deep into the brush. It was everything Dylan could do not to leap and grab it, thinking it would harm her, but her gentle squeeze on his arm prevented his action.

"Bloody 'ell! Let's get out of here!" he whispered breathlessly as he guided her away. Nik looked back to see if she could see the snake, but it was gone. "What were ye doing there, ye divvy? Don't ye know it could have struck and there's no way I could have gotten ye back in time for serious help!" Feeling his role as the protector and defender, he found himself actually scolding her.

"The rattler had no desire to *attack* us, Dylan. It was only *afraid*—just like you. Life holds so much more than fight or flight, darling. If there really is only God in everything, then God within the snake heard me and knew I had no intent to harm it. Real macho of you to want to sacrifice yourself for me, however—though I'm grateful you checked yourself before either of us got hurt."

How did she know I was thinking of leaping and grabbing the thing? Crow wondered with his face screwed up in frustration.

"Were you thinking of rattlesnakes by any chance, Little Crow?" she asked.

"As a matter of fact—been thinking 'bout them since we began the ride!"

"Well, I guess we have you to thank for the lesson then, don't we?" she said, smiling wisely.

"What do ye mean?" His voice reverberated with annoyance, but sincerity.

"Look, my love…" she began.

He noticed she used the words "my love"—not dear, not darling, not Little Crow—but, "*my* love." The word had not been used between them, save for the Irish public term of endearment: luv.

"...when I talk to you about higher laws, you get as squirmy as that snake. I truly appreciate your desire to protect me, but there *are* higher ways of approaching life—ways that bring harmony, peace, and joy. There are things I could teach you so you'd never be afraid of anything, ever again—but only if your heart wants to hear them."

She stood her ground like an aggravated parent who's been fighting the uphill battle of implanting *new, undesired* information into a rebellious teenager. "I figure if you really want to know some of the things I know, you'll ask me with the intent of actually *hearing* what I have to offer. This exchange of energy between us has to be balanced and I'm not going to drag you down some metaphysical road, kicking and screaming all the way." She spoke with gentleness, but firmness, looking straight into his soul through his matching eyes.

Turning on her heel, she headed back to the mules.

Crow stood still for a moment, feeling a little dodgy, then reached for a cigarette. "What? Does she think she's mi guru or something? '...with intent on hearing!' What a load o' shite!" he muttered under his breath. His pride was bruised and his ego dented. He wanted to hear what she had to teach, but also felt a strong desire to be the masculine, protective hero he'd always admired in his life. The image of himself as strong in body and pride brought tremendous satisfaction. He liked the image of being able to hold his own and being tough. It made him feel powerful. She had made him feel like a powerless git with her lecture.

Stubbing out the butt, he looked about for any more snakes with God inside of them, heaved a deep sigh, then joined her at the mules.

An ominous silence fell between them for a while. Her words

were not spoken unkindly. In fact, she prefaced them with "my love." But, he found a resentment building inside of him. He wanted to veer the conversation to anything but *higher laws* and decided to teach her a song on the remaining drive back to the ranch. She joined right in, like a happy child who had forgotten her boo-boo.

By the time they reached the ranch, darkness had fallen. Bear and Shasta, the Lab, greeted them rambunctiously. As they hauled their luggage in the house, a jet-black cat stood at the opened screen door.

"Py, baby, you come for a visit?" Nikki opened the door and let one of her many cats in. Py sat still, looking right into her friend's eyes, meowing with a consistent concerned voice. Nikki picked her up, looked at her tummy, and commented that she must have delivered her kittens while they were gone. "I always give them eggs and milk when they have babies. All the ranch cats know the rules and come to see me when their babies are born," she explained to Dylan, who stared with fascination at their exchange.

She beat the egg and milk together in a small bowl and offered it to the mewing cat. Py sniffed the milk, then returned to her rigid sitting posture and meowed frantically again. "Show me, girl!" Nikki said, as she opened the door and followed the cat quickly down the dark path. Suddenly bursting back through the door, she grabbed a flashlight and ran back out again.

A few minutes later Nikki returned holding a tiny little fur ball in her hand, massaging what appeared to be a dead kitten. Dylan peered over her shoulder. "I guess that one didn't make it, eh?"

"Dylan, could you trust me for just a few minutes?"she asked gently, but anxiously, as if they didn't move quickly, they'd miss the opportunity of a lifetime. "You can be part of something wonderful you'll remember forever, if you'll just relax and trust me!"

"Sure, yeah—why not?" came his casual response.

She carried the lifeless body to her bedroom and from a drawer in her bedside table, retrieved a little wand embedded with stones and terminated in a crystal. Pywakit followed them calmly. "This is for you to use," she said, handing Crow the wand. "Now we're both going to consciously direct energy to this little thing and see if its soul wants to return. OK?"

"Tell me how to do *that?*" he asked, laughing. To him, the idea seemed a bit farfetched and he wondered about Nikki's psychological balance.

Nikki continued. "See a bright light coming from a glorious, self-radiant being directly above you. See it send light from its heart down through the top of your head, to your heart, back up, and out through your right hand, magnified by the wand and directed into the kitten's body. You're a great actor, Dylan, and I *know* you can visualize and feel this perfectly. Just fake it 'til you make it. OK?"

He tried to follow her instructions and found that, in fact, he could visualize it easily. She mouthed words silently as she held her left hand under the kitten and her right hand over it. He began to feel energy move in a circular motion, swirling between her hands and reaching out to his, like a spiral that had been squashed down. They remained in this focused position for another fifteen minutes, neither saying a word, just focusing energy. A little movement took place in her palm as one back leg began to tremble slightly. Pywakit leapt onto the bed and began to lick her baby. Both Nik and Dylan marveled at its perfect little form, even though the eyes were still glued shut. After a few tender moments with her animal friends, she carried the kitten back to the nest and kissed Py good night before returning to Crow.

"Blimey, Nik! What just happened? Do ye have some weird

power to raise the dead or somethin'?" The experience had both mystified and scared him at the same time.

"My accumulation of light has been drained with all the sex we've had and I couldn't do it without you and some magnification. I merely asked the spirit of the kitten if it still wished the opportunity to use the body. Obviously, it wanted to," she said, offering no further explanation.

He felt tired, but as he crawled into bed with her that night, he found himself thinking she may, in fact, be some sort of advanced soul. *What the bloody hell is she doing with me? What the bloody hell did she mean when she said her accumulation of light had been drained because of all the sex we've been having?* Then he went to the well, drained some more, and fell asleep.

Chapter 9

In the soft, early morning light, Dylan lay studying her lovely little face and smelling her sweet breath. He never knew anyone to have sweet breath in the morning. Inhaling it deeply, he stared at her in absolute awe.

Crow's thoughts vacillated between the poles of deepest adoration to that of resentment founded on fear. *If there is actually such a thing as twin flames and Nikki is, in fact, mine, I'd be a fool not to hear what she has to offer. I know she believes we're destined to be together, but I just don't know if I'm ready to be with a woman who seems leagues ahead of me—a woman over whom I have no control.*

He had dreamed all night of snakes and kittens. The previous day's events had elicited from his psyche both exhilaration and trepidation, both love and antipathy. His brain felt raw from the pinball game that had pinged him from one goal to the other. *Surely,* he thought, *if I don't do something soon, I'll go stark raving mad.*

The peaceful expression on her face told no tales of powerful, mind-altering darkness; rather it held the signs of a soul with a clear conscience and sure knowledge of her relationship to something pure. Even though she slept, he drew her to his chest and the energy within his heart began its, now familiar, expansive throbbing as the desire to pull her inside overwhelmed him yet again.

Nikki opened her eyes dreamily, smiled, and whispered, "Good morning. I'm taking Pegasus to the mesa for the sunrise. You want to come, or stay here and rest?"

He opted to stay.

After the jingle of the bells hanging on the front door announced her departure, he rose from bed and started pacing around. Caught in this eddy of things he didn't quite understand, his feelings could neither be explained, nor denied. To him, there existed a terror that approached sacredness when he opened himself to any form of mysticism. Though he knew none personally, he had read of others who met their own insanity as they braved direct religion. The thought of accepting the responsibility for delving further into these mysteries filled him with angst. He seemed to be looking into a fathomless pit of abstraction and speculation that set itself above the dogma with which he'd been raised.

Dylan sat on the edge of the bed, holding his aching head in his hands. *Maybe I should pack up and get out while the getting's good. After all, mi life was doing just fine before I met her. In fact, I'd never even heard of the concept of twin flames until* Nikki's friend, *Grace, introduced the idea! Maybe the two of 'em cooked this whole thing up for some private agenda!*

As suspicion mounted and fear built a wall of defense, he could think only of calling Peggy to come to the rescue—delivering him to the nearest airport as fast as she could drive. An excuse of urgent business could be used to cover his tracks and his departure could be expedited within a few hours!

Crow located Peggy's card in his wallet, reached for the phone, and began to dial—then slowly hung up the receiver. A framed photograph of Nikki embracing one of her dogs had attracted his eyes. The look of devoted adoration in the dog's eyes moved him. Animals *always* sense the truth about humans.

"Keep ye'r hair on, lad," he said out loud. "What is it ye're so bloody afraid of? The lass is just a funny, adorable nanism filled with goodness and love. She hasn't done ye harm. That woman fills every day to the brim with good thoughts, constructive feelings, kind words, and decent actions. She hasn't *asked* ye to believe what she believes! 'Tis only ye'r bruised ego speaking, ye lout! Now be a true man, and quit trying to *control* everything! Don't be denying ye'rself the gift that's been handed ye on a silver plate."

Dylan drove to his cottage to obtain fresh clothing to store at her home. Wanting to wash some things, he determined to work the machines without Nikki's instructions. Strutting like a peacock upon her return, he reported his brilliance with the washer and dryer.

She just laughed. "Speaking of your wardrobe, did you bring a suit or a tux in one of your many bags?"

"Aye, in fact. Why? There a formal in town tonight?" he asked, charmingly cocking his head to the left.

"I need a little time on my own today. You mind entertaining yourself 'til about six? We can wear our fancy duds and make a good night of it. OK?" She searched his eyes, hoping she'd not hurt his feelings.

"Perhaps I could drive into town for a while. May I borrow that trashy jacket again?"

Obviously, they both needed a little space, and each gladly gave it to the other. Although their budding relationship bordered something of inestimable value, they both sensed they were on the precipice of blowing it.

She sent him on his way and began making phone calls. At noon she took a swim in her pool, then set off to her screened-in room to sculpt for a few hours.

Calling forth a form from within a stone always proved to be an exciting event for Nikki. She let the stone show her what it wanted to be. Never considering her art as work—only playful creativity—she painted or drew when inspired, wrote prose or poetry when her heart needed to be expressed out loud, and sculpted or gardened when she desired physical creativity. This day she chose to play with the stone she titled *Trinity*.

☯

As Dylan drove around he reflected on the sum of his life. He had everything he *thought* he ever wanted. He was a healthy, good looking, and talented bloke with a fabulous career he loved, and from which he made more brass than he ever dreamed he could make in his life. Unexpected fame had been his constant companion. He claimed good and loyal friends. Unlimited supplies of beautiful women were at his beck and call, as were many other forms of entertainment. Though he owned his share of vices, he also possessed all the trappings of success that he, and the world at large, *thought* should make any man happy and complete. But, something was missing in his life—and he knew it. That *something* that made him feel slightly anxious all the time. Dylan had often wondered if the void represented a stable relationship or a family.

He thought back to the night Nikki plucked cactus needles from his leg and how she tried to comfort him about his loss of Anne-Marie. She'd said something about "Divine discontent" coming from something deeper than relationships. *Am I missing mi spirit connection?* he wondered.

He considered himself a pretty noble soul: kind, compassionate, generous, and honest, (though he sometimes had difficulty in being completely honest with himself.) Feeling he could be considered courageous, dependable, loyal, and loving, he measured himself as a man of high ideals. *So, what's missing?*

Once again, the desire to pray for higher guidance swept over him. "Lord, there are forces at work in mi life right now that I don't understand. If it's true there are no coincidences, then the things that have led me to Nikki's door must hold some meaning for me. I want to understand, but I'm afraid to understand 'cause it may mean lettin' go of some beliefs that have held me pretty steady on mi course so far. I just want to know the truth. Can ye take the fear out of mi heart so I can hear the truth?"

As the last word of his prayer emerged from his lips, he noticed a large tourist-trap rock shop and thought perhaps he could find an interesting stone to buy for Nikki. She certainly loved all things that came from the earth.

When he parked, a white dove landed on the hood of the truck, pausing to engage his eyes through the front window. The bird took flight as soon as Crow opened the door, but he noted the direction in which it flew and gave chase. Entering an exterior display area, he found the delicate creature perched atop a small statue of St. Francis of Assisi. He stepped slowly toward it, fully expecting a flapping of wings, but it showed no signs of timidity. When Dylan extended his finger, the dove flew right to his shoulder. It stayed only a few moments before it flew out of sight.

He gazed down at the statue and began to chuckle. "I guess I'm supposed to buy this piece, eh? Now, this would make mi Nikki smile. She could easily be St. Francis reincarnated as far as I'm concerned."

When he carried it in the shop to pay the cashier, he commented, "That white dove of ye'rs is pretty friendly, isn't it?"

The cashier looked at him askance and replied, "Sir, we don't have doves in this area of the country."

After Crow's day of solo exploration, he pulled in the driveway and went looking for Nikki. Hearing music from the pool area, he followed its notes until he saw her, clad in bathing suit, safety goggles, and leather gloves. The hilarious sight drew a great belly laugh straight to his lips. She raised the goggles onto her forehead and joined his laughter, knowing she must look like an alien who'd just been for a dip.

Crow pointed at the piece she'd been sculpting. "I saw that piece the first day I came here. I like it. Does it have a special meaning?"

"It does for me," she explained, "but all art draws forth different meaning and different emotions from those beholding it. Don't you think? Like your work; every once in a while after you've listened to a million people pick apart a performance and analyze what *you* were *trying* to convey, don't you just find yourself laughing?"

"Aye, I guess I do."

"That's one of the reasons I never took any art appreciation classes. Like—who gave the guy at the podium the authority to tell *you* how to judge someone's act of creation…same with music or literature. I think all mankind must, by his very nature, *create*. *You're* a master of creation!" she said, smiling lovingly at him.

"Some people's art is finance, some acting, some healing—you know? Everyone must create. The passion inside of us needs to be expressed and when one works with passion, his work blesses not only himself, but also everyone around him. Too many people work hard, but with no passion, accepting employment that pays the rent and fills the coffers, but leaves an empty heart."

"Anyway—even though this holds a special meaning for me, it isn't necessary to define it for anyone else." She turned away to return her tools to their leather case.

Dylan stepped quietly behind her, gently touching her bare shoulder and turning her toward him, lovingly connecting eye to eye. "I only asked because I wanted to know what it means to *you*." He pronounced "you" with a distinct American accent. "I just want to know *your* motivation." While smiling, he spoke softly, attempting to honestly draw her out.

Searching his eyes to see if he feigned sincerity, she answered, "You really want to know?"

He nodded and laughed at the redundancy of her question.

Nikki hesitated, and then caressed the piece as she spoke. "It's

the trinity of existence. It represents to me the I AM Presence—
God Individualized in man—as the large outer figure embracing
the next two levels, but distinctly contributing to the Intelligence
of the lowest. See how its arms reach full around the central character but come to rest on the head of the small figure? The central
form represents to me our higher mental body—our Christ-self,
the great intercessor—who, while completely held within and part
of the I AM Presence, reaches in full embrace to the lowest figure,
distinctly contributing to the heart. The small figure represents
the physical, or lower self. It's God, Holy Spirit, and Christ. It's the
father, mother, and child. It's Intelligence, Wisdom, and Love. It
represents all the trinities of creation. Now you know." She lowered her eyes for fear her words might just be the proverbial straw
that breaks the camel's back. She understood his confusion from
the prior day's experiences and the last thing she wanted was to
drive him away from her, believing her a zealot of some sort.

He stepped closer to the sculpture and stroked each of its
smooth lines, allowing himself to move into her heart. The major
component of communication is not listening, but hearing, and
he had decided he would *hear* her. He wanted to understand fully
by listening attentively while honoring and respecting her value,
even if he didn't comprehend or agree with everything she said. *If
I have such an intense desire to have her inside of me*, he thought, *it
must go way beyond wanting her physically.*

Turning to her, he gently touched her face with the back of his
hand. "Ye have a bit of dust on that pretty cheek of ye'rs." Without
passing any form of judgment or offering comment, he simply
allowed her opinion without debate. He admired the excess of love
and serene benevolence that she extended beyond humans and
animals to even inanimate objects.

"I brought something for ye," he exclaimed like an excited child as he led her to the truck to expose his gift. "Ye remind me of this great saint," he said. "Can ye find a place in ye'r lit'l kingdom to give him a home?"

She jumped around and made such a fuss, you would have thought he'd given her a twenty-karat diamond. Its value exceeded that of a twenty-karat diamond, for she knew he had been thinking hard about the incidents with the animals. Throwing her arms around him, she kissed him all over his face.

Now there's a woman who knows how to accept a gift! he thought to himself. It made him feel so happy to have given something that brought her that much joy. Nikki had been right—just doing something with love did return with more—at least from her.

"It's four forty-five, little miss," he declared in his John Wayne voice. "I'd best go iron mi tux!"

"Oh, my! You have been acquiring a lot of nerve today! First, the washer, and now the iron?" she questioned giddily. She spoke with childlike gaiety, one of her many charms.

While looking like a fairy in the garden trying to find just the right spot for St. Francis, joy radiated from her whole being. Her bright yellow bathing suit with red flowers was not particularly revealing, yet Crow felt passion welling inside him again. *Give her a break, lad!* he scolded himself and settled for a squeeze on her bottom as he pulled her to him and kissed her. "I'll be back with the pumpkin and three mice at six, Cinderella!" They both laughed as she returned to the statue and waved good-bye.

☯

At pumpkin hour, Dylan let himself in and waited for her to make her entrance. He looked too handsome for words, and knew it. Occasionally he liked to dress up. While busy stroking his own ego, Nikki stepped into the room. Struck dumb, he absorbed the vision that appeared before him.

Her simple, deep purple, knit dress hung from dual spaghetti straps, hugging her petite form to mid-calf. A delicate shimmering violet shawl hung loosely over her arms at the elbows. The manner in which the dress' style flattered her form took his breath away. She wore no jewelry, save for the tiny gold band above the middle knuckle of her wedding finger, the one she wore to remind her she was not yet complete. Her hair had been lifted from her neck and clipped into a French twist and the scent of her, while subtle, elevated his senses to a peak of clarity he had never experienced before.

Suddenly, she became the most beautiful creature he'd ever seen. Crow had attended unlimited gala affairs where the women had spent thousands, in fact, sometimes, hundreds of thousands of dollars on a single costume—but none compared to the jewel before him.

She stepped toward him, complimenting him on his appearance. As words were unavailable, his kiss told her he enjoyed hers as well. How this woman could tweak his heart, whether in blue jeans or an evening gown, delighted his soul.

Insisting they take the Lexus for their chariot, Nikki explained she just didn't have time to turn the pumpkin and mice into coach and coachmen. He laughed and with his massive hand contacting the velvety skin of her bare back, gently ushered her out the door.

Though he drove, she instructed him to turn toward Kolob instead of town. Bewildered, he knew from having been that way a few days before, there weren't any restaurants in that direction. When they approached a sign that read *Smith's Mesa*, she directed him left onto a dirt road, and they drove ten miles over washboard conditions. He serenaded her all the way with his glorious voice, though the rough road gave it new definition.

A small hill lay before them and as they reached the crest, a blue canopy came into view on the mesa. Nothing else appeared in sight for miles.

"Stop here, Dylan."

As they emerged from the car, he walked closer to discover a lovely surprise. Underneath the canopy lay a large, thick oriental carpet, topped with an elegantly set table, complete with candles, china, crystal, and silverware. An ornate silver cooling vase filled with ice chilled a bottle of champagne. The boom box she'd used the day they had dined on Kolob Mountain sat perched on a near-by boulder. The extraordinary evening view of Zion National Park completed the elegant setting in the middle of the desert mesa.

Surely, the gods of Zion descended from their mountain thrones to place everything just for our pleasure, he thought.

They ate while the sunset painted the adjoining mesas with sur-real shades of light and color. The carefully chosen music comple-mented the romantic backdrop. When darkness fell, Nikki lit the four small propane lamps that hung at each corner of the large canopy, as well as a candle for the table and a free-standing propane heater.

The early stars peeked through the inky fabric of the night sky while the couple sat intently gazing into each other's eyes. Nikki had created a world apart from the other to share with her beloved and he appreciated her effort.

"Close ye'r eyes," he instructed with a kind smile.

When she obeyed, he fastened the little silver bracelet he had bought onto her wrist. Glistening tears filled her eyes as she admired it. When she gained her emotional balance, she spoke. "Do you have any idea what it feels like to have someone observe you close-ly enough to see what you admire and then surprise you with it? You have an enormous well of generosity inside of you, Dylan Crow, which goes so far beyond material things. No wonder you've thought of yourself as the 'king of love unreturned.'"

She understood, because, at least in this regard, they were absolute twins. Her love nature insisted on giving, and giving, and giving. But, she had spent a good deal of her life on the lower side of that teeter-totter and for years had thought others did not appreciate her generosity. When she delved into a complete understanding of what she had created in her life, she understood that she had created the blockage *herself*. Life is a constant giving and taking, as with each breath. Accepting yourself as someone *worthy to receive* is a hard lesson for many souls.

Leaning across the table, she kissed him in gratitude. "I will never take it from my wrist."

"Would yew care to daence, Miss Scarlett?" he drawled with a Southern accent.

"Why, Mr. Butler, I can think of no other thing that would bring satisfaction to the pitter patter of ma lit'l heart!"

Standing, he stretched his hand out, then pulled her to him like Fred Astaire. They rocked to and fro to the rhythm as he pulled her left arm up close to his chest and held her hand over his heart. He buried his face in her neck in their dancing embrace and kissed it softly, allowing his lips the sheer joy of touching her delicate skin. Then he whispered, "Heart of my heart, soul of my soul, flame of my flame—I love ye with a love so Divine, it puts all human love to shame."

Nikki stopped dead in her tracks. Her heart stopped. Her breath stopped. She seemed paralyzed. He smiled down at her face and kissed her with utterly sublime gentleness.

"How...how long have you known?" she asked in a hoarse whisper, searching his eyes as if *they* held the answer to this great mystery.

"Since the day ye arranged for me to have a stone-laying on

the grid at the spa."

She wept tears of relief and joy, as he swept her off her feet and danced around with her in his arms like a small, weightless child. There were no more masks between them. He made love to her on the oriental carpet under the stars, never wanting the night to end—reluctantly leaving only when she explained how cool it would be in another hour.

Upon their arrival at her home, he literally carried her to the bed where the magic began all over again. It was as if he saw her, and she, him, for the first time, for a new vision came from the clarity in their hearts.

Kissing her feet and working his way up her body until he came to her breasts, he suckled and nuzzled like an infant with moans of ecstasy while her body responded lovingly to every embrace. The electricity building between them threatened to crest and he feared if he didn't join her soon, it would be too late. Then, to his amazement, the electricity and frequency changed noticeably another notch. The sensation of a sustained orgasm overwhelmed him for over twenty minutes, while their hearts exchanged the energy between them, shifting it back and forth in a flood of perfect giving and taking. Finally, with shuddering completeness, they both screamed little cries of joy as an explosion of energy filled their whole bodies with absolute and utter ecstasy, an ecstasy that so far surpassed a physical orgasm, he couldn't comprehend it. While it held their bodies paralyzed, it freed their souls and they both wept in gratitude in each other's arms. A deep calm filled the room.

He never knew the human body or soul could experience such heights of joy. It went beyond his body, however, and that much could not be refuted. Even though he had experienced sex in every form man could imagine, he had never experienced love making with this type of physical and emotional intensity.

"Nik, luv, ye know so many things I won't even pretend to understand, but I'm curious to know if when we make love together, ye notice anything unusual in ye'r heart or head?"

Smiling wryly, she asked with sincerity, "Do you really want me to tell you about what you've been experiencing—or will my sharing it just encourage you to apply a few more bricks to that wall you started to build during our trip to Salt Lake?"

He felt a little ashamed, but so much love poured from her eyes, he felt certain she wasn't being judgmental or putting him down in any way. "Babe, ye intimidate me a bit. It's like trying to go to university when I'm only prepared to enter kinder-school. I'm used to being the one in charge of things and ye make me feel like a wee schoolboy. I don't mean to be buildin' a wall 'tween us. In fact, I'm trying really hard to just flow with things 'cause I find there isn't anythin' I wouldn't do just to be around ye. Do ye understand?"

"You didn't answer my question, love. Do you want to comprehend what you're experiencing, or just enjoy it?"

"Tell me what ye think it is, then," he answered while turning her back to his chest and spooning with her.

She recognized the move as one of distancing their eye contact. *Well*, she thought, *he did ask, so I guess I have an obligation to answer.* "Do you remember when I spoke to you about the four lower bodies?"

"Aye," he whispered softly as he nibbled her ear.

"Each chakra—or energy center—in your body relates to different aspects of your being. The energy centers for the four lower bodies are located below the heart. The higher aspects—or Divine energy centers—begin at the heart and go upwards. As we are *Divine lovers*, so to speak, each of these centers is magnetically

drawn to the same in the other. When the higher centers are acti-
vated while exchanging energy, whether or not we make physical
union, the electrons within the chakra become excited—expanding, and increasing in vibration until the center experiences an
orgasm of sorts. Divine love doesn't even pass below the heart,
angel face. I must admit, however, I truly enjoy uniting with you
on *all* levels. I guess you could call what we're experiencing *sacred*
sex."

"Like that eastern tantric sex stuff ye see in the New Age book-
stores?" he asked.

"The original purpose behind the tantric information was to utilize a method that would raise these frequencies—but the majority
of what is commercially available still focuses only on a heightened
physical orgasm at the lowest chakra.

"When the light of *our* chakras merge with the other's complementary energy, a double helix, similar to that of the DNA strand,
is formed. It completes an encoding sequence, which acts like a
tumbler on a bank vault security system, unlocking our joint spiritual potential. Together, we can create without limit, being the
fullness of the reflection of God, the pure image in our complementary activity of the Divine Masculine and Divine Feminine
energies. This encoding is unique only to individual sets of twin
flames. That joint spiritual potential cannot be reached by choosing just *any* person to be your partner. We were created as separate
halves of one whole. Individually, we can be complete in our at-
one-ment with our I AM Presence, but without our other half, we
are not complete as the perfect reflection of God."

She turned in his arms and began to kiss each area where his
chakras were located and explain them in more detail. Most of what
she said flew right over the top of his head, but the sound of her
lovely voice drowned all his resistance to the unfamiliar concepts.

He cared only about his overwhelming sense of bliss on every level when they joined "their energies."

Chapter 10

Nikki woke Dylan early the next morning, requesting he meet her at the barn in an hour. She intended to take him someplace very special.

After his shower and a light breakfast, Crow arrived at the barn to find Nikki loading Jake, Pegasus, and Lucy, the jenny, into her horse trailer. "Going to cover some distance today, are we?" he asked with one eyebrow raised in question.

After locking the door to the trailer, she scurried up to him. "I'm really going to push you today. I'd like to teach you something, or at least have you *experience* something as a gift from my heart. It will require that you trust me absolutely, however. Do you feel you can honestly do that, or should I unload our friends here?" she asked inclining her head toward the trailer.

He began to croon, "Baby, I'm yours and I'll be yours..."

It tickled her heart to have him so adorably answer the question by singing the old Dusty Springfield tune.

They drove the Tundra and trailer up the road toward Kolob, parking their vehicle at the Wild Cat turn-off. Jake and Lucy were already saddled, and Pegasus wore only a blanket. The jenny was loaded down with big leather sacks with a long copper tube tucked between the flap and the bag. Without questions, he let Nikki lead the way.

Two and a half hours later, she guided him into what he had imagined could only be *the place of beginning* as described in the movie. Her enthusiasm indicated her willingness to share yet another sacred spot and he approached with reverence. "What are ye up to, luv?" he half teased her.

Dylan retrieved his pocket camera. When Nikki turned with one hand reaching to him, and the other pointing above her to the area where she wanted him to follow, he caught the image on film. "That's the first picture I've taken since we've been together!"

Nikki untied the leather strings on the jenny's saddlebags and withdrew and unwrapped a number of large quartz crystals. Measuring the distance from a center point at which they should each be set, she positioned twelve stones in the sand with their termination points directed toward the sky. Though it appeared as a perfect circle to Crow, she had actually created a twelve-pointed energy grid. Next, she took the copper tubing, which had been bent at a ninety-degree angle on one end, and secured it in the ground in the very center of the circle. At the base she placed a medium sized crystal, also pointing upwards. Then she walked to the jenny's pack and withdrew the same *power stone* that had been used over his heart during his work with Grace.

"Do you trust me, my love?" she asked, searching his eyes for any sign of doubt.

"I trust ye as God above. Just tell me what to do."

Seating Crow so his spine touched the earth, she stretched his legs around the central crystal, bending them as if he were in a rowboat with oars. "Hope I don't have to hold this position too long!" he said. "It's a bloody tough back exercise."

Nikki sat opposite him, reaching up and hanging the power stone between them, over their heads, and in perfect alignment with the stone between them on the ground. The *power stone's* terminated end faced toward the earth.

Nikki crossed her legs over the tops of his, bringing their sexual centers as close as she could without disturbing the crystal. She took the copper wire from the power crystal and slipped it under the small stone directly beneath.

"You're going to have to follow my words consciously," she instructed. "Visualize everything I describe as clearly as you can

and let no other distractions enter our space. Do you trust me?"
she asked one last time.

Quite seriously, he answered, "I do, Nik. I do."

She wrapped her arms around his back slightly below the heart
level and instructed him to do the same to her. It balanced their
weight perfectly so neither felt any strain whatsoever. Dylan closed
his eyes.

Tilting her head toward the heavens, she declared: "Mighty I
AM Presence, through thee, and in thy name, I call forth the higher mental body and I AM Presence of myself and my twin flame,
Dylan Crow, the Lord of the Violet Consuming Flame, Jesus
Christ Sananda, our guides and angels, and all those who can best
serve this day's purpose. Magnify the light within our hearts and
the field that surrounds us in purity, perfection, and protection. I
AM our tangible, audible, visible enlightenment as to our joint
contract and purpose together while incarnate at this time. In the
name of the Light, I AM our union, serving to anchor one hundred per cent pure light here and through us, that our highest
good may be obtained and utilized to bless all.

"Breathe deeply, my love, and let your breath synchronize with
mine," she instructed softly. When they were in tune, she called
for the energy from the earth mother to rise between them. The
energy pulsed so strongly, Crow feared he would have an orgasm
right there. Just at the moment of release, however, she instructed
him to take the energy to the area just below his navel.

"See the light rise and fill your belly with a ball of light so
bright, vibrating so quickly that it must, of its own energy, explode
any second!" Again, at the moment of release, she brought the
light and energy to his abdomen—his feeling center—creating a
vision with her words regarding the intensity and speed of the
vibratory action of the light.

Dylan could feel the energy bouncing back and forth rhythmically between his abdomen and hers and thought they must be rocking each other with its force.

Just as the light reached a climax in his feeling center, she brought the light to their hearts. This sensation he recognized completely and fully, as if rising to the heart center, he no longer had an awareness of his body.

"These hearts are one," she continued. "See within their chambers a small flame with three plumes. The center plume is yellow, the right pink, and the left, blue. Though they are small, I want you to help them grow." She verbally directed his vision until his heart flame became the size of his chest. When the heart could no longer sustain the frequency and began its energetic crescendo, she moved the energy and the light to their throat chakras.

"This light will be held self-sustained within this center when you hold your attention on your higher self. Then, my love, every expression you give forth to this world will bless all humanity and the whole of God's creation."

The energy at their throat areas bounded between them so rapidly Crow thought his ears would explode. She told him to increase the size of the heart flame so it would rise from the heart and engulf his throat chakra, and again, just in time, she moved the energy to their third eye area.

Dylan saw light radiating like a glowing sun. He felt clarity and lightness of being, allowing the energy to flow from his third eye to hers. Spectacular displays of color intermixed with the white light as she instructed him to raise the level and size of the heart flame to include the third eye.

With the deftness of a surgeon, Nikki raised her left hand and touched him at the base of his skull, cradling his head while commanding the light to rise to their crown charkas—the point of entry into the material form for the light of God. As the ball of light increased in intensity, filling the entire top of his cranium, she instructed him to increase the size of the heart flame, yet again.

She called forth the light of God to be sent from their I AM Presence, through their higher mental bodies, and down to join the light that had risen from the earth mother.

When she pressed the spot where her left hand made contact with his skull, Dylan heard a "pop" as she commanded the light to rise, yet again, to an area one hand's width above their heads. He felt completely released by the light, becoming himself the light, becoming the flame that had been rising from his heart. He saw it leap above his physical body and envisioned it doing the same with her.

"Allow our flames to dance together, to complement each other in their double helix of perfect harmony."

In Dylan's consciousness they had become the flames. For the first time in his life he felt complete. He didn't know how long their flames danced together and reluctantly returned to his body when Nikki softly commanded the light from above to come back in its concentrated form to their hearts and maintain perfect harmony and balance.

"As this flame returns to your heart, Dylan, know always that everything now perceived through your other energy centers is defined by and through the perception of this heart flame."

When the overwhelming experience ended, Dylan collapsed to the ground in a deep sleep. While he dreamed, Nikki collected all the tools and re-packed them in Lucy's saddlebag.

She silently thanked their helpers with all the gratitude of her heart and went to watch over her beloved as he dreamed.

Crow had a vision that a great light went forth from his third eye, throat, heart, and through his hands, blasting around the entire planet, enveloping all within his perfect Love. This love circled the planet repeatedly and every time it came back to the point of beginning, he experienced an orgasm of the heart. Each time, the orgasm grew stronger and stronger, until his whole being became encased in a great oval of light. Within the white fire ovoid he beheld his twin flame. She held a book in her hands, which she pressed into his heart. The words of the book came through his voice and spread from his throat chakra and out to enfold the whole of humanity. He turned to his beloved and heard her say, "Well done, my dearest love—heart of my heart, soul of my soul, flame of my flame."

When he awoke an hour later and all evidence of the experience had been cleared away, he thought perhaps he had dreamed the whole thing. Nikki assured him he had not, gently explaining the opportunity they had taken for a "glimpse" of a higher cosmic purpose together. "I couldn't sustain the connection and vision for very long due to the decrease in the light in my field from our lovemaking. When we both increase the light in our fields, we won't require the use of these tools. We can be the tools."

Nikki moved behind Dylan and wrapped her legs around him while he lay back. "Making love—completely connecting with another soul in co-creation—is an extraordinary gift. It is a repetition of the act of creation on cosmic levels. Mostly, humans use their sexual energy only at the lower center for *sensual satisfaction*—squandering both their seed and energy with no thought to the expense it's costing them. I just wanted you to see and feel for yourself what it feels like to raise that energy to the higher centers and utilize it for the goodness, the Godness of the whole. It's not that sexual relations are in some way wrong. It's just that people participate in sexual practice more as a habit than as a conscious intent to join with another soul. It's the habitual release of *undirected energy* that's squandered. In consciously directing that energy to some constructive end, it, of course, follows the great circle of life, returning to us magnified. That's why the Law of True Love is one of *giving*.

"We can use that incredible energy and build it within our own force fields and draw upon it to perform seeming miracles if we desire. We can send that power out with direction from Divine Love and Wisdom to heal and prosper all mankind. Or, we can use it to procreate, making a temple for a beloved soul to enter and achieve his purposes. There's virtually no limit to what we can co-create together, my love.

"We can raise that energy to any of our chakra centers for any purpose by consciously holding the creative thought while we make love. It's the joining together of the complementary forces of creation with conscious intent. The same act of creation exists throughout the universe. As above, so below.

"The sacred energies that are exchanged in a sexual union were intended to be spiritualized. If the union consecrates the love of God, it brings forth the Son of God, whether it be in the form of a child, an idea, a work of art, inspiration, or a successful endeavor. If the union is not spiritualized, the partners can experience physical pleasure, but the energy is squandered."

Crow turned to face her. "So, ye're sayin' without proper intent and direction of that energy, it basically just spins off somewhere into space or somethin'?"

"That's it! It's not held in our fields to maintain our youth, beauty, health and strength, or utilized to increase the light in our fields for future accomplishments, or directed to anything useful. It's simply…lost."

"I never realized the true value and importance of the sexual union before, luv."

Dylan stood and brushed the sand from his clothing. The

experience had been profound and life-shaking, and he could speak no words on their journey home.

Chapter 11

Crow felt no desire to communicate with anyone in the outside world. As he'd asked Peggy to get in touch with his family and agent to allay any fears regarding his safety, he had no concern about connecting with them. It felt like the most beautiful pause of his life. He couldn't believe three weeks had already passed. In fact, he felt certain time stood still just for them—endless and full. Instead of his usual sense of urgency, only profound peace permeated his psyche.

Their days were filled with little chores and cavorting with each other, the earth, and the nature spirits. Dylan began to trust everything she did and said. When she initiated a discourse of sorts, he truly listened.

They could talk about anything easily, for he found no form of judgment coming from her. Curiously, in Nikki's presence, his very thoughts and feelings had become absent of criticism toward anyone or anything. She didn't indulge in idle gossip about individuals or the world at large, though she had her opinions and voiced them with authority. Because he felt safe, his soul completely relaxed with her.

For the first time in two years, he felt like himself—completely himself. Acting out roles for so much of his life, at times he wondered who or what he really was. He felt whole in her company. Crow admitted things he'd never told to anyone before in his life, including family, friends, and lovers. When confessing incidents he was certain would horrify her, he found only relief, for she looked upon all experiences as opportunities to learn. Nikki looked at him through the eyes of love, and he knew it, felt it, and appreciated it. It made him want to *be* the very best, most noble, character that ever lived.

"I keep waitin' for someone to shake me and tell me I've just been dreamin'," he declared after a particularly cathartic session. He realized his soul had been starved for the kind of love and affection he felt from her.

"Angel face, did you ever read any of Frances Hodgson Burnett's works...like *A Little Princess,* or *Little Lord Fauntleroy,* or *The Land of the Blue Flower?*" Nikki asked.

"Might have when I was a lad, but I can't remember, Nik. Why?"

"I have a BBC production of *Little Lord Fauntleroy.* Let's watch it this afternoon and you'll know why I asked. O.K.?"

They settled comfortably on her bed to watch the flick. Any excuse to prop up the pillows and hold her in his arms was acceptable, so he agreed to participate. Whenever Nikki suggested a movie, the story she chose always had some profound moral to it. Dylan was keenly aware she utilized his medium—something he understood completely—to teach him, though she never said as much.

When the film ended, she looked to him in anticipation.

"What?" he answered.

She looked shocked that he could have missed her purpose in having made him watch it. The point had not been missed, but he delighted in yanking her chain. He just wanted to hear *her* version.

"Wasn't it wonderful how, through his innocence, Little Lord Fauntleroy saw his grandfather through eyes that held him as the most kind, most loving, generous, and wise man that ever existed? Wasn't it magical how, by having just *one* person hold him in his heart and mind that way, a space was created in which *he became* those things?"

"Is that what ye do for me, Babe? Do ye hold me in ye'r vision and heart in such a glorious place that it makes me want to possess every noble virtue that ever existed?" His eyes pooled with tears, knowing the answer before he asked the question.

"You already possess all those virtues, Dylan. All those 'noble virtues' you refer to are self-sustained within your I AM Presence, just waiting for the opportunity and invitation to be expressed. Perhaps the greatest tragedy is that we see ourselves as separate from God's Divinity; that we see ourselves as miserable and lowly, unworthy creatures being tossed and blown by outside circumstances. When you can see yourself as God in Action, you'll find those virtues govern your entire existence and all your experiences. The only difference between *my* vision of you and *your* vision of you is that I *know* your perfection, and you only hope for it. To me, you're absolutely beautiful, through and through."

"Do ye remember all our past lives together, Nik, 'cause I don't remember any of 'em?"

"I don't remember all of them, but enough of them. Most of my memories are…how can I explain it? Well, it's more like I remember the *essence* of our lives together. Sometimes that essence felt loving and constructive, and many times it was anything but! I do have lucid memories about the lives when we knew *what* we were. As I chased you through each life, I missed those times most of all. I missed you—the real you—most of all. That we are both conscious of our relationship to one another now is no coincidence, angel, even though it felt like an odd series of events that brought us back together.

"It's certainly no coincidence that you've spent this lifetime in two vocations through which you share what you know through mass media. The ability to transfer concepts and principles through your acting, speaking, singing, and writing, can be used to serve the highest and most noble goals for all mankind. I have no doubt whatsoever that our joining at this time is to help you remember your destiny to serve the light with your talents. It's no coincidence that your voice is so luscious and affects people the way it does."

She suddenly lit up like a little child as she tried to imitate his deep, melodic, harmonious tones.

"Oy!–Is that how I sound?" he asked holding his ears. They both laughed as she pulled his hands from the sides of his head and began to whisper little nothings in his ear with an Irish accent.

"There's only one thing I want to hear ye whisper breathlessly in mi ears, Nik."

In a dulcet angelic voice she whispered, "I love you, Dylan Crow. I love you yesterday, today, tomorrow, and for all eternity."

Chapter 12

Playing Sam's guitar in her studio, he created music while Nikki sculpted. "Do ye play any of the instruments I see around this house?" he asked while plucking absentmindedly.

"I love music! Never had any musical training, however, and always figured *someone* had to be in the audience to enjoy the great talents of those who *can* play and sing." She sat down next to him and withdrew the guitar from his arms, posturing with it herself. As she strummed the strings, Dylan showed her some basic chords.

"Wait a minute," she said excitedly. "This is a perfect opportunity to share something amazing with you." Nik placed the guitar between them and became very tranquil and quiet, asking him to be still as well. Though her lips did not move, he could tell she had sunk into a deep form of meditation or prayer. Her eyes were closed as she sat motionless for about fifteen minutes in absolute silence. Finally, Dylan wondered if she'd fallen asleep.

With eyes still closed, she reached between them and drew the guitar to her, holding it like an expert musician. Her fingers pressed, plucked, and strummed an entire concerto of classical origin with absolute mathematical precision, impressed with all the passion of the composer.

Dylan, transfixed, beheld the scene: his little, musically untrained, twin flame playing with all the finesse and perfection of a master. When at last she finished and opened her eyes, he was too stunned to do anything but stare with his mouth agape.

"I thought ye said ye *couldn't* play!"

"I can't. Of myself, I've had no training and possess none of the knowledge necessary to perform the piece played for you. I just connected through my Mighty I AM Presence and Universal

Consciousness with a musical master and asked him to perform the piece through my brain and hands. How did you like it?"

"Nik, ye really do scare the shite out of me! Ye got any more lit'l tricks hidden up ye'r sleeves? I mean—can ye channel Elvis, or somethin' groovy?"

She realized she had perhaps introduced the lesson too early, for though he attempted to interject humor, she discerned in his eyes honest-to-goodness fear.

"In God consciousness all things are possible, Dylan. You just have to believe that! I don't do parlor tricks with smoke and mirrors. I merely used this as an example to show you the unlimited nature of our beings, to demonstrate our connection to the whole. It wasn't necessary for me to reinvent the wheel—only to connect to another part of the whole that possessed the knowledge, training, and talent to bring something into this domain. It doesn't preclude me from personally learning and sharing anything I desire with the whole, dear. It's just one of the unlimited possibilities of our extraordinary lives."

They talked about their ability to create and Nikki explained how thought began the process, but how nothing could come into form until it becomes clothed in feeling. She made clear the critical power of learning to control what is allowed within one's feelings, for that is the area where discord makes its entrance.

"Have you ever known people who destroy everything around them that's beautiful and good because they can't control their temper—people who use volatility as their primary means of expressing emotion?" she asked.

"In the thirties James Allen wrote a book titled *As A Man Thinketh* addressing this very issue and it's as profound today as when it first came to press. He wrote about 'self-control as strength, of right thought as mastery, and calmness as power.' He likened a man's mind to a garden, which could be cultivated with intent or allowed to run wild. Allen said, whether cultivated or neglected, the 'mind will bring forth the fruition of the seeds that are left there, whether they be useful seeds, or weed seeds.' It's his message that prompted me to weed my garden so often, just to remind myself to eliminate my own useless thoughts and feelings."

"Nik, luv," Crow interrupted, "we're exposed to unlimited trauma and drama everywhere we look. We can't possibly control *all* the images and *seeds* that are planted in our brains."

Nikki stood and stretched as she continued. "Ah, but my dearest, we *can!* First, and foremost, we can *choose* much of what we are *exposed* to! Who chooses the novels and publications we read? Who chooses the movies we watch, the news we listen to, the music we hear, the parties we attend, and the company we keep? True, there are times when you simply can't get away from the muck by voting politely with your feet, but even then, we have the ability to transmute the energy of the situation."

Nikki reached for a popular magazine he'd been reading, and kneeling beside her lover, began to flip the pages. "The tragedy of our mass media today is through story, whether written, sung, or acted out, we've become addicted to the volatility of destructive behaviors, viewing life as one great painful drama, as evidenced by ninety-eight percent of that which is written in America's favorite magazines and what appears on our televisions—eh?

"Though that is *a* pathway of learning, it's just as powerful to observe people rising over dilemma and trauma to the best within themselves—just like the Hodgson Burnett stories. Instead, the media serve up a feast of judgment, condemnation, and criticism that creates a feeding frenzy among the populous. Remember how people were glued to the television during the O.J. Simpson murder trial? Meanwhile, with the public distracted, they neglected to notice the truly important things going on around them... like the President of the U.S. eliminating the last shreds of our constitution.

"Mass media could be the most remarkable means by which to enlighten people, but it has *definitely* been infiltrated by nefarious forces that consciously utilize it to hold the populace in a mesmerized state of fear, hate, anger, and resentment. In this constant state of discord, people have difficulty connecting to the truth of their relation to God and one another and end up looking for someone or something else to lead the way.

"Those who finance the film industry and the major publishing houses are concerned only with the bottom line, and they, too, have become addicted to how much money can they make by pushing people's emotional buttons. The majority of them, consciously and devotedly, seek stories imbued with violence, lust, greed, selfishness, infidelity, dishonesty, and a thousand other destructive emotions—because it 'sells!' Most of the time when they choose the lighthearted approach to life, they express it through vulgarity or absolute stupidity, creating a fool of the otherwise noble human spirit."

"Wait," Crow interrupted her diatribe, "go back to that page." He reached for the magazine and flipped back a few pages. "It's not all bad, luv. See, there's mi smilin' mug from last year's Golden Globes. Hmmm...guess they didn't have an updated photo for this article."

"Hold on there, buckaroo. As I recall, this article is chuck-full of *crapola,* not only about you, but also about the other 'stars' whose smiling faces are printed here."

"In mi business, it doesn't matter if the word is good or bad, luv. Keepin' ye'r face before the public is the *only* thing that matters." Crow scanned the article. "Ye're right, as usual, however. It is...what did ye call it? Crapola?"

Nikki pointed to the magazine. "Well, according to this article, you've impregnated and abandoned at least ten women, you're bi-sexual, a hopeless alcoholic, and I think it says something about beating up small children. Hmmm? Let's see, now...is that the kind of energy you want people to hold for you?"

"Nik—it's a bloody game! No one believes that drivel."

"You'd be surprised how many people believe 'that drivel!' Look— all I'm saying is that life is joyful. Life should be celebrated. Every *advance* we make in life should be celebrated *constructively* by the whole. Our novels, entertainment, news, and media in all its forms, could reflect the attributes and values that *increase* our light instead of decreasing it. They could seek and print that which is life-enhancing instead of life-damaging. Instead, the majority of what's placed before us holds little or no true value to our souls."

Nikki rolled the magazine and tapped Dylan over the head with it. "Facing our seeming dilemmas in life with a sense of light-heartedness and humor is the fastest way to rise above our perceived problems, so I'm glad you view this 'drivel' with lightheartedness. If it *could* press your emotional buttons, it would send you straight to a hellish existence."

She looked deep into his eyes. "Look at how many parts you've played in which your ONLY job was to be angry or passionately out of control, creating violence as the pathway to solving your character's quandary. Great example for the masses, eh? Yet, when I hear the lyrics to some of the ballads *you've* written, I recognize God coming through. You have a depth of love, insight, and a sense that life continues in the face of disappointment with more rainbows on the horizon. I see more of your true self in your original and authentic creations than I do watching you play out someone else's drama.

"You're a fabulous actor, Mr. Crow, and you've proven to yourself, and the world, that you possess a remarkable talent. Your ultimate genius will be shared with the world when *you* are the author, director, and actor of your own works: when every aspect of your performance is your authentic creation! And, my dearest love, I'll be the first to applaud your Divine art, because I *know* what you contribute will be *noble*."

Chapter 13

Nikki sent Dylan to her basement to collect a can of black beans for their supper. As he flipped the switch, the light illumined her secret library. Hundreds of books on every conceivable subject lined two walls of the huge room. He took so long, she came to investigate.

"Found it!" he blew at her as if he'd just won a sleuthing prize. The upper house exhibited all manner of books, including many about the Latter Day Saints religion, but he had seen evidence of spiritual, esoteric, and metaphysical literature only on her bed stand. He knew she must have resources that went beyond the few things he'd seen. The library selections ranged from spiritual and metaphysics to physics, geometry, astronomy, geology, and philosophy.

"It wasn't hidden, dear. You just never asked me if I had any reading material," she responded, smiling graciously. "Besides, the best and only completely reliable information comes from the education you receive directly from your I AM Presence."

"Any favorites?" Dylan asked.

She responded only with a shrug of her shoulders.

Attempting to discern whether some books looked more used than others, his eyes were drawn to a series bound in green leather: *The I AM Discourses*, by St. Germain. Some of the titles offered credit to *Godfrey Ray King, the Great Divine Director, Victory,* and other lofty names and titles that seemed to Crow a bit bizarre. "Ye think I should read any of these?" he asked, willing to have her guide him.

"That's up to you. If you feel attracted by something, take it." Nikki became visibly nervous and felt compelled to leave the room, for in watching him thumb through her favorite books, she had an insight with such clarity that it shook her entire foundation. "I better check on our supper," she said, excusing herself. She located the black beans and headed slowly up the stairs, trying to steady her emotions.

Lingering behind, he opened books randomly to see what treasures lay upon their printed pages. He chose the first volume of the St. Germain series, perhaps because he'd heard Grace call upon this being during his stone-laying. It was titled, *The Magic Presence*. He leafed through its pages and then withdrew several other volumes. One had artist's renditions of Angelic Hierarchy throughout. Flipping the pages to the back of the book, he found one of the man with the violet eyes he'd seen in his dream on the grid. With heart thundering in his chest, he raced up the spiral staircase to the next level, charging into the kitchen to share his news with his love.

"Blimey! Look what I found, Babe!" he blurted out excitedly. "This is the guy—the one I told ye 'bout! Remember mi past life dreams I had on the grid? I swear it's the same fella!"

Nikki glanced at the rendition of St. Germain. "You're fortunate to have met this master, even if only in a dream. If you need guidance, he'll help you any time you call upon him through your I AM Presence. But to receive his assistance, you must invite it."

Crow helped her make a salad to go with their supper, but he couldn't wait to start reading the book he'd brought up. He wolfed down his meal like a kid trying to get out the door for a soccer game. She laughed at his antics and offered to do the dishes alone, just this once.

"Nik, remember on our trip to Brighton ye said when I was ready to hear ye'r tale with an open heart and mind, ye'd be glad to share it with me? Seeing that library and scanning the titles of all the books ye've read triggered somethin' inside o' me—somethin' that

has me confused about ye. Do ye trust that I love ye enough to tell
me 'bout ye'r personal spiritual evolution?"

"Darlin', do you think you can truly hear me without moving
into a space of judgment?"

"Well, can't I ask questions or anything?"

"Sure—in fact, I welcome your questions. I'm not willing to
argue or debate with you, however. You don't have to agree with
my beliefs or experiences, but I ask you to sincerely honor them.
We each see through different eyes and that's OK. I'm not claiming to own all the truths in the world or asking you to follow my
path. But, when I share my experiences with you, it can multiply
your own, vicariously."

"Alright, then, Babe. Start at the beginnin', from your childhood training."

"Well, it's not a three minute story, Dylan. Wouldn't you rather
read that book you found for a while and talk later?"

He stood with the book in his hand, then reached for hers and
led her silently to the bedroom. After placing the book on the
night stand, he removed his shoes and got comfortable on the bed,
signaling her to do the same.

"I have kind o' an inner sense that it's important to know why
and how ye've come to where ye are before I delve into this book,
Nik. It's obvious ye've read the books in that series more than just
a few times. They must hold a special place in ye'r education.
Though I'm dyin' to crack the book, somehow I know I'll get
more from it if I understand why it means so much to ye."

Nikki piled the pillows high behind her as Dylan crawled
between her legs and reclined in her arms. As she began her tale,
he softly stroked her fingers.

"All good tales begin with 'Once upon a time,' so, Once upon
a time, a little girl named Nikki was born into a household where

her mother, though raised as a Mormon, did not participate in her religion. Nikki's father had been raised as a staunch Catholic, but as an adult, also did not participate in his religion. Since Nikki's father and mother divorced before she reached the age of two, Catholicism played no major role in her life. As Miss Nikki grew, her friends and neighbors were all Mormons and wanting, as all children do, to be accepted in the community, she also participated in the Mormon church. Actually, it is not the 'Mormon' church, but rather The Church of Jesus Christ of Latter Day Saints—but most folks call them Mormons.

"At the age of eight, with the *wisdom* of an eight year old, Nikki decided to be baptized into this particular organization and, with confirmation, became a full-fledged member. Her membership brought many fine relationships with good and caring people who did their very best to teach her their beliefs. It also kept her off the streets for they offered a wide variety of activities from sports to dances and mid-week meetings for the youth of the church.

"As Nikki grew, she began to notice the handsome boys who had become Priests, Decons, and Elders: degrees of both responsibility and authority which are confirmed upon male members of this particular organization. She never questioned why these positions were held only by the male folk, for it had been deeply ingrained from youth that this organization believed in the patriarchal order and that females, although honored, were only recipients of the highest blessings by their alliance with the priesthood through marriage."

"Can't women hold the priesthood?"

"No. And for a long time, neither could people with black skin. But one day, lo and behold, their prophet and president had a revelation that changed the belief that had so long been held that black people held the mark of Cain and were not 'worthy' to hold the priesthood. Oddly, it coincided with a threat from the U.S. Government to change the church's tax status for obvious reasons. But who was I to question the words of the *prophet*, a man who recieved divine inspiration and revelation for the entire church from God himself."

Dylan shifted in her arms and looked up with one raised eyebrow. "Surely there must 'ave been some rebellion from the followers!"

"If so, it was kept quiet. But then, remember, our Nikki is still but a teenager and terribly disinterested in politics, so she neither knew, nor cared.

"That particular incident, however, sparked her first questioning as to organized religion and authority figures.

"By age sixteen our girl decided that her church was indeed the 'one and only *true* church upon the face of the earth.' After all, everyone around her said so, and said it with such conviction that she began to repeat the same words until she unquestionably believed them herself. After making an appointment with her Bishop, she advised him of her desire to serve a mission. He smiled kindly and asked if she had even read the Book of Mormon all the way through. With a pat on the back and an assurance that one day she would be the wife of a man who served an honorable LDS mission, he told her that her greatest calling would be as a mother in Zion."

"Ye mean he prophesied that ye'd have Sam and live here in Zion?"

"No, dear. Zion is the term they use to describe the coming kingdom of God populated with faithful Latter Day Saints. His reference to Zion didn't indicate my living in a particular geographic location.

"Disappointed that her Bishop tried to dissuade her zealous enthusiasm, she took his advice and read the Book of Mormon, The Old and New Testament, and attempted to discern their hidden treasures. Although she found many beautiful truths, she also found one contradiction after another. How could a God who claimed to be omnipresent be separate from mankind? How could a God of justice send people out to perform acts of unfairness and prejudice time and time again? How could God claim to love all his children yet claim elite status for a few? How could God, the great creator, be a God of utter destruction? How could a God of love and peace condone and order murder in order to have his plans prevail? One who we say rewards, then punishes? One who we say accepts without judgment in unconditional love and then, rejects? Who brings all good and then visits evil upon his children when they disobey his will? How could this God, in whom I believed, be both benevolent and malevolent at the same time? What these scriptures described was, in fact, the behavior of man.

"Completely discouraged by these three books, little Miss Nikki sought truth in other quarters. Naturally, she first sought it through her father's religion—Catholicism. But their beliefs were based on the Bible, which she had already studied and discovered had been bastardized over time to control the masses. After studying about the Nicean Council and how they altered original writings, even deleting a few, etc., Nikki knew that basing her spiritual beliefs on these books would simply not be enough."

"So, what did ye do?" Now completely engaged, Dylan rolled to her side so he could see the expression on her face while she told her tale.

"Like any devotee on a pilgrimage, our character set out to look at *other* organized religions. Drawn by the tenets of Buddhism, she quickly became aware that having been born in western civilization, she lacked both the ability and aspiration to depress her wordly desires in order to reach enlightenment. Somehow it seemed not only too physically restrictive, but also spiritually restrictive, as if their God detested all the Earth and those upon it. Once again, her studies led her to believe that original teachings had been manipulated to meet the needs of the organization.

"Next came the Koran, which proved to her once again that these organizations were created from revelation received by individuals that had been altered either through their own consciousness or that of their followers. Should a modern day visionary print such things, the words might be taken with a grain of salt. Covered with a few hundred or thousand years of dust, these visionaries' writings seem to be taken as absolute truth by those who are touched by their words or who have had the words repeatedly ingrained from birth.

"Each of the major world religions that she studied only represented God in man's image, and at first, she came to abhor all organized religion. What may have started as one person sharing their amazing spiritual experience with others soon became a vehicle through which to teach. The sheer mass of followers required an organization and the organization required people to accept positions of responsibility toward the followers. Soon this responsibility became authority, and before you know it, you repeatedly had people *following* instead of finding out for themselves. With authority and power, inevitable abuse of power follows. When doctrine claims God as a being who forever remains elusive and separate, man is forever seeking an intercessor. Alas, the advent of the 'one and only son'(yet another separate being) through whom we must receive some miraculous undoing of every poor choice we've ever made and who will 'save' us, since we are evidently incapable of doing so ourselves. In other words, Nikki came to view organized religions as vehicles that started with good intent but ended up as self-serving organizations interested in survival. They could only survive, both corporeally and economically, with followers—hence the salesmen—missionaries."

"Wait, Babe. Are ye sayin' ye don't believe Jesus is the son of God? Ye can't just arbitrarily define God or his son, ye know!"

"Quit jumping to the end of the story, darling! You wanted to hear my tale, so be patient enough to listen to all of the tale. OK?"

With a childish shake of his head, he bit his lip and refrained from his cherished act of debate.

"So Nikki concluded that by all appearances man did, in fact, *arbitrarily* create God in *his* own image—the image of duality consciousness. In so doing, man created the moral authority to demonstrate duality. Good/evil, love/hate, peace/war, acceptance/rejection, etc. You see, if God can be these things, so can man. If God can destroy entire populations to meet his plans, so can we—right? All these contradictory beliefs are securely in place in every single major organized religion and their spiritual writings. All of them! The constancy of our societies is based upon granting ourselves the authority to behave as God, and in claiming that God *conferred* upon us the authority to do so."

Unable to contain himself, he exclaimed, "Whoa, lass! Are ye sayin' ye think all these great spiritual leaders upon whose teachings these religious organizations are based were self-serving frauds? Are ye sayin' Jesus was a fraud?" The look in his eyes reflected torture.

"Not at all, love. Now, you promised to listen, didn't you? Let me continue for a bit and I think your question will be answered fully."

"OK, OK. It's just that..." he sighed heavily, "well, OK, Nik. I'll be quiet for now."

"But our Nikki felt in the depths of her soul that she, and all life, had been created by an intelligence of order and supreme consciousness. She hoped she was, in fact, made in the image and likeness of God, but could not understand how God could possibly *be* this duality that surrounded her. Also, the belief in the ominipresence of God inspired her, for that would mean God existed within her as well.

"From her childhood training within the LDS Church she remembered that its founder, Joseph Smith, had read a scripture in the Bible which inspired him to go into the woods and pray for guidance regarding which religious organization to join. From James l:5 Smith read, 'If any of you lack wisdom, let him ask of God, that giveth to all men liberally and upbraideth not; and it shall be given him. But, let him ask in faith, nothing waivering...' His sincere prayer brought a direct experience with God in which instructions were given to unearth certain hidden golden plates. These ancient plates had been inscribed by the native people and told not only their history, but also provided ancient spiritual instructions in an unadulterated manner.

"Perhaps due to my childhood training, I believed that Joseph had, in fact, experienced *something* very real. But even in his experience, Joseph described what he saw as God the Father and Jesus Christ appearing as *separate, individual beings with tangible bodies*. Regardless of the contradiction to most religious beliefs, even in this, the words of James ran repeatedly through my head until one day, completely discouraged with the ways of the world, I too knelt down to ask in faith as to the truth of things.

"God did not appear to me, nor did Jesus, or any angelic beings. I spent many nights in prayer in complete anticipation of some marvelous being appearing in my bedroom. Somehow, I just knew there must be a Divine creator who cared enough about humanity and about me individually to answer my questions.

"The years passed and no answers came—at least no direct answers that I recognized. Later, I realized just how many ways I had been answered, but my mind was so rigid, I wouldn't allow the gentle teachings that came from unlimited sources.

"I ran from guru to guru, to astrologers and psychics, to New Age leaders and the like, hoping to find some semblance of a God I trusted among them. Although interesting and sometimes great fun, I still felt a deep sense of dissatisfaction and betrayal.

"While attending a spiritual retreat in Florida and listening to a channeled entity named Ola, I heard some truths among the many deceptions. This being challenged things inside of me, however, for she continually placed responsibility for my Godness and my relationship with All That Is on my own shoulders.

"I left the retreat early, but a friend of mine who stayed called and gave me a list of books recommended by Ola. I wrote down the titles, but had no intention of purchasing or reading any of them.

"A few weeks later I found myself in an old used book store looking for information on English country cottages. The owner sent me to a dark, dusty part of the basement storage to find what I sought and while in the architectural section scanning the book I had chosen, another book fell from one of the shelves above, right into my hands—literally, into my hands. The title seemed familiar, and then I realized it was one among those recommended by Ola; *The I AM Discourses, Vol. 3*; the third volume in the series you found today."

"Ye're teasin', right Babe?"

"No, Dylan, this is a true story."

With a look of incredulity, he quietly allowed her to continue.

"Something possessed me to purchase the book and when I started reading, it felt as if my heart would leap out of my chest. I recognized, with great joy, everything that I read—like recognizing an old friend. The book did not leave my sight until every page had been read and, even then, I began to re-read and highlight favorite passages immediately. I called the bookstore and asked if they had any other volumes and they informed me that they had none; that, in fact, they had no record of having purchased the one I acquired only a few days prior."

"Doodiddlydoodoodoo," came the notes of mystery from Dylan's lips as he sneared in disbelief.

"Would you like me to stop?"

"Hell no, I find this highly entertaining."

"Then behave!"

"Right," he said, placing his hands together in a prayerful fashion, as if acting the part of a saint.

"I could not find these books in any store in Salt Lake or in the library, so given that this time period was pre-internet and Amazon, I dialed information and asked for the number of the publishing house; The St. Germain Foundation in Schaumberg, Illinois. I promptly ordered the entire series and began a new course of study. Completely intrigued, I decided to pay a visit to their 'temple' in Chicago to investigate their organization. Once again, I found myself repelled by the organized side of a religious activity. After three days, I returned home slightly despondent.

"Every time I read the books, however, I would be elated, overjoyed, and overwhelmed with a sense of being home—knowing truth. This much could not be denied. Within the writings, God was represented as All in All, All That Is. Repeatedly the writings told of the illusion under which mankind has lived, and reported that many have risen above the illusion of duality, becoming masters and ascending into a new state of consciousness. They represented that the 'only begotten son of God' is Love and We *are* that

Love, incarnate, and Love is truly *all there is*. All else is illusion. Atonement no longer represented suffering and sacrifice, but at-one-ment; at one with All in All, consciously remembering who one is. Christ became Love—not just Jesus, our beloved brother who came to remind us who we are and who provided through example a pathway home. In being Christ-ed, he became the living incarnation of Love *in complete remembrance in action*, of his relationship to, and with, God. He established a pattern of mastery for those, who would, to follow. Jesus walked our same pathway of earthly embodiment and became an Ascended Master: a being who has mastered himself, his environment, and the elements. Like many of the great spiritual leaders who have trod this planet, he loved mankind completely and became a way-shower.

"Most of the Christian religious groups hail Jesus as the *only* son of God, when even he stated emphatically that he is *our brother*; we are the same as he and capable of the same, and more, than he achieved. Clearly, I could see that it has been the *belief* that we are *separate* from God and that Jesus, some special being, is the *only* son of God, that has kept us from rising into our true estate.

"Answer me true, lass. Do ye believe Jesus is the son of God?"

"Absolutely, for if I could not see him as the son of God, neither could I see you or myself as the son of God."

Narrowing his eyes in thoughtful consideration, he allowed her to continue.

"So I asked about duality consciousness, since it is all I have known. Because of my new state of thought and feeling, I began to magnetize the information I required. This information came from all kinds of sources: conversations, books, articles, and direct information through prayer and meditation. I could not stop the flood.

"One day, while in mediation, I received an amazing 'ah-ha,' when told that duality consciousness has been our way of learning. That we agreed to an education that involved free choice on a gameboard that included duality. Our education in becoming individualized Gods within God had to be completed in a fashion where we chose to live intentionally, to be the Cause instead of acting at the mercy of Effect. That from the cycle of awareness of wholeness, we have cycled into a belief in separateness and are now beginning our return to the consciousness of wholeness. This growth, this evolution, has been our way of learning and becoming more. Naturally, mankind created God in his image in order to justify his way of learning. But mankind's definition of deity bears no resemblance or relationship to what I believe God actually is.

"Now, our Nikki, though bold and brave in her own spiritual quest, certainly knew that challenging the *God created by man* would be considered blasphemous, at best, by any and all organized religion, so she quietly studied on her own.

"She came to believe that all religions are right—exactly right— for those who participate within their structured existence. That all spiritual writings hold beautiful truths and beautiful falseness, the discernment of which comes down to each individual. An organization cannot force you to grow spiritually. You do not grow by artifice or by another's efforts. Nor does one grow spiritually by virtue of the fact that they are handed membership to some organization with their diapers. The *group* can no more *grow* you than they can eat your supper for you.

"But I also learned that it certainly isn't necessary for me to challenge religious groups and their beliefs. Instead, I learned to honor each of them and found that what I had gleaned in my private education merely *expanded* my understanding beyond that which those organized religions provided. When people join together to express Divine Love and expand God's perfection, limitless possibilities unfold because the energy is multiplied exponentially. If this magnified energy is directed to bring harmony to All That Is, it can only be a good thing. If used divisively or to harm any part of All That Is, one should challenge it directly and forcefully.

"It is not until the individual cries 'the emperor wears no clothing!' that he can change his own consciousness. One must rise above the chaos and say, 'this no longer makes sense—I'm going to choose another pathway!' One can grow and evolve without the bitter activity of judgment, destruction, disaster, or unhappiness. Duality is not the only pathway of learning. Growth can leap forth just by preference. Perhaps today I painted a great picture and tomorrow I hope to paint an even better one. Do you see? I do not have to view my creation with unhappiness or disappointment. I can merely make new choices based on desire or preference."

"But, Nik, ye have to live *in* this world. People are assholes all the time. They can threaten ye'r security, ye'r happiness, and even ye'r life. How can ye react to someone behavin' badly or out of duality?"

"Look, my love, I can choose to *be* love, to see past the illusion, even for those who behave badly. I can act as a mirror to remind them who they really are and give them an opportunity to step into that role. In order to do that, however, *I must remember who I Am and act like it.* If someone attacks in any way—verbally, physically, psychologically, or emotionally—they are merely screaming for help. This is a great opportunity to learn to heal one another through forgiveness, collaboration, and resolution."

"Ye mean to tell me if someone killed ye'r son or someone ye loved dear, ye'd just stand by and say, 'that's OK, sweetie. I know it's not the truth of who ye are'?"

"Well, actually Dylan, it would be impossible for either my son, or me, to magnetize such an experience. Our energy, our focus, is on creating a space of love, and that kind of destructive energy simply *cannot* enter our personal fields. Because of this, I am ever seeing only the truth of *who* people are, and nothing they can do can blind me to that. We are all ONE, my love. Just as you and I are ONE, so are you ONE with the spiritual masters and the Hitlers of the world. Each is merely a part of the whole, experiencing different things and different realities in order to further their education. You create your own reality. God speaks to you and through you, and every other single being on this earth—not just a select few.

"When one believes in God as All in All, they recognize themselves as part of the whole. As their consciousness changes into *unity consciousness*, they behave differently, knowing that every thought, feeling, word, or act on their part affects the whole, as well as themselves. They learn to honor and celebrate all of life and no longer require legislation of their morality or behavior. They won't wait for, or worse, create, some apocryphal disaster from which Jesus or any other master must 'rescue' us. They will recognize themselves as the *joint creators* of this world."

"Blimey, Nik! Yer views are surely diametrically opposed to mi own, though I'll admit that my perspective originates from mi own ingrained spiritual education. Personally, I've found no reason to challenge the God I know, and I hate that what you say makes sense because it means I have to think about it and maybe do somethin' about it. I do want to explore; in fact, I *need* to explore this further. Ye've made me see that I needn't berate another's belief or insist that they believe what I do. Historically, people *have* destroyed one another by conquering, condeming, dividing, and killing whole civ- ilizations who did not agree with their concept of God.

"I'll be makin' ye a promise right now not to do that, mi darlin'—not to berate yer beliefs to make miself feel right. But, I must
confess, I am now somewhat terrified to open this book. Could be
Pandora's box, ye know?"

Nikki wrapped her arms around him and held him tenderly,
offering no further information or advice. Kissing him gently and
gazing deeply into his eyes, she silently thanked him for his
courage.

As she hugged him, she looked out the window and noticed
the large crow that had landed on the branch of a small tree. They
made eye contact before she closed hers tightly, wishing it would
go away.

☯

He became completely absorbed in his reading and, for the
most part, paid no attention to Nikki at all. She merely watched
to see how he reacted to the teachings. Her heart grew heavier and
heavier, however, for she had something to do that she did not
want to do.

After four days of non-stop reading, he came to her one night
and laid his head upon her lap. "I can't quite get miself to believe
this stuff is real. I've read so many books and scripts that it almost
makes the material seem like a play. In m'industry, everything is
fabrication based on some form of reality—yet it's still fantasy, ye
know?"

"Have you seen in me any of the truths you've been learning?"
she asked.

"I have and that is the *one* thing that shatters mi doubts, or at
least shakes 'em up a bit," he answered, turning his head in her lap
so he could look into her beautiful eyes.

"How old do you think I am, darlin'?" she asked him.

He looked at her inquisitively. "Ye told me we were born the same day."

"Now that you know I'm your twin flame, doesn't that make sense? Haven't you noticed the dates of my life experiences as I've shared them with you don't add up to your age?"

"Oh, aye," he sighed and then looked at her warily. "Tell me ye're not, like, hundreds of years old, or something, and goin' to turn into an old, ugly hag as ye come out o' Shangri-la!"

"No dear, but I did precede your journey by a decade," she confessed.

His expression revealed shock. *How could this beautiful young lady be nearing fifty years of age?* he wondered. *She looks younger than I!* He thought back to the lesson she tried to teach him about youth and beauty on their trip to Salt Lake. He silently wished his foolish resentment had not interfered with his attention that day.

"I've chased you, lifetime after lifetime, trying to coerce, force, plead, and beg you to follow *my* pathway. I came ahead of you this time, not planning on becoming your lover, but only your friend. As fate would have it, I have not only Divine Love for you, but my outer self, my human nature, also holds for you an enormous well of love. This passion, this desire, that comes from my lower self, could easily distract and interfere with my higher purpose with you. I find myself having thoughts and feelings that do *not* come from the God within me—thoughts that include possessiveness and fear of losing you.

"What I'm about to say will no doubt upset you, but I ask for your trust, knowing I love you completely, and want only that which is *perfect* and *good* for you and our relationship."

A sickly lurch turned his stomach with a subliminal knowing. "Something awry, mi luv?"

"When I saw you looking at my pathway of learning in my library, I knew with certainty you would have to find your *own*

pathway without any interference or teaching on my part.
"I'm but a novice, my love. In the ancient mystery schools,
they wouldn't even let students speak to each other. The Ascended
Masters understood when a student is building up a momentum
of light and knowledge, someone casting a shadow of doubt or
confusion on their learning could shatter all they had acquired. If
we were to stay together at this juncture, it would be too easy for
both our lower natures to make you feel you were coerced, once
again, and I would surely lose you for another lifetime.

"I know the wisdom within directs me to point you to the
simple laws by which you may learn to wield your own scepter of
victory and complete dominion over your outer self and your
world. But, to do this *for* you, or give you a place where you lean
on me as an outside source, would only retard your spiritual
progress and make you weak.

"I want to be with you in *every single, possible way*, with
every fiber of my being. You *know* how deeply I love you,
Dylan. Nonetheless, I'm asking you to leave me and seek the
truth for yourself. When you can meet me half way, I'll reach
with wings of angels, and you and I shall journey inseparably
the rest of the way home."

"Why can't ye be with me while I'm learning, Nik?" he asked
earnestly. "Why can't ye be at mi side, and inside of me? Ye can't
just throw this away, Babe. I won't let ye! It's an absolute miracle
we've found each other this way and ye can't deny the magnetic
quality that binds us together. Ye said if I'd just relax and trust ye,
ye'd *take* me safely home. I think that it's ye who doesn't trust and
have faith in me and mi love for you!" Induced by a sickening fear,
the tenor of his voice had reached a booming shout.

"It's because I have *absolute* faith in you that I send you from
me now, my love—so you can return of *your own free will*," she

explained softly. "I've built up, through many lifetimes with you, karmic energy that needs to be dissolved. This karma relates to my trying to *coerce you* to join my pathway. The great cosmic law, however, absolutely requires that we must first individually identify with God before we can *unlock* our joint spiritual potential within our twin flames. Because this karma lies between us, we must individually develop a certain level of mastery and oneness with God—with our real selves— before we can be together. In one another's presence, the very thing that gives us power as twin flames would amplify our negative energies or patterns. As much and as deeply as I love you, I desire our full and perfect union, which can only be fulfilled first through our individual pathways—yours without my coercion, but with my complete support, fidelity, and divine love; and mine, in the willingness to relinquish any attempt to control your choices."

He fell silent and pensive, with eyes swimming in sorrow, then retired to the bedroom—alone. She followed and lay next to him on the bed so she could comfort him. "Darlin', you've chosen for yourself the hardest, but fastest possible pathway to enlightenment. You've chosen a pathway of temptation to abuse your God-given powers in such ways as the standard mortal *cannot* comprehend. Yours is the Armageddon of the soul in the truest sense.

"The power of words, either spoken, written, sung, or by edict of sword, affects the course of history and millions, maybe billions of lives. The sacred responsibility of use of power in this position staggers the mind! *This* is the art you've chosen to share with the world, at large. You must *choose* between the earthly accolades announcing what a terrific actor you are, enticing you to play even the part of the vilest characters well, where your influence depicts the lowest possible nature of man, or playing parts that ennoble and raise the consciousness of the whole.

"Your ego daily accepts the praise for your talents and hard work, and yet you're tempted never to give credit where it's due. Without the life, light, and breath of God within you, you couldn't think a thought, speak a word, or even animate your body. It's so easy to stand at the podium accepting applause from your public and peers, feeding your ego to the point of ultra self-importance. You have to *decide* if you wish to pay tribute to your ego god, or in humility, pay tribute to the true God within you.

"A self-made man, such as you, darlin', thinks his strengths lie in his persistence to achieve what he's done in the face of tempestuous odds; but what created that strength inside of you? What gave you courage to bypass the good opinions of others and free yourself from the tribal thinking in the first place?

"You're exposed to the possibility of abuse of your sexually creative powers, for the limitless number of people standing in line wanting a piece of you, manipulating and distorting truth to serve your appetites. The temptations of the flesh appetite are, indeed, strong within you, because of your creative energy. You've focused a great deal of energy to your lowest chakras. It's what makes you a great actor. You're in an industry where the body beautiful is thrown at you daily as a sacrificial offering. It's an energy you can learn to honor, control, and utilize for higher purposes, or squander on an endless stream of sensual gratification. Squandering that amazing life force will ultimately contribute to imprinting upon your flesh disease and aging and, if used without spiritualization, condemns you to taking on the karmic burdens of all those with whom you have sexual relations.

"You're exposed to the possibility of abuse of your physical and emotional bodies through the use of narcotics, tobacco, and alcohol —used to heighten or numb your senses. You must *choose* between the height, clarity, and perfection of the God light that animates your very being, or those things which arrest your ability to create perfectly, that inhibit the free flow of God's light.

"The possibility exists for you to abuse the power of money to serve only as a vehicle for your private entertainment and lavish lifestyle, never allowing it to move beyond selfish use, attempting to get more gain. You must *choose* between the understanding and proper use of the Law of Abundance and its continual outpouring to bless all mankind, or its use to create a kingdom for your ego.

"With your God given talents and beauty, you're exposed to the possibility of abuse of power through pride and vanity. You must *choose* between acknowledging the God within you as the source of your beauty and perfection, or allow your ego full due. You must learn to be so benevolent, people forget your handsome air, or at least look upon it as a gift from God, rather than boasting it vainly.

"Your lower self is so afraid it has no purpose it tempts you to believe in separateness from God at every turn of the hand. It struts like a peacock with unwarranted vanity, especially in light of the fact that without the spirit of God within you, you have no life, no animation, no ability to think, or feel, or speak, or BE!

"When you're unhappy, you're exposed to the possibility of abuse of power by the ease with which you can transfer responsibility for your misery, never accepting the part *you* play in fashioning your weaknesses. You must *choose*, of your own free will, to understand the height of responsibility for every single thought, word, feeling, and deed, and how *these* are the true fashioners of your world.

"Someone once wrote that 'success is a hideous thing.' I can't remember the quote exactly but it was something like, 'its false similarity to merit deceives men. To the masses, success has almost the same appearance as supremacy.' Receiving admiration from your peers and fans, creating mass notoriety, does not presuppose your talents have made of you a capable spirit, my love. You know, from having observed others in your profession falter, that admiration and notoriety is nothing more than nearsightedness on the part of the viewer. You must allow for your talent and creativity without confusing it for supremacy and self-importance. I can't even begin to imagine how difficult that would be when the whole world seems to be applauding your every effort, angel.

"On the other hand, you may turn the possibility of abuse to *right use* of that power, and utilize every stumbling block placed before you as a launching pad to rise to great heights, serving the whole of God's creation to the highest and best possible good through the spoken, written, and sung word, delivered through mass media. And Dylan, a soul who transcends this much possibility of abuse of Power is indeed a magnificent and noble soul.

"Doubts and fears wreak havoc upon the student who's just beginning to understand and utilize his God light properly. My love for you is supreme and I *will not* allow any part of my lower self to interfere with your chosen course. I, too, have much to do to reunite fully and freely with you, my dearest love."

Nikki stroked his hair and continued speaking, even though his eyes were held tightly closed, as if wincing in pain. He refused to respond to even one comment.

"You wrote the script yourself. You brought your soul here into this body, into this schoolroom, for learning and soul testing so you could transmute and make righteous changes to expand the light of God within you. It's your way of reaching for heaven and no one can stop you from creating heaven or hell in the process. That unfed flame within your heart that beats in unison with mine, *is* the spark of the Divine element that is incorruptible in this sphere and immortal in the next. It can be developed by goodness; it can be kindled and lit up and made to radiate so no evil, that either your ego or any other can create, can touch it!

"This is a cram course you've created for yourself to get your degree in right use, or 'righteous' of God's unlimited Power.

"The choice you made in *Little Crow* was noble. It helped release some of the karma you saw in the dreams St. Germain guided you through. It's because you came to this place of knowing I feel I can trust my future in your hands, and if it takes another eternity, I *will* wait for you."

She had delivered her well-practiced, but agonizing speech in a measured, but firm tone.

Silence filled the atmosphere for a few minutes until he sat up, faced her directly, and held her small shoulders in his great hands.

"Nik, luv, I truly believe that there have been people like Jesus, Buddha, and St. Germain—and maybe, even ye, who have walked this planet and achieved the things I've been studyin'—but I also believe those who have done so *were* and *are* **special** souls, foreordained to achieve these things. I honestly don't believe the standard man, (and by that, I mean miself,) can do all this stuff! Being with ye has been like a miracle, day after day. But, the miracle has been ye, luv. *I* have not been the miracle. I have witnessed these things with mi own eyes and felt them with all mi heart, but I haven't the faith that I can do, or rather that *I am worthy* to do these things! I also don't know if I want mi life to be that of an ascetic. All I do know is that I don't want to be without ye.

"Love has let me down, time and time again, Nik. Now, here ye are, the one woman I believe is the love of mi life, essentially saying I'm not good enough for ye. Saying that when I can catch up with ye, perhaps ye'll think about givin' me leave to be ye'r partner."

Nikki winced at his callous remark. "That's your ego talking,

Dylan. You know in your heart the truth of the things about which I'm speaking. *I will not stand in the way of your free will!* Nor will I allow this powerful union of our twin flame activity when there is a chance we could misuse the atomic energy we create together. In order for our union to be a blessing to ourselves and the world, we must come from a space of total committed love— for God, one another, and all creation. I cannot force your conscious choices, thoughts, and feelings to align with these truths. You *must*, of your own volition, without *any* outside pressure from me, enter these gates by yourself."

"Look, luv—I'm but a mortal. Perhaps I drink too much, or argue too much, or a thousand other things—but, basically, I'm a decent fella. I do love God. I do love you. And, I love mankind— well, most of 'em, anyway. Isn't that enough for ye?"

Nikki stopped speaking. She had clearly conveyed her intent and any debate that would ensue from following his lead could only muddy the waters more.

She felt his heart breaking, because he, also, understood he would have to consciously choose his pathway of his own free will and intent without her interference, but also without her physical presence. The love she held for him allowed her to see that his defense was his attempt to hold them physically together at any cost.

It would surely be her tribulation as much as his, for parting from him felt like more than even she could bear.

☯

He made rough love with her all night long, as if trying to punish her for sending him away. Only one energy center responded to their union, and even that paled by comparison to what they had previously experienced. Like an errant puppy, Crow woke her around four in the morning, begging her to let him stay a while longer. It was everything he could do to accept the arrangement with utter submission. They agreed he would leave in five days.

Chapter 14

The phone rang early the next morning, and since their night had been so restless, Nikki slept in.

"Mom! What the heck're you doing in bed at this hour? I never saw you lie in bed past six-thirty! You're not sick, are you?"

"Hi sweetheart," she said quietly, so as not to wake her lover. "I just had a rough night and fell back to sleep in the early morning. What's up? How are things going there?" She rose quietly from bed and carried the remote phone out of the room so Dylan could sleep.

"Listen, I've got a tournament in Vegas in a couple of days. Wondered if you'd like to come down and watch?"

"Oh, I'd just love to!" she answered joyfully. "It feels like I haven't seen you forever. I'd swim the ocean to be there!"

"I have to stay with the team at the dorms, but I thought you could stay somewhere nearby and we could grab a couple of meals together between matches. It's scheduled for Thursday through Saturday at the UNLV Tennis Center. We're playing against USC for the regional championships."

"I have a guest staying with me. May I bring my guest?" she asked tentatively.

Due to his slight hesitation, she knew he pondered if her guest was male or female.

Sam figured since he caught her in bed, it had been a man who had kept her up late, but respected her privacy and made no further inquiry.

"That'd be great, Mom. So, call me and let me know where you get reservations. OK? Gotta go! Love ya—bye!"

"Love ya—bye….," Sam's original hyphenated word that expressed not only his deep affection for his mother, but also the urgency of his life. It stood as a private joke between them, for he never waited for her farewell, always hanging up first. Somehow he felt that in so doing, his mother would be granted the gift of eternal life, ever and always awaiting his next call or visit. He feared that if she said "goodbye" it would mean forever. The last word his father had spoken to him was "goodbye."

Nikki and Dylan spent the next two days in bed with each other, neither wanting to leave to even shower or eat. They were two starving souls consuming with the voracity of those told this would be their last supper.

Dylan agreed to join her in Las Vegas to watch her son play tennis for Stanford. She made reservations for a bungalow at the Regent in Summerlin; an infinitely more private and secluded hotel than those on the strip.

While assisting Dylan to pack, Nikki hid the first three volumes of *The I AM Discourses* in one of his bags. As she helped stow the overwhelming number of suitcases in the car, she turned to him with one raised eyebrow. "My dear, it's time for you to quit carrying around all this unnecessary baggage."

He realized she referred to more than his luggage.

Consumed with joy upon seeing her son, Nikki threw her arms around him, while he twirled her through the air. Dylan felt the contagiousness of her energy and happiness and decided to postpone any thoughts about his impending departure. Sam had, indeed, been duly surprised to find a super movie star with his mother. Both his mother and her "friend" seemed lit up like Christmas trees. Never had he witnessed this type of happiness in his mother before now. However, an underlying current existed between them he could not quite put his finger on, and he assumed it had something to do with Dylan's scheduled departure on Sunday morning.

Sam spent as much time as he could with them between matches, which he won, one after another. He charmingly told his mother he still hadn't found the "right" girl yet, but had his name on the school bulletin board requesting a woman with a list of virtues to match hers. There just hadn't been any qualified takers.

The three days passed far too swiftly. By Friday, evidence that neither his mother, nor Dylan, had been sleeping at night showed on their faces. Sam assumed they spent their nights making passionate love. Oddly, he felt no sense of infidelity towards his father. Instead, he was so happy for her he could burst and secretly hoped he could find that kind of love one day.

Saturday night Sam kissed his mother and newfound friend good-bye and joined the team on the bus to drive back to Palo Alto with his first place trophy in hand.

"He's really quite good, isn't he?" asked Crow.

"He ought to be. He took up every night of my life for seven years to get here!" she said, laughing.

"Ye mean to tell me ye coached him?" he asked.

"No—we just lived too far away from anyone else to use as a practice partner. He beat the socks off me every night," she said, giggling with a deliberate half smile.

As the bus drove away, so did the distraction that had held them whole for three days. They skipped dinner and went back to their bungalow to spend their last night together.

At eight-thirty Nikki asked if he wanted her to order room service. Dylan had been pacing back and forth around the room, out the sliding door for a cigarette, then back again to start over. She could think of nothing to do except maintain her calm attitude and try to project it to him.

He didn't want food; he only wanted alcohol. Crow called room service, all right, but had them deliver a bottle of Jack Daniels instead of a meal. Drinking alone, he swallowed a third of the bottle, straight up.

Nikki sat in a chair reading, sneaking glances at him until she could stand it no longer, and stood to encircle him in her arms.

"I've got an idea," he said frantically through slurred words. "If I just work on things alone and we never discuss it, ye can come with me to Ireland. I'm taking some time off and it'll give me a chance to really focus. I promise not to ask ye anything. Ye *have* to come with me, Nik! Can't I make ye see that? I just have the most terrible feeling if I get on that plane tomorrow I may never see ye again. I'm all twisted inside!"

"I believe in you, my love. I believe *in* your love. I believe in your goodness. If you can't hold yourself in that perfection, then know there is someone who's holding a focus there for you. You can stop accepting my heart light as I send it to you, but I promise, I will never stop sending it until we are one again."

There was finality about the way she spoke to him. Dylan could tell by her tone she would, without doubt, make him get on that plane alone, and to him, it felt like some terrible, cruel and excessive punishment.

"Nikki," he said in a choked voice, "I don't know that I can stretch to believe in a God who would allow me to feel this much love, to experience such overwhelming joy, and then say, 'Sorry bloke, it's really just a cosmic gag! Ye can't have it!'" Inside, he'd been fighting with this God for days, and would have won too, except for the fact that he equalled only half of the equation. If Nikki could not be convinced, he would lose anyway. "This is a moral misery that seems absurdly distorted to me, luv. I can't hold on much longer—it's pulling me to ribbons! We should be puttin' things together, 'stead of ripping them apart! I don't give a bloody rat's ass about this postponed clemency ye offer me, Nik! I want ye *now*. I honestly believe I deserve the pleasure of ye'r company *now*!"

Within him stirred a seething darkness, a great storm of wild unconscious tumult: an endless, ceaseless churning of truculent waters. He could not be comforted.

"Sit down, angel face, I want to tell you a story." She gestured to a chair opposite hers. Dylan filled his glass, yet again, while she continued:

> *Once there were two old men, Edward and George, who were the very best of friends. They loved each other and spent time together every day. They would sit in the park in the mornings and watch the birds and the children and the animals and tell each other funny things. They spent a lot of time laughing and smiling with each other.*
>
> *On Tuesdays, Edward would pick George up at his apartment and they'd go to the same café and treat themselves to a night out. They would laugh and tell stories and share their opinions, which each respected. On Fridays, they would meet at the matinée and watch a movie, even if it meant seeing the same movie twice. They just enjoyed and loved one another's company and each realized that it was the most valuable asset they possessed.*
>
> *One day, Edward came to George and told him sad news. He intended to move to another state where he could be close to his son, whom, he felt, needed him.*
>
> *George felt crestfallen and angry that this man, whom he loved, upon whom he depended for happiness, would be willing to leave when he needed him as well.*

Every thought of Edward made him so sad, that George began to droop a little in the shoulders and the corners of his mouth took on a distinct downward sag. The lids on his eyes seemed half shut most of the time and he started to shuffle, rather than walk. He spent most of his time in a chair, mindlessly watching television. Without his friend, the world and his life seemed an empty place.

Years passed, and one day as George walked home from the store, with cane in his hand to assist his unsure steps, he heard someone yell out his name. He shakily turned to see his old friend, Edward, whose appearance remained just as he remembered. He stood tall and erect with strength, striding toward him like a youthful man.

"I thought it was you, old friend!" said Edward joyfully, as he grasped his friend's hand and patted him on the back with the other. "I'm so happy to have found you already. I just got back to town today! My things are being shipped and I move into a new apartment right away! I've missed you and have looked forward to this reunion with all my heart!"

George stood with tears running down his cheeks in disbelief. He eyed the man up and down to ensure his imagination played no tricks on him. Edward, however, noticed George had become such a sad and aged man that he hardly recognized him. He helped the old man with the shuffle to his apartment and they put his goods away, and then strolled very slowly to the park, for George no longer had the ability to move quickly.

They sat upon their old, favorite park bench and Edward finally found the courage to ask what had happened to bring on such a drastic change.

George explained, "When you left, I became the saddest

man in the world. I tried to come to the park, but the thought of you made me too sad, so I stopped coming. I tried to go to our favorite café, but the memory of you eating across from me made me too sad and I was angry that you left. I never went back again. I even went to the Friday matinée, but found the thought of your absence left me feeling hollow and sick inside, so I stopped going to the movies altogether. Every time I thought about you, I became sad and lonely and angry, knowing the best friend I ever had, had abandoned me."

Edward looked down at his hands and touched his fingers together. There were tears in his eyes, but he looked up and spoke to his friend anyway. "George, I had to go. I had an important responsibility and I trusted what you and I had together would last forever. Whenever I went to a park, it made me think of you and all the good times we had, and those thoughts made me smile with happiness. Every time I ate at a café, I thought of you and the things we shared; how we always disagreed on politics; how we always agreed on beautiful women—and it made me laugh and brought joy to my heart. I went to the movies a lot, because going to the matinée reminded me how we were too cheap to go to the later shows. It reminded me how we used to eat popcorn and talk over the movie, laugh at the stupid parts, and then discuss every detail of the show afterwards and, George—it always made me happy. You see, old friend, the thought of you brought me joy. I, too, was saddened by our parting, but looked forward to our reunion, holding you in a space of love and happiness in my heart."

"Do you remember me telling you about an angelic being, named Aurora, the first day we met?" she asked him.

"Aye, a bit," he answered despondently through his drunken stupor.

"This story is one she once told me that helped me understand we can *choose* our feelings, *choose* our course and attitude, for what we think and feel creates our world. Where our attention is held, either through vision, hearing, thought, or feeling, and how we qualify or hold the focus of the light within us, is *what we become.* It *becomes* the *reality* of our world. This life force is impersonal. It doesn't care who uses it or what it creates. You can create misery or you can create happiness—both being a distinct *choice* of free will," she said gently, kneeling in front of him and putting her head in his lap.

He wouldn't touch her.

Nikki's embrace was one-sided and she felt her own heart sinking for heaviness, knowing how the battle inside him raged. It was his hour of bitterness and dark clouds. She asked for higher assistance for both of them, but also knew that he'd have to learn *he* had to do the work himself. No one could do it for him. He would have to call upon the God anchored in his heart. When she could see no point in remaining in her position, she rose in a dignified manner and prepared herself for bed.

Crow drank some more and when he finally joined her, he passed out. Their last night together dissipated into thin air— wasted in self-pity, the ultimate nefarious force.

She lay in the bed next to him, holding his non-participating body, and she too, wanted to trash the whole idea and go with him. It took every ounce of courage to call forth her I AM Presence to ask that it hold dominion over her feelings, which were definitely on strike.

They overslept and were running late for the plane and barely arrived at the airport on time. His ridiculous luggage took up another twenty minutes.

As she ran with him down the concourse to catch the shuttle, Crow stopped in his tracks, turned to face her, and with a shock-wave of anger, hissed through clenched teeth, "Don't bother! If ye're leaving me to make it on mi own, ye might as well start now!" He turned and hustled down the ramp without a good-bye—without anything except cold, hard anger.

She had no choice except to entrust him to God's care.

BOOK III

Chapter 1

Through all his flights Crow drank, and drank hard. He desperately sought to numb his senses and deaden the pain in his heart. He didn't want to feel anything. Part of him thought she betrayed and abandoned him; the other part knew she was right and wanted to do everything in his power to join her again.

Within a few days of arriving in Schull, having greeted his family and friends, he began the laborious chore of unpacking. What a chore! It felt more like moving. Nikki had been right—time to get rid of some of his excess baggage. He discovered the books she had hidden among his things, stopped working, and began to read. Dylan still had difficulty believing all that had happened. It seemed with every passing day the experience became more and more ephemeral, like a dream. He promised himself to read the books cover to cover, and called the St. Germain Foundation in Schaumburg, Illinois to order the full set he'd seen at Nikki's.

☯

His best friend and co-conspirator in his musical career, Braydon Hatch, possessed talent without equal. Although Braydon had a little trouble with alcohol and drugs on occasion, he was a good man with a sincere heart, who always cheered for the underdog—the kind of a man you wanted protecting your back in a scuffle. When the two had met in their teens, Braydon told Crow they had once been great warriors together in another life, but their strength came from the balance between their talents. One simply could not survive without the other. Dylan laughed at the idea, yet, during Braydon's bouts with stimulants, it repeatedly surfaced in the form of a story that improved with each telling.

Braydon pounded relentlessly on Dylan's door until his friend finally roused from his deep sleep. "Hey ye bugger, it's eleven o'clock. Get ye'r lazy arse out o' the sack!" he shouted. He pounded until Crow unlatched and opened the door with only a grunt for a greeting.

"The lads and I are takin' a lit'l sail this afternoon. Thought ye'd like to come 'round and spend some time wit' ye'r low-life mates. ...'sides, Cort's invited a few *shagalicious* women who've agreed to accompany us."

"Cort must 'ave paid 'em. He couldn't get laid if 'is dangler was made o' gold!" Crow said sleepily.

As he walked to the kitchen to brew some coffee, Braydon sheepishly remarked, "Well, to be honest, I think he might have mentioned the possibility of some famous ugly bastard showin' up."

"Nothin' ever changes, does it? Ye farts 'ave been using me like a pimp since ye were acne-faced teens!"

Braydon sounded his throaty, honest laugh. "If ye can't use ye'r friends, what're they good for, mate?" When the coffee maker made it's final hiss, he opened the fridge to retrieve a carton of milk. As he opened the container, a distinct sour odor filled the room. "Jasus, mate...how long's this been in here?"

Ignoring Braydon's complaint, Crow reached for a cigarette, but his fancy titanium lighter wouldn't work. "Could I trouble ye for a torch?"

Braydon poured the steaming coffee into two large mugs, handed one to Crow and sat across from him. Pulling his own cheap, red plastic lighter from his shirt pocket, he tossed it to his friend. "I guess that piece o' shite of ye'rs can't hold a candle next to mi dependable Bic, eh?" As he sipped his coffee, he grimaced. "Jasus, this stuff's nasty without cow juice. Got any sweet?"

"Aye—to the left of the stove—top cupboard. While ye're up, hand me the Irish, will ye?" Crow sucked a long drag and held it for a while before he blew out a ring and watched it float to the ceiling.

Braydon sat down again, noticing the far-away look that had been in his friend's eyes since his return. Crow took the Irish whiskey and filled his half emptied coffee cup to the brim.

"What's up, lad? Never seen ye take a sip o' the Irish this early in the day."

Crow remained unresponsive, gulping down the brew to the last drop, as if he'd been challenged to swig a pint without stopping. He licked his lips, smiled weakly, and pounded his cup back onto the table.

"Ye've been acting real queer, mate. Me 'n' the lads have noticed ye're not quite here. Somethin' bad happen to ye in Utah?"

Crow narrowed his eyes, took another drag, but remained silent.

"Known ye since ye were hungry, boyo, but can't ever remember a time I've seen ye sufferin' so," Braydon said empathetically.

The alcohol on Crow's empty stomach took a non-stop route to his brain. A comfortable buzz relaxed both his tongue and the constant ache he felt in his heart. When he looked into his oldest and dearest friend's eyes, he saw true concern and compassion. Dylan wasn't sure if he could trust Braydon with the tale of his spiritual adventure, but as the whiskey began to do its job, the opportunity to allow wisdom to guide him was lost. Instead, he told the whole story to his friend.

"Jasus, mate. Sounds like ye got ye'rself into some kind o' cult thing, or worse! Sounds like some sort of devil-worshiping, mind control, woo-woo to me. Damn lucky ye got out when ye did. She's just trying to get her claws into ye, lad."

"Are ye a shockin' deaf idiot? If that were so, *why* did she send me away, man?" Dylan nearly spit out. That question kept going through his head like a phonograph that repeated the same song over and over again. *How could she send me away?*

"Why?—Why? I'll be tellin' ye, sure, boyo! Now, ye listen to ye'r ol' mate, 'n' listen well! I'm not meanin' to throw sand *in* ye'r eyes, lad—but rather to help ye clear ye'r vision. Straight off, she's a woman and *all* women have an agenda of some sort. Jus' like mi Jessica—remember? Sure, 'n' didn't she insist we get married when she was with babe. Then, sure as I put a roof o'er her head, she finds some swell, legally procures mi home, is granted custody o' the babe, plus the blinkin' alimony and child support—and *who* was sittin' in the street with nothin'—no luv, no babe, no house, and *no bloody brass* to make a new beginnin'? *All* women have an agenda, lad! Haven't met one yet that didn't."

"Nikki didn't ask me for brass, man!"

Braydon slammed his palm onto the table. "No, lad—far worse —she asked for ye'r soul!

"Let's look at the whole picture, mi lad! I don't doubt ye when ye say the lass seemed to be full o' miracles 'n' all, but mi mum knows a witch in Inishowen who's been known to restore life to plant 'n' animal. Ye oughta talk to Darby O'Shaughnesey. He's been to India 'n' firsthand seen them bloody fakirs throw a rope in the air, stiff as a board—callin' a lad from the crowd to climb it.

Said they've *proven* it's a form of mass hypnotism—a mind control thing. Them dreams ye had with the Indian lady could 'ave been part o' some elaborate scheme to make ye 'think' ye'r lass was 'the one 'n' only' woman for ye. After all, ye did say the shaman knew ye'r lady, now, didn't ye?

"... 'n', as far as the lass miraculously playin' the guitar—well, now, truthfully Dylan—don't ye think it's possible she may have had years o' trainin' and was yankin' ye'r chain a bit? After all, ye mentioned not only a guitar in her home, but also a piano!

"Take that incident with the snake—come, now—isn't it plausible that by 'oldin' still and lettin' the creature take its time to decide if it was safe, that it might o' just taken the pathway that crossed ye'r lady's foot? ...'n' the kitten? Sure 'n' the massagin' she did probably revived the wee thing!

"As for the woman's age—we both know that 'alf the bloody population 'as been to the plastic surgeon for the reconstitutin' o' one part or another!

"Dylan, I don't discount that ye had amazing sex, 'n' all, but couldn't that just 'ave been ye'r own feelin's wellin' up inside so strong that ye made ye'r own 'eart feel as if it were explodin'? Everyone's experienced some kind o' overwhelmin' emotion that's carried them off into a state of bliss at one time or another."

Dylan stared steely-eyed at his coffee mug, just contemplating his friend's words.

"... 'sides all that, lad—ye're one o' the finest men I know! Why, there's more honor and goodness in ye'r heart than all the men in this county put together. Ye're a loyal friend, sure. No one knows better than I of the generous nature of ye'r soul and 'ow many times ye be doin' good things for people without 'em even knowin'! There's a love in that heart of ye'rs that can wash over any situation or person and leave 'em feeling good 'bout themselves.

"So what if ye partake of the libations or the *O*-ccasional pharmaceutical preparation when opportunity affords? All men on this bloody planet need a way to release the pressure valve so's they don't explode. Ye haven't done anyone harm, save for the rare fistfight—'n' even that's just provin' the Irish in ye, lad. 'n' as for the lasses, well, hell, boy!—ye're jus' doin' what comes natural. Man wasn't meant to be monogamous. Jus' takes ye'r Bible stories. Not a one o' them chaps went without a concubine. The ladies are blessed by ye'r very touch and each one o' them 'as a story to tell their gran'babes when they're old enough." He raised his voice like an old lady's. "'Oh, aye, it's true. I was shagged by the famous Dylan Crow!'"

Braydon reached over and punched his friend in the arm, causing both of them to break out in uproarious laughter.

"What lass in her right mind wouldn't want either a piece o', or to own completely, the world-famous, Oscar-winnin', rich, 'andsome, omnipotent Dylan Crow? Jus' think about bein' the power behind the power o' a man like ye'rself. Wow, Dylan, can I be ye'r lover?"

"Sod off, ye fag!" Dylan said through his laughter.

"Trust me, ol' friend. The lass *has* an agenda. If she sent ye away, 't'was only to reel ye back in. She's just givin' ye a bit o' line to make ye think ye're free…that's all."

"But, Braydon, it felt so right, so good, so…I don't know—so true!"

"Be honest man! Do ye know o' any couple who's maintained that lovin' feelin' ye're talkin' 'bout? Sure, 'n' they all feel it in the first blush o' their relationship, but anyone who still pretends to feel it later is only a good actor. Relationships are bloody 'ard, lad. Takes real work to keep a marriage together. Men and women are jus' too different! People stay together for reasons other than the type o' love ye're describin'. They get a history together, or they get comfortable in their misery, or so financially intertwined that it doesn't make sense to part ways. Or m'be they stay together to create some sense of stability for their youngun's. But, all in all, I know of none who stay together 'cause o' *true* love, lad. There's a kind o' feelin' that we give the name o' love that comes from commitment, but it's not the same as ye've been describin'. What ye're talkin' 'bout exists only in the short-lived fantasy of people seein' one another through rosy lenses—'n' that's the fair truth of it, Dylan."

Braydon stood to leave, deciding to let his words seep into his friend's head on a time-release basis. He stretched and slapped Dylan on the back. "Well, gotta fly, boyo. Let me know if ye'll be joinin' us, will ye?"

☯

As Dylan stood beneath the pounding massage of his showerhead, he thought about Braydon's perspective. While his friend had planted all the seeds of doubt and fear necessary to shake him loose of his moorings of self-pity, he had also helped him remember that he was a pretty decent fellow after all was said and done. *Well, lad, chalk it up to experience and get on with ye'r life!* As the lather of the soap rinsed free from his body, he determined to rinse his mind free of Nikki's memory.

☯

Later that afternoon, Crow relented and agreed to join the sailing party. His best friend told the whole story to all twelve people aboard. They crowned Nikki with the titles of "The Virgin Princess," and "Voodoo Nikki." Crow, by his indiscretion, had sent a terrible energy in her direction, and even though he regretted it, found himself joining in with their obscene little jokes. One particularly seductive blonde even approached Crow proposing she acquire some crystals so they could try "that kinky sex thing" together. Somehow making light of his experience boosted his ego. The tribal thinking had won, again.

☯

Dylan left Nikki's books on his bed stand, unopened. He set an ashtray on top of them and, for the most part, forgot about them within two weeks.

The course of a broken heart, or spirit, often takes one down the road of self-pity and self-destruction. He had traveled these roads before. Crow began to regret having opened his heart to her. "Damn her! Damn her to hell and beyond!" he shouted to the night skies that had lost their magic since she no longer stood by his side.

☯

Dylan began drinking hard and smoking three packs a day. Sometimes he popped pain pills, chased by the Irish. Perhaps it was his way of inviting death, as opposed to the relentless pain he could not escape. Calling his uncle, a local doctor, he requested more pills, moaning that his back ached and his surgeon could not be reached while traveling abroad. His ruse worked like a charm, for the pharmacy even courteously delivered a large supply of narcotics to his door. Feeling such a deep sense of injury, he yielded to despair.

Mic was alarmed by his brother's declining appearance and behavior. "Ye need some professional help, Dyl," he said one day when he found him lying in his own vomit. "What's happened to ye, mi lad? Ye need to get off ye'r behind and do something constructive. Come help me brand today. I can't do it alone and Mason'll be gone for two weeks."

Crow lay unresponsive.

Mic dragged his little brother to the shower, shoved him in, turned the cold faucet on, and stomped out of the house, slamming the door behind him. *What happened to him? What could be so bloody terrible that he's stopped livin'?* he wondered.

Mic, Dylan's lone sibling, had always been a good, true friend, and confidant. His brother's silence regarding his obvious pain confused him. Mic had the wisdom, however, to allow his brother the space to work things out for himself, trusting if Dylan required his support, he'd ask for it in his own time. He knew the innate goodness of his brother's heart and prayed that whatever haunted him would, by some miracle, disappear soon from his consciousness and allow him to get back on track.

During his occasional days of sobriety, Crow spent time with his mum and da. Da didn't look too good and Dylan wondered if his health had declined since his last visit. If so, neither he, nor his mother, said as much. Then again, his da was not the kind of man who complained. His parents were simply content to see their son under any circumstance, for before his return, they had seen him a total of four days in two years.

As he watched his mother cooking dinner one evening, he offered to help her sauté the onions and make the roux for the gravy. Since he'd never participated in the kitchen during his youth, it startled her. She stopped stirring the mélange in her pan, and turned to determine his sincerity. "D' ye know how, mi lad?" she asked doubtfully.

"Aye, I know a few things, Mum…and as a special treat, I'll prepare a Waldorf salad for ye," he offered.

He discovered he liked doing simple things. The act of helping to prepare a meal for all felt, in fact, rewarding. As he provided his parents with a home and had been supplementing their income for years, he had thought his financial contribution served as more than enough participation in their lives. The simple act of cooking a meal for them, however, made him think about how much they had done over so many years, all the survival things parents do for their brood. Usually children never think about those things until they have offspring of their own. The heart of the son began turning to the heart of the father—at least his mortal father.

Mic rang Dylan early the next day to help him with some minor repairs on Da's house. Da had a hard time breathing and didn't do too many of the physically strenuous things that are necessary to maintain a home.

Although Crow began working the ranch with Mic, he still drank hard and smoked non-stop.

☯

"Da…Da…Wake up!," whispered one of Mic's small boys at two in the morning. "Da, there's a frightful noise comin' from up the hill by uncky Dyl's house."

Annie rolled over and opened her eyes. "Josh, are ye ill, son?"

"Says he can hear a scary noise comin' from Dylan's house. I'd best check it out. Probably just that ornery old ewe stuck in the fence again," Mic whispered. "Just go back to sleep, luv. And ye can hop back in ye'r lit'l cot, mi lad. I'll go untangle 'er." Both the speed with which he haphazardly clothed himself and the fact that he retrieved a rifle from the rack on the wall, betrayed the calmness in his voice.

"Ye think ye really need that?" asked Annie in a concerned tone.

"Probably not. I've been able to get her out without breakin' anythin' before."

"Mic, ye're thinkin' it's something besides that blasted ewe, aren't ye?"

"Everything's fine, mi luv—really. Close those beautiful eyes and I'll be back before ye fall asleep."

The ranch security remained minimal, for Dylan rarely came home. Due to his overwhelming notoriety and the fact that Dylan refused to hire personal bodyguards, Mic felt uneasy about his safety every time his brother stayed in Schull for more than a few days. He made his way through the house without any illumination. If there were intruders, the element of surprise would be the best way to lay hold of them, for he had no intention of giving them leave to depart peacefully.

As soon as Mic opened his door, he could hear the sound his child described. The high pitched screeching sound came from Dylan's recording studio, an old remodeled barn located within walking distance of his brother's home. Mic charged up the hill like the hero he was and stormed into the building. The sound of the screeching reached deafening proportions and his brother lay prostrate upon the floor next to the sound mixer.

Mic rushed to his side, looking for signs of foul play as he checked his brother's pulse. Dylan's eyes were dilated and he appeared nearly comatose. An empty bottle of Jack Daniels lay on its side atop the sound mixer, and a bottle of prescription pain pills had been spilled across a nearby desk.

"Ye bloody bugger—that's the coward's way out! Ain't nothing *that* bad in life, mi lad," Mic whispered, choking back the tears.

Reaching up with one hand, he turned off the power to the sound mixer, terminating the earsplitting sound, while his other hand stretched for the phone to dial his wife. "Annie, call doc O'Donohue. I think Dylan's tried to do 'imself in. Make sure he doesn't call over the landlines for an ambulance. We've got to keep this quiet. Just get him here with a stomach pump as fast as he can come. He's still alive." After pausing a moment, Mic whispered, "Annie, mi luv, don't say anythin' to Mum, Da, or our wee lads. Right?"

He knelt and cradled his little brother in his arms, rocking him as he did when he was a small lad, scared in the night.

☯

"Hello, pest. Guess it wasn't ye'r time to go, eh?" Mic said reassuringly as Dylan's eyes fluttered open forty-three hours later. "Actually, it was, but St. Peter said ye were a pain in the ass, and sent ye back."

Big brother never left his side, nor spoke a word about the condition in which he found Dylan to anyone, save the doctor and his wife. Mic knew his parents couldn't bear to think of their "golden child" as one with warts, and he wasn't about to let the tabloids in on his brother's private suffering.

Dylan said nothing, but turned his head away and began to weep.

"Ye're obviously strugglin' with some feelings ye've no wish to expose, mi lad, but that's not the way to handle 'em. There ain't nothing in this world that's worth snuffin' out the light of a candle as bright as ye'rs. ...'sides, it'd be bloody awful boring without ye."

Mic rose from his bedside chair, sat on the bed, and held his brother tightly as he wept. Stroking his hair, he softly hummed the old Gaelic tune he used to sing to put his three-year-old brother to sleep when he was, himself, a lad of thirteen.

Chapter 2

Crow spent more and more time with his band and began to compose again. His lyrics ranged from the saddest, heart-wrenching words to angry, spiteful ones. Many a night he spent away from home in the company of loose women who were more than happy to satiate his lustful appetite. Dylan never brought any of them home, however—not to his special place. He didn't want *just anyone* there. He wanted Nikki there. Though trying to keep busy, when the thought of her snuck into his consciousness, he continued to numb it with alcohol and drugs.

Late one night, with brain unclouded with debilitating stimulants or depressants, he lay alone in his bed, staring at the ceiling, simply allowing the thought of Nikki to come into his head and heart. He visually relived the night they danced on the mesa; the night she looked like an angelic princess and he confessed his knowledge of their twin flame relationship. With longing, he recalled their lovemaking: every sincere glance that concealed nothing, every scent in the air and upon her skin, every savory kiss, every curve of their entwined bodies as the firelight defined them, the expanding energy that exploded in every chakra of his body, the limitless sensation as if they were truly one being, with no beginning and no end. He experienced it all over again, even though alone. The pulsating feeling in his heart began to expand, which he felt sure could be attributed to the light his dearest love promised to send. He relaxed into it and fell asleep as if in her arms.

The dreams of Nikki played all night long, dreams of being with her, in her, part of her. When the morning sunrise woke him, he tried desperately to get back to sleep to dream of her again, but he could not. She had disappeared. The sunlight had stolen her away.

Crow rose from his bed and reached for his old favorite guitar, which hung from a bracket on his bedroom wall. Locking himself away for three days, he composed a song called "Heart Fire."

A few days later he called Braydon and asked for some help with the rhythm and secondary instrumentation. Braydon, completely unaware of its source, hailed it as the best work Crow had ever done. They spent another three days creating just the perfect background to his lyrics and original tune.

The band had spent sufficient time together since Crow's return to generate and perfect a total of twelve new songs. They agreed to cut another CD. Braydon arranged for a professional studio in Dublin for the original tracks, which took two weeks. Dylan insisted they send it off for final mixing and polishing to the U.S. recording genius, Hal Weinberg.

When Crow and Braydon were actively engaged in their music, they seemed too occupied to use stimulants. The creative power inside of them appeared to fill a need. When idle, they tended to fill that need with destructive behaviors. With their work completed, however, "party time" returned with a vengeance, complete with drugs, alcohol, tobacco, and shagalicious women.

Braydon had a way of subtle flattery with Crow that led him to do things he might not otherwise do. These ranged from experimentation with different drugs to fast money schemes. He could work Crow's ego into a state of self-importance like no other. Oddly, he honestly believed his unusual support helped his old friend get his confidence back and pull him out of his occasional funks.

The non-stop party continued for a week before Crow decided to sleep in his own bed. With his body cells well steeped in alcohol, he turned the key in the lock, grateful to be home. The phone persistently rang and he staggered toward it, anxious to terminate the nagging intrusion.

"Oh, mi angel, thank the Blessed Mother ye're there! Ye'r da's fallen and I fear he's damaged. I found 'im unconscious on the floor of the loo. I woke him with a bit of cold water in the face, but I can't move 'im.

"Mic and Annie went to Dublin for the night. Their lads are here, but they're too small to be of much use. Can ye come straight away?" Crow's mother sounded breathlessly frantic. She wasn't much good in emergency situations, and worse still if they related to someone she loved.

In spite of his drunken daze, Crow understood the situation. "Be right there, Mum. Don't worry." His head miraculously cleared as the adrenalin surged through his system while he bolted down the hill.

With his upper torso wedged between the toilet and the bathtub, his father seemed weakly conscious.

"Da? Da, ye all right?" Crow calmly asked. He'd helped enough of his friends out of similar physical situations when they had passed out.

Jack looked up and his eyes brightened at the sight of his son. "Oh, I'm grand, mi lad, just grand. That bloody sciatica o' mine must 'ave buckled mi knees or something. I think I knocked mi noggin.'"

"Well, first let's just get ye from under the toilet and back to bed, shall we? Can ye get ye'r right arm around mi neck, Da?"

"Aye, mi boy. Just get me standin' on mi own two feet and I can make it to the bedroom."

Crow gingerly pulled his father to a standing position, but his left leg was completely useless. Crow lifted him bodily and carried the old man to his bed. "Mum, lift the covers, will ye?"

"Such a fuss over a bit o' nothin'!" Jack muttered. "I'll be good as new by mornin'—ye'll see. Just need to relax the muscles around the nerve, that's all."

"I think we should call Mum's cousin, Da, just to make sure."

"Doc O'Donohue? That ol' quack doesn't know his right from his left. Let it be lad—the restin' will take care of ye'r ol' da just fine!"

Crow looked at his mother's face, ashen with fright. He could tell more went on than met the eye.

"Now, mi darlin wife," Jack said tenderly, "ye'd best get Mic's lit'luns back to their beds, and if I could trouble ye for a cup o' tea to settle mi jangled nerves, I'd be most grateful. Besides, maybe I can get mi lad to stay and chat with me for a minute. Takes a bloody emergency to get an audience with 'im anymore, so I'd best be takin' advantage of the situation."

Maryssa obeyed his commands and closed the door gently behind her to give the men some privacy away from the listening ears of her two grandsons.

"Pull up a chair, mi boy."

"I think ye scared mi mum, Da. Ye had the look o' death about ye."

"I could say the same for you, mi lad—and the stench that goes with it! What the bloody hell is that smell?" Jack asked wrinkling his nose.

Crow looked down at his stained jacket. Due to his inebriation, he hadn't noticed the appalling odor. "I guess ye'd say I'm wearing a soup of alcohol, tobacco, and Cort's chuck. He spewed all over me tonight. It is pretty awful, isn't it?"

"Remove the foul thing and throw it out the door, so we can talk without chuckin' ourselves!"

Crow laughed as he stood and removed the unwanted garment. As he opened the bedroom door to toss it in the hallway, his mum signaled him to come out. He stepped down the hall into the kitchen.

"I called Toby O'Donohue, but Iris says he's delivering Mrs. Porterman's baby. Said she'd send him straight away when he's done, but it could be another hour or so."

"I'll see if I can keep 'im awake, Mum, in case he has a concussion or somethin'."

"That's mi good lad—but don't overexcite him—right?"

'I'll take good care of him. Ye just tuck them lads away for the night, then."

As he returned to the bedroom, his father dozed. He shut the door loudly to wake him. "Ye still awake, ol' man?"

"Ol' man? Why, ye lit'l cub, I can still show ye a thing or two," Jack returned with the spunk of twenty-year old, playfully shaking his fist at him. "Is it disrespect ye're tossing at ye'r sire now?"

Crow laughed as he sat next to his father and held his hand. "Just playin' with ye, Da. Wanted to see if that bump on ye'r head diminished ye'r wits any!" Crow smiled with loving tenderness at his aging father. He couldn't get over how much older he looked now than he had several years ago. There wasn't a man in the world he respected more than his ol' da. Jack had been a pillar of strength, both physically and morally, and yet he had the kindest heart hidden beneath his rough facade.

"Oh, aye. Speakin' of 'diminished wits,'" whispered the old man, as he pushed himself to a sitting position, "there's rumor screamin' 'round the village that ye've done nothin' but drink ye'r way through pub after pub and ye've been spreading ye'r seed far and wide. They're all scared o' sayin' somethin' to ye 'cause ye're famous 'n' all, so they give ye a wide berth. But that's not the moral lad ye'r mum 'n' me raised, now is it?"

"Da, I'm not a boy any more. I'm thirty-nine years old. For

Godsake, are you really going to lie there and lecture me on mi
morals?"

"I'll say mi piece this once, and this once only, son. Ye'r rowdy
and promiscuous behavior won't serve ye. I'd call it takin' liberties,
I would!"

"Liberties, Da? With the ladies? They're old enough to know
what they're doin'!"

"Yes and no, mi boy. When ye take a lass to ye'r bed just to sat-
isfy ye'r lust, a piece o' both o' ye'r souls departs. Ye're taking liberties with ye'r own soul, as well as the lady's, son! Ye keep it up,
and I assure ye, its light will soon be strugglin' to see its way to the
surface. The world's heavy for reflectin' the darkness in mens'
hearts right now, mi lad. Don't burden 'er with more!"

Crow looked past his father and stared at his parents' wedding
picture that hung on the opposite wall. The old man followed his
son's gaze.

"Listen, mi boy. Ye seem to be forgettin' that I know ye well.
T'was a miraculous gift from God when ye entered ye'r dear mum's
womb. After the birth o' ye'r brother, Mic, the doctor told us he'd
most likely be the only wee one we'd ever claim from heaven above.
But ten years later, ye'r mum come to me with great tears o' happiness fillin' her bonnie green eyes, telling me she was with child. Ye'r
very age, she was, mi lad. So certain we'd been bless with a miracle,
it never occurred to us to be concerned about her age!" Jack chuckled as his eyes bore into his son's. "When her cousin, Toby, delivered
ye, he swore ye glistened like gold and ye'r mum has privately called
ye her 'golden child' ever since.

"We knowd ye were special since ye first drew breath, for we
saw a strength in ye; a strength of heart, mind, and soul, mi lad.
Ye've the heart of a lion in ye, and there's none can deny it. So,
what I'm thinking—is that ye're tryin' ever so hard to run away

from somethin'—or someone. Is ye'r ol' da right, boyo?"

Dylan's eyes pooled with tears as he looked to his feet like a child who's been caught in a lie.

"The heart is an especially unusual organ, Dylan. It can't be filled, until its been broken open. One day ye'll wake to find it overflowin' with love again. In the meantime, remember the love that ye do have about ye. Ye'r family and friends love ye true, mi boy. When ye start bein' grateful for the things ye do have, the heavens are opened and pour more abundantly into your life that for which ye're grateful."

With a light tap on the door, Dr. Toby O'Donohue stepped in. Crow carefully stood, facing away from the doctor, as he wiped his eyes and carried his chair back to the wall. "Well, doc, ye must 'ave pulled that baby out with a come-along!"

"False alarm. Baby's not due for another two weeks anyway." He set his bag on the bedside table and looked sternly at Jack. "Oh the joys of being a country doctor, eh? Iris tells me ye took a tumble, Jack. That right?"

"Did mi wife ring ye after I specifically told 'er not to?"

"That she did, ye old fool! Worried ye might have a concussion or somethin'." The doctor pulled a small flashlight from his bag and began checking Jack's eyes.

"Away with ye, ye ol' quack! I'll be good as new by sunrise!"

"Ye are, by far, the most *recalcitrant* patient I have, Jack Crow! Were ye not mi cousin's husband, I'd let ye rot!"

As the two men engaged in their cherished banter, Dylan excused himself so the doctor could make a thorough job of his examination.

Half an hour passed before Toby stepped into the kitchen where Dylan and his mum were drinking coffee and speaking in hushed tones.

"He's asleep now. I don't see signs of a concussion. It may be worse, however. Maryssa, has Jack been takin' his medicine regular-like?"

She stole a quick glance at her son, and then threw a furtive glare at her cousin.

"Blast it, woman! Answer me true!"

When she avoided the question, he seized her shoulder. "Maryssa —*has* he been taking the medicine I gave him?"

"Could ye excuse us, son?" she said politely as she stood.

"Mum..." Crow said sternly, lowering his head like a butting ram, looking at her from under his thick black eyebrows. It was his father's look of disapproval, which he mimicked perfectly, *and* which brought her cowering to her seat again. "What's wrong with Da?"

Turning abruptly to the doctor, she spoke forcefully. "Toby O'Donohue, ye know how Jack feels about burdenin' his lads with such nonsense!"

"Nonsense? Nonsense? You listen to me, woman! Ye'r husband may be in jeopardy, make no mistake about it, and his lads may have more influence over him than ye seem to have. As a doctor, I'm bound by oath not to reveal anything, but as kin, I'd say it's bloody-well time this family of ye'rs stop hiding so many crashin' secrets!" He looked unsympathetically into her eyes and then into Crow's.

"Well the cat's out o' the bag anyway, ye old fool!"

Maryssa tucked her chair closer under the table and reached for her son's hand. "Ye'r da thinks it's nothin', lad, but Dr. Toby disagrees. Da insists the med'cin' is only a placebo, so in answer to ye'r question..." she turned to face her cousin, "no, he's not been takin' it at all."

"Disagrees with what?" Crow demanded, looking to the doctor

for a more lucid description of his father's condition.

Toby looked to Maryssa for some form of consent and after a pause, she nodded. "Ye'r da has an inoperable congenital heart anomaly, which, in and of itself, has caused him no harm during his life. However, he now suffers from high blood pressure, which can exacerbate the problem and cause either a terrible stroke, or worse, death. Looks as if he may have suffered a small stroke tonight. He suffers weakness on his left side, but it may return to full strength on its own." He turned deliberately to direct his next comment to his cousin. "And—if the bloody fool won't take his medicine, he'll *surely* be departing the society of his beloved family *soon!*"

Maryssa, now sobbing, pulled a hankie from her apron to stem the flow of tears.

"I want him in my office tomorrow morning for further tests. Right? And, Maryssa, don't ye let him charm his way out of this. Understand? I'm talking life and death here!"

"We'll have him there, doc." Crow stood to shake hands and escort O'Donohue to his car.

The night was crisp and clear for a change. Crow heaved a sigh. "Thanks for bein' so conscientious and patient with us Crows. Mi da's a proud man, sir. He's only known good health all his life. I'm sure the thought of not aging gracefully offends his very spirit, ye know?"

"Aye, Dylan. Pride runs rampant in *ye'r* family! They still don't know of ye'r lit'l bout with death, do they?"

"No, sir—and I'd like it to remain that way. 'Twould serve no purpose except to aggravate mi da's condition and set mi mum to worryin'."

"Son, ye may not have a physical problem with ye'r own heart, but I'd say it's in as much danger as ye'r ol' da's. I know a doctor in Dublin that specializes in cases where suicide's been attempted."

"I wasn't tryin' to off miself, doc. Honest. I'd taken the same amount o' pills with alcohol before without dyin'! It's true I've been lately buried under mi own pathetic desires, but mi heart's as strong as mi da's and I can see this through by miself."

"Don't ye be fooled by that kind o' thinkin', lad. What may have started out as an escape from somethin' can end up takin' on a life o' its own—demandin' all ye'r attention and money, until one day it swallows ye whole—body, mind, and spirit. But, I'm not ye'r priest, son. Ye'll have to deal with the demon ye'r own way."

As the doctor swung his legs under the steering wheel, he looked up and made one last comment. "Oh, by the by, nurse Anderton tells me she refused ye a prescription for pain pills earlier this week. I guess ye've learned that it won't be me who'll be helpin' ye drown ye'r sorrows, son."

Crow laughingly responded with a nod of his head and shut the car door.

Toby rolled down his window and shook Dylan's hand one last time. "Lord keep ye, then, mi lad and ye make bloody-well sure that da o' ye'rs is in mi office come sunrise!"

Chapter 3

Six months after Crow's return from the States, he heard from his agent, Robert Dansboro. "Say, old friend, have I got an opportunity of a lifetime for you! Now, just hear me out. OK?"

A disinterested, "Hmmm" sounded from Crow's end of the line.

"I know you wanted to take some time off this year, but hey, man, you've been sitting around for more than half a year already, and that should have given you enough time to recoup!" Robert hurried into his next line, so there would be no debate forthcoming. "I got a script today I want you to look at. Peter O'Leary was cast for the part, but his wife has been diagnosed with ovarian cancer and he quit the show. I think you're perfect for it. They want you to play the brain behind the brains in the world drug industry. The location is Singapore. And this is the best part—who have you always claimed as the best and most beautiful actress in the known universe?"

"Janet Langston, hands down, mate," Crow answered.

"Guess who your co-star would be?" Robert grinned on the other end of the line, hoping this bit of trivia would cinch the deal.

"No way, man! Ye're not trickin' 'bout with me, are ye?" Crow asked tentatively.

"Man, when you stay home for a while, that Irish accent gets thick, doesn't it?"

"Let it slide, mate. What's the deal?"

"It gets better, friend! Part of the contract says you get to… what's that word you guys use? Shag? Yeah that's it—shag her under the intimate glare of all the lights and in front of a working crew of approximately one hundred people. Really—just you and

Janet with no porno backups. The sex scenes are very explicit full body shots, so they don't want to use any doubles. Here's the best part—she's already agreed to you as her new co-star! *You* ought to be paying to be in this flick, man!"

Robert waited, knowing his client all too well. Crow had confessed more than once that Janet Langston met his ideal of a *real* woman. She was two years his senior, a graduate from Vassar, the most beautiful woman in the world, famous beyond famous, wealthy beyond wealthy, and could play a role far better than anyone he'd ever seen.

"What's her husband think about the sex thing? I hear he insists on doubles."

"Don't you get the newspaper in Ireland? No hubby, at present, friend. Her quickie divorce came through last Tuesday. I told you, she's already agreed to copulate with *you!*"

The silence on the phone was deafening as Robert allowed Crow the opportunity to take the bait. As an agent, Dansboro had learned to manipulate his clients well. He knew men forever bait each other with sexual innuendo, and that generally speaking, most men buy into the baiting process for fear their friends will deem them less than worthy on the masculine scale if they are willing to pass up *any* opportunity to dip their wick. Knowing that it's very difficult for most men to free themselves from the good intentions or opinions of their male counterparts, he let the challenge stand.

"And the brass?" Crow asked, though Robert knew the money meant nothing next to the opportunity to do a show with Langston.

"Fourteen million, five, U.S."

"How soon would I have to be on set?" Crow asked while holding his scotch to the light in a toast.

"Yesterday! So you want to take the script sight unseen or have a copy shipped overnight?"

They chatted about the details and, as Dansboro hoped, Crow agreed to head for Singapore within two days. Robert knew all the right buttons to push. The agency would arrange for the tickets and have a limo pick him up by ten a.m. two days hence, and he'd be off for the "opportunity of a lifetime."

☯

Robert arranged for the script to be sent overnight, but it arrived only minutes before Crow departed for the airport in Dublin. Dylan read it during the long flight.

Not a terrific script, as far as he was concerned. He would play the part of the brilliant, suave, mastermind behind the worldwide trafficking of drugs, a highly respected man of business, coincidentally involved politically in major drug producing and consuming countries. Through his subtleties and financial influence, he overpowers all obstacles in his way to provide narcotics mainstream to the general public. His argument, of course, is that those who are going to use drugs, will, whether or not they are legal. He arranges his drug super-highway through political pressures. With his identity held anonymous, he also manipulates his puppets within the drug agencies to reduce the requirement from *prescription to over the counter* on both an addictive pain medication and an antidepressant owned by a company he controls. By applying political pressure on the regulatory agencies, and hiring a large P.R. firm to create a major campaign, he convinces the public any attempt to control street traffic drugs is a useless drain on tax dollars. The financial and medical statistics are blasted through every media possible. By forcing the two issues with the United States Food and Drug Administration, five other countries follow suit, granting the desired approvals.

His power and influence continue to grow to such heights,

even Hitler would have been proud.

Co-star, Janet Langston, plays the woman he can never have, and he determines he *will* have her, regardless. After secretly *arranging* her husband's untimely death, he sweeps in and woos her off her feet, convincing her to be his bride. He subtly begins to control her as well as everything else he touches, until her vision of him becomes clear. When she investigates his secret life, he begins drugging her, forcing an addiction. She becomes useless and he has her eternally committed to a sanitarium.

His financial influence, through legal, but immoral contributions to the world at large, makes him one of the most sought after people in world politics. The final scene portrays his acceptance of a major position in the U.N., which is acting secretly to create worldwide political control. He abuses his power in every conceivable way and wins. The end.

Blah, blah, blah, blah, blah…nothing new! thought Crow.

Before the jumbo landed in Singapore, he had decided to turn back. Nikki's words about his responsibility toward what he sent out into the world haunted him. He knew he could play the part perfectly, but her words disturbed him deep inside.

After being greeted upon disembarking by the producer and his co-star, Janet Langston, he threw all good intentions aside. Alarmingly, he transmuted into a groupie in her presence, as if under a magical spell. She had an air of cultured perfection that made him yearn to become acquainted with her. His conscience simply gave way to his excitement.

Janet Langston was a tall, lanky girl from Georgia, born of a wealthy father and a high society mother. She had spent most of her early life in expensive boarding schools and followed her elementary education with a degree from Vassar in political science.

She had begun acting as a dare from a friend in college, but had been discovered by an executive from Columbia. Even though a pretty decent actress, her beauty and well-endowed, sexy body, encouraged the executive to take her for a ride, so to speak. However, Janet took him for a ride, executing her part as his play-mate well. Within weeks she was cast, even though unknown, in a major role.

The executive from Columbia felt relief when the public perceived her as an excellent actress and the ratings of the show and box office sales exceeded his expectation. In the excitement of her major debut, they were wed. He had insisted on a prenuptial agreement, which Janet signed without reservation. She trusted him implicitly and allowed him to handle all their finances. The scoundrel essentially squandered all the money Janet made from her first film and publicly humiliated her with a high-profile affair with another actress. Janet delivered a male child just two weeks before they decided to separate, nine months later. Although she legally secured some finances for child support, no alimony had been awarded and she was left with a broken heart and an empty bank account. The tender wound upon her soul never healed.

Janet made an issue of getting back in shape and for the most part, gave the care of her unwanted infant over to a nanny. Within a month of the delivery, she set on a course to prove her worth to the world. Suddenly, men of every kind buzzed around this beautiful, intelligent flower, with the well-practiced ability to make men feel like her protector, something she knew made them feel virile and potent. Although she had married multiple times, she never let another man truly near her intimate and vulnerable heart, or her money, ever again!

☯

In her thick Southern drawl, she held out her lovely hand to

Crow to greet him and breathlessly whispered, "Why, Mester Crow, I find it an absolute playsure to make yo acquaintance."

She had sky blue eyes and blond hair cut in a chic, straight style to her shoulders. Dylan had never seen a face sculpted to such perfection. He guessed it had, indeed, been sculpted a time or two, but it appeared, nonetheless, remarkably beautiful. Her seductive Southern accent held a promise of secrets to be shared. Standing about five foot ten, with the carriage of a queen, her body boasted perfect proportions and though slender, her voluminous silicone breasts gave her the image of a soft, welcoming woman. The whole package appeared to be femininity, grace, charm, intelligence, art, and beauty rolled into one goddess. He decided to stay.

The production had been greatly upset with O'Leary's departure, and every scene possible without the main character had been filmed while waiting to replace him. Crow's prompt arrival proved to be a godsend, but they knew they were going to have to push him hard. He had a reputation as a dedicated worker, so they trusted he could handle it.

Though non-stop busy, Crow and Ms. Langston had many opportunities to converse between shots and over meals. Their first scenes together were electric and everyone agreed the combination would work out better than they'd hoped.

Crow had made no advances toward Janet, nor she, him. They had been strictly professional, though friendly, during the filming. Their big sex scene, scheduled for the morning, had Crow doubting his ability to pull it off in front of the camera—not because he was incapable of having sex on camera, but rather, because he had this slight intimidation factor with Janet. In his private fantasies, she aroused him tremendously, but he often felt at a loss in her actual presence. He couldn't bear the thought of finding himself impotent in front of her and the entire cast and crew!

Janet stepped into his dressing room a few moments before the first take and noticed the faraway look in his eyes as he sat staring in his make-up mirror. "Honey, you seem a tad nervous 'bout this," she observed aloud while gently squeezing his shoulders.

Her reflection in the mirror mesmerized him.

"I rememba ma first sex scene on camera. I was so damn scaad—sure I'd fail miserably and they'd fire ma lovely ass on the spot." She continued to massage his shoulders. "I lund a li'l trick to hep me tho and if ya'd lak, I'll share it with ya."

Looking up, he begged with his eyes, but said nothing.

She reached into her pocket and brought out two little pills, putting one in her mouth and waiting for him to extend his tongue. "Now, ya jus' relax and take yo clothes off. I'll meet ya on the set in twenty minutes."

He had no idea what she'd given him, but noticed a distinct sense of arousal and no inhibitions overtaking his senses. Dropping his clothes on the dressing room floor, he marched, fully naked, to the set, causing cast and crew alike to giggle. Ms. Langston, already on the bed and under the sheets, winked as he approached.

"I see yo ready to do some work, Mr. Crow?" She smiled sheepishly with their untold secret as he ripped the sheets off and moved across her as if he owned her.

The director didn't have time to do anything except turn to the cameramen and say, "Start rolling! I don't know how long this is going to last!"

Both Crow and Langston were overwhelmed by their sensuality and lack of inhibition. They were hard and rough with each other, rapacious in nature with powerful consuming lust, while each vied for control second by second. It created such an air of excitement that the observers stood with mouths agape for the sexual energy blasting in every direction. The streams of that energy made contact with all who watched, and many found themselves being aroused. There were some among the group who'd never seen any form of pornography before, but they felt this must surely be what pornography looked and felt like; no tenderness, no giving—just taking, and taking, and taking. The stars looked like wild animals as they bit, clawed, and sucked. He did not make love with her; he violated her. She ravaged him.

After forty minutes, they cut, with both Langston and Crow lying exhausted and laughing on their backs in the bed. Dylan had never experienced anything like it. He turned on his side and looked at her body, head to toe glistening with sweat and asked in his American screen voice, "How was it for you?" To his surprise, she took his hand, directed it to her dark, inner parts, and they began all over again.

Never had the producer or director seen anything like it. The cameramen picked up every conceivable angle they could find.

That evening, while viewing the day's work, the producer masturbated several times as he watched the scenes again and again. To his delight, the sexual energy had transferred to film. Although the rules were changing yet again in the film industry, he knew exactly how to edit this scene to keep both the R rating *and* the sexual excitement.

A connection had been made between Crow and his idol. Their professional behavior had slipped into the realm of an intimate relationship. He noticed, however, each time they engaged in sex, Janet popped a little pill.

Crow, a quick study of character noted that Janet had all the outward appearances of a strong, dominant female, but truth be told, he discovered a frightened and vulnerable child underneath it all. This, alone, made him want to surround her with his protective shield. Like most good actors, Janet had a history as a consummate liar and her *appearances* before the rest of the world were pretty much all a façade.

As he lovingly drew her out, Janet allowed her vulnerabilities to be exposed for the first time since her marriage with the Columbia producer. Crow took seriously his responsibility with this tender and fragile part of his new lover. Underneath her disguise, she was actually quite a lovely woman on the inside as well. He became more and more enmeshed in her world.

Before long Dylan realized he only held onto the tail of this tigress, and did not dare to let go for fear he'd be consumed by the irresistible power she held over him. Janet could be soft and gentle, then cruel on the turn of a dime—switching emotional gears like one diagnosed with a bi-polar personality. Nonetheless, so utterly dazzled with her beauty, intelligence, and ability to turn a phrase, when she walked into a room, he could see only her.

They both smoked a lot. It was a relief not to have someone overtly, or secretly, judging him about his smoking habit. They drank untold quantities of alcohol together and laughed a great deal. Their mirth, however, had usually been initiated at the expense of others.

Crow felt this new relationship had rescued him; had, in fact, been the greatest possible thing that could have happened in his life right then. Janet had a way of making him feel important and he felt she'd be a great asset in his life.

When he asked her to marry him, she wept for fifteen minutes. She had, one by one, exposed her fears and vulnerabilities to him, the first man she had trusted in many long years. Janet longed to come in from the cold netherlands of emotional isolation.

They decided they would marry just as soon as the filming

drew to a close. They told no one, save her attorney, who swiftly arranged the legal documents to protect her estate. She may be willing to trust her heart to this new mate, but the financial part of her life she entrusted to no one!

Janet had signed no prenuptial agreement as related to his estate, though he signed one for her. Crow seemed willing to share everything he had. He owned a few apartments in the states, his ranch, a sailboat, and a number of expensive vehicles. The rest of his funds were, for the most part, managed by an investment firm he'd selected, and they were ensuring him a nice return. Knowing Janet's reputation as a substantially wealthy woman, he assumed money would never be an issue between them.

Dylan had been nominated for the Best Actor award for his role in *The Teaching of Little Crow*. Unfortunately, the Oscars were scheduled during the final week of the Singapore shoot. The production could not afford his absence, but arrangements were made for him to be available on a live feed in the likely event he won.

Chapter 4

Sam happened to be visiting his mother for two days en route to play a tournament in Phoenix the night the Oscars were being aired. Nikki excitedly insisted they watch to see if Dylan would win for his performance in *Little Crow*, though she already assumed he would. Sam had never seen his mother so excited. When the announcer stated Crow's inability to be present in person, he assured the audience he would be available for a live interview from Singapore.

"Have you two been in touch since he went back to Ireland?" Sam asked trying to sound only slightly interested.

"In a way," she said, keeping her secrets to herself.

His mother had seemed more alive and vibrant in the last six months than Sam could remember in his life. She literally glowed. He had seen it the first time he saw his mother and Dylan Crow together. Always respecting her privacy, as she did his, he decided not to pry further. If she wanted to share more about their relationship, she would—in her own good time.

"Why do they always show Best Actor last?" Sam asked while yawning. "You'd think they could control the length of the acceptance speeches, wouldn't you? I detest all that bawling and blather."

After having sat through almost three hours, waiting for the only item of interest to either of them, Dylan Crow won the award. Nikki screamed and danced around the room like a wild woman as she hugged and kissed her son. Pulling him to his feet to dance with her, they waited for the live broadcast from Singapore to be aired after a commercial break.

There, framed in her own television, appeared the face she loved most in the world. Crow looked a little tired and something was gone from his eyes. *Perhaps it's just the time change,* she hoped silently. Nikki suddenly grew very quiet and sat on the ottoman, listening to what he had to say as his extraordinary voice filled both her heart and ears.

"I'm grateful for this supreme honor. It's always a nice pat on the back to have mi peers acknowledge mi work. I thank Peter Laslow for his perseverance and insight, without which this noble piece could never have existed. I'd like to thank all those who helped in the production on every level, because no one performs alone. Oh, and…(he smiled sheepishly)…I'd also like to announce to the world that I'm finally off the bloody market, as Ms. Janet Langston and I will be getting married in one week. Thank you."

Crow waved to his unseen audience, then blew a kiss to Miss Langston, who, caught on camera in her Oscar-esque, shimmering gold, quarter million dollar gown, smiled broadly and blew him a kiss in return.

"Well, that's that," Nikki whispered thoughtfully.

Sam's jaw dropped as he turned slowly to see his mother's reaction. A steely calmness filled the air around her, but all the radiance he'd seen for months had literally drained from her in a few seconds. She sat motionless while he stood to turn off the television. There were no tears in her eyes, or any hint of sadness in her voice. Instead, she appeared calm. Dead calm.

Sam's anger in defense of his mother rose to his throat as he began to berate her, evidently, *ex*-lover. "Those guys have no sense of reality, Mom. They just live in a la-la land where they don't ever have any real relationships or true values beyond that which meets their immediate needs! I'm glad the bum's getting married to someone who deserves him!"

She rose, put her arms around Sam, and hugged him tightly. This amazing son of hers seemed to be present to ease the pain of every major crisis she'd had in her life. His soul entered her womb when she felt no hope in her relationship with Scott and had been there when she reclaimed her power. He'd been with her when she'd been diagnosed with breast cancer and also on the day she healed herself. He sat by her side consoling her the day his father died. Could it be considered a coincidence that he spent the last days with her prior to letting her beloved go, or that he comforted her now when she had to let him go all over again?

"I've never asked you to promise me anything in your life, son, but I'm going to ask you to take a sacred vow right now," she said in a clear voice, her eyes engaging his. "You know the saying, 'If you have not walked in another man's shoes, you cannot know what it is to be on his pilgrimage?' Some take a very long journey, while others seem to ride the fast-track. You mustn't judge Dylan or anyone else for that matter. We're all in school and we're all learning through our own pathways." She paused to see if what she said had any visible signs of having been comprehended.

"I want you to promise me if Dylan ever tries to find me *through* you, you'll *never* tell him where I can be found. You must tell him only that when he *knows* for certain he is ready for me, he must remember the beginning. You must tell him if he remembers the beginning, he will know how to find me. In addition to that, I'm *begging* you to hold him in your own heart with the same affection with which you held him only moments ago. This I ask for you, as much as I do for him."

"Are you going somewhere I don't know about, Mom?" he asked with great concern.

"Not at the moment, honey; I'm right here. I ask you to remember this, however, in the event such a *miracle* ever occurs." Her voice trailed to a whisper on the word "miracle." After he made his solemn vow, she excused herself for bed.

She sat half the night in an upright position, with knees drawn to her chest, sobbing into a pillow, not crying for *her* loss, but for the agony she felt on her lover's behalf, knowing how truly painful his chosen pathway of learning would be.

Chapter 5

Janet had two children from two previous marriages: Katie, age eight, and her oldest, Donald, age nineteen. Donald had been on his own for several years and Katie spent time between boarding school and her father's home. Janet's career kept them separated most of the time and she had to admit to the emotional estrangement she felt with both of her children. It wasn't that she didn't care for her offspring, or that her life was shallow—rather, she found her true child had been her career. To this child she held absolute fierce fidelity.

Her P.R. firm put them on parade when they felt the need to portray Janet's nurturing mother image to the press. Because of the media blitz, both children were pulled from their schools and flown to Paris to meet the next man she intended to marry. They arrived a day early to attend an informal reception where Crow would be introduced to all Janet's immediate and extended family who came to join the celebration.

Donald, though friendly enough, kept his distance.

Katie downright hated Dylan. "Ya thank ya can be ma daddy now? I got a daddy—a good daddy and ya cain't never be ma daddy," she spat at him in a private moment.

Somehow, this beautiful little duplicate of Janet had gotten the idea into her head that if Crow married her mother, she wouldn't be able to see her own father any more.

"Tell ye what," Crow offered, turning the other cheek, and hunkering down to her eye level, "I promise not to be ye'r daddy or to try to take his place. Maybe we can be friends though. OK?" He said it so sweetly and gently that Katie relaxed and took his extended hand.

Crow's da hadn't felt well enough to come to Paris, and his

mum wouldn't leave the old man's side. In fact, none of his family members ever wanted to be a part of his publicity. They decided it would be best if the happy couple would come to Ireland to allow his bride to get acquainted after the honeymoon. So caught up in the event and the buzz that followed the Oscars, Crow didn't even feel slighted when his family waived their responsibilities to come support their son at his long-awaited nuptials.

The elaborate, formal, and supremely elegant wedding/reception was hosted in the Jules Verne Restaurant of the Eiffel Tower. Though considered a *private* affair, it ended up being the media event of the century, outshining even the press coverage of the royal couple's wedding in England.

After the marriage, the kids were shipped back to their respective homes and Janet and Dylan began their whirlwind lives together. They had spent their wedding night at the Georges V in Paris, though they were both too drunk to enjoy it very much. The next day, however, she slipped a little pill in his juice and they had a royal union. From Paris, they'd gone to Rome, from Rome to Genoa, from Genoa to Switzerland, where they spent a delightful few days in Gstaad.

In spite of their decision to take a few months off to be alone together, the paparazzi followed wherever they tried to hide. The pictures and details of their wedding and honeymoon were splashed in every daily paper, every gossip column, every magazine, and tabloid in print.

He was crazy about her. Crow couldn't believe he actually married his idol. A promise had been made to remain by her side 'til death, and he fully intended to keep his commitment, come hell or high water.

They flew from Geneva to his beloved Ireland and spent their first night in Dublin, where Dylan introduced his bride to his favorite haunts. The following day they hired a limo for the four-hour ride through the enchanting Irish countryside en route to Schull. Dylan anxiously anticipated showing Janet the place he loved most in the world.

"What a chamin' li'l o' place," she announced as they drove in. He presented her to his parents, who, though dressed in their best clothes, seemed shabby compared to her. His brother, Mic, and his wife, Annie, and the boys, joined the introduction and Dylan felt as if he'd come home to show off the biggest and best trophy he'd ever won.

Janet behaved in a pleasant, but slightly formal fashion with his family. Nothing of her familiar chic lifestyle appeared here. There was no one for whom to dress up, no cameras flashing—just *real life* family members who ran Crow's sheep ranch.

Unintentionally, Janet spoke down to his parents, as if they were uneducated and required a verbiage change in order to understand even the simplest concept. Jack and Maryssa were uncomfortable with her obvious effort, assuming she suffered in translation. Crow felt a little ashamed, but thought once everyone got to know each other, things would be fine. He knew Janet's career had forced her into certain behavioral patterns to protect her privacy. Dylan had managed to protect his own with a different bag of tricks.

Mic made himself scarce by claiming work had to be done after Janet had spoken to him almost like a lowly servant. "Mic, da'lin'," she had said, "would you bring the luggage to the main house and put it in the masta bedroom." There had been no *please*, no *thank you*, as if having called him "da'lin'," he should do handstands for her upon command. Crow had seen the look in his brother's eyes and read his thoughts. He simply intervened, saying, "I'll get them, dear."

It wasn't as if Crow brought home the girl next door. He brought a media icon—one larger than himself! She had been handled with kid gloves, having every whim granted by the slightest wave of her hand for over two decades. The queen of the screen had unlimited servant-types rushing around her all day long. She chose not to become familiar with any of them, for it would distract her from her work. Unfortunately, Mic seemed the most likely person to wait upon her at that particular moment.

Janet looked around the rooms of Dylan's treasured home with an eye of severe judgment and though she didn't want to hurt his feelings, she simply despised the place. It lacked all the accoutrements of grand beauty that normally adorned her surroundings. As far as she was concerned, her new husband had delivered her to the farthest corner of the world and stuck her in a log cabin without running water or electricity. The ranch represented his dreaming place, however, and she loved him, so one way or another, she determined to survive the visit the best way she could.

"It's jus' chamin', da'lin'—jus' chamin'," she lied. He watched her brush off a chair to have a seat, though the chair was not dirty. "Why, we can just have Marlow come and fix this li'l ol' place up like a palace and you can come here a couple of times a year!" Marlow was her interior decorator, one who managed to spend a goodly part of Ms. Langston's hard-earned money.

Dylan had hoped she would love the ranch as much as he, but it was evident within the first twenty minutes in his precious home that she actually held it in disdain. He'd have to bite the bullet and move into her world. The ranch would be kept, however, because it gave his parents and brother a home and employment. Maybe he *could* visit a couple of times a year, but he felt certain it would be without his wife.

Janet strolled around his home inspecting things to see if they had any monetary value. Some of the paintings on the walls were costly, but some were worth only as much as a corner store poster. It disgusted her to see that he would lower himself to put such, in her estimation, *trash* in his home. As an avid admirer of elegance, she insisted that her surroundings reflect it at all times. Some would have described her as extravagantly spoiled, but Crow saw her only as an elegant queen.

When she entered his den, an unusual wooden box on the desk drew her attention and she proceeded to open it. Crow walked in behind her and saw she had discovered his *lucky charms*. In his haste to leave for Singapore, he'd neglected to pack them.

"And what great popose do thase serve, da'lin'?" she said fondling his sacred charms.

He wanted to snap the lid shut on her hand because he wasn't ready for her to invade that part of his life just yet.

As he approached, she pulled out an indigo colored flower from the top of the box. It looked as if it had just been picked and she raised it to her nose. Its fragrance, a sheer delight, provided her first joy in his home. She assumed the box of trinkets belonged to one of Dylan's nephews.

With doubt it could possibly still have life within it, he literally grabbed it from her fingers and walked to a window where he could inspect it more closely. Janet didn't think much of his antics and continued fingering through the *junk* in the box. She grew bored with her endeavor and continued out of the den to inspect the bedroom.

"Keep it by your bedside until it fades and dies," he remembered Nikki saying. *Could she still be holding a life force focused in this flower after all this time?* he wondered. He felt a familiar longing as he thought about Nikki. His heart started to ache a bit and he walked to the alcohol cart, poured a drink, and slugged it down. Behind his desk he noticed an unopened, long, narrow box on the floor, with a return address from the St. Germain Foundation. "Listen lad," he said aloud, "ye chose another road, and *that* one is no longer an option!" He tossed the flower back in the box and put it high on the top bookshelf, well out of Janet's sight.

Janet asked Annie, in the charming fashion of a supremely talented manipulator, to come over and prepare a meal for them, for she had no intention of taking on any domestic chores. They would be back in Beverly Hills in a week and Dylan would see her full time cook as a great advantage. "After all, weer stas, da'lin'! We don't wanna get our li'l ol' hans dirty in that nasty ol' kitchen sink, do we?" She had said it with her nose wrinkled up in a mischievous manner and she appeared too adorable to argue with!

Annie made their welcome home meal as a gesture of love to Dylan. She did not offer to repeat the performance, though Janet had suggested they would like to have their breakfast late the next day. Crow tried to understand her outlook. It was one thing to be on parade, and another to be in one's home; at least that's how he viewed it. Certainly more earthbound than she, he could see a few adjustments would have to be made in order for them to honor each other's idiosyncrasies and live in harmony.

The ranch was situated on the ocean a few miles distance from the city of Schull. Though a small village, it had some nice restaurants that catered to the yachtsmen and he thought he could take his new trophy into town for a few meals. He, otherwise, would be the one getting his "li'l ol' hans dirty in that nasty ol' kitchen sink." Crow didn't mind. He just wanted to please his beautiful new bride.

After three days at his ranch, Janet became nervous and anxious, pleading with him to take her home. "There's nothin' to do out here, baby," she whined like a two-year-old. "It's like we've been dropped off in East Geesus, and there's no one to take care of us, no one to talk to, nothin' to stimulate us, jus' nothin'! The country's fine for a day or two, but I just desperately need the energy of a city. Understand, sugar? ...'sides, yo too impotent to be here, da'lin'. Ya need to *be seen* in the right places!"

He heard her emphasize the word "important" with her Southern drawl, which came out "impotent." That's how he felt—impotent.

It was a helpless feeling. He wanted to make her happy, but realized the cost of doing so would be walking away from all the things he had held as valuable in his life. She had met and didn't like, or approve of, his mates in the band—had treated his parents like plebeians and his brother and family like servants—hated sheep—and to top it off, wouldn't let that "stanky ol' thang," his beloved Great Dane, in the house. In fact, to his extreme disappointment, she made it abundantly clear she didn't like animals at all!

Contrary to the implied opinions of his family and friends, he knew her intimately and knew this shallow display did not represent the full spectrum of her personality. Between finishing the last film, arranging for their wedding, and being asked to stay in a place she found distasteful, Crow feared any further disruptions to her lifestyle would shoot her right over the edge.

He called for a limo service to get them to Dublin and made arrangements for their early departure, making an excuse of business to his family. Janet said her phony, obligatory farewell to his clan and they drove away. Looking back through the limo window, he wondered if he would ever see his beloved home again.

Chapter 6

Janet's residence, a paltry twenty thousand square foot palace, sat on a five-acre setting. The gardens and lawns were immaculate with a staff of seven just for the exterior. Her spunky Italian cook, Josephina, lived in her own space off the kitchen. A staff of three cared for the interior of the home, and their chauffeur lived above the garage. Crow thought it all a little pretentious for a woman who lived alone and away from home most of the time.

His first months were very rough for he felt like a guest in a hotel. He wasn't even comfortable enough to walk to the kitchen in his underwear to get a drink.

One day, while playing his guitar and trying out some new lyrics, Janet drawled, "Da'lin', yo disturbin' ma concentration. Could you take *that thang* and make *that noise* in another pot of this house?" She raised her hand and gestured for him to shoo.

"Ye're *only* reading a magazine, luv!" he answered, slightly bruised.

Glancing up to see the hurt registered in his eyes, she softened her approach. "I don't mean to be pullin' threads, baby. It's jus' that sometimes I need a little space. Understand, sugar?"

As he departed to give her "a little space," he forcefully jammed his baseball cap onto Shakespeare's head, one of many marble busts that lined the hall outside their bedroom.

Janet's palace was filled with extraordinary art and artifacts collected from every corner of the world. Dylan had once asked Janet to tell him about different pieces, but as Marlow, not she, had chosen each treasure, he realized her home did not truly belong to her. She had not *sculpted* it with things she loved that brought comforting thoughts to her when her eyes gazed upon them. He thought of the little stone walls Nikki had built in front of her home, how she had lovingly collected and stacked thousands of stones to sculpt her yard. As he looked out the window watching the maintenance staff trimming bushes, he remembered how much fun he had mowing lawns with her. *Though she'd lived in the lap of luxury, she chose to live on a ranch and sustain her life and energy her own way,* he thought.

Refusing himself permission to think about Nikki, he opened a bottle of wine and turned on the news for a distraction.

☯

Ennui set in for both Dylan and Janet. The honeymoon now over, he felt working would be the best remedy. *Problem is,* he thought, *if one of us goes on location, will the other follow?*

They spent a lot of time shopping—something to which he quickly became accustomed. Janet loved to spend money and lots of it! She spent a fair share on herself, but also spent a great deal of thought and money on those she held dear in her life. There was always someone on her list that "*this* would be *perfect* for!" Crow liked that part of the game. It made him feel more than generous; it made him feel benevolent.

Three months after their marriage, Janet's agent called offering a script he described as perfect for her. He brought it over to the house at four p.m., and by eight o' clock, Janet had accepted the studio's offer. The location would allow her to reconnect to her hometown roots in Georgia, and she was thrilled. Crow had nothing better to do, so he followed.

While Janet worked, he read and watched and became infinitely more bored by the day. Plenty of women on and off the set were still making passes at him, in spite of his marriage. Crow always behaved graciously and sometimes his new bride mistook his etiquette for flirting. One lovely thing dropped her hotel key into his lap and kissed him on the cheek. Crow looked up in time to see Janet's eyes narrow to near slits and wondered what she must be thinking. Although men were secretly admiring his bride, he noticed no overt attempts on their part to challenge his place by her side.

He hadn't liked any of the scripts that had been offered to him and his restless, agitated state wore thin on his new bride. Dylan began to experience an indifferent state of mind where everything seemed profitless. By making extravagant, expensive gestures toward his wife and her family, he tried to feed the emptiness. He could no longer see beyond the vanities of the world. It became a terrible, disenfranchising state, like being held motionless in a vacuum. His very soul seemed denuded of vitality. But—he had made a commitment to support Janet's career as well as his own, and he would stand by it. Awakening on a rainy morning, he looked out the window and decided to make his own sunshine. *By God, there are plen'y o' constructive things I can be doin', 'stead of sittin' like a toad in the rain!*

Being in Janet's hometown brought even more press than had hounded them since they were married. Like it or not, the press were a big part of their lives. Whether true or false, what is said or printed about a man often has as much influence on his life and destiny as he, himself does. Unfortunately, when you're a celebrity, you find that many people talk, but few think. He felt most of the journalists were petty and self-serving. Both he and Janet knew, however, they had to use the press to their advantage in their profession, and had acquired quite a talent for saying just the right thing and smiling at the precise moment the bulbs were flashing.

Mid-way through the shoot, Janet decided they should move into her father's guesthouse rather than remain at the hotel, because it would afford them more privacy while in Atlanta. Security was beefed up, and once again, Crow found himself under house arrest.

Her mother decided to hold a little soirée to show off her daughter and new son-in-law. All the truly important people in the state were invited and Crow felt obliged to participate. He thought attending the party would make his lovely bride happy, and her happiness mattered most of all.

The Governor topped the list of guests. Crow overheard a small group gossiping that the Governor and Janet had been long-time secret lovers. He wondered at her sweet familiarity with him and when his bride became occupied with other fans, he determined to introduce himself to the right honorable fellow.

"Where's that charming Guv'n'r of ye'rs? I'd like to chat with him a moment," Crow asked his new mother-in-law with a vapid smile on his face.

"Oh, da'lin', he had to leave a while back. Somethin' 'bout a problem over that nasty ol' murderer who is s'posed to be executed in the mornin'."

Crow thought if he could work, even a little, that his enthusiasm for life could be renewed. He called his agent and told him he personally wanted to review all scripts that had been sent for the last two months. Robert obliged and shipped a large box full to Janet's father's home by FedEx. Crow began truly searching for something to do.

Janet's schedule didn't allow for them to be together privately as often as he desired, and he resented the time she spent away from him. One day Janet mentioned a night shoot had been scheduled and because she'd be home a little late, he shouldn't wait up for her. Out of boredom, he called her assistant, Susan, and asked the location of the shoot so he could watch.

Confusedly, the young woman informed him the night shoot

was scheduled in three days. "Ms. Langston left the set two hours ago, Mr. Crow."

Crow poured himself a tall scotch, popped two Demerol, and sat in a chair right in front of the door, waiting for her to come through. At two forty three a.m., his lovely bride sneaked quietly into the darkened guesthouse, holding her shoes in one hand and her bag in the other. He sat there, regarding her eye to eye. No words were necessary between them. No confessions were issued, for all had been said.

He thought he must be responsible for his failure to please her. "What is it ye want me to change to make things better for ye?" he demanded. "Who're ye shaggin' 'stead of ye'r husband, lass? This isn't the way marriage works, ye know?"

She would not dignify him with a response, but crossed to the bedroom, swallowed some pills, removed her clothing, and climbed into bed. *That'll paint his lit'l red philanderin' wagon!* she thought.

His head pounded and his insides twisted into a thousand knots. When he awoke still in the chair the next morning, she had already gone. *How could this be happening to me: the world-renown womanizing, lov-'em and leave-'em, Dylan Crow?* he wondered. *Have I just been reduced to a clinging sap or is that the bride I promised to stand by for better or worse? Guess this qualifies for "worse." She's probably just caught in some stage romance that'll pass as soon as we get out of this crashin' hell-hole!*

Patrolling at every set, he tried to figure out whom to blame. He began protecting his investment, smothering her with attention, and Janet couldn't stand it.

The ten thousand dollar bracelet he bought her seemed to delight her---for five minutes. He remembered how much love and gratitude Nikki had shown him over a seventy-five dollar bracelet which she refused to remove from her wrist.

He talked to Janet about going to his apartment in New York as soon as the film was over to fool around in the big city. Standing guard over his property every moment until they left Atlanta, he hoped they could make things better once they left.

His bride agreed to the trip and the press followed. As soon as rumor flew that they were in town, an invitation arrived for them to attend a gala affair being held at the Waldorf. She looked so beautiful to him as they breezed into the event, with all eyes turned to see the lovely couple. He felt great pride at having her at his side. Holding her tenderly in his arms, they danced throughout the evening. Crow remained glued to her instead of circulating with the others. As he looked around at the prestigious guests, he remembered "the where to be, if you're a *wannabe* temple," and laughed at the reality.

"Honey, why don't ya jus' say howdy to summa those nice people who invited us to the party!" she said, trying to shake him loose for three minutes. "I'll jus' go powder ma li'l ol' nose and ya can handle the niceties. 'Right, sugar?" She did go to the ladies parlor and sat down to have a cigarette, aching to be free of him for a few minutes. Janet felt like she was choking, so she stayed in the room for half an hour, while he kept the door in sight, anxiously awaiting her return.

Something had snapped inside of Janet the day she saw her new, beloved husband openly flirting with some young "thang" after she brazenly dropped her room key in his lap. When he disappeared fifteen minutes later and returned to the set after an hour's absence, she assumed the worst. Every feeling of distrust, fear, pain, and anger that she had buried in her heart since her first marriage surfaced. Any betrayal on his part was absolutely unpardonable, *especially* because he *knew* she had opened her heart completely to him. She had wanted to hurt him in return. *Men! There's not a one o' them worth this sickenin' feelin' in ma heart! He's jus' like all the rest o' the bastards. I can't bear the sight or touch o' him,* she thought as she forcefully stubbed out her cigarette.

Finally alone in the room, she stared at her reflection in the mirror. Her otherwise proud shoulders sagged and she reached for a tissue to wipe the tears that were surfacing. Janet didn't want to close off her heart to Dylan, but felt herself falling swiftly back into her old habits—those habits that held all men and all intimacy at a distance. Somewhere in the back of her mind a small voice whispered, *Give him a chance, girl. Ya haven't truly loved a man fo' years! Give yo'self permission to love and be loved by that da'lin' boy. All that female attention jus' comes with the package of a man as famous an' handsome as Dylan. Ya gotta learn to trust again.*

Chapter 7

They re-established themselves in Beverly Hills, settling back into the palace. Enough space existed that she could escape him when she felt like it, and he knew her location, so no longer hovered over her every second.

While still wading through the boxes of scripts Robert had sent, he found one he truly liked: a remake of *El Dorado*. Crow called his agent to see if they'd cast the part yet and his return call assured him the studio would be thrilled to have him play the lead. Production would begin in twelve weeks.

Janet had Katie shipped home during school holidays and attempted with all her heart to be a good mother. She had Marlow create an extravagant girl's room for her daughter and though everything looked the part, there wasn't much mutual affection between Katie and Mom. The natural cause of separation showed its effects as the two strangers played out the roles of mother and daughter. Janet tried to offset things by buying "her precious baby girl" anything and everything she wanted, but even an eight-year-old knows when she's being bought off.

Dylan suggested a trip to Carmel during Katie's visit. According to the media, they were the perfect little family. People magazine splashed photos of the happy trio romping in the waves and building a sandcastle at the beach, and to the world, these three were bonded and joyful. Janet's guilt over her lacking maternal instincts induced a subliminal need to escape—which she did by drinking. No one saw or reported how heavily both Janet and Crow were consuming alcohol. Crow felt relief on Katie's behalf when they put her on a plane and shipped her back to her father's a week before school.

❦

When he accepted the role in *El Dorado*, Dylan fully expected Janet to go with him on location to Mexico. After all, he'd supported her in Atlanta. To his extreme disappointment, she said she wanted to stay in Beverly Hills because she never liked Mexico anyway. "Too many Mexicans!" she had said. Having already signed his contract, he packed and left alone.

Janet truly struggled with her feelings. She *wanted* to embrace Dylan with heart and soul, but a lot of water rushed pell-mell under the fragile bridge of their relationship. Worse still, she felt she had no control over her emotions. She had been receiving secret love messages as a result of her vengeful tryst in Atlanta, which only compounded the emotional upheaval. Having her husband away would give her time to figure things out.

❦

While filming *El Dorado*, Crow found he couldn't sleep, so someone on set arranged for some downers, which he took every night. However, this type of good night's sleep often left him drowsy and not "with it" on time in the morning—so he began taking uppers.

Because of a few mechanical problems in the third week of shooting, the producer offered Crow three days off. He decided to surprise Janet by flying home. The surprise was his, however, as he discovered *his* bride in *his* bed with the Governor of Georgia, apparently their houseguest for the weekend. Dylan looked blindly past Janet, picking the Governor up by his throat and thrashing him soundly. Luckily, the press didn't catch wind of the story. The Georgia media merely reported a painful spill which the Governor took down the stairs of his mansion.

"Look, Janet," Crow said resolutely as he walked out his front door the next morning, "I love ye—but ye'd best be gettin' ye'r heart straight with me, or start packin' mi kit. I know the temptations of our crazy lifestyle—but there's not been a minute of infidelity on mi part, and I *will not allow* ye to be unfaithful to me—ever again. We made a promise, we did, lass. Whatever it is that's twistin' ye'r thinkin' needs to be re-evaluated. I know ye've been hurt before, mi girl, but it wasn't me and not *all* men are bastards! If ye have any feelin's for me at all, there's only one way I'll be playin' this game with ye. That's all I'll be sayin'." He stepped over the threshold and shut the door firmly.

Janet sat in a confused daze on the bottom step of her elaborate spiral staircase. She held her head in her hands and wept.

☯

Upon his return to the *El Dorado* set, Crow patiently waited daily for her call, but it never came. The next move had to be hers. He felt trapped between the emotions of love, anger, disappointment, and betrayal.

Occasionally he would snort cocaine; socially at first, then just to feel normal. During one scene his horse bolted unexpectedly and he was thrown, causing unbelievable pain to his back. Dr. Paulo Guzman, production physician, prescribed his old favorite pain pills—a generic oxycodone. Between his drinking, the pain pills, and his frequent use of recreational drugs, everyone noticed his morose behavior. He played his character well, however, so no one said a word about his new conduct—at least not to his face.

Meanwhile, Janet immediately accepted a movie offer while Dylan worked in Mexico. Having never seen him enact any form of violence before, she feared his return home. Her agent, concerned for her safety, ensured her location would be far, far away in Brazil. Once established, she finally placed a call to let him know where she was.

☯

The first year of marriage proved to be as rocky a road as a man could travel. He knew now the madness of two flaming egos, each trying to control their private lives The word *divorce* had not yet entered their conversations, however, and he determined, yet again, to meet his commitment to her as a husband. He thought she had slept around because she suspected him of infidelity or he had somehow failed her sexually. The subject would be broached when he had a chance to see her in person.

When his movie wrapped in Mexico, Dylan flew to Brazil. Janet had softened toward him and they got along as well as they had when first they met, though she continued to use drugs to have sex with him. When he asked if she felt dissatisfied with his performance, she assured him he was the finest, most considerate lover she'd ever had.

"Janet…if that's so, why do ye need that lit'l pill?"

She avoided his eyes, as if ashamed. Then she stiffened her back and smiled. "Well, da'lin', I jus' wanna pleasure ya to the highest heights, that's all!"

"An' ye'r affair with the Guv? Is that o'er, mi lass?"

During their phone conversations the subject had been blatantly avoided. Janet had hoped it would never be brought up again.

"Dylan…" she choked out, "what I did was terribly wrong! Do ya 'member that day on the set in Atlanta when that hussy gave ya her room key?"

"I recall the look on ye'r face, luv."

"Well, when ya disappeared fo' so long, I concluded that ya had taken her up on her offer. I felt so hurt and mad, all I wanted to do was strike back at ya! Alan and I have known one another fo' a long, long time—helped each other through some bad marriages and some nasty divorces. He seemed a likely and safe candidate for ma accomplice. I jus' wanted to teach ya a lesson, that's all. Problem was, Alan took it serious-like and says he's always been in love with me. The whole situation was very confusin' and when ya told me ya had never been unfaithful to me I wanted to die for havin' jumped to conclusions and hurt ya so bad. Yo violence sca'd me to death, howeva, and all I could think o' was runnin' as fast and far away as I could go. I haven't talked to Alan since the day ya beat him to a pulp!

"I do love ya, Dylan, but sometimes I wonder if I have ever had the ability to trust anyone enough to let them all the way into ma heart."

☯

During the first few days together Dylan babied his back to the point of distraction. Janet arranged for the production physician to prescribe some pain pills. She couldn't bear to see him so uncomfortable. "Baby, ya'd best see that back doctor o' yo's when ya get home."

☯

In Janet's current role, she portrayed a Catholic nun serving in a remote Brazilian village in the early 1800s. Crow asked if he could stay and watch for a few weeks.

One particularly outstanding and touching performance by Janet caused him to open a new territory of conversation between them—God.

After their late supper, Janet donned a slippery little nothing and slid next to her husband under the covers. Apart from the glow of ash on the end of Crow's cigarette, the moon provided the only light. "We've been together for over a year, lass, and I've never once heard ye speak about God or spirit—yet here I find ye playin' the part o' a nun with all the devotion of a real one! Do ye believe in any particular religion or have ye ever practiced one?"

"Ain't got much use for God or religion, baby. I've come to believe that it's jus' folks hidin' behind somethin' so's they don't have to accept responsibility for their own choices or actions. God ripped me apart as a young thang and quite frankly, da'lin', I don't trust any one who represents themselves as God-fearin', bible-thumpin', devotees."

"What do ye mean...'God ripped ye apart'?"

Janet sat up and lit a cigarette of her own, distancing herself from Dylan by a few feet. She drew her knees to her chest and wrapped her arms around them. "When I was 'bout thirteen years ol' 'n' off at boardin' school 'n' all, we had this Southern Baptist priest who taught ma Sunday School class each week. He was the most handsome man I had ever clapped eyes on. Sunday became ma favorite day o' the week, as I'd sit starry-eyed, gazin' at that man. One week, after he had stirred ma lit'l ol' soul to the height o' lovin' everyone an everythin' in sight, I was stupid enough to ask him if I could stay behind an' help him clean up the church. I developed rather early and I think ma buddin' femininity was perhaps flirtin' with him a tad. Anyway, he agreed and told our bus driver that he'd personally deliver me back to the school.

"I didn't know nothin' 'bout nothin' then. Inside of thirty minutes he had violated me in ways I pray no child or adult ever experience. I was terrified. When he was through rapin' and sodomizin' me, I curled up in a ball in the corner o' that ol' stone church and wept and wept. He told me it was Satan that possessed him and that he was sorry 'n' all...but I must never tell no one. Said he'd kill me an' himself were I ever to reveal the horror o' that Sunday afternoon."

She took a long drag of her cigarette and stared blankly ahead. "This is the first time I've ever breathed a word to a livin' soul. I guess somewhere in ma lit'l heart I thought I'd asked for it by flirtin' with him and askin' to stay. The guilt I felt was consumin'! Anyway, never had much use for God or religion after that."

She turned to see Dylan's reaction and the moonlight bounced off the tears streaming down his face. He reached for her and pulled her close to his chest and stroked her hair while he tenderly embraced her.

That night Janet made love without the assistance of her pills. She silently wept through Dylan's climax, never having reached one herself. When she thought him asleep, she tiptoed to the bathroom, closed the door and turned on the faucet to drown out the sound of her retching.

Dylan rolled over and stared out at the moon, realizing just how truly fragile and vulnerable his wife was. It brought forth every desire within him to protect her from the world that had created the need for her emotional walls.

Before he left Brazil, Dylan asked what she thought about making a family of their own and Janet made it clear she had no intention of having any more babies at her age. Though he'd once been involved in a paternity suit early in his career, the DNA testing failed to show the child as his. Now he desperately wished for his own family—one created in a space of love. He thought if Janet had another child, she would settle down and they would live happily ever after, storybook style. After their conversation, however, he surrendered to the idea of *never* having a family.

☯

Janet's work would keep her out of the country for another three weeks, so Dylan headed home to handle his business affairs. As he walked through the front door of the Beverly Hills palace, the phone rang. He rushed to pick it up, hoping it would be Janet. The caller ID registered Mic's name and number in Ireland.

"Hey, bro! What's up? Haven't talked to ya foreva!" answered

Crow in his new stylized Southern accent.

Mic's voice trembled. "Da's dead, Dylan. Can ye come home?"

☯

Janet would not leave Brazil, even though the studio had actually given their consent for her temporary absence. She just couldn't stand the thought of having to go back to "East Geesus" ever again, and since she had only met her husband's father the one time, she did not feel obligated to attend the funeral. "Dylan, da'lin', I just can't break free. Ya'll have to go alone. Please extend ma condolences to yo family fo' their tragedy," she drawled over the phone. "An' baby, I'm truly, truly sorry for any pain yo're feelin'." At least the last thing she said was sincere.

☯

During the long flight Crow plied himself with alcohol and pain pills. Just as his old uncle had once predicted, the "demon" had taken on a life of its own.

Mic stood in shock when he saw how much his brother had aged. Deep, dark circles drooped beneath his lifeless eyes, and gray hairs peeked out all over his head. His skin looked sallow and it appeared as if he hadn't eaten in a year. He even slurred his speech. Mic wrote part of it off to grief and managed to get his brother back to the ranch. Putting him to bed and turning out the lights, big brother hoped Dylan would be able to cope during the funeral in the morning.

Everyone noticed the absence of any kind of joy in Crow, especially his mum. Again, all assumed it had to do with the death of his beloved father. In fact, his father's demise had devastated him, though his appearance resulted from a combination of the emotional trauma he'd endured during the previous months and his constant use of narcotics.

He sulked around his ranch house for a few days and called Janet several times trying to find her. Finally, he located a young girl who, while delivering a costume to Janet's dressing room, answered the star's cell phone just because it rang. "Do ye know where mi wife is?" he asked.

"I thought she was with you, Mr. Crow. I heard she left several days ago to attend your father's funeral in Ireland!"

Someone shshed her and snatched the phone.

"This is Lyla Arken, sir, your wife's assistant. Your wife didn't head for Ireland. She's here, sir. I'll leave word for her to call you back. It might take me a while, because she's out on location today. Where can she reach you?"

Though he continued to leave messages on her cell, it took twelve hours for his wife to return his call. Janet worked diligently to convince him she'd been busy with a shoot and just barely picked up his messages on her phone.

He stayed at the ranch for only five days. It felt too painful to look at all he loved knowing he could never be there. "Mic, I want ye to put it on the market," he told his brother over a glass of wine. "I'm not anxious to do this, 'cause I know ye'r family and Mum have made a home here. I've enough money to set ye up anywhere ye want to be and take care of Mum too. I've made a commitment to Janet and she just hates this place. Can't see any reason to keep it if I can't enjoy it."

Mic, a man of honor and principle, told his brother he'd put it up, but he and Annie would make it just fine on their own. Mum was another story. Dylan's financial aid for their mother would be appreciated, but even if Crow wouldn't help, Mic would take care of her.

"What price ye want, Dyl?" Mic asked.

"Get it appraised and ask two to four million more. I figure with mi name, we might get it," answered Crow as he twisted the stem of his wineglass between his fingers.

Mic stared into Dylan's eyes, wondering who this stranger was sitting across from him.

.

Chapter 8

Upon returning home, Janet responded with enthusiasm when Dylan mentioned selling the ranch, eagerly asking how much he could get for it. The quoted price had been set at twelve million dollars, U.S. It had appraised for only eight, but he failed to explain that little point. "Well, we can jus' take that money and build us a love nest on Maui, baby. It's a lot closa than I'land," she said excitedly, thoroughly delighted with the prospect of spending his money.

The Schull property sat on the market for nine months without a bite because no fool would offer to pay his asking price or even honor it with a counteroffer. Mic called him one afternoon with some news, however. Some U.S. corporation had sent a solicitor by to take a look at it. "Ye really want to stick to that ridiculous price?"

"I dunno, Mic," answered Dylan. "I know I need to get it out of mi blood, so maybe we better just see what they offer. We haven't had a single nibble up 'til now. Say, tell me what ya'll been doing?"

A long silence sounded from Mic's end. Dylan always had the distinct ability to change his voice and behavior like a chameleon, but Mic got a sick knot in his stomach hearing this Southern drawl drip from his brother's lips.

"Not too much—usual stuff around the ranch. Annie got tickets for a few of the matches at Wimbledon, so we flew over for a few days with the lads."

"Yeah? Watch any of the biggies?"

"We don't have that much brass, Dylan. They're scalping tickets for two hundred quid a seat for the dumb matches! We did see a talented young man from the States who looks pretty promising, though." Mic said, though he knew his brother didn't really follow tennis.

Dylan really missed his brother and attempted to draw him out in order to hear his voice a little longer. "Yeah? What was his name?"

"Sam James, it was. I think he's fairly new on the big circuit though. Heard the press say he had really struggled between getting his degree first or playing professional tennis."

Crow experienced near paralysis at hearing Sam's name.

After they hung up, Crow asked his chauffeur to purchase all the latest tennis magazines he could find. The driver returned thirty minutes later with six magazines. Dylan read each thoroughly, but found only a small mention of Sam's name and no pictures. The magazines were carefully wrapped in black plastic bags and placed in the trash pile. As he turned off the garage light he thought, *I can't bloody believe that I'm even thinkin' 'bout Nikki. Don't know why I'm hidin' these like I'm ashamed. Never told Janet 'bout Nikki anyway. Cowboy up, lad—for the queen awaits ye in bed!*

☯

Three days passed before Mic called back with a bona fide offer. "The solicitor claims the corporation buys strictly for investment and no one would be coming to live on the ranch. They offered eight million, five, U.S., with the strict proviso that I stay on and manage the place. Offered me a higher salary than ye're paying as well, and, get this Dyl, they said Mum could live in 'er house as long as they owned it. What do ye think?"

Dylan breathed a sigh of relief knowing his family would not be uprooted.

"Oh, yeah," Mic added, "they also insist that nothing be changed in ye'r home. They want to keep it as a guesthouse in the event anyone in the company wants to come for a visit. They said we could even keep guests there occasionally if we needed to." Mic hesitated a moment. "I don't know if this is the right time to be tellin' ye something else or not," Mic said a little nervously. "The McKenzies' are finally selling out."

The McKenzies' were his adjoining neighbors to the south. Crow had always wanted to purchase their ranch because he felt it complemented his perfectly. Mic half hoped by delivering this news, his brother would decide not only to keep his ranch, but buy the other as well.

Crow winced, as if someone had opened an old wound. "I'll send ye mi power of attorney by FedEx tomorrow and ye can close it at eight, five." Crow hung up, staring blankly at the phone as he realized he'd just sold the place he loved most in the world.

☯

"Eight million five hundred thousand? Yew fool! With yo reputation and big name? That was jus' stupid, baby!" came his wife's response. "We' gonna have ta supplement the building in Maui from somethin' else, 'cause it's gonna cost us at least twelve million!"

Janet had been dreaming up plans for an extravagant beach house in Maui ever since he told her he'd put the ranch on the market. She had teams of architects working round the clock and Marlow was already in the Far East picking up a *few* little things for their nest. They had found the perfect spot and the asking price of the raw land was only five million two hundred thousand. "An incredible deal!" the realtor assured Crow.

Chapter 9

Crow's substance dependence became more severe. Though he drank freely in her presence, he tried to conceal the pain pills from Janet. His behavior told all, however. Through the next eight months his dependence on the oxycodone had her concerned. He refused offers to work, insisting his one priority was to get the house completed in Hawaii.

Janet thought they had a real breakthrough in the marriage while in Brazil. She wondered if he harbored any ill-will over the fact that she had not attended his father's funeral in Ireland—wondered if he had somehow discovered she had, instead, spent those few days secretly meeting with Alan to iron things out.

The drugs interfered with their intimacy, though Crow seemed attentive enough. Although he tried to make her feel protected and safe at all times, he simply wasn't truly there for her anymore.

The movie icon had enough to deal with in her relentless pursuit of her ambitions and nourishing her vanity. When they appeared together publicly, she treated him with doting affection in front of the snapping cameras, but privately she became more discouraged.

Janet received an offer to perform in a film that would primarily be shot on a set in Hollywood. Although entrenched in a hectic schedule, she came home at night. Dylan found pleasure in playing house with her at last.

He took it upon himself to get the nest built in Maui while she finished the film. He had withdrawn money from his private investments to cover the additional amounts to complete the house. The final construction cost amounted to over fourteen million dollars. Marlow's damage would add an additional burden of eight million. So, all told, Janet's *little love nest* cost him over seventeen million dollars.

He considered it a privilege to provide for his wife in an elaborate fashion, and thrilled at the thought of creating this place she dreamed about. A plan formulated to present it to her as a gift in the secret hope his flamboyant gesture would re-ignite the initial spark that drew them together. Perhaps her cooling interest related only to the long hours she kept at the studio.

When Janet finished filming, they flew over to the final product to spend a month so she could regroup. On their first night in the nest bed, he handed her the deed to the house in *her* name alone. She coo'd and lavished her kisses all over him in her gratitude for his generous gift. Slipping him a little pill, she ensured their wild, passionate sex for two hours.

Crow behaved openhandedly at all times with his wife. It was his nature. He paid all of their expenses, which were, indeed, extravagant. Though he had made obscene salaries on his last eight films, both their lifestyle and his drug use were sucking the money out faster than he could bring it in. The thought occasionally crossed his mind to ask Janet to participate financially, but his male/provider pride never allowed it. Besides, they had enough problems in their rocky marriage without adding the additional weight of finances.

Having been so dedicated to building the nest, he hadn't accepted any new offers. Because there were no demands on his time schedule, using narcotics had become a way to get through the whole day—from the minute he rose, to the minute his head hit the pillow. Surreptitiously, Crow still hid his narcotics, like most addicts in denial.

The days turned into months, the months into a year. Because he showed signs of damage, the decision makers in Hollywood made very few worthwhile offers.

From year to year, Crow's soul had progressively withered, slowly, but inevitably. He had begun to feel a relentless indifference that produced an ineffable mental state. Only one who had experienced something similar could understand.

Janet had wrapped herself in the security of the one thing she trusted—her work. She loved Dylan, but could see no way to reach him through the fog of his addictions. Though never unkind or even sloppy, he just wasn't there for her any more. She wondered, one morning when she found him passed out on the bathroom floor, what held their marriage together. *"Baby, if ya can hear me in there, I'm getting' to the bottom of this!"*

She made a personal appointment with his surgeon while he was in San Diego.

"Dr. Reichman, thank ya fo' takin' a minute to speak to me. I know it seems a tad unusual to be seein' ya without ma husband, but I'm concerned fo' his health. I know he doesn't think I see what he's doin', but he's eating those pain pills ya been givin' him like candy and he seems to be ignorin' all possibility of work. His eyes are glazed all the time and he slurs his speech. Worse still, I can never trust that what he's tellin' me is the truth any more. I'm at the end of ma rope! Can't ya just operate or somethin' and fix his back?"

The doctor looked a little confused. He excused himself for a moment and returned with a chart in his hand. "Ms. Langston, I haven't seen your husband as a patient in over nine months. As I told him, that little bit of swelling from his fall had nearly subsided on his visit and there was no damage to his previous surgical site. And, as for the drugs, according to his chart here, I only gave him an anti-inflammatory equivalent to aspirin to use for a total of ten days after he left my office."

"Where the hell is he gettin' all those pills? He's been complainin' o' pain and poppin' pills fo' a *very* long time now. Told me ya were monitorin' his condition and ya thought surgery might be in order!"

"I'm sorry, Ms. Langston." The doctor looked sympathetically into her eyes. You wouldn't know the name of these pills, would you?"

"Oxy somethin' or other."

The doctor shook his head in disgust. "Oxycontin or oxycodone?"

"I'm not right sure."

"One is a time release form of codeine and the other is the straight, hard thing. Doesn't matter. Half the damn country is addicted to it. Terrible stuff—makes any pain ultimately worse and creates the need for more and more drug. I *never* put my patients on it and I've written several papers to suggest that prescribing it causes infinitely more damage than the original symptoms. If your husband is addicted, he'll most likely go to any lengths to justify its use. Those addicted swear they need it for their unbearable pain; they engage the sympathy of health care providers, their families, their pharmacists, dentists, and any and all sources that can provide it for them. The symptoms you're describing fit it to a T. I'd suggest you find out the name of the physician who's prescribing it for him and join forces to *help* your husband."

☯

When Janet returned home from the doctor's office she combed through the bathroom cabinets, but found only one small prescription bottle with four tablets in it. "Dr. George Hansen" appeared as the physician's name on the bottle and the prescription had been outdated by nearly six months. She searched through all the drawers in the bathroom and dressing room, to no avail.

While taking her afternoon tea she asked Josephina if she had seen any medicine bottles lying around.

Josephina, certainly not blind, but carefully trained to discretely guard the privacy of her employer, only looked down at her hands while she bussed the table. "No, Miss."

Janet's eyes pooled and she began to sob uncontrollably as she confessed the full details of her conversation with Dr. Reichman.

The cook had been with her for fifteen years and had grown quite fond of the queen. In her pity she took Janet's hand and led her to Dylan's study. Pulling a few books from the shelves, she exposed all manner of drug paraphernalia.

Aghast, Janet frantically pulled more and more books from the shelves exposing literally hundreds of bottles of pain pills, cocaine, marijuana, and other drugs with which she was unfamiliar. Some bottles were full, some empty. They had been procured under the names of over twenty physicians and the addresses of the supplying pharmacies ranged from San Diego to Modesto. Worse still, the patient name on several of the bottles did not read "Dylan Crow." Dylan's secret life lay revealed in all its darkness.

Janet turned to her cook. "Don't say nothin' 'bout this to Mr. Crow, Josephina."

☯

After several failed attempts to force Dylan into therapy, Janet gave up. When she found him stoned on his den couch at three o'clock one morning, she stood over him in contemplation. "I'm takin' the very next thang that gets dropped off in ma lap, baby!" Janet said while covering him with a blanket. "…And I'm not talkin' 'bout a movie!" Her words fell on deaf ears.

☯

Janet received an offer to co-star with James Baldwin in a romantic comedy. The location would be in New Orleans and she felt relieved to get out of Beverly Hills and away from Dylan for a while. Confirming a filming date in eight weeks, Janet planned a two-week visit with her parents in Atlanta prior to the shoot.

Chapter 10

Crow received a call from his old friend, Braydon, who insisted the CD they cut three years previously be released. Braydon needed the money, as did the other "Overs." Since Dylan had, for all intent and purposes, severed their relationship after his marriage, his old best friend told him he'd find the money to finance the endeavor, even if Crow didn't want to bankroll it this time around. Overwhelmed with guilt for the estrangement, Dylan immediately agreed to reach Hal Weinberg in Texas to see what happened to the master.

Hal not only had the finished product in his files, but also agreed to ship a copy by overnight express. Weinberg, by contract, always kept the originals.

When the disc arrived, Crow put it on his CD player and kicked back to remember the words from his past. It shocked him to hear how angry and sad most of the tunes were. Then he heard the one titled "Heart Fire." He tilted his head back, closed his eyes, and listened carefully to the words and the music inspired by a dream, and realized it was the best thing he'd ever written. With sincere enthusiasm, he called Braydon to suggest a few changes he felt would improve the CD and contribute to the current commercial atmosphere.

Without delay, Braydon flew to the States and they rented a studio to lay down the final tracks. Luckily, Janet was in New Orleans while his "shaggy" mate took up residence as a houseguest. She hadn't liked Braydon one bit, and whenever his name surfaced during Crow's conversations, she referred to him as "that *shaggy* friend of yo's." Crow never asked if she referred to his appearance, or the fact that he spent all his spare time *shagging* any woman who would consent.

The presence of his warrior companion returned Crow's strength of heart. Most of the uneasiness between them had passed during their phone conversations prior to Braydon's arrival. They resumed the silliness of their youthful camaraderie as if no time had passed between them.

Braydon introduced his friend to some new stimulants he sneaked past the airport SS, and in general, once they completed recording, they behaved like juvenile delinquents for an additional week.

"Say, mate, if this CD has any success, will the ball 'n' chain let ye hang with the lads long enough for a wee tour?" asked Braydon tentatively as they drove to the airport.

Crow grew as somber as he'd been prior to his friend's arrival. "Don't know, Braydon. Things are kind o' tenuous between us lately. I wouldn't want to do anything to break the last fragile strands that are holdin' mi marriage together."

Braydon moved into his own heart before he spoke. "I know we frolicked like younguns the last two weeks, but that's not who I am anymore, Dyl. I guess I was so nervous to see ye again I thought the drugs and alcohol would bring back the ol' days. In a way, they did. I just don't have the desire to destroy mi body and brain like I used to. Ye see, I've met me a young lady who's changed mi views about life and I'm finally ready to settle down. I think we'll even make a family. What I'm sayin', lad, is, even though I personally believe that wife o' ye'rs is Satan in a red dress, I understand ye'r need to keep things balanced at home. If ye change ye'r mind, let me know."

As Braydon grabbed his luggage from the trunk and bear-hugged his old friend in one last farewell, Crow choked back the tears.

Crow financed the CD again. They had made enough connec-
tions in the music industry during their last hoorah that he felt
they would have much less trouble getting this one on the market.

He discovered Hal Weinberg had expanded his business
beyond mixing and now offered production and marketing services. With a little financial incentive, Hal shifted the gears into
high to fast-track the Rollovers' "Heart Fire" CD, guaranteeing its
release within five to six weeks.

Within two weeks of its release, the single, "Heart Fire," hit the
number one spot—not just in Ireland, but also in the U.S., Canada,
Europe, and Australia. Crow felt rather confident that they'd win a
Grammy for it.

Chapter 11

As Crow descended the spiral staircase he saw the florist in the foyer arranging an enormous bouquet of flowers on the central table. The display equalled any he'd ever seen in the entry of the most luxurious hotels. Josephina supervised.

"That was thoughtful of ye, Josephina," he whispered as he came behind her. "The missus just loves fresh flowers when she arrives home from a long absence."

The florist overheard and shot a glance at Josephina.

"Why, sir…you ordered these flowers yourself three days ago!"

"Did I? Well, then—I guess it was thoughtful of *me*!" he said, chuckling at having forgotten.

❧

An hour later Janet opened the front door of her home. Dylan stepped out of his den with some letters in his hand and looked up, somewhat startled to see her.

"What a lovely surprise! Wasn't expectin' ye 'til three or four. So ye got away early, did ye?"

Janet noticed the flowers immediately. "Those for me?"

"Aye. Nothin's too good for mi lady."

Crow noticed through the open door the limo's engine still idling and the driver sitting behind the wheel. "Are they sendin' ye'r stuff later, luv?"

"No, Dylan. Ma early arrival isn't ma only surprise today." Her face exhibited no hint of a smile and Crow shifted nervously.

"I'm pregnant."

He stood still for a second while the unfathomable idea registered and then jumped in the air and whooped and hollered for joy while running to embrace her.

"Guess mi last visit to New Orleans did the trick, eh?"

Since no smile graced her beautiful lips, he stopped short. "Ye're not gonna abort *our* Babe, now, are ye, lass?"

"I have no intention of committin' murder," she said sharply, "but the baby is not yo's."

Dylan froze, too stunned to speak or move.

Janet softened her tone. "Quite frankly, Dylan, the infidelity between us destroyed our marriage right from the beginnin'."

"I have *never* been unfaithful to ye—not ever!"

"Ya took on a mistress I couldn't compete with, da'lin'. I can't fill yo bloodstream with some form of bliss that makes ya give the rest of life away. I tried lovin' ya through it all, baby, but somehow I fell between the cracks when that harlot got her hooks into ya. Ya been lyin' an' sneakin' 'round to be with her, jus' as sure as any mistress! When I tried to hep ya, ya refused. I jus' can't take it no mo'.

"I'll be wantin' a deevorce—instantly, if ye get ma drift. I see no need to muddy ma publicity, so let's jus' get this over with so the tabloids can show me happily married and makin' babies with ma true love."

Crow dropped his head. "And...that would be?"

"Oh, ya 'member the Gov? I rekindled that ol' flame when I went to visit ma parents in Atlanta. Alan and I are two similar creatures. He understands me, and mo' than that, he needs and *wants* me. Hasn't got yo international reputation and he's not very photogenic, but I'm 'fraid, ma dear, he's the man who owns ma heart. We'll probably have to live off ma money, 'cause politikin' doesn't pay much, but I guess that's the price of love."

"Ye'll give him a child, but ye'd never give me one?"

"I came home from Brazil resolved to make a baby with ya, da'lin', but by then ya couldn't take care o' yo'self, let alone another human bein'. I had already failed miserably as a mother twice befo' and I woulda been makin' that baby for ya to raise primarily by ya'self, da'lin'.

"Ya see, Alan got me to seein' this nice therapist who's changed ma life, Dylan. I'm not gonna be feelin' guilty 'bout leavin' ya, 'cause yo been gone from me fo' so long, I cain't even 'memba a single reason to be together. She's helped me to see how ya been tryin' to compensate for the emptiness 'tween us by yo generosity. Hell, yew've only been reflecting ma own behavior with ma kids. But there's a new girl in this skin, I'm tellin' ya...and that new girl's gonna give it all to ma new husband and our adorable child. Ya know, I can even have sex without drugs *and* without vomitin' now! That's a huge breakthrough fo' me!

"I ain't sorry fo' our time together, da'lin'. It's been most educational. I'm jus' graduatin'—that's all.

"Now, I'm taking the next flight to Atlanta today and when I get back in a week, I want ya outta ma house and outta ma life." As she opened the door and stepped over the threshold, she turned back. "An' to quote a famous actor I once loved... 'That's all I'll be sayin'.'" She walked out and firmly closed the door.

Crow stood in stunned silence for another five minutes, just staring into space. Then he sat down on the bottom step of the spiral staircase. *I can't feel anythin'! Nothin'! Is mi heart even beatin'?* He put his hand to his chest and could feel no throbbing. No tears fell. No feelings registered; no anger, jealousy, resentment, or pain— nothing. He had become numb.

"Ladies and gentlemen," he announced in a loud voice when he finally stood to climb the stairs, "once again, love proves itself a fraud!"

Crow pulled several chests from the dressing room and began to pack the essentials. He would leave within the hour. Unlocking the vault, he removed his valuable items, and then turned his attention to the case where he and Janet kept the costume jewel-ry. While he collected the few trinkets he wanted, he came across a necklace that belonged to Janet—a silver heart shaped cache with an ornamental hook. He remembered the day they bought it at a funky New Age street fair when they had taken Katie to Carmel. Opening the latch, a prize was revealed within. A small double terminated quartz crystal protruded from the blue velvet lining.

Dylan held the stone to the sun at the window and watched the colors refract and dance on the walls. The crystal triggered an old, familiar longing. Softly he whispered, "Nikki, mi dearest…if ye could only see me now. A man without a heart; a man without a soul; and a man without a bloody home! Somehow I doubt ye'd be seein' mi perfection at this stage of the game."

☯

Crow snapped that night, right in two. It had been the last bit-ter blow.

He moved to the Wilshire temporarily, waiting to find out what their legal nitwits could negotiate. It was simple. She want-ed everything. Janet already had title to her house and he'd given her the title to the nest. Since he was a big star and there were no children at issue, the suits decided it would be best for both of their publicity to just let things ride. Knowing his client had squandered most of his fortune, however, Crow's attorney consid-ered the negotiations lucky because no alimony was requested.

☯

Feeling himself begin to unravel and thinking it best to keep busy, Dylan accepted the offer to tour with his band. The booze and drugs hadn't interfered too much with his ability to function so he felt he could handle it.

The Rollovers went on a six-week tour in Europe and an

eight-week tour in the U.S. Every performance sold out, though Crow appeared stoned through most of them. The overwhelming supply of alcohol, drugs, and women on the concert tour made every vice easily accessible.

Braydon felt sincere concern for his old friend, as he could see Crow spinning completely out of control. He confronted him, suggesting he get straight. They had a parting of the ways at the end of the tour that left a bitter taste in both of their mouths.

Chapter 12

Crow took up residence in his New York apartment.

Peter Laslow called out of the blue, asking him to look at a script. He was intrigued by the premise and knew Peter never took on a project that didn't have some moral goal. They discussed the possibility of joining forces once again, and Peter promised to put a bug in the casting director's ear to see if they would offer him the starring role. The final choice, unfortunately, would be up to someone else.

Peter laid his own neck on the line, for everyone in Hollywood knew Crow's condition. By leveraging his own position and agreeing to a few behavioral guarantees in the star's contract, he finally convinced the studio to employ Dylan.

Laslow personally called and offer him the lead role in *Three Weeks on an Island*. He explained they would be filming on a small island off the coast of Florida, rather than the original location.

In the first week of shooting, Crow showed up late every day— *really* late. He couldn't remember his lines and consistently slurred his words. Between his arrogance and volatile temper, he drove everyone batty. He'd arrange for nightly parties and ensure that anyone present had ample drugs and alcohol to keep them happy. On top of everything else, he'd become a dealer. In addition, each morning he awoke with a new, unfamiliar female lying naked next to him in his bed, some of whom were definitely under-aged.

One evening, Peter asked Crow if he would join him in his room for a drink. Upon his arrival Dylan sensed an uncharacteristic anxiousness in his respected friend. Crow was sliding down off some speed and began looking for alcohol. He helped himself to some scotch from the mini bar and plopped down on the Floridian-style divan. "So, mate, what's really up?"

"Dylan," began Peter in a sincere tone, "I've some bad news. The studio is pulling you from the movie. They left a loophole in your contract, which you *evidently* didn't notice, about the use of drugs and alcohol while working. They have your replacement on a plane as we speak."

"Those sons of bitches!" shouted Crow, jumping to his feet. "Don't they know *who* I am? I've won *two* bloody Oscars! TWO, mate!"

"Come with me, Dylan. I want to show you something." Peter calmly led his irate friend to another seating area in the suite. "Sit down and let me show you what we filmed this week."

Even Crow could see how pathetic he looked. The evidence was inarguable. He felt truly ashamed.

"Dylan, I really like you and, as a friend, I'm genuinely concerned for both your welfare and well-being." Peter crossed over to the desk. "I'm going to give you the name of a little place in North Carolina that I think can help you. It's not a rehab center or AA. They can help you heal the wounds in your soul, and, my friend, I've never seen a soul as wounded as yours. It breaks my heart to see you this way, 'cause I remember the man I worked with on *Little Crow*."

He wrote down two names: one of an institution, another of a doctor, and one telephone number, all of which his secretary had acquired earlier that afternoon. Peter's brother had participated in their programs when he spun into a severe depression after his wife's death. He came home from the center a new man.

Too humiliated to see or speak to anyone, Crow literally packed his bags and stole away like a thief in the night. He got in his Porsche and drove, and drove, and drove, heading back toward New York. As the sun rose, his exhaustion overwhelmed him and he registered at a lovely hotel in Virginia. The surprised and delighted manager offered their finest accommodations to their famous guest.

Dylan lay upon the bed in a daze, wondering how he had become this frightfully lost soul, now reduced to little more than an empty clay pot. He couldn't quite remember what had started the entire slow, numbing process that brought him to this place in life. An aching deep within his heart shouted "I want to *be* again!" His mind, however, struggled with an inner turbulence that threatened to wrench the last breath free from his lungs, leaving him soulless. His body had become both his burden and his ultimate temptation. This disenfranchised state of existence made him long for the grave. Crow felt like a prisoner of war; like a man who has suffered long and hard—psychologically, emotionally, and physically—looking forward to death, and yet, hanging on to any thread of life.

A thought skipped through his brain repeatedly: *If I could just talk to Nikki, I could find mi way back.*

Rising to locate a phone, he passed the open french doors which led to his veranda. There sat a large crow on the rail that eyed him curiously, but remained fearlessly on his perch.

"Hello, old friend. Time for a change, eh?"

The bird squawked and tilted his head to the right, as if listening intently. When Dylan picked up the receiver, the jet black creature took to wing.

He dialed information and asked for her number in Virgin, Utah. When the operator could find none listed, he asked for the Red Rock Canyon Ranch. To his great relief, the operator clicked the auto switch and the electronic voice not only gave him the number, but also dialed it for him.

"Red Rock Canyon Ranch," answered a deep male voice. Crow's heart fell. *M'be she got married!* he wondered, unexpectedly shaken.

"Hello. I'm trying to reach Nikki James. Would she be at

home?" he asked.

"Couldn't say friend, she hasn't lived here for a while now," answered the stranger, chuckling, thinking his answer amusing.

Crow questioned the man in hopes of tracking her. "Do ye know where she moved, by any chance?"

"Sorry, I only worked with her attorney. His name was Gubler, or something like that...out of Salt Lake. Maybe he could help you locate her. Sorry I couldn't help you, friend." The line went dead and Crow slumped in his chair.

He dialed Salt Lake information and requested a number for any attorney named Gubler. There were seven. He took all the numbers, but after a solid hour on the phone, could not discover a single attorney named Gubler who had either Nikki James or the Red Rock Canyon Ranch as a client.

He threw himself on his bed and wailed like an infant, pounding his fists and screaming into his pillow.

The next morning, he placed a call to Dr. John Whitting at the New Millennium Center in Durham, North Carolina. He tossed his bag in the back of his Porsche and drove without stopping until he arrived at their driveway.

Chapter 13

"It's a pleasure to meet you Mr. Crow," Dr. Whitting offered as he reached to shake his hand. "I'm an admirer of your work in *The Teaching of Little Crow*. Truly, it will be considered a classic."

Crow, thoughtful, but nervous, appeared somewhat fidgety. "Ta. 'Twas a wonderful story wasn't it? I think I learned more about life the year we shot that film than just 'bout any other."

"Sometimes we learn with wonder and joy; other times we learn through trauma and drama. Which pathway held sway that year?"

"A bit o' both, I'm afraid. So..." Crow had hoped for more than something similar to a magazine article interview, "tell me how this place works."

Dr. Whitting signaled his guest to a chair and sat next to him. Whitting never liked to speak to someone from across a desk. Somehow it seemed disrespectful and demeaning. "Why don't we just have a little chat before you get settled? I don't know how much you know about our facility or our approach to helping people heal themselves, so I'd like to share our philosophy with you. Who knows, you may want to back out of this right now!" he said, laughing.

Crow shifted uncertainly in his chair and lit a cigarette. "Would ye like one?"

"No thanks. I quit years ago."

"Do ye mind, then? Most people who quit wig out when I torch up." Crow actually behaved in a considerate manner. Lately, he hadn't given a damn about what anyone thought or felt.

Whitting held himself in a relaxed, poised manner. "If a bit of smoke bothered me, I don't think I'd be qualified to run *this* facility. About eighty per cent of our guests arrive smoking."

"Sorry for the interruption, doc. Do go on."

The kindly doctor's face possessed an air of indescribable goodness. His voice exuded calmness. "Well, you see, we think the cause of *dis*-ease of any kind originates deep inside and unless one addresses those inner issues, a complete healing *cannot* take place."

"Oh, ye mean, like, ye have a group of shrinks analyze mi childhood nightmares and shite, right?" asked Crow.

"Although we have qualified psychologists on staff," Whitting continued, "we have a slightly more holistic approach to helping people find their way through the maze. We use a combination of many methods which are custom designed *for* and *by* our individual guests. What might work for one may not be the pathway of another. Every soul who walks through our doors has a completely different need, because no two are exactly alike.

"We're an alternative healing facility, Mr. Crow, and offer somewhat unorthodox methods of treatment. We emphasize spiritual healing, though we certainly don't tout any particular organized religion.

"Insurance programs don't cover the costs of your stay with us, however, so you'll personally be covering all the expenses. We don't force our guests to stay and you're free to leave any time you wish.

"This is not a de-tox center—it's a healing center. We won't search your room for drugs, alcohol, or tobacco, and if you choose to use those things, you do so of your own free will."

What kind of loony bin is this place? Crow wondered. "Doc, just how do ye expect me to get off this merry-go-round by miself?" His voice echoed incredulity.

"Did you get on it by yourself?" asked the doctor. "Don't misunderstand me, Mr. Crow. You wouldn't be here if you hadn't personally decided to get off 'the merry-go-round'. If you'll just relax and trust us, we can see you safely free of these demons."

Oh mi Lord! thought Crow. "What did ye just say?"

"I said, if you'll just relax and trust us, we can see you safely free of these demons." Whitting smiled knowingly and his whole persona took on an aura of profound serenity.

Dylan decided to admit himself.

Crow expected to be filling out all kinds of papers, answering questions, pouring out his intimate history, etc., but not a soul asked him to sign any papers, waivers, or releases.

Dr. Whitting suggested a tour of the facility to help Crow understand the layout better, and also to help him choose where he'd like to live during his stay. "And, Dylan," added Dr. Whitting, "everyone here is as important as the next person. Unless you instruct us otherwise, you'll be referred to only as 'Dylan,' and I hope you'll feel comfortable enough to call me John."

The Center had been built like a wheel with the central hub being the largest building. It reminded Crow of the layout of Paris. From the hub radiated twelve spokes, or roads, each leading to an exterior gate of the walled compound. It was a miniature city, minus the commercial section. None of the gates were locked and one could enter or exit through any of them.

John referred to the hub as the "Center" and its design made it appear almost like an ancient temple, though Crow could not identify the architectural style. It simply had the flavor of an ancient era. Four great pillars stood in front of the structure, which was covered in a luminescent, white stone. A dome served as the roof on the Center and appeared to be either painted gold or covered in gold leaf.

Just another shockin' scam to take money from addicts with means, Crow thought. *"We don't take away ye'r drugs, or alcohol, or cigarettes…ye can stay as long as ye want,"…Aye, probably at fifteen thousand quid a day!*

Each section of buildings between the radiating roads consisted of smaller temple-looking places, though they appeared dissimilar. John explained that every building had been created to concentrate a focus for a particular type of *therapy*, a word, Crow noticed, John qualified by the tone of his voice.

Further down the road from the central hub, small, but lovely houses came into view, with beautiful trees, shrubbery, and flower gardens covering the entire landscape. The whole little city looked like a jewel.

"Each neighborhood has an energy of its own, Dylan, and it's important to allow yourself to open up to feel it as we tour them. You'll be attracted to one, and there you'll stay until such time as you feel drawn to another," explained John.

"Dr. Whitting, I mean, John," said Crow with skepticism, "I didn't know places like this existed. Seems a little weird to me and I expect the next thing ye'll be telling me is mi stay will cost mi entire life savings and you cannot guarantee I'll drop the addictions!"

"This is how it works, Dylan," John began. "Once you find the area in which you wish to live, you can choose from a variety of places to stay, which vary from modest to extravagant—both in cost and surroundings. You'll pay rent on your place for as long as you stay, which includes your electrical bill and grounds services. Personal expenses will include such things as phone bills and any damages or breakage for which you're responsible. You'll buy your own groceries and provide your own meals or leave the compound and go out where you desire. You may clean your own unit, do your own laundry, or hire someone on the staff to do it. The cost of each service is listed in a book inside the rental. In the event you wish to have groceries delivered, that can be arranged. However, our staff will *not* purchase alcohol, drugs, or nicotine for you. You're not allowed to bring any guests within these compound walls and we ask you to honor this rule. Oh, and we'd like you to leave your cell phone in your unit when you go out. Ringing chimes and people talking through lectures is the height of impropriety."

"How much do the services cost?" asked Crow, waiting for the grand slam answer.

"The greatest sacrifice of all, Dylan—*control*. By that, I don't mean you're going to give everything you have up to me or anyone at the Center. I mean you're going to hand things over to God, and that'll be the biggest challenge of your stay here. As to the monetary end of things, we don't charge for the services. We were taught freely how to help people, and we teach freely. We accept donations only if people wish to give them to us. No one is ever coerced into financially donating to the Center."

"Are ye screwing about with me?" asked Crow indignantly.

In spite of the fact that he used vulgarity, John's face remained perfectly calm. "That's it, Dylan. That's how it works. You see—those who serve here at the Center are paid only after all expenses are met. No one receives a specified salary. We act as a non-profit organization."

"How can ye stay in business?"

"We're not a business, Dylan. We're a healing center, and as you can see, God's unlimited abundance flows freely and we've not found ourselves wanting."

It was a new paradigm for Dylan and he couldn't quite digest the idea. Certain a catch lay hidden somewhere, he vowed to keep his eyes open.

Situated on about four hundred acres of land, every square inch of the Center was beautiful to behold. As they drove through the neighborhoods, Crow tried to *feel* the energy of each place, but couldn't seem to connect with anything in particular.

"How many buildings exist in ye'r lit'l kingdom?"

"One hundred forty four."

"Got plans to build more?" Dylan asked trying to determine if they were making all their brass on rentals.

"Nope." John kept his hands on the wheel and gazed forward as he spoke. "What we teach and the way in which we help people, they, in turn, take out into the world and teach again, and the exponential geometry allows for healing on a larger scale."

Crow shook his head. "Ye're either daft or brilliant, man." He stared out the window for a minute. "Doc, I can't feel anything as we drive through these areas. M'be I should get out and stroll about or something, ye reckon?"

"Splendid idea, Dylan…and I'll just drive back to the building where you first met me. If you get lost, knock on any door and they'll tell you how to get back. You comfortable with that?" John asked, looking directly into his eyes.

"Aye, I can handle it, mate."

Crow paced the streets, astonished to see the variety of architecture present side by side within the same compound. Yet, oddly, nothing looked out of place. Had he seen this in a development he would have been horrified. The homes ranged from approximately three thousand to five hundred square feet in size, though each had its own unique and beautiful garden areas that complemented the style of the house wonderfully.

He walked through two more sections of the compound and came to a cul de sac. Just before he turned back, his eyes were attracted by some small, rock wall gardens filled with indigo and yellow colored flowers. He moved steadily forward until the full structure came into his view. The walls were irregular in height and snaked around the front of the yard. He smiled, thinking of their similarity to Nikki's stone walls.

The home situated behind the walls looked like a fairytale

cottage from a Brothers Grimm story, completely isolated from
the other houses by its landscaping and foliage. A winding, stone
pathway led to the door. An overwhelming sense of profound
peace swept over him, something he'd felt in only one other location in the world—the Red Rock Canyon Ranch. Everything
about the place felt old, wild, and enchanting, just like Nikki's.

"This is it!" he said to himself. "*This* is the one for me."

An elderly woman stepped around the east side of the house.
Blast! he thought. *It's occupied!* Though the woman appeared to be
in her late seventies, she moved easily and swiftly toward him.

"May I help you, young man?" she asked sweetly.

"Just arrived and was scouting for a place to stay. This place
looks charming! I'll bet ye're enjoying it," Dylan answered.

"I have enjoyed it very much," she said, smiling at the house
like an old friend, "but alas, today I'm ready to go home. Perhaps
you'd like to come inside and look around?" she offered, taking his
elbow and leading him to the front door. The thick, carved oak
door led into a small entryway where she hung her straw hat on a
coat stand. "Come in, dearie, come in."

She guided him down three small steps to a living area which
included a fireplace and comfortable furniture arranged in conversational style. Three steps up delivered him into a petite kitchen and
dining area completely glassed-in by French doors. The kitchen
floor had been constructed of heavy planks of wood, and had been
topped with a variety of lush area carpets.

"This is nice," he said, turning to find the woman smiling at
him as though she had created the place and took pride in her
work. She directed him back through the living room and up a
small flight of stairs.

"Here's the bedroom and bath," she said, pointing. "This is
my favorite room of all."

The smallish bedroom contained a queen-size bed, covered with a satin comforter and adorned by pastel-colored pillows. The headboard had two corner posts carved with designs of dancing bears. A small sitting area looked out onto the property and had been furnished with a white couch and a welcoming chaise, over which a violet, chenille throw had been tossed. Crow crossed to the window and viewed a pond built of the same stones that created the walls in front of the house. There were several chairs in the garden and the landscape was informal, as if someone had simply cast flower seeds here and there and just let the fairies do the work.

"Do ye think they'd let me move in here when ye leave?"

"There're no coincidences, young man. I'm certain the reason you're here is because *you* are the next tenant. I pray you well," she said kindly.

"How much does this unit cost?" he asked.

She walked to a little desk in the corner and picked up some papers, then donned a small pair of reading glasses. "Well, it doesn't have a laundry room, or television, or some of the fancy things the others have, so it's quite reasonable. Before I pay for any phone bills or cleaning bills, I've been paying five hundred a month."

"Ye're playing with me, right?" he said, instead of his usual vulgar response.

She handed him her checkout statement and he confirmed what she told him. "How can they make any bloody money around here?" he asked.

"They don't exist to make money. They exist to make a difference in the new millennium. I'm sure they charge enough to cover the maintenance of the buildings and pay taxes, however."

"But how could they cover the costs of the construction?" he asked thinking about the millions upon millions he'd spent to build the nest in Maui.

"The land and cost of the buildings were donated to the center. Now they mostly have to cover the costs of maintaining it," she explained.

Have I just been dropped into the Emerald City of Oz? he wondered. "Why wouldn't every grunt in the entire state be trying to rent one of these places?" he asked sincerely.

She winked as she smiled. "You'll understand soon enough, son. Would you like to stay a while longer, or escort an old lady to the administration building to pay her bill?"

"I do have to go back there and I'd appreciate havin' ye lead the way." He offered his arm and they descended the stairway, past her packed luggage, and walked out the door without locking it. "Must have great security around here, eh?" he commented.

"The very best!"

As they walked, he held her elbow. Other people were strolling around as well, the majority of whom seemed to be heading toward some definite goal. There were a few cars, but surprisingly few, given there were one hundred forty four buildings on the compound. It took fifteen minutes to walk to the administration building and they parted company with a congenial handshake.

Crow knocked on Dr. Whitting's door.

"Come in."

"I found a remarkable, wee bit of a fairy cottage to move into just as soon as the occupant leaves today. Will that be all right?"

"Oh, yes...that would be Mrs. Ammot. She goes out to bless the world today!" said John staring into space.

"Look, mate," Dylan barked gruffly, "I gotta tell ye, all this seems a bit off the road to me and I'm pretty uncomfortable, not to mention put-off, with the language and New Age indications I see everywhere."

"No one's forcing you to stay, Dylan. You can leave any time you want. That's what free will is all about." John stood and stepped around his desk, taking one of the two chairs sitting in front, and motioned Crow to the other, once again. "This is a place of *self*-healing. If you allow our help, it will facilitate *you* to heal *yourself*. When one is whole, one loves the whole, and can do no less than go out and bless the world."

Crow saw no diplomas on the walls. "What kind of doctor are ye, anyway?" he asked suspiciously.

"Well, in the world of academia, I have a medical degree, a naturopathic degree, and a theological degree. It's been helpful to have this formal education, but it represents only a small part of the type of healing we do here. There will be no time, during any of your chosen stay, wherein you'll be *forced* into *any* type of treatment. You'll be drawn to that for which you're guided, just as you were drawn to the house you chose this morning. This may take a daily leap of faith for you, but you must trust the intelligence within you to be your guide. You're going to be inviting your ego to step aside, and it may get a bit peeved about that." John laughed at his own words.

Dylan had noticed he felt calm and hadn't lit a cigarette, nor had he been scrounging through his pockets looking for some sort of pill. Whatever this place offered was already starting to have some effect upon him and he decided to "relax and trust them to take him safely" …*Where? Home? Mi self? Mi sanity? Mi health? Maybe all!* he thought.

☯

The secretary explained that it would be several hours until he could move in and suggested he explore the local markets for his provisions. A preprinted map of the compound, along with a map of the surrounding area, noting such things as grocery stores, gas stations, malls, etc., was supplied.

He jumped back into his Porsche and drove toward one of the gates to investigate the village. Again, he wondered what type of security they had because it appeared that anyone could walk or drive into the facility. It made him somewhat edgy. He could not bear the idea of the media peeking through the windows and asking questions of the staff. Donning the stupid hat and sunglasses incognito program, he headed for the store.

First filling his basket with fruits, vegetables, meat, bread, and bottled water, he then found himself drawn to the liquor department. *What are ye doing, ye git? Ye're here to get off this bloody stuff!* he thought. Nonetheless, he bought a case of his favorite Merlot, and a carton of his preferred fags. He proudly resisted the hard liquor, however.

Two hours later he became entrenched in his fairy cottage and left alone. *Now what?* he wondered. Crow sat around reading the material about the facility and then began pacing a little. He picked up the phone and dialed the administration office. "Say, I just got in mi house and wondered if there's some sort of schedule I'm supposed to follow or somethin'?" After a pause on the other the end of the line, Crow was politely asked to hold for a moment.

John's voice answered the line. "Hello, Dylan. Happy with your little cottage?"

"Aye," he answered, "but now what do I do?"

"Follow your gut, Dylan. Just follow your intuition," came the reply.

When John hung up, Crow felt both severely annoyed and alarmed. "This is the craziest damn place I've ever seen in mi life!" Crow shouted as he slammed down the receiver.

He didn't have an intuition to do anything, so he took a nap. When he awoke, he lit a cigarette and poured a glass of wine. Dylan refrained from drugs, though his hands were trembling and his head hurt something wicked. In spite of his addictions, he still had a tremendously strong will.

First he paced around the house inspecting every detail, and then moved his discovery to the outer perimeters. Sitting in the teak rocking chair near the pond, he listened to the gurgling water and watched the koi swim about while smoking another cigarette. *What am I doin'? I don't know what to do!* he thought. Then an idea struck hard and he hustled back into the house.

He called his agent to ask if he would try to track someone down for him. Crow had no idea how much work would be involved, but promised to make the effort worthwhile financially.

"I've been talking to attorneys all morning about your situation, Dylan. I think we can get around their legal loophole and get you back on the show," Dansboro said, without having paid the slightest attention to Crow's first request.

"No, Robert! They're right. I've got to get cleaned up. Mi whole life's out o' control and I'm not gonna keep driving down that mucky road! It leads nowhere, and if I keep it up, we'll both be broke, mate!"

The agent just laughed. Crow had made him a multi-millionaire and he was grateful. Through the years they had become more than business partners; they had become dear friends, and Robert truly loved his client like a brother.

"Where are you, man?"

"I'm at a kind o' rehab center in the Carolinas. Goin' to be here a while, so I want ye to have the number, but I'm disengaging mi cell, 'cause too many people know how to reach me that way. Ye're the only one to whom this number will be given, understand?" instructed Crow.

Robert got it—loud and clear—no relatives, no friends, and

certainly, no media.

"So, what was it you wanted me to do for you again?" he asked.

Crow sat by the pond with his remote phone and explained that he wanted him to find someone by the name of Nikkol James, last known address in Virgin, Utah. "If ye can't locate her, find her son, Sam James. He's presently on the pro tennis tour and can't be too hard to trace. I want telephone numbers and addresses, if possible."

"You want to hire a private investigator?" Dansboro asked, audibly chuckling under his breath.

"I thought maybe Brenda could do a little leg-work first, ye know…call around Utah, call the IRS, or someone who'd have access to financial stuff," Crow pleaded.

"You're lucky she likes you man, 'cause she wouldn't do it for just anyone! I'll get on it and get back to you. Get well, friend."

Darkness had fallen and it had been hours since his conversation with his agent. Crow feared getting too far from the phone because it didn't have an answering machine. He stepped outside the French doors and left them open so he could hear the phone ring. Half an hour later, it did.

"Mr. Crow," said Brenda, with confidence in her voice, "I was able to track her son. You can't just hack into the IRS for names and phone numbers, but I did call to see if a listing appeared anywhere in Utah. I could find no listings in any city in the state. But—the son's name is Samuel Scott James and he lives in La Jolla. I told the head of the USTA you admired Sam's talent and wanted to speak to him personally. Guess your name got me through the door, because they didn't hesitate giving me his phone number and address. Amazing, isn't it?"

Crow wrote down the information and thanked her profusely. Nervously, he dialed.

"Hello," answered a pleasant female voice.

"Hello, I'm looking for Sam James. Have I the right number?"

"Who's calling please?" the woman asked, politely screening Sam's calls.

Crow wasn't certain if he should reveal his name to this stranger, then he just blurted out, "Dylan Crow, Ma'am."

"Please hold, Mr. Crow, I'll see if Sam wishes to speak with you."

Who does that lit'l cub think he is? Crow thought. A stab of shame hit his belly for all the times his phone had been answered in the, *I'm a celebrity, don't bother me* way.

"Hello, Mr. Crow," Sam said somberly. "What do you want?" His voice reflected formality and coldness.

"I'm trying to find ye'r mother, Sam. Called the ranch, but they said she moved a while back. Can ye be telling me where I can find her these days?" asked Crow, like an old family friend.

"I could, but I won't."

"Why not?" asked Crow, his face flushing with anger and frustration.

"Listen, Mr. Crow," Sam said angrily, "there isn't anyone on this planet I love more than that woman and there's no way in hell I'm going to watch her get tangled up with you again!"

"What's ye'r meanin', lad?"

"Look, my mother has only truly loved *one* man in her life," began Sam. Crow expected the boy to defend his father, but astonishingly, he stated, "That was *you!* I don't mean my mother didn't love my father, 'cause I know she did. But there was something between you two I've never seen between two other people on this planet, something that made me long to possess it myself. I guess I was wrong, though."

"Ye've the sound of long-held anger in ye'r voice, lad. Better say all and have done with it."

"Ok... you asked for it. Mom had been lit up from inside in a way I'd never seen, Mr. Crow... right up until the night you announced your engagement to Ms. Langston to the whole world. I was with her that night and witnessed that light disappear in seconds—I mean seconds! She's still her wonderful self, but it felt as if a part of her soul abandoned her that night. Mom never said a word against you, though. In fact, she asked me to hold you in my heart with love. Can you believe that?"

"Plow on, lad. I can tell ye're not done. Ye've a keg o' dynamite that seems to need blastin'."

"Damn straight, I do. After I'd gone to bed that night, I heard a noise and got up to investigate. Walked through the dark to the hall by my mother's bedroom and found her holding herself in a little ball, crying into a pillow. Quite frankly, Mr. Crow, I've wanted to beat the shit out of you every day since!" Sam had obviously finished venting his disgust and anger.

Crow choked up envisioning her sitting with her son and watching him on television. When Nikki sent him away it never occurred to him she could feel the same depth of pain he felt. With obvious emotion in his voice, Dylan spoke. "Sam, 'twas ye'r mum that sent me packin'. It wasn't mi choice. I can only ask ye'r forgiveness for having hurt ye'r mother or ye in any way. I really need to find her, mi lad. Please help me."

"I'm not 'your lad,' Mr. Crow," Sam spit out, not believing his mother could love someone that much and send them away. "There's only *one* thing I'll tell you." Sam breathed and spoke slowly to ensure he met his promise properly. "Mom said when you were truly ready, you would *know* how to find her if you remembered the beginning. She actually made me take a vow to relay this information were you ever to call. So, now I've met my obligation to my mother, and I'm afraid that's all the help you'll be getting from me, Mr. Crow."

The line went dead.

I would know how to find her? Remember the beginning? What could she possibly mean? Crow wondered. Try though he may, he couldn't figure out her puzzle and the thunder in his brain sent him reeling to his bed with nausea. He lay staring blankly at his gabled ceiling and closed his eyes, trying to see her face. "Nikki, mi dearest love, I need ye." Then he wept.

Chapter 14

Dylan awoke when the sun's brilliant rays flashed over his eyes. The light felt welcoming rather than invasive as it played upon his closed eyelids. Still too early to call Robert, he determined to challenge the pain in his head and the tremble in his hands by participating in life. The overwhelming sense of desperation and claustrophobia made him want to leap out of his skin. He dressed, scrambled some eggs, drank two cups of coffee, and repeatedly commanded the ache in his head to "bugger off." The pain could not be reasoned with, however. The open French doors admitted the freshness of the morning air and he decided to take a walk, hoping the exercise would help his condition. Before he left, he raced up the stairs and found his medicine bag, expecting to find some aspirin among the narcotics, but there were none. The temptation to pop the pain pills was severe, but he forcefully zipped the bag shut and tucked it in the back of the cupboard beneath the sink.

Crow had already smoked several cigarettes by the time he walked out the front door. Hands trembling, head throbbing, and sweating like a racehorse, he felt like he had the worst possible case of the flu. Nonetheless, he marched out the door and began his stroll. He headed in the direction of the "temples," as he'd come to think of them.

He passed some of the smaller buildings and one, in particular, caught his eye. The door to the temple had been lit from behind, highlighting an inlay of opalescent stones in geometric designs. It appeared as beautiful as a stained glass window in a cathedral. Dylan didn't know if the colors, the shape, or its uniqueness drew him, but he opened the door for his first encounter with his intuition.

An orator could be heard further inside the building, and since no people could be found in the entry hall, he followed the voice. In a circular room, about twenty feet in diameter, thirty or so people sat in a half-moon around a young woman at a lectern. She looked up, indicating a welcome to Crow, but continued her speech. He quietly found a seat and waited to hear what she had to offer.

"As I was saying," she continued, "everything is made up of light; an energy, which when oscillating or vibrating at a particular rate of speed, takes on different qualities. This light is literally God substance. By moving that light with consciousness into particular geometric patterns or forms, we obtain the basic platonic solids, or the building blocks of our material manifest world. These act as matrices, so to speak, for the movement of directed light and literally compose the electromagnetic network within your body and your surroundings.

"Every time you think a thought or feel a feeling, you instruct the light within you to move along the matrices of this electromagnetic network. Thoughts and feelings are nothing more than energy in motion as waveforms. You cannot see them with the naked eye any more than you can see a radio wave. Nonetheless, they are real and very powerful energy forms.

"As the intelligences within your physical body receive your instructions, they obey by releasing whatever chemicals are required to achieve your given command. Likewise, thoughts and feelings create energy forms within your thought, emotional, and etheric bodies. With continual energy directed to these thought and feeling forms, they eventually manifest in the physical body, your experiences, and environment.

"The most important thing to understand is this energy is *impersonal*, as are the intelligences I referred to in your body. This energy and these intelligences have no conscious discerning ability and have no concern as to *who* uses the energy or *how* it's used. A similar example would be the use of electricity. The electricity itself cannot determine if its purpose is constructive or destructive, nor does it have attachment to the one *directing* its use. It simply acts by following a natural law. If you, through your conscious direction declare to the energy of which you're comprised, 'I am sick,' you have just instructed the light to move and create this condition.

"The two most powerful words in the universe are 'I Am.' They are the most ancient of words, handed down from the *first* language spoken on this planet. It is the very name of God in action within you and to command anything within this universe with 'I Am' should not be taken lightly. Now perhaps you understand why taking the Lord's name in vain can be so disastrous. 'I Am mad, I Am sick, I Am poor, I Am unhappy, I Am an addict, I Am dumb,' etc. The very vibration that is released by the emotionally empowered, audible, or silent use of these words, literally acts as an encoded preface to create whatever follows. No one can stop you from creating a disaster for yourself. Likewise, you can create what you *want* by qualifying that energy in a constructive fashion.

"These electromagnetic matrices exist in all four lower bodies —your physical, thought, emotional, and etheric bodies. The four pillars in front of the Center represent these four lower bodies, which are the areas our healing facility addresses. Even though it seems these bodies are separate, they cannot be divided. What affects one, affects all. They are part of the whole, and are therefore affected by the whole.

"There are many things which can bring an imbalance to these four bodies. The densities the mental body encounters in the physical body—ranging from the harmful residue of nicotine, drugs, and impure food, or even the substance of fear or doubt, or a mental rebellion that has accumulated from past lives—clogs the brain cells and imprisons the light of the atom. This prohibits the free flow of light to the physical consciousness and impairs the function of one's mental faculties. Alcohol actually creates a short-circuiting of the electrical system, and of course, as you all know, its long-term use acts as a fatal poisoning to certain organs. What would normally move as God's perfect light, doing its perfect thing within you, has now been re-clothed and re-instructed and/or re-circuited by some form of pollutant.

"Imagine if you will, an artificial intelligence being that's been circuited to do anything and everything you command. Then, see a glass of water or a cup of mud spilled into the mainframe. What happens? A nasty interference and short-circuiting of electrical impulses that were intended to send information and instructions to the parts of the machine. Right?

"Well, that's what you are—a great big, soft computer. The power source is this light energy—your source of electricity. It's projected from your I AM Presence, which is God individualized at your particular point in the Universe. This light enters your physical body through the crown of your head (remember the baby's soft spot when they're born). From there, it moves through your body's energy centers, also called chakras, to literally give life to your four lower bodies, including the animation of your physical body. When this *light* is withdrawn from the body, regardless of how amazing and complex the body is, all *life* is withdrawn—just as if the plug is pulled from the computer.

"Through thought and feeling, you clothe that energy and create exactly what you want. You are literally a co-creator with God, having been endowed with both the ability to create and the substance with which to create. Each being is part of a hologram, and within each is contained the imprint of the whole. 'As above, so below.' So the most valuable thing one can do is to *be responsible* for *managing* this energy in a way that is *constructive*, both to yourself and the *whole* of creation.

"In addition to clogging your atomic structure, introducing physical, mental, and emotional pollutants affects your light bodies in such a way as to create holes or tears; holes through which thought and entity forms may enter and attach themselves to you, acting like parasites that feed off your negative energy. When you find yourself behaving in unexplainable ways, or being completely drained of your energy, it usually has a direct link to these 'clingons.' And, I'm not referring to any Star Trek characters. Some of you in this room may be old enough to remember a comedian named Flip Wilson, whose famous line was, 'The devil made me do it!' In a way, I guess you could say the density of these energetic attachments, in fact, creates such a low vibratory influence, that you may be prone to do or say something less than constructive.

"We can help you open up these 'jammed' or 'short-circuited' areas in your energy centers, but *only you* can keep them from getting 'jammed' again. We can teach you how to eliminate the parasites, but *only you* can keep your fields intact and whole so they cannot enter uninvited in the future.

"In order to do this and maintain your connection to the light in an unobstructed way, you'll have to call upon your higher mental body to step in and take control over the energy. Your lower self, or personality, will try to convince you with a thousand different tacks that everything is under control and it can handle its creations just fine. By your very presence here, it is evident your lives are *not* just fine. You are here because a higher part of yourself is desperately trying to raise you above the very low frequency at which you've been existing.

"Your primary sources of qualifying this energy are your feelings and thoughts, your vision, hearing, and spoken words. These are the instruments through which you create your reality!

"Now, I've basically been talking about physics here. If you were drawn to this lecture, it's because the language of science is comfortable to you. Within this hall of healing, we use the natural laws of physics, quantum physics, and *new* physics to teach you how to access and clear those jammed areas in your four lower bodies. For those of you unfamiliar with the term *metaphysics*, it means *beyond* physics—or a Higher Law. There's no mumbo jumbo here and we can easily educate you about the physics of our methods. We work with the color rays, stones, sound, scent, symbols, and force fields created through sacred geometry. These are only tools, however, and you have the power within you to *BE* the tool instead of using one. So, even if you allow us to facilitate an understanding through our methods, *know* that you must ultimately take responsibility for *BEING* that which we teach you.

"I will be here at nine every morning to offer a different discourse, and if it feels right for you to come, please join. If it doesn't, don't. If you sense you're in the wrong place once here, please quietly depart so you'll not disturb the others. If you wish for a facilitator to perform a service for you, an appointment can be made through the administration office. If you were drawn to this facility, but don't know what you want, I'm available to speak to you after the lecture." With her last words, she looked directly at Crow.

He waited for the others to leave, as per her visual command. Without rising from his chair, he addressed her at the podium. "So, what do I need?" he asked, half laughing.

She took the seat next to him rather than standing above him, and offered her hand. "Hi, I'm Ashley."

"I'm Dylan," he returned, wondering if she already knew *who* he was. If she did, she didn't appear overly impressed, though she seemed sincerely interested and concerned for his welfare.

"Is this all new to you, or does it seem vaguely familiar?" she asked.

"I'm not exactly certain if I understand ye'r question, Ashley. I guess the closest I've come to the type of service ye seem to be offering was a stone laying an Indian shaman once gave me over a grid of some sort. I also experienced a very special meditation while encircled by crystals once."

He shifted uncomfortably in his chair. "What that's got to do with why I'm here is beyond me, for the truth of the matter is I've become overwhelmingly addicted to pain meds, alcohol, nicotine, and sex, and I've no idea how to address the problem. Ye don't have a de-tox center, nor do ye offer a medication program to bring me slowly down. I see no signs of an AA group sitting about telling their horror stories, declaring that all present will be considered eternally *recovering* alcoholics. I honestly don't know what it is ye do here!" he stated in earnest.

"Dylan," she began gently, "it is not *we* who do the work. *You* do the work. We *all* have the responsibility to encourage the light to expand in each other, but only *you* can open the door. Your whole system of worlds that makes up what you are is in chaos and is seeking balance. The addictions are just the symptoms of the underlying disorder, which is most likely, of the spirit. Balance and harmony is the natural state intended by the Great Creator, and we're going to try to help you get there through any means necessary.

"If you feel you need to be placed in a locked space to come down, I'm sure Dr. Whitting would oblige, but, our methods aren't structured to deliver even more trauma than you're already experiencing. You know how when you've been hurt, it doesn't take much to make the injury really sensitive again. Throwing you in a drunk tank and forcing the chemicals out of your system is certainly *a* pathway; but, I think if you'll just trust us a bit, you may find you have the ability to quit all by yourself in a way that communicates love to all that you are. We believe the best way to eliminate something from your life is to take your attention completely away from it and put it on something higher."

Ashley said her piece, refraining from sermonizing or moralizing.

What she said made sense. When a man has a wound, isn't it most sympathetic not to touch it at all? It was the first time someone had suggested *resisting* a pathway that lacks compassion.

"Here, in this hall, we offer some physical means by which we may open up your chakras in a gentle way. Do you know this word?"

He nodded. "Aye."

"If your chakras are closed down, there's a reason for it. You may have closed them to energy outside of yourself as a defense, and it may be inappropriate to just fling them wide open again. Our facilitators will work with your higher mental body and your guides to properly diagnose what's going on and head in a direction that'll help you heal yourself.

"Basically, the entire New Millennium facility is an energy management center. There's no judgment or criticism here about where you've been or what you've done. There's only the understanding that things are out of balance and a desire on our part to help you put things back in order. OK?" She reached out and touched his arm gently as an act of compassionate connection.

"May I have a diagnostic session then?" he asked.

"Sure. I'll call and see if Marsha can take you today, if you feel like it." She rose from her seat and headed for the phone on the wall.

"Ye mean, it's not ye'rself who performs the 'diagnosis'?" he asked, as he had an aversion to repeating this process and conversation with yet another person.

Seeing his discomfort, she tried to ease his mind. "Dylan, I think it would be best to utilize Marsha's particular gifts at this juncture. She won't be asking you a lot of questions, but she will be giving you a lot of information. A recording of your session will be made and you will receive the only copy."

Ashley dialed the phone and made an arrangement for eleven thirty. Dylan nodded his head in approval and stood to leave.

"Let me show you where to go for your appointment," she offered while leading him further into the building. They walked past seven doors, each painted a different color of the spectrum, and stopped in front of the eighth, which was white. There were no numbers or names on the doors.

"You can let yourself in here at eleven thirty and Marsha will join you." Ashley opened the door to expose a completely white room with a white massage table positioned in the center. Quartz crystals of varying sizes and configurations lined the shelves and a large one had been placed underneath the table. The open shelves of the cupboards contained various colored candles and small vials of oil. He wasn't uncomfortable with it, but he wasn't exactly comfortable either. The vision of his experience in Zion canyon with Nikki and the crystals popped into his mind and his opposition mellowed.

Crow headed back to his cottage, smiling and nodding at people as they passed him. He lit a cigarette and, with trembling hands and pounding head, dialed his agent's office to leave a message on the machine. "Robert, it's Dylan here. I *do* want ye to hire a private investigator. Nikki's son wouldn't tell me where she is and I've just got to find her. There's no machine here, so I'll check back with ye later. Thanks."

He could stand the pain no longer and headed up the stairs to retrieve his little black bag.

☯

At eleven thirty on the dot, Dylan pushed open the white door and could see he was alone. Sitting on the edge of the massage table, feeling slightly foolish, he had no idea what he'd gotten himself into. He studied the crystals in the room and though tempted to handle them, decided against it. Nikki told him crystals could be programmed just like a computer and he didn't want to interfere with whatever "program" they might contain.

"Hi" said the woman as she entered the room. "I'm Marsha." She looked to be of East Indian descent, in her early twenties, standing five foot four with long, dark brown hair tied back in a knot.

Crow nodded rather than responding verbally.

"Have you done anything like this before?" she asked gently as she directed him to lie down on the table.

"Aye a bit, but, to be honest, I've no idea what ye intend to do," he answered.

"Well, I'll explain things as I'm going. I promise I won't be rough with you!" she said, winking.

Her funny crooked smile helped him loosen up a little.

Seeing how tense her patient seemed, Marsha changed the energy in the room by playing an Enya CD softly in the background. She then draped a thin white blanket over his body to keep him warm while she worked.

Standing at his head, she softly explained, "I'm going to be doing a little bit of work with my higher self, your higher self, and our guides. Guess you could say I'm clairaudiant and they can see parts in all four bodies that need addressing. I have no foreknowledge of what will be said, so our session will be recorded and you can use the information to determine which direction to take while here. OK?"

He responded only with a nod, because he really didn't understand, nor did he necessarily believe she could access these things. But, this did not feel like the right time for debate. Since his conscious participation did not appear to be required, he closed his eyes and listened to Enya sing her song, *Pilgrim*.

The lyrics spoke of the long pilgrimage each soul chooses to discover where his true treasure lies; how each fork in the road takes you to different destinations—some leading to the riches of the material world, while others take you only to what you've been told—and how every soul wonders which pathway's true. The lyrics confirmed that one cannot change the past, but one can choose the future, and for most, the journey to find out who they are, is, indeed, long.

Overwhelmed by the coincidence of the lyrics providing what he needed to hear at that very moment, tears began to flow down his cheeks from his closed eyes.

Marsha hadn't spoken a word yet, but stood at the top of his head and touched his crown gently as she moved into a prayerful, meditative state. A few minutes passed before she pushed a button on a recorder in her pocket and spoke into a small microphone clipped to the collar of her shirt. She inhaled deeply and blew the air out of her nose, and after a few moments pause, spoke:

"Dylan Crow, I AM the only Intelligence acting in this room this day and will bring forth that which you must know for your own journey.

"You have fashioned the chains of your own bondage, none of them being real. They are as ephemeral as the light from the sun. Your heart is open to the memory of my presence in you, and yet you have stubbornly closed the door, again, and again. Still, I wait. What you are *searching for* is the fullness of what I AM, and can only be received by turning your attention to me.

"Call to me and I will fill you with the strength and courage to master your lower self. *Be consciously aware* of my unlimited love, which I pour through you. I AM your power. I AM your valor. I AM the light within you. I AM the Command of Obedience within you to every requisite which makes for your Freedom.

"In all the Universe there is but One Intelligence, One Authority, One Light, One Substance. I AM the power of the Godhead announcing its authority at your individualized focus in the physical octave.

"To every expression of pain or disturbance in your body, feelings, or mind—any perceived limitation whatsoever—say to the illusion, *'You have no power! I know* the perfection of my God Presence, my Mighty I AM.' Say to your pain, 'Be still!' and call upon your Mighty I AM Presence to annihilate all cause, all record, all effect of this illusion!

"*Feel* this, *know* this, *do* this, Dylan. *Stand firm* by your I AM Presence and the Presence will stand firm by you! *Do not surrender* to conditions or illusions which have frightened you and made you believe you were under their power! You are under no domination of limitation of any kind! *You are not!* Believe this, live in this, and you may find your *Sovereignty* now!

"I AM the only Intelligence acting in your world and all whom you have called forth today, thank you for this opportunity to call your attention to every endeavor to help you and your brothers. The rest is up to you. I AM ready to assist, but you must invite that assistance, whether it be *from* your own I AM Presence, or *through* your I AM Presence to your guides, or any of the Angelic Host of Light. I AM releasing the Power, the Energy, and the Intelligence for you to act. To the very degree you accept and feel it, will it produce Perfection in your world.

"I AM enfolding you now and forever in the Glory of the Light of Infinite Power, Intelligence, and Love."

Marsha remained still for a few moments, and then breathed deeply again. After turning off her recorder, she stroked Crow's head gently, touched his forehead, and whispered, "You may remain here as long as you need to." Quietly, she removed the tape from the recorder and placed it on the blanket over his abdomen.

The energy in the room still felt as if it were swirling as Crow tried to consciously absorb it into his physical body. His heart expanded the same way it had with Nikki, though time had numbed his memory of the extraordinary sensation.

Crow wasn't sure he could remember the few words that were spoken to him. It felt as though they were spoken not only to his mind, but also to the very atoms that comprised his body. He lay there until he could feel the pulsing energy no longer. To his bewilderment, what had seemed like hours was only half an hour. Clutching the tape, he removed the blanket and sat upright. He tried to regain his bearings, though he felt a little light headed. The music had ended and the room filled with a quiet and digni-fied peace. He stood, looked around the room one last time, and then walked back to his cottage.

Bolting up the stairs, he located the small, portable stereo sys-tem under the top shelf of his nightstand, inserted the cassette and listened to it again, then again, and yet again.

He became immersed in thought. *These were the same type of words Nikki used in her whispered prayer over me the night I pretend-ed to sleep,* he thought. *Is it conceivable all these things are coinci-dences? Has mi life been directed one scene at a time to bring me to this understanding? Nik spoke about the 'great whip of life' that brings us back to our knees in humble appeal to understand the truth. So, here I am God, or perhaps I should say, here, I AM GOD…tell me the truth.*

As the evening skies began to darken, he wandered around his little cottage contemplating the words Marsha delivered to him. *Is it possible,* he wondered, *this is a compulsory journey all souls must make?* He thought of the words to Enya's song. *Can man, created perfect and good by God, become wicked by forgetfulness and survival? Is it possible for human nature to be entirely transformed and transmuted from inside and out? What is this mystery of the rise and fall of the soul?* He turned inward to his own conscience to think things over. Stepping out into the night air to look at the stars, he contemplated these grand and mysterious wonders, thinking night is a good time to look into the endless heavens and contemplate such things.

He listened to the tape one more time before he fell asleep on top of the bed. At two-thirty in the morning he awoke sweating profusely, overcome with feelings of desperation. Heading downstairs for a cigarette and a glass of wine, the words on the tape suddenly struck him. In the kitchen, he poured the wine, then laid a cigarette next to it and said aloud with great conviction, "Ye have no power! I AM the only intelligence acting here and I AM the perfect harmony of mi body, feelings, and thoughts!" Then he summoned the grit to walk away from his temptations and return to his bed.

He didn't know if it had worked, or if he was just too tired to care, but he did not lie awake craving a hit of any kind.

Chapter 15

When the birds' song gently coached the sun into the sky, Dylan rolled over and pulled a pillow over his aching head. His hands were trembling severely. *Jasus, Mary, and Joseph,* he thought, *help me get rid o' this bloody freight train that's runnin' between mi eyes!* He forced himself to rise and headed for the bathroom. Studying his lifeless eyes in the mirror made it difficult to even think about his I AM Presence, let alone decree anything. The reflection inspired only hopelessness. As he averted his eyes from his pathetic appearance, a booming voice pounded through his consciousness as if the voice came from someone standing next to him. The words came loud and clear:

> *"Seek not to find the truth in the illusion,*
> *but draw thine eyes to my perfection."*

He braved the mirror again, engaging contact with the soul behind his eyes until he remembered his own perfection.

Determined to quit cold-turkey, he knew that allowing *any* medication in his system would only give more power to the demon he was bound to eliminate from his body and mind. He couldn't believe the sense of desperation that surfaced second by second, building to a crescendo, only to be quelled by his determined affirmations. With body aching and his stomach cramping, his skin became so sensitive that he could barely tolerate the feeling of clothing upon it. Once again, the cottage seemed to be closing in on him, so he grabbed a quick cup of coffee and strolled toward the "temples."

He consciously allowed his feet to walk and his eyes to draw him where he *should* go. The interesting experiment distracted his attention from the tremors and sweating that consumed him.

The morning's stroll delivered him to a building whose entrance had been created with an inlaid violet stone he'd never seen before. It looked stunning. He simply *had* to go in. As a gentleman smiled while passing, Crow touched his arm and gestured to the interior with his chin. "Say, mate—what's in this buildin'?"

"You new here?" asked the man.

"Aye. Only been in one buildin' so far."

"I've only been in a few, myself," said the stranger. "I hear people sometimes never go in more than one while they're here."

"Been here long?" Crow had begun to wonder what the average stay was.

"Six weeks," the man whispered.

"Sounds like someone's givin' a speech. Can ye tell me where to go?" Dylan asked, understanding from the man's whispered tone that their conversation perhaps interrupted something. The man pointed and Dylan followed.

"Welcome friends," said a small, elderly, white haired man. "My name is Walter and today's subject is karma." He saw Crow standing by the entrance and signaled him to take his seat.

The rectangular room contained only twenty seats, but as Crow sat, he filled the last one—coincidentally vacated by the gentleman to whom he'd just spoken. The lecture hall had been decorated in shades of violet. Through a skylight in the ceiling, which appeared to be encrusted in amethysts, the sun filtered through in purple streaks.

"Many of you are at the Center attempting to assess certain aspects of your life which have created imbalance. Some cannot seem to put a finger on which particular activity or event initiated your descent into the mire from which you wish to extricate yourself, and to that end, I'd like to address the concept of *karma* this morning.

"Karma can be defined as energy and consciousness in action. It is the law, not only of cause and effect, but also retribution. Some ancient traditions referred to it as the *Law of the Circle*, which essentially means whatever you do inevitably goes around the great circle, collecting similar energy and returns to you, magnified."

Now there's a wee lesson that keeps poppin' up for me! Crow declared silently.

The old man continued. "The Law of Karma necessitates that the soul re-embody until all karmic cycles are balanced. Thus from lifetime to lifetime one determines one's fate by his thoughts, feelings, words, and deeds. In other words, it's accepting complete, *one hundred percent* responsibility for the way you use energy.

"Through many Eastern religious constructs it is taught that there is a Karmic Board which dispenses justice to this system of worlds, adjudicating karma, mercy, and judgment on behalf of every lifestream. Every single soul must pass before this Karmic Board prior to, and after each incarnation on earth; receiving their assignment and karmic allotment for each lifetime before, and an overall review of their performance at its termination. The Lords of Karma have access to the complete records of every incarnation of every soul. These are referred to as the akashic records, which are an energetic imprinting of your entire life.

"This board determines who shall embody, as well as when and where. They assign souls to families and communities, measuring out the weights of karma that must be balanced. The Lords of Karma, acting together with the I AM Presence and Christ-self, or higher mental body of each individual, determines when the soul has earned the right to be free of the wheel of reincarnation.

"Now, I have just given you an overview of karma as seen through the eyes of most Eastern philosophies. Fact is, karma, or at least this concept that one must balance every tittle and jot relating to misdeeds by *counteracting* those deeds is a man-made concept. It is true that with every thought, feeling, word, and deed you *create* something—at least an energy form of some sort. Because energy is magnetic in nature, it attracts similar energy and by the time it travels the great circle, it does come back to the creator magnified. Now, that's the truth of karma.

"In this nursery of *time* and *space*, where we are allowed to grow into our individualization of God, duality has been the means by which we have educated ourselves. It has been the tool by which we have discovered the difference between using God substance to create with love and what the world reflects when we don't. Once a lesson has taken hold, allowing you to choose the constructive use of this substance, there's no need to repeat the lesson. But, as humans, oh, how we love to hang on to our creations instead of surrendering them to love. The problem with hanging on to them is that they magnetize and magnify the experiences as they follow the circle and tangibly re-enter our lives in one form or another.

"A special dispensation was granted for the elevation of the consciousness of mankind, who was so steeped in its mis-creations, that the appearance of 'light at the end of the tunnel' seemed an impossibility. This dispensation allows for a means by which anyone, or all, of mankind may speed the process by which they can dissolve and consume prior negative mis-creations and their resulting karmic (or magnetic) bonds.

"Saint Germain, the Chohan of the Seventh, or Violet Ray, holds the responsibility for this particular activity. It provides an accelerated path of transmutation of negative, misused, and misdirected energy and its resultant forms by the violet flame of the Holy Spirit. The use of this flame transcends the rounds of rebirth through the path of the Individual Christhood, leading to the ascension as demonstrated by Jesus. It is the *'baptism by fire'* referred to biblically, which not only dissolves the undesirable energy forms, but also immediately replaces them with Love. It is the road, ultimately, that all men must travel to free themselves from their binding mis-creations.

"Even as Jesus, as an incarnation of the Christ Consciousness, interceded in such a way as to provide a grace period by which you could work out your individual karma, so does the Ascended Master, St. Germain, oversee another grace to assist you in transmuting your misdirected energies into pure light substance once again.

"Inherent in the transmuting quality of the violet flame is the ability to dissolve and consume all cause, effect, and record of your past mismanagement of God's energy. It serves to physically and etherically dissolve the energy forms that have wound so thickly about your four lower bodies, holding you in a form of bondage. Each soul is responsible for what he creates. Through this method one may *un-create* his *mis-creations.*

"Every single ensouled being, as Son of God, *must* learn to manage the unlimited substance of God's energy in a constructive way. Nothing can stop you from coming back time after time, experiencing a relentless stream of trauma and drama to *try* to make things right…if that is your soul's desire. If you're someone who loves soap operas, it may, in fact, be your pathway of choice."

The group, as a whole, laughed.

"BUT…it's possible to forgive, dissolve, and consume the mis-creations, which, in this world of polarity may have served to further your soul's education, but are now no longer required. A pathway of learning, or choosing, to use this energy constructively in a way that expands God's perfection and expresses Divine Love may be more appropriate at this stage of your soul's development. There's no reason, save addiction to drama, to carry around all that excess baggage which weighs so heavily upon the soul, constantly acting as a magnet to draw more darkness into your world.

"As all children of God have free will, the choice is, of course, up to the individual.

"Those who are drawn to this facility may be dealing with conditions that have been brought forth from other lifetimes, or they may have misused their power in this one. Most likely, all here are dealing with a bit of both. You're not in this room listening to this discourse by accident. You are present because your higher mental body and your unseen assistants have brought you here.

"If you wish to learn the use of the violet consuming flame, also known by the names of the *Law of Transmutation*, the *Law of Divine Love*, and the *Law of Forgiveness*, you may return to this theater tomorrow and we'll begin your instruction. Although the words I've just spoken may sound a little 'out there' to some of you, you'll soon discover the conscious direction of this ray is merely one of the most profound laws of the physics of energy.

"If you're not quite comfortable with the concept and wish to educate yourself further before utilizing the ray, I suggest a bit of preparatory reading in the library, where you'll will find a series of books titled *The I AM Discourses*. These, I believe, may be of use in introducing the idea to both your mind and heart."

Just as the day before, the lecturer purposely hesitated, directed his vision toward Crow, making conscious eye contact.

"If, however, you're bent on the course of reincarnation, we have facilitators who can help you access and review past life information directly related to specific questions you may have. To make an appointment to meet with a facilitator, please call the administration office."

His monotone voice had droned on as if he were reading a

boring financial report before a group of sleeping bankers. An odd experience, to say the least, but Dylan believed his presence had been no coincidence. The lecturer had pointedly indicated his need to read *The I AM Discourses*. He walked away from the building laughing out loud. "OK, OK, I GOT IT!"

He'd never even opened the box of books, which still sat, he hoped, in the den of his old ranch house. He trusted Mic would have at least stored his personal effects, rather than throwing anything away.

Crow asked for directions to the library. He knew what the books looked like, but the library was much larger than he anticipated and filled with thousands of books. Upon asking for help, a lovely, elderly lady gently took his arm and escorted him to the right section.

"Ye only have one set?" he inquired.

"Actually, we have about twenty, but most of them are out right now. Would you like to peruse them to see if you'd like to check the set out?" she asked.

"Very much, thank 'e!" he responded, taking the first volume, *The Magic Presence*, from the shelf and sitting down to read it.

He wondered if Nikki somehow influenced his circumstances now. No, he decided. *That's why she sent me away. She wanted me to decide for miself!*

Chapter 16

Deeply immersed in the *Discourses*, Crow kept company only with himself as he voraciously consumed the information in the books. *No wonder Nik told me she didn't have the right to teach me*, he thought as he read. *It really would have been easy for her to inter-ject her personality and interpretations. Thank ye, mi love*, he thought.

Daily facing the obstacles that clouded his mind and body still proved to be a challenge. After four days of physical hell, includ-ing diarrhea, his body seemed to have passed through the worst of the biological stages of withdrawal. His psychological habits did *not* magically disappear. It seemed as if every day he boarded the boat anew, setting sail, making both major and minor adjustments to the course with the rudder. It was, however, the first time in his conscious memory that he *had* a rudder. No longer drowning in grief, Dylan felt exalted and dignified through hope.

One day, while leafing through something in the library, his eyes were drawn to an insightful and appropriate quote. No particular author had been given credit, as is often the case with words that speak to all men's souls. Crow memorized it as a personal mantra.

A soul, knowing its own weaknesses, and knowing and trusting that strength can be encouraged and developed by practice and patience, will begin to exert itself, adding effort to effort, patience to patience, strength to strength, and never ceasing to develop, will, at last, grow Divinely strong.

The Discourses taught him to take his attention completely away from his addictions and direct it to the perfection of his own I AM Presence. Where his attention was, so was he. What his attention was upon, he became. Crow learned to consciously flip a switch in his brain, redirecting his attention when required.

His education included creating the new *habit* of controlling his thoughts and feelings in a constructive manner.

Astonishing changes began to take place from within. The concepts were so simple, but, then, he believed the greatest truths in life were, without exception, the simplest. Crow read and memorized decrees as if he were committing a script to memory, understanding that without the feeling nature attached to the decrees, they would serve no purpose. As he'd spent his career acquiring the ability to put *feeling* and *intent* to *word*, the effort came easily.

☯

Three weeks passed before he heard from Robert.

"Sorry, old pal, it's like she dropped off the planet or something. Rumor is she moved out of the country, but we haven't been able to discover where she's gone, and that son of hers is as tight lipped as he can be—so's his wife."

"So, Sam got married, did he? Must've been his bride who answered his phone."

Dansboro continued, "We'll keep trying 'til you tell us to stop, Dylan. OK?"

"Right," Crow muttered. Then an idea struck. "Say, Robert, she used to spend time every year in France and Switzerland. Could ye arrange to check over there?"

"I'll call the firm to see if they have a sister or referring agency in Europe." Robert hesitated for a moment, wondering if the time was right to inquire as to his client's progress. "Now—how are things going with you?"

"Amazing place, man," Crow responded sincerely. "I think I may have found God or somethin'."

"Whatever it takes, pal, I'm right behind you."

Crow had expected the third degree, or at least a cruel, derisive snort, but certainly not "whatever it takes, I'm right behind you."

He thanked him aloud for his assistance, and silently for his compassion, then hung up the phone and went back to his homework.

He didn't intuit the need to participate at any of the treatment centers at all, feeling he'd been delivered, as Nikki would have said, "all the answers on a silver platter." Contemplative study and meditation *was* his *treatment* for another six weeks.

Though free from his *need* for stimulants, alcohol, cigarettes, and mindless sex, it didn't stop him from *wanting* them. To destroy the abuse was not enough. Habits must be replaced by other habits; old mental programs replaced with new—so he determined to start with the habit of turning his attention to his I AM Presence every time he felt the desire for anything self-destructive. He'd immediately check himself by saying aloud, "I AM the Resurrection and the Life," one of the most powerful mantras spoken by Jesus. He knew he must *become* the cure. Though the whole process created a complete paradigm shift, Crow felt as if he'd unlocked a door that led to reality.

A feeling of *sustained* inner peace permeated his consciousness for the first time in his life. The cause of his addictive behaviors had been the vacuous space in his soul. Now, as he began filling that space with light, it freed him from his self-imposed bondage.

Crow started to observe his thoughts, feelings, and actions from outside of himself, almost in the same way he'd observed his past life experiences in his dreams on the grid. He'd risen to a place where he could survey them from a higher level without judgment, and, in fact, laugh about the antics of his lower self.

The teachings of the Ascended Masters, most particularly those of St. Germain, held deep understanding and explanation of the baptism by fire, or the *Law of Forgiveness*. To Crow, this means by which one could clear the spiritual path, made sense. He came to understand this activity of the Holy Spirit (or Whole I spirit) provided an avenue by which one could physically dissolve and consume both unwanted energetic forms and bonds of negative karma by utilizing a natural law of physics. He now understood it as a frequency that transmutes and transforms these mis-creations, returning them to their pure essence; literally *recycling* the energy.

When Dylan searched for information within the Discourses about twin flames, he discovered the key to transmuting or changing his past karma and rejoining his beloved twin flame, involved the conscious use of the violet consuming flame. He daily visualized and affirmed its use, not only for himself, but also for Nikki. Though he understood he could not do Nikki's work for her, anything he did would magnify her own efforts.

☯

Crow pondered his rebellion of the orthodox religious training of his youth. The words Joe Chatauk had spoken to him regarding a rebellion about organized religion versus a spiritual rebellion surfaced consciously. In Dylan's heart of hearts, he desired his spirit connection above all other things. He felt compelled to visit the library to secure a copy of the King James Version of the Holy Bible and sat at one of the private study tables in a secluded corner to enter the "closet of his soul."

As he looked out the window and watched the play of sunlight on the garden, he uttered a silent prayer: *Mighty I AM Presence within me, remove from mi heart the shackles of mi youthful rebellion and help me to see God's presence in these ancient words with new eyes.* He simply let the book fall open where it may, trusting he'd be led by the wisdom of God anchored in his heart.

The pages, in fact, dropped open to specific reference to the Wholeness of God and the inseparability of man from God. He found profound wisdom within texts of scripture with which he'd completely disagreed in his earlier years. Allowing his eyes to find the words that were intended for him in that moment, instead of reading the scriptures as a whole, provided a new depth of understanding.

His newfound knowledge from the teachings of the Ascended Masters did not appear much different from what he found in the scriptures. However, it seemed as if the parts in the Bible that cast confusion simply disappeared from the pages—as if an inner knowing told him the scriptures were much like texts encrypted in such a way as to unfold wisdom in accordance with one's level of growth, adding line upon line, precept upon precept. As one who approached as a novice, he looked upon himself as basically learning a spiritual alphabet. He trusted when his heart and mind were ready for deeper understandings, the encrypted messages would make perfect sense. For now, he felt content to accept this elementary education.

While reading the words highlighted in red in the New Testament (those supposedly spoken by Jesus of Nazareth,) it became evident how often his most profound statements were prefaced with the words "I AM." Crow realized Jesus referred to the God within—"the Father within me"— and not his *personal* self.

His childhood training always presented Jesus as the *only* son of God, the intercessor, holding mankind once removed from God, always looking to *this being* for mercy, instead of looking to the God within. After reading the teachings of Jesus with new eyes, he could see his brother had only taught about the God within all mankind. When he understood Jesus' reference to the Universal Christ Consciousness as the intercessor, suddenly, "as above, so below," became crystal clear. This great and holy being, by his example, came to remind us we are, in fact, One with God, and have the *Father* anchored right within us, and the Christ-self acting as the intercessor between the lower self and the Mighty I AM Presence—God individualized within each man.

Toward the glorious master, Jesus, he felt overwhelming love and gratitude for the ancient knowledge received with vision free from prejudice. Jesus' words, "I AM the open door that no man may shut," became a living reality. He knew now that Jesus referred not to himself, but to the very living light anchored within him from his individualized God Presence. Crow's gratitude to Jesus for incarnating as a pure example of Christ Consciousness was truly heartfelt.

☯

Every time that Dylan "knocked," the door opened for him. Repeatedly information arrived as if on a "silver platter." As long as he fully expected the word of God to come through unlimited sources, he found it at every turn. Sometimes answers would come in a magazine article, or a book that would literally fall open to a page inadvertently, delivering exactly what he needed to know. Sometimes, the truth came through the lyrics of a song. Once, when perplexed by a concept he'd prayed about, the answer came through the voice of a small child in front of him in line to pay the cashier at the grocery store.

He felt completely supported by the Universe, as if in reaching to God, the whole host of heaven reached for him. From the depths of his soul, Dylan knew what he desired, desired him just as much!

Swiftly, a return of his moral integrity and his intrinsic worth pervaded his consciousness until at last he felt ready to face the world.

Crow felt gratitude toward his I AM Presence and all those seen and unseen helpers who had brought him to the understandings that cleared his mind. Feeling indebted for the Center's very existence, he wondered how he could ever begin to repay God for the opportunity to discover all he'd learned in its supportive, protective, and gentle environment.

Such thoughts helped him re-evaluate the Law of Tithing. His new education regarding the Law of Abundance leant a fresh perspective to the old concept. Tithing could be given to anything—not just a religious order. It could be given with time and service, and even as prayer and meditation prior to any act. It could be given in the world's terms. He understood, for the first time, the Law of Tithing is actually selfish, and sacrificial only in the sense that one should make of it a sacred offering. Every blessed and loving thing you freely put out to the world, whether it be thought, feeling, words, deeds, or money, returns with more of its kind. *No wonder Jesus Christ instructed us to love our enemies. What we send out must come back to the creator, magnified*, he thought.

☯

With a clear head on a cloudless morning, Crow drove to the administration office and knocked on Dr. Whitting's door.

"You're leaving aren't you?" asked John.

"How did ye know? I just came by to tell ye I think I'm ready."

"Just a little game I play," said John with a wink. "Besides, someone asked if they could rent your cottage this morning, and as you've learned, there's no such thing as coincidence."

"Didn't notice anyone lurking 'bout, checkin' out the place. Ye know, I've been meanin' to ask ye 'bout ye'r security 'round here. I haven't noticed intrusive strangers, or press, or anythin' that smacked of offense. Neither have I seen any patrol cars. What do ye do?"

John smiled wryly and said, "If God ain't watching over us, no one's watching over us!"

The déjà vu hit him like a cosmic joke, with the whole host of heaven laughing at Little Crow.

"We sort of *charge* this place with a certain energy that will draw those who need us and repel those who are just curious."

From having read the *Discourses*, Dylan understood. "Well, whatever it is ye 'charge' the place with, I've found miself turning a major corner, and I'm grateful ye'r Center gave me both the insight and the surroundings in which to seek some healin'. I just wanted to leave this token of m'appreciation with ye personally." Crow reached to the inside pocket of his jacket and handed a white envelope to Dr. Whitting.

As Whitting stood to shake his hand in farewell, Crow had an insightful sense that what enlightened the doctor came from his heart—the wisdom formed from the light inside his heart. He felt inclined toward respect for him and silently gave thanks such men existed. There was something unconsciously noble about Whitting: something truly Divine.

When Dylan left, John opened the envelope to discover a check in the amount of one hundred thousand dollars. He just smiled, turned his gaze upward, and expressed his gratitude to God for the unlimited abundance that made the Center possible.

Chapter 17

Dylan packed his Porsche, paid for his rental, and drove straight through to his apartment in New York. Before he'd even tossed the car keys on the bureau, he picked up the phone and dialed Mic.

Mic's voice was flooded with relief. "Dylan, mi lad—been worried 'bout ye! How ye been keeping? The press's been giving ye a pretty bad time of it. From the sound of the crashin' fabrications, I feared ye were good as done for! Ye been hiding out or somethin'?"

"Aye, sort of," answered Crow. "But I'm doin' grand now. There's lit'l I can do 'bout the press. Hope it didn't embarrass the family too much."

"One o' the blighters snuck into the ranch to see if ye be here. But I set him straight…'Let 'im be', says I, 'after all he's just a wee bit of a fella.'"

They both laughed.

"Say, Mic, remember when ye said the corporation that bought the ranch allowed ye the occasional visitor? May I come be ye'r guest for a bit? I've just got to come home."

"I've been prayin' ye'd come back after that fiasco with Janet," said Mic with concern. "I knew it was over 'fore it ever started, little brother. I know ye think ye loved her, but *that* kind of love a man can do without."

"Ye read her belly holds another man's child, then?" asked Crow, somewhat embarrassed.

"Like I said, Dyl, *that* kind of love a man can do without! Come home. It's evident ye be needin' someone to look after ye. Come home today and I'll drive to Dublin to get ye."

"I'll call to see if I can get reservations and get back to ye. Lord keep ye, mi fine brother."

"And ye, mi brat."

❧

The flight from New York to Dublin seemed interminable. Though anxious to touch foot to homeland soil after his long absence, Crow still felt grateful the powers that be provided him with a lone seat in the front row of first class. No fans or curious onlookers interfered with him on the long flight. The stewardesses were friendly, but noninvasive, and for the first time he could remember, none of them flirted with him. When the wheels touched ground, he thought he'd split out of his skin.

Mic stood waiting with open arms and a bear hug that made Crow feel like he was, indeed, *home*. Packed to the brim, the airport bustled and they had to push and shove to get through to the luggage carrousel.

"Christ, the whole o' Dublin must be here! Take off ye'r hat and glasses, lad. Maybe they'll give the big celebrity some room!" Mic thumped his little brother on the head with the magazine he'd been reading while waiting.

The drive to Schull took four hours, but Dylan, eager to be home, chatted non-stop all the way. He enlightened Mic as to his whereabouts for the last ten weeks, describing what he'd been learning and how life changing the whole experience had been for him. Mic breathed a sigh of relief, 'cause baby brother was back and better than ever!

As Dylan crossed the threshold of his beloved home, he realized nothing had been touched or rearranged. For the most part, everything remained exactly as he remembered. It appeared someone had begun the process of packing things in his den, but quit mid-box. He turned to Mic with a questioning face.

"Aye, I started packin' ye'r kit when ye told me to accept the offer, but when they said to leave ye'r things, I just gave up. Since no one from the company ever came to stay, I never bothered to put things back. Sorry.

"Don't get settled yet, lad. Mum and Annie said they wanted to see ye as soon as ever we arrived." Mic dropped Dylan's luggage on the floor of the master bedroom and pushed him out the door.

Maryssa looked well and healthy, but in her joy to see her son, cried for five minutes. "What did that terrible woman do to ye, mi darlin'? I'll teach 'er to tamper with one o' mine, I will!"

"Hey, Mum, we're all responsible for our own choices. I did it to miself. Settle ye'rself now, mi dear. I'm grand—honest—just grand. Janet's leavin' turned out to be the best thing that could've happened, 'cause I don't think I had the courage to leave her."

"What he means to be sayin', Mum, is there's too much loyalty running through his veins to have left her, even if he should have done so donkey's years ago!" Mic slapped Crow on the back, trying to lighten things up.

Crow's eyes searched the room. "Now, where are mi lit'l uns?"

"We weren't sure what kind o' shape ye'd be in, so I sent the lads to stay the night with their friends. When Da died ye were looking pretty rough 'round the edges and I think it gave 'em a bit of a fright. Christ, wait 'til they see how ugly ye are now!" Mic laughed as he punched his brother's arm and pulled him into a headlock.

"Ye've always been jealous 'cause I got the looks *and* the brains, ye toad!" Crow squawked as he tried to free himself.

"I've a great pair of sons, I have!" Maryssa chuckled at her sons' youthful banter that never seemed to change, regardless of their ages.

Annie gave an unnoticed wink to her husband, acknowledging that Dylan appeared not as a broken chalice, but a man who knew where he was going. Mic nodded his agreement.

After a family supper in the stone cottage, Crow took a solitary stroll around the ranch to reacquaint himself and see what stock remained. Two lone horses were housed in the barn—one, being his old pal, Red. "Glad I am they didn't sell ye, mi boy," he said, patting his friend's neck. "We'll go riding tomorrow, we will."

The sunset on his ranch always tugged at his heartstrings and it tugged hard enough to bring tears to his eyes the night of his arrival. Although filled with a deep sense of joy for being there, he also felt deep remorse for having ever sold it.

That night he unpacked the box of books that had long remained unopened on his den floor. After retrieving his favorite volume and preparing to head for the bedroom, he caught sight of a photograph jacket on his desk. He thumbed through the pictures of Utah taken years before. In the last photo he found his Nikki, reaching toward him with one hand and pointing above with the other. "I'm coming, mi love," he whispered, kissing the print. "Wait for me." He took the picture to his room and decided to use it as a bookmark in the most precious book he'd ever opened.

Suddenly a thought occurred to him that gave wings to his feet as he literally ran back to the den to find his *lucky charms*. The box remained entombed on the high shelf where he'd hidden it from Janet's view on her first, and last, visit to the ranch. He dragged the desk chair to the case and stood on it, carefully lifting the box out of its dusty grave. As he lifted the lid, the most delicious scent filled the room, and his perfect, very much *alive* flower greeted him. Holding it gingerly by the stem and inhaling its fragrance, he danced with it like a woman in his arms. When the dance ended, he rummaged through the box to find the gold disk pendant with the double terminated crystal attached. Pressing it to his lips, then his heart, he headed back to his bedroom with both prizes in hand.

❧

During conversation over tea, Maryssa offered to introduce Dylan to the nice widow-lady who lived next door. "She really is the sweetest thing. We all just love 'er, dear."

"No thanks, Mum. I'm really *not* ready to be 'round women right yet. Ye understand?" he asked her, hoping not to hurt her feelings. He wasn't prepared to disclose that his personal agenda would not allow for a romantic relationship with any woman other than his beloved Nikki.

"She bought the place 'bout the same time ye sold this one," his mother continued, as if she hadn't heard at all. "Checks on us regular-like to see if we need anythin'. She's a pretty thing and all the single lads, and some of the married ones, 'ave been trying to 'ave their way with her since she arrived—though she pays not a one o' them any mind. Serves in all manner o' community service too, and the whole blinkin' village thinks she's a Godsend."

He screwed up his face in exasperation.

"Well—m'be when ye feel ye'r heart has mended, ye'll let me introduce ye—though she may have no interest in *ye* either." She stood to put the kettle on to boil, feeling deflated because her well intended attempt to rescue her son's love life failed miserably.

Crow was interested in one woman, and one woman alone, and he would find her if it took him the rest of his life.

❧

Dylan had been hunkering down at the ranch for about a month when the phone rang with a call from Peter Laslow.

"Hello, Dylan. Glad to hear you're back home. Heard rumor you'd sold it, though."

"I did, but they kept mi brother on. I'm just here as a guest," explained Crow.

"Well—did you call the New Millennium?" Peter hoped for

an affirmative answer, followed by a roaring success story.

"I did, Peter. Just came home from there about a month ago, in fact. I think ye saved mi life, man. Can't begin to tell ye how indebted I am to ye for what ye did. There are no coincidences, are there, mate?"

"So…are you all right now?"

"Better off now than as a lad!" Dylan answered honesty.

"I had hoped so," Peter continued, "because I have a script I want to produce and I think you're the man to play the lead. Moreover, I'd very much consider it an honor if you would co-produce and direct it with me."

Crow felt flabbergasted, but flattered and honored at the same time. The man he most admired in the film industry just asked him to co-produce and direct a film with him. A thick knot tied in his chest, remembering just how far he'd let his friend down on the last one.

"Do ye trust me that much after mi last failing, Peter?"

"I have that much faith in you, Dylan!"

Crow wept openly, glad Peter couldn't see him.

Peter heard, however, and tried to send as much love as he knew how.

To have one's life and dignity restored by another's trust was a gift Dylan desperately needed, and it would have been difficult to accept without the gratitude of tears.

To distract his friend, Laslow began speaking about the project. "This is a story about a guy named Brigham Young, who became the prophet and president of the LDS church and literally made it what it is today."

"Ye mean the *Mormons*?" Crow questioned with incredulity, wiping away his tears with his sleeve.

"Yeah, yeah…just let me tell you more before you make a

judgment. OK?"

"OK—ye've got m'attention."

"You know how the Catholic Church or any Christian-based church wouldn't even exist if it hadn't been for Paul? Well, this is the 'Paul' of the Mormon Church.

"The story begins with the conversion of Brigham Young, followed by the martyred death of their original prophet and organizer, Joseph Smith. Then it takes you into the subsequent service of Brigham Young. He has to organize and lead his people far to the west to escape the persecution that has destroyed their homes, their businesses, their lives, and their families. It's the exodus! It's Moses taking his people into the wilderness. He gets them to Utah and they suffer from drought, Indians, military, and every conceivable hardship imaginable. *But*, Brigham's faith is completely untouched.

"He starts the largest immigration of people westward until the Goldrush of '49, importing converts from all over Europe to settle Salt Lake. Then he sends groups of them out to settle throughout the western part of the United States, Canada, and Mexico. Because of his initial work in holding the infant church together along with the missionary efforts he initiated, the Mormons have grown to be a force with which to be reckoned.

"It's the story of *undaunted faith*, Dylan. In fact, I'm toying with the idea of using that as the title. It's the story about a man standing in the face of hell, insisting he knows the truth, and defending and living it at all costs! It's not about proselytizing for the LDS religion. It's about undaunted faith, the undaunted faith within our mortal souls to rise to the Divine.

"I really think you'd love it, Dylan. Are you at all interested?" he finished.

"Any brass? I'm 'bout wiped out, ye know!"

"Well, I've been putting together financing myself. I'm having a hard time selling this one to the studios," Peter said slightly chagrined. "Even if I can't get anyone to buy it, I'm going to do it myself, anyway. That could only mean a split in the proceeds after it's out. I think I can get enough to handle most the production costs. You willing to go out on a limb with me for something that's worth putting on celluloid?"

"I've decided from now on to apply mi craft *only* to works that can help raise the consciousness of those who watch, Peter. This sounds like a great place to start."

A perceptible awe reverberated from Peter's end of the line.

"How soon ye wanna start?" Crow asked while searching for a pen and paper.

"I can get a crew together within four weeks if you can get back here. There aren't any special effects—only spectacular landscapes, some studio work and, of course, a hell of a lot of good, passionate acting. That's why it needs you, Dylan."

After agreeing to the venture, Dylan spent the next few weeks trying to assess his finances, wondering if he could scrape enough together to buy back his ranch from the T F Corporation. He had his apartment in New York appraised so he could borrow money against it and checked with his investment broker to see where he actually stood after all the divorce dust settled. An Irish appraiser brought him up to snuff on the value of the ranch, reporting the current market value at nine million two hundred thousand, U.S.

Crow asked Mic for the name and number of the solicitor with whom he'd been dealing since the ranch had been sold, and made an appointment to meet him in Dublin.

Mr. Croxford had acted as the sole representative of the T F

Corporation in all the ranch affairs, the only one who'd ever made contact or checked on sheep and wool sales and financial requirements. His firm paid Mic directly, though apparently the money came from a trust through the T F Corporation.

Crow appeared in a very handsome suit, well shaven, and as dashing as ever he'd been.

The old Mr. Croxford, being a self-proclaimed student of classic literature and proudly unfamiliar with modern theater and movies, hadn't been overwhelmed when his secretary told him of the appointment. He sat behind his desk wondering what the man across from him wanted.

"Mr. Croxford," Crow began, "ye've acted as the legal representative of a U.S. firm that purchased a ranch from me a ways back, the T F Corporation."

"Oh, you're that Crow," interrupted Croxford. "I know your brother and mother, Mr. Crow. Fine people, fine people. Now, how is it I may help you?" The rotund and balding man leaned back in his chair, crossing his legs in a more relaxed posture, once he assumed Crow's presence related to pleasant matters.

"I want to buy it back, Mr. Croxford. I'd like ye to take an offer of nine million two, U.S., to the T F Corporation to see if they'll consider selling. T'would have made them a handsome profit, and since it appears *that* was the reason for their purchase, I'm hoping they'll accept." Crow had sounded so businesslike. He rather liked playing the part of a businessman.

Croxford leaned over his desk and hit an intercom button. "Alice, can you find the file for the T F Corporation and bring it in, please?

"Well, we'll just take a look at the papers and see what the original documents look like, shall we, Mr. Crow?"

A few minutes later, a slender, aging secretary walked in the room and handed a rather sizeable file to Mr. Croxford. "Thank you, Alice," he said, as she departed quietly.

Rummaging through the pile, he wondered if he'd be able to put his fingers on the desired information before his next appointment arrived. "Ah, here it is," Croxford said as he thoughtfully perused the document. He just wanted to confirm if what he remembered was correct. Croxford peered over his reading glasses and exclaimed, "Mr. Crow, to attempt to re-purchase this property would be the height of foolishness."

"Why? Have they tied it up as collateral or somethin'?"

"No, sir. It's just that it appears *you* already own it. It's been held in trust for you by the T F Corporation since the date you, or I should say, your brother, signed over the deed," explained Croxford.

Crow leaned forward, literally grabbing the papers out of the old man's hand. Then he pulled the whole file toward him to discover the identity of those behind the T F Corporation. An address was listed in L.A. and one in Dublin, which he recognized as Croxford's. He could see no principals named, but felt bound and determined to discover *who* truly owned the T F Corporation. Then he came upon one piece of stationery, one that had no address— only a brief typed note. At the top, above the corporate name, appeared a logo of two flames, each with three plumes—one pink, one yellow, and one blue—intertwined.

What could it mean? Could this have anything to do with Nikki? he wondered. He remembered how she described their twin flames residing in each of their hearts. T F? *Twin Flames?*

"Mr. Croxford, what do the initials 'T F' stand for?" he pleaded rather than asked.

"Can't say as I know, Mr. Crow. I Never felt curious enough to ask."

"How do ye contact the T F Corporation?"

"Well, we only work with their L.A. attorneys, Mr. Crow. I'll be glad to give you their names and number if you wish," said Croxford as he stood. As he jotted down the name and number, he added, "Now, if you'll excuse me, I do have another appointment waiting." The old man extended his hand in a farewell gesture.

Crow knew he'd be stopping by L.A. after filming the Brigham Young story and intended to pay the offices of Gerlacher and Schmidt a personal visit.

Chapter 18

Crow packed lighter than usual for what he knew would be at least a two-month job. The important things—his favorite books, his *lucky charms*, an indigo flower, a crystal pendant, and a small photograph of Nikki—were placed in his carry-on luggage for safekeeping.

In his first meeting with Peter, Crow described what he'd learned over the last several months of his life and the difference it was making. Peter could see the change. Dylan appeared to be a renewed man. Laslow asked to borrow one of the books described and Crow happily obliged.

They began working with each other from a new level, operating out of their higher selves instead of their egos. Each day began with heartfelt decrees, which they performed together. They found it empowered the entire production. Never had either of them experienced such perfection in every step required for a work of this magnitude. They both attributed the smooth success of the filming to God's energy moving perfectly through them, unobstructed. Crow taught Peter how to hold a field of protection over both the project and all the people who worked on it. By amazing coincidence, not a single misfire or accident occured during the entire shoot.

Dylan felt the reason Peter swiftly accepted the new concepts was due to both his brother's and his own remarkable behavioral changes. He allowed Peter to learn directly from the books, even as Nikki had done with him. Recognizing himself as a student, Crow did not want to have his views lend any confusion to Peter's ability to understand the teachings.

They filmed in three major locations and a few small ones along the way, beginning in Missouri, traveling to Salt Lake City, and ending in Brigham's winter quarters in St. George, Utah. After five days of shooting in St. George, they wrapped the project and Peter sent the cast and crew home.

"I'm heading to L.A. to edit this thing," Laslow said, beaming, fully expecting to hear Crow ask what time they could catch a flight.

"Peter, there's somethin' I need to see here 'fore I leave. I'll meet ye in a couple o' days. OK?" Crow's serious face indicated that Peter's company would only intrude upon his business.

"Sure, friend. You've got my number. I'll just wait to hear from you," he answered. "You know, you're truly welcome to stay in our guesthouse, Dylan. I hope you'll consider it."

"Thanks, mate. I'll let ye know."

The day wore late after Crow saw Laslow off at the airport. He decided he'd make his little side trip in the morning.

☯

At sunrise, Dylan drove toward Zion, turning north on the road that led to Kolob from the city of Virgin. Nikki's lower ranch had been turned into a new, elegant, gated community, complete with a private golf course. His heart fell to his knees.

Driving further, he felt thrilled to see the old *Red Rock Canyon Ranch* sign had remained just as he'd remembered it. The gate stood open, so he drove down the long, steep drive. A large tennis facility with at least a dozen courts had replaced Nikki's rental cottages. Small adobe units dotted the landscape here and there with some across the stream where he'd hiked barefooted.

He invaded further in hopes of seeing *anything* Nikki had created. There, on the volcanic boulder, sat her sculpture of the large lady holding a broken heart full of stars. Excitedly, he jumped out of his car and stepped through the raised garden to caress her art as if Nikki were somehow inside. The plaque that conveyed her hard-won insight was fully buried beneath a mound of Mexican primrose. He reached under and pulled it right out of the ground.

> *Whenever life hands you experiences of disappointment or betrayal and you feel your heart is broken beyond repair, turn your attention to God, and he will fill your broken heart with the illumination of his Divine Love, Intelligence, and Wisdom. Then will this world appear to you as the illusion it truly is, and all experience will serve only to teach and enlighten you.*

After reading it three times, he wondered what it is about human nature that responds with its best only when confronted with tragedy and despair. He pinched the plaque, sliding it beneath his jacket in the car, then continued on foot with his tour.

The small units appeared to be rentals. Peg's log home still stood, but remained well hidden behind trees and shrubbery. He wouldn't have noticed it at all, had he not known it was there. Crow strode hopefully toward it, daring to believe Peg may still claim it as her residence. Then a sign that read *Jack and Sue Anderson's Log Haven* caught his eye and he knew, she too, had abandoned the ranch.

He drove back to the fork in the road, turned right, and headed the quarter mile to Nikki's home. The equipment and chicken sheds had been supplanted with a carefully measured line of trees, and the old, white, wooden fences had been replaced by modern, small, vinyl ones. The pastures toward the main house still existed, though no horses could be seen within them.

What he saw when he reached the apex of the hill made his stomach lurch. Though the pond remained, everything else had been completely removed and replaced with a Santa Fe style log and stucco mansion.

Gone were her precious rock gardens and the rock pillars with cedar logs. Gone was the vegetable garden surrounded by the purple fence. The charming little walkways and her beloved flowers, angels, and paintings had all disappeared as though her life there had never existed. The picnic area and sculpting studio had vanished. Even the pool had been re-dug to make way for a lap pool. The petite, secret cottage feeding-shed had been replaced with an oversized three-car garage. Nothing of hers remained; nothing, save the sculpture by the tennis courts. Her cherished world, created by her own two hands, had been swept off the planet like a Buddhist monk's sand mandala.

Crow got out of his car and walked around in abject disappointment.

A gentleman opened the front door of the mansion and marched toward him almost threateningly. "What can I do for you, sir?" The man stopped short as he recognized him. "Aren't you that Dylan Crow feller?" he asked.

"Aye, that I am."

The man reached out his hand and grabbed Dylan's, shaking it with a heavy, masculine grip. "It's a real pleasure, sir, a real pleasure. Are you lost or something?"

"Nay, it's just that I stayed here once and wanted to see it again," he explained.

"Big improvement, huh?" asked the man.

All Crow could hope was that Nikki had never come back to see what they had done to her place: the place she loved more than any spot on the planet.

"What happened to all the trophies that were here?"

"A woman by the name of Mrs. James owned the place before we improved it. She donated them to a museum in St. George after she moved," said the man. "Sorry, I didn't introduce myself. My name is Howard Holbrook. I own this place."

"Do ye own the tennis facility down the road as well?"

"I, and a couple of other partners," he answered. "Would you like to stay at our facility?"

"Nay. Actually, just wondered if ye'd be willing to sell me the sculpture on the volcanic rock down there. It's one I admired when I visited here and I'd sure like to have it. I knew the artist personally."

"Never thought it much fit in with the tennis center anyway. How much you willing to pay for it?" asked Holbrook taking on the air of a real financial wizard.

"Would ten thousand cover it?" Crow asked, not knowing its value. He wanted it, regardless, because it was a piece of Nikki.

"Sold, man! Can you arrange to have it moved?"

"Aye—I'll send some experts up to crate it and ship it to me." Crow followed the man into the house and wrote him a personal check.

"Would ye mind if I hike around a bit?" he asked while handing the check across the counter.

"Be my guest." With a wide sweep of his arm, and still grinning from ear to ear, Holbrook gestured that the ranch was Crow's to explore.

Crow drove his car down the steep hill to the barns. They'd been covered with an earth-colored stucco. Although every stall had an inhabitant, no horses "played" in the pastures that ran adjacent to the stream. Parking his car, he headed toward the gate where they had delivered Pegasus day after day.

He wondered if, following the stream, he could find the waterfall again on his own. His feet edged forward, but his heart and mind leaned backward. As if it were yesterday, he remembered his first meeting with Nikki: the funny, little lady rancher in the middle of nowhere. Though she'd come from high society and high finance, accolades and expertise within her own industry, elegance and tastefully decorated homes, and all the vanities of the world—of her own accord, she moved to the country and connected to the earth. She had risen above obsession of the body beautiful, and extravagant adornments of both her body and space, of ambitiously striving to be in first place, and even above being visibly and publicly philanthropic, to find her own spirit—the God within her. Nikki had surrounded herself with absolute authenticity. Everything around her had been touched with her authentic creativity. Her personality was authentic. Her love was authentic. Her heart, soul, and character were authentic.

Having done battle with his own Jungian experiences, he truly admired her courage to have faced the world and said, "Sorry, it's just not enough. I want more. I want truth."

He understood completely why she insisted he find his own pathway, for only he, alone, could have made the choices he had.

After forty-five minutes of hiking, he found the waterfall. He climbed to the flat boulders above the falls and sat in the sun, reminiscing. Though he could recall every touch of their lips and bodies, his inner longings ran much deeper. He felt like an impoverished man who had been introduced to abundance and luxury, and then had it forcefully taken away. He'd experienced a corner of paradise in their union, a place where he felt whole—and his soul demanded a return to the fullness of the experience.

"I *will* find her!" he insisted to the sky.

Chapter 19

Crow flew to L.A. the next day and called Peter to see if he could stay with him. He had sold his California apartment when he and Janet were married. It seemed somewhat redundant to have two places so close together. Laslow welcomed him and helped him get situated in his guesthouse located directly above his editing studio.

"I've been going through this and you know, I think it's the best thing either of us have ever done!" said Peter.

"Maybe we didn't do it by ourselves, mate! Maybe we should give credit where credit is due, eh?"

"Hey, let's do it with a dedication at the end, shall we?" Laslow suggested. "Something like, *'This film is dedicated to the God dwelling within all, and to those whose undaunted faith manifests that Divine perfection.'*"

"Ye think it's Oscar material?" asked Crow, lifting some film to the light.

"Absolutely. In fact, I'd like to show it to DreamWorks to see if they'll buy it now. You know, they were too scared to finance something with you in it after the rumors flew from the last bit of trouble. But now that we've covered the cost of production, I think they'll take it," said Peter.

Dylan stopped short. He hadn't realized what a truly good and dear friend Peter had been to him. Laslow had handed him back his livelihood when no one else would have touched him with a ten-foot pole.

"Well, they do have the reproduction facilities in place and the network distribution. That would save us a lot o' time and money. Ye already have someone working on the soundtrack?"

Peter stood and walked to his desk, lifted the receiver of the phone and dialed his friend, Hans Radcliff. Radcliff had created the musical score for *Marrakech* and both he and Crow felt his talent exceeded that of anyone else in the business. "Hans, it's Peter Laslow. You get a chance to look at it yet? Yeah? You mean you'll do it? Great! You know we've got some finances to work out, but I think we're going to try to sell it to DreamWorks. Once they see it and know you've agreed to do the score, I think I won't have any trouble getting what you want. Fabulous! Fantastic! You made my day!" he said as he hung up the phone.

Laslow smiled like an excited child. "Yep, I got someone working on the soundtrack."

☯

They stayed together for another two weeks editing the film so it would be absolutely perfect for the big boys' review. Radcliff had finished the introductory music and they plugged it in just to demo the work. Peter called Forrest Alderman at DreamWorks. The three of them sat down in the reserved screening room to watch the preliminary production, unaware that DreamWorks' C.E.O. sat in the film room watching as well.

As the last scene ended, Alderman enthusiastically turned to them, asking, "What terms do you want?"

They both smiled. An up-front cash settlement of forty-five million dollars was guaranteed to cover the costs of production, along with an eight million dollar contract for Radcliff. In addition, they secured sixty per cent of the net proceeds forever and ever, amen. Laslow and Crow departed on cloud nine. At that particular moment they had no inclination of the fortune that would ensue, nor that each would receive an Oscar that year.

☯

His part of the work completed, Dylan chose to return to Ireland. Before he left, however, he privately divulged to Peter the

mysterious conditions under which a U.S. corporation had purchased his ranch and held it in trust for him. He explained his
attempt to discover who the principals were before leaving Dublin,
but that he'd hit a brick wall. With his best British accent, he admitted his intent to contact the L.A. legal firm who represented the
group and do a little "Sherlock-ing."

"Which firm is it?" asked Laslow.

Dylan opened his briefcase and rummaged through the papers
until he found Croxford's hand-written note. "Here it is—Gerlacher
and Schmidt."

"I know Schmidt!" Peter claimed proudly. "We golf at the
same club. Want *me* to call him?"

Crow stepped to the phone, grabbed the book beneath it and
handed them both to his friend with a smile. "There are no coincidences, mate."

☯

The phone rang while they were having dinner. Paula, Peter's
wife, had made tetrazzini and they were all sitting around the
table, holding their bellies, complaining they'd eaten too much.

"Al…what did you find out? Yeah, yeah, OK. Got it. Thanks
pal, I owe you one." Laslow hung up the phone and handed a
piece of paper to Dylan. "These are the principals who signed on
the original corporate papers."

Two of the names Crow did not recognize, but the third was
Samuel Scott James.

☯

Dylan dialed La Jolla information, but discovered Sam's number unlisted. He had not kept the number his agent's secretary had
provided, for after Sam had so vehemently refused to help him, he
could see no use.

He wanted to try one last time to communicate with Sam to

learn about the T F Corporation. Crow called his agent's secretary the next morning, pleading with her to schmooze the USTA again to see if she could obtain the number. It worked a second time. By ten in the morning she returned his call with phone and fax numbers, as well as an e-mail and physical address.

Crow jumped in the car and headed for La Jolla determined to confront Sam face to face. He didn't know if he'd be home, so dialed the number from his cell. Recognizing Sam's voice, he hung up and kept driving.

☯

"What are you doing here?" Sam asked coolly when he answered the door. An old yellow Lab pushed his way through the entry, wagging his tail in friendly recognition.

"I've gotta talk to ye, mate. Please…just give me five minutes," Crow implored as he patted Shasta on the head.

Sam obviously had no intention of inviting him in his home, as he merely leaned against the doorframe and looked at his watch.

Crow really liked this kid and most especially admired his fierce protection of his mother. It felt comforting to know someone watched out for her until he could.

"I want to talk to ye about the T F Corporation."

"What about it?" Sam asked nonchalantly.

"Ye'r name is listed as one of the organizing principals."

"So?" he said disinterestedly.

"So, ye'r corporation has been holding mi ranch in Schull in trust for *me* for several years now." Crow watched Sam's eyes as they hardened like steel.

"So what? You still have your damn ranch, and my mother sacrificed hers. What else do you want to know?" he spit out.

"She…sold…her ranch…to buy mine?" Crow asked, with eyes tearing from the truth.

"Yep—to people she said she'd never sell out to—the land-rap-
ing developers!" Sam said the last word with disgust in his voice.
"It was the only way she could raise enough capital to meet your
ridiculous price, and quite frankly I don't think it was worth it."

"Ye've been there, then?" Crow asked.

"Mom made me go see it after I played at Wimbledon. When
she found you'd put your 'precious little heaven' on the market, it
just broke her heart, and she rushed to the rescue. You really are
an asshole, Crow. I can't imagine what she sees in you!"

"Look, mate, I admit I've made some really poor choices in the
last few years, but I've also made some really good ones. I love ye'r
mum, Sam. I want to marry her. I want to be with her forever. Why
won't ye tell me where she is?" Crow begged like a small child.

"You look, '*mate*,'" Sam said, mocking his Irish accent, "as I
made abundantly clear previously, it was *she* who told me not to
inform you of her whereabouts. I'll only tell you what she told me
to tell you those many years ago, and that's it...*mate!*"

"Tell me again, Sam. Please, tell me again."

"She said, if by some *miracle* you ever came looking for her
through me, I was to tell you, and I quote: 'When he knows he's
truly ready for me, he must remember the beginning. If he remembers the beginning, he will *know* how to find me.'" With those final
words, Sam turned and stepped into his house, shutting the door
behind him—but a knowing smile crossed his lips.

"The beginning. The bloody, blinkin' beginning of...what?
What could she mean...the beginning?" He asked himself the question out loud all the way back to Peter's guesthouse.

The Teaching of Little Crow

Chapter 20

Crow bid his fond farewell to Laslow and Paula at the airport and waited for his flight back to Dublin. He called Mic and told him what time to meet the flight, then settled in for the long haul.

As usual, the flight from L.A. to Dublin consumed an eternity. Sitting on a plane proved to be truly exhausting—especially without alcohol.

He didn't unpack for three days, but when he did, he found his books, his flower, the photograph of Nikki, and the crystal pendant and placed them lovingly by his bed so he could look at them at night.

Crow called Braydon to beg his forgiveness for the damage he'd done to their relationship.

"Are ye free of the monster that's been eatin' ye'r soul, then, boyo?"

"I believe I am, Braydon. Can ye ever forgive me for bein' such a bloody fool? I treasure our friendship, man. Ye've always said our strength came when we teamed up. Would ye consider teamin' up again?" asked Crow.

"I've always known ye'r heart, lad. Ye're too fine a soul to be kept down long! I've missed ye too. How 'bout I bring mi lovely, *pregnant* wife to meet ye on Friday?"

"Congratulations, man! I'm truly happy for ye. About seven, then?"

Mic warned Dylan their mother was about to launch a full-frontal approach to get him to agree to meet the widow-lady next door. "She's in town and Mum's determined to get ye two together," said Mic.

"I have to tell ye some stuff, Mic, but I don't want ye to make light of it, or share what I'm about to tell ye with *anyone* else. I made a huge mistake telling Braydon about it years ago, and he and the lads twisted it into something ugly. Nothing could have been further from the truth. Ye're the only one I trust to hear this story."

Crow began at the beginning, that day when the car stalled above her ranch, beautifully describing each intricate detail, right up to his marriage to Janet. Also, he revealed his attempts to discover her whereabouts through her son and Robert's private investigator. During the two-hour story, Mic noticed Dylan never once mentioned the lady's name. "This woman sold her ranch and bought this place, Mic. It's been held for me in a trust. Were ye aware of that?"

"Nay…honestly…I didn't know, Dyl, or I'd 'ave told ye," Mic responded.

"This—*this*—is the lady I want by mi side. I'm not interested in Mum's widow-lady next door. Ye've heard the quote, 'The heart has reasons that even reason doesn't understand'; well, I think it applies here."

"What did her kid mean when he said 'remember the beginnin'?"

"I'm not sure. Been trying to figure it out for months now," Dylan said as he walked to the sink for a glass of water.

Mic turned in his chair with a thoughtful look on his face. "Ye began ye'r tale tonight with 'the way it began.' Could it 'ave somethin' to do with the first day ye met her? I mean—she rescued ye on a big Pasafino, ye had that thing happen in ye'r chest, ye drank her Mexican coffee, ye hiked 'round her place, ye had a dream, she gave ye a present of a flower and a pendant, and ye drove off. What's in that first day that could make it possible for ye to find her?"

The color drained from Dylan's face. "I'll have to think about that tonight, Mic. Thanks for not laughing 'bout the things I told ye."

"Laugh? Bloody 'ell, brother, I'm jealous! I honestly hope ye can find her, 'cause this is definitely a lady I'd like to meet."

As soon as Mic left, Crow hustled to his bedroom and picked up the pendant. Nikki had said, "You'll know when to use it!"

What was it the characters did in mi past life visions with the pendant? Think, lad, think! Then it came to him. He remembered they'd put it to their forehead. It was worth a try, so he lay upon his bed and placed the gold to his third eye and began by calling upon both his I AM Presence, and hers.

"I AM here and I AM there. Through and in thy name, Mighty I AM Presence, I call upon the I AM Presence within Nikki James. I call upon her higher mental body and command a connection between us. Nikki, I AM ready. I know I AM ready to meet ye half way. I don't know everything ye know yet, but I AM on ye'r pathway of mi own volition and anxious to learn. Please come to me! I AM OUR INSEPARABLE UNION NOW!"

He repeated his call with more and more feeling, projecting a light from his third eye chakra to hers, from his heart to hers. He felt it with all of the intensity of his soul until sleep overtook him.

☯

The phone rang at seven thirty a.m., waking Crow from a deep sleep. Startled, he discovered the disk still in place on his forehead. He grasped it and held it in his left hand while sleepily answering the phone.

"Sorry to wake you so early, Dylan. This is Robert."

"Hey, mate. It's all right. What's happenin'? Any word yet?" asked Crow, stifling a yawn.

"I think we've found her in Switzerland. Tony Jenkins heard

from Geneva yesterday. A woman by the name of Nikki Wright, U.S. citizen, was located living in Lausanne. That was her professional name. Your Nikki had an agency called 'Wright Advertising.' Did you know she only changed her name to James after her son was born? I think this is her, man! They're checking into it further and we should know within twenty-four hours!" The enthusiasm in Robert's voice betrayed that he couldn't wait to find this mystery woman for whom he had searched so diligently. He truly desired his friend's happiness.

A huge smile crossed Crow's face with an overwhelming sense of victory. "Dear God, please let it be her!" he whispered under his breath. "Fabulous work, mate! Please, the *instant* you hear, no matter what time, ring me. OK?"

"Gotcha buddy. Take care."

The line went dead and Crow lifted the flower and smelled it, then picked up Nikki's photograph and kissed it. "Please let me find ye!"

☙

Dylan decided to take Red to fix the fence Mic said needed mending between the widow-lady's property and his. First, he double-checked the answering machine so as not to miss Robert's call.

He gathered the mending materials and tools and threw them in a saddlebag on Red's back. "Hello, old fella. How long's it been since we had an adventure together?"

A bull Mic had agreed to pasture for a neighboring farmer had smashed down the barrier, so Dylan had to dig a temporary post-hole and stretch the metal fence again. The strength required for the manual labor made him realize he'd gotten a little out of shape. Sweating profusely, he removed his jacket, and as he tossed it over a pole, his eye caught the jet black color of the bird in flight over his head. The crow circled three times before it came to land on the post only three feet from where he worked. As it landed, Red jumped back and the tether holding him jerked free. The horse ran headlong back towards the barn.

"Blast ye, Red! Do ye know how long a walk it is back to fetch ye?" he yelled.

The crow held its ground and cawed as it raised its wings. Then while tucking them back into place with great dignity, the creature eyed Dylan curiously.

"Haven't seen ye for a while, ol' friend. Would ye be here to announce yet another change in mi life? Given that ye've left me without a ride, I hope this isn't an ill-fated omen!"

The crow hopped closer and cocked his head side to side as if thoroughly engaged in the conversation. Dylan went about his work and chatted with the large bird as he would an old acquaintance. Completing his task, he surveyed the tools and decided they were too heavy to haul back on foot. He piled the supplies neatly and tied his bandana to the fence as a marker. The quickest route of return took him toward the beach, over to his dock, and up the road again. He decided to return later with a truck for the tools.

Walking the fence line, squinting in the dazzling morning sun, he heard, rather than saw, the horse approaching on the widow-lady's side.

"Hey," (as opposed to 'hello,') said a lovely familiar voice. "You just enjoying God's country, or are you in trouble?"

Dylan put his hand over his eyes and tried to move so he could see. He looked at her with an expression no human tongue could describe. Heart in throat, he reached across the fence and pulled her from her horse, right down on top of him, so they both fell to the earth.

"*Ye're* the widow-lady? Mi dear Lord, *it's really mi Nikki!* Ye came! Ye fell right out o' heaven!" He was kissing her everywhere his lips could touch, as tears of joy streamed unabashedly from his eyes.

"I think we both fell from heaven, my love!"

"Why didn't ye contact me before now! Sure, 'n' ye were right next-door the whole time!" he said clutching her to his chest.

"Just got your call, darling," she said calmly.

She was as youthful and beautiful as he remembered. The light from each of their hearts acted like great magnets drawing them together in a dynamic embrace of profound love as they joined the dance of fusion and combustion. The overwhelming desire to join swept over them with a passion of spirit, mind, heart, soul, and body as they married in the sweetest love dance. There was nothing left to bar their hearts or bodies from one another.

Crow kissed her tenderly. His hands roamed her entire body, as hers roamed his. He ached to be inside her again and began to pull her clothes from her body as if it were his last chance to ever make love with her, tolerating no barriers whatsoever. He couldn't pull her close enough. His breath was hard and fast, and he could hold his excitement no longer as his very soul seemed to drain into her.

Once again, his heart exploded like a nuclear reactor, as he was held paralyzed by the extraordinary bliss of their union. They lay gasping and laughing, then crying, then, laughing again. Time stood still and he knew in the depths of his spirit that this was just the tiniest bit of the joy they would experience together—God's perfect design manifest and joined in the physical octave. They lay there for another hour holding each other in sweet reunion, too overwhelmed by their gratitude to even speak above a whisper.

Dylan reached for her left hand and took her wedding finger into his mouth and withdrew the small band above her middle knuckle with his lips. He tossed it deep into the grass and pulled his own ring from his finger and placed its bulk over hers. "This is to remind ye ye're no longer incomplete." Her eyes were laughing, observing its gargantuan proportion over her small finger.

"I owe ye m' eternity," he softly whispered in her ear. "Would ye consent to marry me, Nik?"

"We're already married, my love. There's nothing in this Universe that could ever part me from you again."

His mouth widened into a satisfied smile. "Nonetheless, I'd consider it the greatest honor of mi life to display our Divine Love to the world in the example of marriage—even if it's only a *man-made* institution. Besides, mi mum's been trying to marry me off to the 'widow-lady next door' for a while now!"

"I really love your family, baby. I'd be proud to change my name to Crow."

"I can't believe ye sold the place ye loved most dear in the world to purchase this ranch back for me."

"It was a sacred offering, Dylan. There was something I held dearer to my heart than a piece of land," she whispered.

"How did ye know I'd ever come back?"

"I told you. I had faith in you!"

"Why did ye buy the McKenzie's place?" he asked, nuzzling her neck.

"Because the two pieces fit perfectly, and one was not complete without the other." Her smile punctuated the joint affinity.

"Ye're mi perfect complement, Nikki. Have I met ye half-way? Are ye through testing me?" he begged to know.

"I was never 'testing' you, my love. I just gave your soul the freedom to come to me with full intent and a full heart, without coercion of any sort from me." She laid her head upon his chest and stroked his arm. "It was as much a raising of my own consciousness as it was yours. We've so much we can do together that we can't do alone, and I've prayed for this moment every second since you got on that plane in Vegas. Together, with God, we form a trinity of limitless co-creation and can cross the divide of duality consciousness."

She gazed deeply into her lover's eyes. "I told you once that I had faith in you and faith in your love for me. Without faith in Love, it would be impossible for any of us to be satisfied with ourselves or with any of our relationships. We both had to meet Love's standard in order to meet half way."

"Can ye ever forgive me for having married Janet?" he questioned with the embarrassment of a caught criminal.

"Don't you see, your marriage to Janet is one of the things that brought you back to me? Had the course of your love run smooth and joyously, you would have never hungered for something better.

"I love you, Dylan Crow, with a love so Divine as to put all human love to shame. There are many things about Divine love that I don't even understand yet, darling. All I know is the way I feel for you has the elements of devotion and constancy, of virtue and taintlessness. What I feel is penetrating and expansive: it's enveloping and transmuting. It's been tolerance, and patience, and sometimes, long-suffering, but this Love is absolute gratefulness, understanding, and merciful forgiveness. It's my full approval and support. It has *become* non-possessive and includes all the qualities of God as I understand God to be."

"I know I also loved you with a selfish-love, which is *not* Divine Love. I had to gather the courage to defend True Love against all enemies, and to know that only Divine Love, not only for you, but toward all creation, would sustain me."

He lay in her arms contemplating her words and realized how much selfish love existed within him still, for there was nothing he wanted to possess more in the world than this woman. Dylan knew he could not claim undaunted faith on his part, but felt he was on the right path to attaining it.

"If your horse has made it back to the barn by now, they may come looking for you. We better get dressed, angel face. Want a ride back?" she asked, helping him to reclaim his clothing.

All the anxiety that had split his soul disappeared. He knew they would never be parted, ever again, and his heart relaxed in the purest joy.

She hopped across the fence to Pegasus, who had been patiently waiting. Nikki pulled herself up and offered Crow her hand and foot. "Come on, my love, there's still a long road ahead, but if we'll just relax and trust each other, we'll find our way home, together."

Epilogue

As he rode with his arms around her in perfect communion, he asked. "Are ye too old to have children?"

She smiled, and turned in his arms. "There's no aging, no time, no space, no limits to either of us, darling." Feeling the life force he'd just planted within her womb, she whispered, "Worlds without end shall we make, my love, and populate them all."

ONLY THE BEGINNING

Appendix A: Glossary of Terms

These brief descriptions are by no means all-inclusive, but relate to the way in which these terms have been used within the story.

Ascended Master—a being who has, through the process of incarnation, mastered his lower-self and has risen into the state of perfection in his own I AM Presence, abiding in the Ascended Master's Octave and assisting those souls evolving through the four planes of matter in the four lower bodies. All Ascended Masters are part of the Angelic kingdom.

Aura—the electromagnetic field surrounding life forms; the soul's light force as it manifests through the body; the extended energy around the human body, which alters in radiance and color depending upon the state of the physical, mental, emotional and spiritual health.

Chakra—energy centers in the human body associated with various states of evolution, consciousness, physical organs, glands and stones, colors, notes and geometrical formations; any one of seven main energy centers in the body.

Christ-self—see Higher Self

Clairaudient—the ability to hear sounds beyond the reach of ordinary experience or capacity.

Clairvoyant—a paranormal activity of seeing beyond the ordinary range of vision or experience.

Dimension—an octave of reality; a level of existence; a realm of consciousness; infinite in number with each successive dimension forming the foundation for the progressive evolution of the next.

Etheric body—the non-physical, energy or force field, which contains the energy forms of thoughts, feelings, and past experience. Often referred to as the "memory" body.

Great Central Sun—the omnipotent eternal source of light existing in the center of the infinite universe, out of which radiates the entire panoramic creation; the power that creates the infinite universe.

Guides—individual spiritual assistants and teachers.

Hierarchal Orders—the Angelic orders of God.

Higher-self—Christ-self; intermediating body between lower self and Mighty I AM Presence. Attuned and aligned with the source of power and truth within the Self; the neutral aspect of awareness that identifies with spiritual light and is fulfilled by creatively manifesting that light through thoughts, feelings, words and actions. Acting as a transducer and transmitter of Divine energy to the lower self.

I AM Presence—God, individualized and anchored in the heart of all mankind.

Karma—energy and consciousness in action. The law of cause and effect and retribution.

Lower-self—lower consciousness or lower mind, unawakened to soul qualities and energies; existing in the unfulfilled desire state; seeking fulfillment solely from external sources; egocentric, caring only for the self; consumed and indulgent with sensory gratification and transitory pleasure.

Reincarnation—rebirth of the soul in a new body. A new incarnation or embodiment of a soul.

Shaman—(esp. among certain tribal peoples) a person who acts as an intermediary between the natural and the supernatural worlds known to use magic to cure illness, foretell the future, control spiritual forces, etc.

Stone laying—ancient art of laying stones onto vital nerve centers, chakra areas and plexus points of the body, acting as a catalyst to magnify specific frequencies of colors and vibrations into the subtle energies of the human aura. A method by which an aura may be cleansed, releasing suppressed trauma and connecting a person with his own source of truth and power. Used in some shamanic traditions to bring to the surface old memories and feelings to be expressed to release the true causes of disease or discomfort in any of the four lower bodies.

Sweat lodge—spiritual tradition among Native Americans in which one purifies the four lower bodies in order to receive direct communication from the spirit world.

Tantric—(as relates to sexual practice) practice and ritual of sexual union based on the Hindu texts of the Tantra.

Tripartite Heart Flame—the Sacred Heart Fire from the Great Central Sun, consisting of Divine Intelligence, Wisdom, and Love. Flame of God's purity issued forth from the Mighty I AM Presence, (God Individualized,) through the Christ-self and physically anchored within the physical heart, from which all outer life derives its energy and light. The seat of the soul.

Twin Flames—God's extension into individualization, created from a single white fire body. This body was separated into two hemispheres of being; one with the masculine polarity and the other with the feminine polarity, but each with the *same* spiritual origin and unique, identical blueprint of identity. The Cosmic Law requires that each half define their own identity in God before they can unlock the joint spiritual potential of their twin flame activity.

Universal Consciousness—a unified force field containing all knowledge accumulated from all life throughout the universe.

Violet Consuming Flame—purifying light of the Universal Christ. The Energy and Substance of Divine Love from the Great Central Sun, which each one's own Mighty I AM Presence draws into a concentrated focus as a flame and blazes through the bodies and aura of the personality to set everything into Divine Order of Perfection, that the Presence may express through the mind, the feelings and the body, out into the world of the Individual. Referenced in esoteric and religious writings as the "Baptism by Fire," "Law of Forgiveness," and "Law of Transmutation," and "The Law of Love." The raising, transforming, purifying, vivifying activity of Pure Divine Love from the Heart of God. The frequency of vibration in this light is such that it will dissolve and consume within physical or energy form that which is discordant, returning it to pure energy.

Appendix B: Suggested Reading

The I Am Discourses
St. Germain Series, Vols. 1 to 18
St. Germain Press
1120 Stonehedge Drive
Schaumburg, Illinois 60194
1-(800)-872-1932
www.saintgermainpress.com

Life And Teachings Of The Masters Of The Far East
Volumes 1 through 6
Baird Spalding
DeVorss & Company, Publishers
P.O. Box 550
Marina del Rey, California 90294
www.devorss.com

As A Man Thinketh
James Allen
Running Press Book Publishers
124 South Twenty-Second Street
Philadelphia, Pennsylvania 19103
www.runningpress.com

Souls & Soul Mates
St. Germain through Azena and Claire Heartsong
Triad Publishers Pty, Ltd
P.O. Box 731
Cairns, QLD.4870
AUSTRALIA
www.triadpublishers.com

Soul Mates And Twin Flames,
The Spiritual Dimension of Love and Relationships
Saint Germain On Alchemy, *Formulas for Self-Transformation*
Elizabeth Claire Prophet
Summit University Press
P.O. Box 5000
Corwin Springs, Montana 59030
1-(800)-245-5445
www.summituniversitypress.com

Say "Yes" To Love, *God Explains Soul Mates*
Say "Yes" To Love, *God Unveils Soul Mate Love & Sacred Sexuality*
Say "Yes" To Love, *God's Guidance to Lightworkers*
Say "Yes" To Love,
God Leads Humanity Toward Christ Consciousness
Yaël & Doug Powell
Circle of Light
3969 Mundell Road
Eureka Springs, Arkansas 72631
1-(866)-629-9894
www.circleoflight.net

Twin Souls, *Finding Your True Spiritual Partner*
Patricia Joudry, Maurie D. Pressman, M.D.
Hazelden: Transitions Bookplace
1000 West North Avenue
Chicago, Illinois 60622
1-(800)- 979-READ (7323)
www.transitionsbookplace.com

Re-member, A Handbook for Human Evolution
Steve Rother & The Group
Lightworker
P.O. Box 1496
Poway, California 92074
1-(877)-248-5837
www.lightworker.com

The Ancient Secret Of The Flower Of Life, Volume's I & II
Drunvalo Melchizedek
Light Technology Publishing
P.O. Box 3540
Flagstaff, Arizona 86003
1-(800)-450-0985
www.lighttechnology.com

The Crystal Connection
Randall & Vicki Baer
Harper & Row Publishers,
San Francisco, California

The Crystalline Transmission, *A Synthesis of Light*
Crystal Enlightenment
Katrina Raphaell
Aurora Press
P.O. Box 573
Santa Fe, New Mexico 87504

Subliminal Learning
Subliminal Communication
Thinking Without Thinking, *Who's In Control of Your Brain*
Dr. Eldon Taylor
RFK Book
P O Box 1139
Medical Lake, Washington 99022
1-(800)-964-3551
www.innertalk.com

Order Form

Please send _____ copies of *The Teaching of Little Crow*
@ $25.95 + $4.50 for S & H first copy.

Quantity discounts: 5-9 books, take off 10%. 10 or more books, take of 20%. (Prices are for the USA. For more than one book shipped to the same address, reduce S&H for each book by $1.00. For price and postage to other countries, please e-mail us first.

Ship to: (Please Print)
Name:_____
Address:_____
City _____ State/province_____
Zip Code _____ Country _____ Phone_____
E-mail address_____

Please send check or money order in US currency payable through a US bank, or send international money order made payable to Heart Flame Publishing. We do not accept foreign currency or checks drawn on a foreign bank.

If using a credit card, you may submit this form by mail or fax your order with credit card to: (435) 635-2613, or go to our web site www.heartflamepublishing.com.
Acceptable cards: (please circle) Visa, M/C, Discover, Novus

Name on card: _____
Credit card number _____Ex. _____

We will ship your order by the best carrier. Some carriers do not deliver to P.O. Boxes, so we must have both your street and postal address.

Heart Flame Publishing • P.O. Box 790038 • Virgin, UT
www.heartflamepublishing